STRANGERS *on the* SHORE

STRANGERS *on the* SHORE

STEWART BLUME

Advantage™

Published by Advantage, Charleston, South Carolina.
Member of Advantage Media Group.

ADVANTAGE is a registered trademark and the
Advantage colophon is a trademark of Advantage Media Group, Inc.

Printed in the United States of America

ISBN: 978-1-59932-028-1
Library of Congress Control Number: 2006940049

Dedication

This book is dedicated to Charlie Dickerson, a good friend who guided me through the process and helped me in many ways.

And to Lib Bernardin who was the first person who referred to me as a writer and offered me a wonderful critique; and Ann Summer who edited and tweaked my book to make it as good as it could be.

I would be remiss if I didn't give some credit to my wife, Carol, who allowed me time away from her to write, and my wonderful daughters, Cathy, Judy and Leslie, who contributed so much without knowing it.

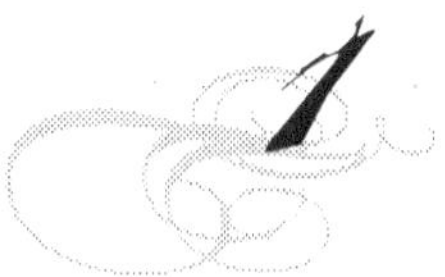

From my loft window I stared at two magnificent live oaks, their leaves hanging in bunches on gnarled, muscular branches. I refused to cut them when I built my office, preferring to wrap them, letting them define its footprint. Their verdant lush foliage was silhouetted in muted tones against the gray monotone the evening rain created. Leaves danced rhythmically on swaying branches courtesy of an Indian summer breeze, but it was just a matter of time before fall arrived and turned them various shades of brown and red and winter stripped them bare.

Rain fell almost invisibly, signifying its presence with moving patterns of dimples in ponding pavement depressions, and soft, drumming sounds as it struck the window. It was a pleasant rain, unlike the blustery ones that visit South Carolina in September courtesy of the hurricane season. It was 1962 and Alma had threatened, but she managed to miss us. Since childhood I've loved rainstorms, especially those in the summer that come with rolling thunder and cracking lightning that light up a threatening sky with its fiery pyrotechnics. As a child when storms were in progress I remember spending hours by an open door or window in a hastily contrived tent of bed sheets stretched over chair backs, reading books or indulging my mind's imagination. This make-believe sense of shelter against the elements was perhaps the source that led me to architecture.

Refreshed by diversion, I turned back to my drawing board, and laid a sheet of sketch paper over the survey of the Cutler property at Bear Creek. Contour lines snapped out under the thin paper, along with symbols locating and identifying larger trees on the property that I wanted to save. Photos of the individual trees and a meandering creek that traversed the rear of the property from east to west were taped across the top of my drawing board for reference.

I grabbed a blunt 5B pencil, my weapon of choice, and spoiled the pristine whiteness of the paper by indicating arrows for north, south, east and west in the margins. I closed my eyes and my minds eye took over, visualizing the site in three dimensions. The creative process was beginning for me as it always did; find the perfect location. Nature had much to offer – topography, arc of the sun, seasons, beauty and much more – and I wouldn't be satisfied until I had used them all to my advantage. This building had to grow from the ground in harmony with nature. Anyone can place a building on a site, but that's the wrong way to do it.

Unfortunately, creativity is a thought process, and when I'm on a roll I run through ideas like snowflakes in a blizzard without recording what I've considered, discarded, or deemed worthy. That's a serious flaw. It's dogged me throughout my architectural career even though I've recognized it and tried my best to overcome it. I guess I'll have to live with it. Fortunately, my short-term memory is good.

The telephone rang, interrupting my thoughts, and I reluctantly picked it up.

"Design Concepts, Terry Forte speaking," I said.

"Mr. Forte, this is Maria Champion. My husband and I need an architect to help design our home. I've been looking at houses and the ones I like are your designs. The Blair's house is my favorite. They were kind enough to give us a tour, and I fell in love with it. We'd like to schedule an appointment with you at your earliest convenience." She had a pleasant, no-nonsense voice, which was definitely not Southern. It was well modulated with little accent, suggesting the Midwest.

"Certainly,." I said, "but it will have to be next week. How about next Thursday........ say two o'clock?"

"Great! I'll call you early in the week to confirm. If you need to get in touch with us, our telephone number is 787-3041."

"Thanks, I'll see you Thursday. Goodbye." I hung up the phone, wrote *CHAMPION* in my calendar for Thursday at two o'clock and returned to work. I didn't know it then, but that appointment would be the beginning of an adventure that would change my life forever.

At promptly 2:00 o'clock Thursday, Mrs. Champion and her husband walked into my office. She wore a tan dress suit, ecru blouse, and dark brown high heel shoes. Her brown hair was piled on top of her head and her green eyes twinkled with a smile. She moved across the room with the fluid motion of a cat and extended her hand. "I'm Maria Champion. This is my husband, Patrick." She was tall, leggy, and attractive.

I accepted her hand and said, "Terry Forte, nice to meet you." I turned and shook hands with Mr. Champion. "Please follow me." I led them to the conference room and asked them to have a seat.

Mr. Champion was a tall man with balding salt and pepper hair and a slim build that indicated proper exercise and diet. He was wearing a tailored navy blue business suit with red lining in the coat, white shirt and a red, white, and blue striped tie. He said, "Mr. Forte, I work for Network America. I was sent here two months ago from California to set up our new plant. Maria and I haven't had much time to meet people or become familiar with the area, but we've decided to build a home rather than to buy an existing one. We think this might be our last move with the company. We want to do it right this time and use an architect. We like your work and hear good things about you." He had an engaging smile.

"Thanks, Mr. Champion. I prefer clients familiar with my work….. it reduces culture shock. My designs are not eclectic period pieces. I'm not good at historical architecture. I like indigenous architecture that respects natural surroundings and embraces the owner's lifestyle. I'm pretty much dedicated to the 'form follows function' philosophy."

Pat smiled and said, "I don't have the architectural awareness or vocabulary to express it that way, but we recognized that your designs make a different statement from other architects' work we've seen in the area. Coming from California takes us out of eclectic architecture and, frankly, that's why your work appeals to us." He chuckled and said, "The first thing you must do is call us Pat and Maria if you want to learn anything about our lifestyle. We aren't formal people."

I smiled. "Great. Likewise, please call me Terry. Now that we've cleared that hurdle, Pat, let me ask you and Maria some questions. Have you purchased a lot?"

"No," Maria said. "Our first priority is to be in an area with good schools. We have two children, one in elementary school and one in junior high. We had hoped that since we're not familiar with the area you might help us with our choice."

I frowned and shook my head. "I would prefer that you look around for an area that you like. I may burden you with too many of my prejudices. I've lived here all my life and I'm not always objective. Sometimes the natives can't see the forest for the trees. I'll give you an opinion, if you like, but I'll be more helpful with site orientation, drainage, utilities, and other physical properties. You know that thing about 'location, location, location' that developers and real estate agents talk about? Talk to a few of the better real estate agents. They'll give you a comprehensive evaluation of all the areas. They'll be calling on you anyway as soon as they find out you're setting up the factory. You'll be a great source of leads for them, so they'll be delighted to help you. John Haskell at Camelot Realty and Gus Cannon at Cannon and Sons Realty are good ones to contact. They know the area well, and they handle about ninety percent of the local real estate transactions between the two of them."

"I know Haskell," Pat said. "I played golf with him when I was looking for potential plant sites. He was representing the Chamber of Commerce – Committee of One Hundred I think. I would feel comfortable calling him. He seems like a nice guy."

"The best, and he's a straight arrow. He won't give you any bad information to make a sale. I'll need a good topographical survey as soon as you select your site, but I can take care of that for you if you wish. In the meanwhile, I have a questionnaire I'd like for you to fill out. It'll start your thinking about what you want in your house and will help me understand how your house should function. Your home must embrace your lifestyle and create a sense of shelter for you that will be comfortable and functional. My function is to make that happen." Maria nodded her head in agreement. Pat picked some lint off his sleeve, but his eyes hadn't glazed over. That was a positive.

I lit a cigarette after offering my pack to both of them and decided to pick up the pace. I blew smoke over my shoulder and said, "A house will drive you crazy if it lacks dedicated space for storage, hobby areas or private spaces. Families who enjoy conversation should have comfortable areas to gather; those who like quiet space for themselves for reading or listening to music should have it. That's common sense. My job is to ferret out data and design around it. That's the purpose of the questionnaire. Answer all the questions and add anything you think is important. Don't be hesitant because you think it's dumb. Everything's important. This is the part of design that I call the psychological phase. I must think like you in order to understand your needs."

Maria said, "Wow, That sounds complicated and a little frightening. I understand what you're saying and I agree. I didn't realize how much effort goes into planning." She seemed eager and was taking in every word. Pat was listening, but he was still quiet.

I laughed. "It's really not that complicated. I'm trying to impress you."

She leaned forward before she spoke. "Well, you have," she said quickly. "Explain to me why the selection of a site is so important. I mean, in the physical sense. I understand about neighborhoods and schools, but I have no concept about physical attributes."

I leaned back in my chair, scratched the back of my neck and thought for a minute before I spoke. "The important things are orientation, drainage, size, shape, vistas, topography, soil type, location and types of trees, and available utilities." I stopped for a moment. I knew that was a lot to absorb.

"Lots, if possible, should have primary vistas to the south. There are a few exceptions, but for sure you never orient glass areas to the west, particularly in South Carolina. The sun travels in a southerly arc from east to west, more vertical in the summer than the winter. This means that on the south side, the sun can be controlled with roof overhangs in the summer when it's hot. With its lower arc in the winter, the sun will be allowed to penetrate glass areas when it's cold. This is the principle used for passive solar design that helps conserve energy in the winter. The heat from the winter sun is stored in collectors or absorbed by material mass to assist in heating the building. Western sunlight can be controlled with vertical elements in the summer, but that destroys the view. It also is a source of tremendous heat gain that overloads your cooling system. Large areas of glass on the western side of a home are not desirable and should be avoided."

They listened attentively and Maria was scribbling notes on a pad as I continued. "Topography defines drainage because it indicates the profile of your property. To make it simple, water will not run uphill. If the topography is shaped like a bowl, you have a problem. If your interests are tennis or swimming, and you are thinking about a tennis court or a swimming pool, you don't want a hilly site. Changing the contours to accommodate a tennis court or swimming pool or any other use that requires well-drained flat planes is expensive."

Pat nodded in agreement. He was listening and understood.

"Size and shape are obvious. This defines the size and shape of your home. It also determines where your home will be located on the site. I prefer rectangular sites of at least an acre. Wedge-shaped lots are difficult to work with but sometimes add a special quality if handled well."

"Soil types are usually overlooked by builders, and may create serious foundation problems. Generally, we have good soil in this area, but it's good insurance to request a few soil borings before you buy. If the property owner will do it, fine. If not, do it yourself. It's not expensive. They provide the bearing capacity of the soil, the nature of the subsoil, and the water table. If city sewers are not available, you'll need a septic tank. It's imperative that you have soil that will provide absorption and oxidation of effluent for a septic tank to function. Heavy shale and clay sub-surface deposits are not always visible and make excavation and septic tank installation very expensive. All of this information is indicated in soil borings."

I subbed out my cigarette and continued. "Trees are important; they can't be replaced. It takes a lifetime to grow a tree. You'll want to save as many as possible, so their location on the site is critical. Perimeter locations are preferable. Deciduous trees, particularly on the south side, make good shade trees. Pine trees are not as desirable."

"I hope this doesn't bore you, but this is the kind of information you hire me for." I laughed. "I've given you a short course in Architectural Site Selection 101. Most of this is overlooked by developers who are building tract houses, but it's all important and should be a major part of site selection." I paused for a moment. "I'm sorry I got carried away, Maria. You'll think twice next time before you ask me to explain anything."

She grinned and turned to Pat, expecting him to comment. "No, I asked and you answered. Actually, I appreciate the information, but I'm not sure I'm ready for that much detail. I really do want to learn as much as I can. It sounds fascinating and challenging!"

I gave her a smile. Then I turned to Pat, "I'm sure you want to know about fees. I charge eight percent of the contract cost for total services and frankly, I don't accept commissions without providing total services. I made that mistake on one of my first projects and didn't recognize it when it was completed. I promised myself I would never do that again."

Maria asked, "What are total services?"

"Twenty percent of the fee is for preliminary planning, fifty-five percent is for contract documents, five percent is for the bidding process and twenty percent is for construction observation. Contract documents are working drawings and specifications. Working drawings are what blueprints are made from. Fees from any consulting engineers are included in the architectural fee. Construction observation is what we called job supervision before lawyers got involved in architecture. Trial lawyers insisted that 'job supervision' implied architects were responsible for any error or omission made by the building contractor. Obviously, architects would have to be on the job continuously during construction work if this were true, and that's impossible. Clients couldn't afford to pay for that. Our lawyers recommended the change of wording. It's a game they play to justify their existence. Job supervision is still the same thing it always was. We just call it something else."

Pat laughed heartily. "I'm familiar with that chicanery. He lit a cigarette and reached for the ash tray. "Do you have a contract for your services? I've had some experience with architects who do commercial work and all of them have some written agreement."

"I use the Standard American Institute of Architect's form. I'll give you a copy before you leave. Read it and highlight anything you question or want explained. If you're comfortable with it, I'll draw one up and mail it to you. You may want your attorney to look it over before you execute it. After you sign it, we'll schedule a conference and get things moving. Keep working on that questionnaire. In fact, jot down notes whenever you think of anything important. But please, don't start collecting pictures from magazines. Architecture is not a jigsaw puzzle."

Maria made a face and said, "I guess I can throw away my scrap book of the last ten years of *House Beautiful.*" She laughed when she saw my reaction.

"I deserved that," I said. I was going to like her.

Pat stood up and extended his hand. "We better go and let you get back to work. It's been a pleasure meeting and talking with you. I'm excited about getting started and I know Maria is. She's been working on me for the last month like Hitler was in Sumter."

I laughed. "Well that's only forty miles away. We'd better hurry. I'll start working on the contract this afternoon and have it in the mail tomorrow. Pat, do you have a card with your name on it? I sure want to be sure I spell your name correctly."

Pat reached into his wallet and slid a business card across the table to me. Then he moved behind Maria and slid her chair out.

Maria stood up, straightening her skirt with her hands. "We'll be back soon. If I have my way, we'll be looking at lots this weekend."

Pat laughed and said, "Terry, that's a true statement.

I walked them to the door and watched them cross the parking lot to their car, a new Buick sedan. It was after four, and I had a few more tasks to complete before leaving. Jane would be expecting me home early. I had promised to take her shopping for school clothes for the girls.

I got into my car, rolled the driver's side window down to let the heat escape, pulled out onto the inside lane and headed east listening to the Beatles singing *I Want to Hold Your Hand.* Our house is twelve miles from town in a new area called Oaklawn. So new, in fact, it is one of only two houses in the subdivision. My children, Laurie and Janet, don't like living so far out, but lots are cheaper away from town and struggling architects just starting out look for bargains. A drawback was that sooner or later I had to buy a car for Jane, and I wasn't sure I could afford two cars. A plus was that it gave me a chance to showcase my architectural ability. Nothing is easy.

I passed the large twin oaks laden with Spanish moss and an umbrella of green leaves and turned on to the road to my house. As I stopped in the driveway, Janet came running out of the house. "Daddy, Daddy! Laurie! Daddy's home!" Janet was starting the first grade and a total tomboy. Her long blonde hair was in a ponytail and bounced from side to side as she ran toward me.

"Hey Jumper," I said as got out of the car. I picked her up, hugged her, and put her down.

"Can we walk in the woods?" she asked. "This morning I saw a rabbit near the sassafras tree. Maybe it's still there. Can we go look Daddy? Can we please?" Her big blue eyes were full of anticipation and excitement and she was hopping from side to side.

I smiled at her. "Let's ask Mama first. You know, I promised to take ya'll shopping for school clothes tonight. We may not have time. Maybe if I told her we could stop at the drive-in for supper, she might say OK."

"I'll tell her Daddy," she said turning and running ahead to the door, her pony tail bouncing with each step.

Jane was laughing and watching the drama from the front door. She was silhouetted in the doorway in a yellow sundress which exposed her slender but ample figure. Her blue eyes were twinkling as she said, "Don't hang that on me, Big Shot. If you can do it in 15 minutes, go to it. Who am I to stop the great white hunters?"

"Lets go," I said to Janet. She held my hand and led me to a line of chinaberry and ligustrum saplings (a gift from bird droppings) under the power line. She jumped over a narrow ditch, pulling me along, and pointed to a thicket of wild plums. "That's where I saw the rabbit. He was under the edge of the plum bushes by the sassafras tree. He was brown and had a white tail," she said.

"He's gone Jumper. We'll try again tomorrow. Maybe we'll have better luck. Why don't we give him a name? What do you think?" I said.

"Thumper, Daddy, like that movie." She seemed pleased with that.

We turned and walked back to the house. The eastern horizon was a band of gray but overhead the sky was still a delicate robin's egg blue with puffs of cumulus clouds turning pink in the west. It was the end of a beautiful day.

Friday morning I awakened feeling refreshed and ready for the day. I lay quietly, listening to Jane's shallow, rhythmical breathing. She seemed so fragile lying there. I wanted to reach out for her, but my desire to do so was diminished by thoughts of her lack of enthusiasm for anything physical in the past few months. Perhaps getting the girls ready for school along with keeping the household running and the heat of the waning summer was getting to her. I was prepared to give her the benefit of the doubt but was becoming a little frustrated. We needed some time to ourselves, maybe a weekend at the beach or mountains. Perhaps I could entice my folks to keep the girls for a long weekend. My mother loved to keep them occasionally, and they hadn't had them for a while. Food for thought.

I got up quietly and started my routine. Shaved, showered, and dressed, I walked into the kitchen. Jane was fixing breakfast and the air was filled with the aroma of eggs, bacon, and coffee. She had started breakfast while I was in the shower. I walked up behind her and put my arms around her, letting my hands stray. She laughed, pushed me away and said, "Stop that. I don't have time for foolishness this early in the morning."

I wondered silently *when do you have time*, and reluctantly moved away.

"Fix your plate. I'm going to see if the girls are ready for breakfast. Probably can't pull them out of bed yet," she said.

I went outside for the newspaper and set it on the table before fixing my plate. I buttered some toast, covered it with Jane's homemade blackberry jam, and began to eat. It was delicious and I was hungry. Laurie appeared in her pajamas rubbing her eyes, and said, "Good morning Daddy." Unlike her sister, she was quiet, studious and feminine. She had the same blue eyes and blonde hair, but she was four years older.

"Good morning to you, Sleepy Head. Did you stay up too late last night?" I asked jokingly.

"My dumb sister kept me up talking about a stupid rabbit she saw in the woods. She thinks it doesn't have any food and she wants to take lettuce to it.

Can you believe that, Daddy? That rabbit probably eats more than she does." She shook her head, walked to the stove and fixed her plate.

"Well, we'll just have to humor her a little. You know how she is about animals. I think she misses Tinker, not that we all don't. Maybe we should get a puppy. Let's talk about that tonight." I knew that Laurie was upset more than anyone else when Tinker was killed and she might profit more from a new puppy than Janet. We got Tinker when Laurie was three, so she felt like he belonged to her. She didn't like sharing him with Janet but he tended to follow her because she was in the yard more, and he liked the outside.

"Could we get another cocker? Maybe a black one this time?" she said. "They're so cute when they're puppies."

"Sure, but let's see if we can find a pure blooded one." I thought for a minute and said, "Check out the want adds in the paper. Sometimes you can find adds for puppies in there. But talk with your mother before you get too excited. She may not be happy about a new pet in the house. If she says it's OK, we'll start looking. Now, I've got to go to work. I've got eggs to lay and chicks to hatch."

"Oh Daddy, that's silly," she said in mock disgust and returned to her breakfast.

I backed out of the driveway and turned onto the highway. The sun was beaming but the air was just cool enough to suggest the approach of fall. The sky was a crisp September blue without even a trace of clouds. It felt good to be a healthy 30 years old and on the way to work doing something I loved. Hell, I probably would have done it for free if I had to, but being paid for it was frosting on the cake. Space was my medium and manipulating it was drama to me. Almost anybody can plan in two dimensions but the interplay of space is what makes architecture special. Texture and color enhance space, and adapting buildings to nature make them appealing. But space is king. That's the difference between good and magnificent architecture. Gothic architects understood it, and Frank Lloyd Wright made it his trademark. His vacation house for Edgar Kaufmann, Sr., *Fallingwater*, embodies the best of all magnificent architecture and has always been my icon.

I exited off the highway into the suburbs, turned right on Peake Street for four blocks and left into my parking lot. My grandfather, bless his soul, left me a small lot in his will to help with my education. Fortunately, a basketball scholarship allowed me to keep it, and I built my office on it when I felt I was competent enough to start my own practice.

I built around two oak trees forming a "U" on three sides of them with a reception area, small conference room, and a drafting room for three draftsmen. My office was in a loft area over the drafting room, creating the feeling of a tree house mingling with the branches of the oaks. The lot was just large enough to provide parking for six cars and the rest of the lot was covered with indigenous plants. I brought in some large rocks from the river, piled them up around a small pool at the base of one of the oak trees and installed a waterfall system to pour water over the rocks. On quiet mild days I opened windows to hear the soothing sounds of the cascading water.

Martha's car was in the lot. Martha Wilhoit was my part-time secretary. When I was working for Bayer-Kline in my apprenticeship years, Martha was our best secretary. She retired shortly after I started my practice. She did some typing for me by the hour, and when my practice began to grow I asked her to work part-time for me. After the untimely death of her husband she wanted something to do, and agreed to work from eight to twelve each day. That was enough to take care of typing my specifications, routine correspondence, billing and bookkeeping. She answered the telephone with an impeccable, professional voice – giving the illusion of a larger office. She was an immaculately groomed 62 year-old, but she appeared much younger. In the year she had been working in my office, she had worked wonders doing the many chores that were routine for her, but very difficult for me. In fact, she had taught me how to run an efficient office. I knew when she decided to retire again I would have great difficulty replacing her. She was a godsend for a young practitioner, and I was fortunate to have her. She looked up from the typewriter as I walked through the door. "I ran copies of the spec sheets I've typed and put them on your desk. Mark them up for me so I can finish this section today. Oh! The ink for the mimeograph is low, so I ordered some. Office Supply said they would deliver it today, probably after lunch." Martha was not much on "good mornings" or "good-byes." She was all business and I liked that.

"Mrs. Champion called. She would like to stop by this afternoon after three. I told her it looked like your afternoon was free, but you would call if it didn't suit."

"OK. I have a Sertoma meeting at lunchtime, but I should be back before three. I'm going to Bear Mountain this morning to look at the Cutler property and I may not get back before you leave. I'll proofread the specs before I leave. I'd like to get this job finished by Monday or Tuesday. I'll need about twelve sets of bid documents, so type up the covers but don't print any specs. When I review the drawings, I may see something I want to change. It shouldn't be major. I'll help you run the specifications Tuesday."

"Oh! Call John and Walt and remind them to have their drawings and specs here by Tuesday. Tell them their review sets look good, and give them a commission number and a date for their documents. I think I forgot."

"I did that yesterday," she huffed as though I had insulted her. I smiled at her and left it there. I know better than to patronize her.

It was 2:15 when I returned to the office, and a package of mimeograph ink was by the door. Martha's car was gone and the door was locked. When I walked into the reception area, it looked like no one had been there. Her desk was clean, the typewriter was covered, and the flowers she kept on her desk were garden fresh.

I made some notes about the Cutler site and put them into the job file. As I finished, I saw a green and white ford pull into the parking lot. It was a '62 Ford Fairlane. Maria slid out of the door, closed it and walked toward the building. I met her at the door and opened it for her.

"Hey there, is this part of the service?" She smiled coyly.

I returned her smile and led her to the conference room. She still moved with that fluid motion I remembered from our initial meeting. She put a folder on the table, sat down, and said, "I need some advice. Pat's got too much on his plate to help me find a lot. Getting the plant set up is his first priority, as it should be, but I don't think we can wait that long to get started. I'll have lots of free time now with the children starting school and I could use it to get things moving. Sooner or later, he'll tell me he doesn't have time and suggest that I do it, anyway. The problem is I don't feel comfortable finding a lot, but I know that's the first step. I know you don't like to be involved, but please help me find something," she sighed, "or we might be months getting started."

I smiled. I understood what she was implying. Men don't place as much importance on planning as women do, but they usually do get involved in the selection of a lot. Closing a deal is a '"man" thing, and buying property falls in that category.

"Maria, call John Haskins and get him to show you some lots. I'll critique their physical properties and rank them on merit. Just don't tell me how much they cost. You and Pat can make the final choice as you see fit and Pat can work out the sale. If you think that will help, I'll be happy to do it."

"Oh Terry, you've made my day. You don't know how much I hated to ask you to help. I couldn't sleep last night worrying about asking you, but I felt I don't have any choice. I promise I won't make any problems for you."

Her green eyes were compelling and her sincerity was the coup de grace. I laughed. "It's OK, just don't tell anybody. I don't want this to become an expected part of my services. If you can hold off till Wednesday, I can handle it. I've got a project to get out and it's going to take some serious overtime to get it done. If I work this weekend and Monday night I should be finished by Wednesday."

She squeezed my hand gently as she stood up and said, "You'll never know how much I appreciate your doing this. I'll make it up to you. I hope this isn't the reason for the overtime."

"No, of course not. It goes with the territory. Architects are natural procrastinators, but they still must meet deadlines." I laughed and said, "I guess I just found another deadline."

"Is that normal for architects? Working overtime?"

"It is if you are a one-man firm. Probably the same for bigger firms with bigger work loads. I have a few guys who work for other firms who help me part time when I get behind or when I have a larger project. They work at night or on the weekends. I'm here when they are. Actually, I go home for supper a lot of nights and come back for two or three hours. More often than not, I work Saturdays and Sunday afternoons. My wife doesn't like it, but she understands that when I have work, I have to get it done. We bill about four times during a project, and it may last a year from start to finish. That can be tough on cash flow. Architecture is the original 'feast or famine' profession."

How in the world did you go into architecture?" she asked. "Did you know anything about it?

"Not about cash flow problems. That only comes with experience. I worked for my father in the hardware business each summer as a youngster and was around construction constantly. Architecture was a natural progression for me. I was exposed to many architects and was impressed with them. I was quick to notice how much they were respected by contractors and builders… and by my father. I had a king-sized case of hero worship. What really got me was all of them dressed well and drove big cars." I laughed. "How's that for misplaced values?

"Sounds normal to me," she said chuckling. "After all, you grew up just after the Depression and were in high school in the late forties, right? Opulence wasn't part of our lifestyle, so why not be impressed with affluence?"

"Absolutely. The most popular kids were the ones with access to automobiles. It didn't hurt to be part of the "in crowd" or be an athlete. Money didn't hurt either, but family name and wealth reigns supreme in the South. It still does, to some degree, but I think allowing the returning war veterans to have a free college education is putting a serious dent in that. It certainly is spreading wealth to a larger base, and I know that's good. So much for Socialism."

"Pat would agree with you. Not the Socialism bit, but he was in the navy during the war and used the GI bill to pay for his education. I think being in service helped him settle down or he probably wouldn't have done it. Actually, that's where we met. His being older and settled appealed to me."

"I was kidding about Socialism," I said. My feelings are entirely capitalistic. If you run a business, your goal is to turn a profit. It doesn't always go that way, but you won't last long if you don't. The government gets enough money from me now, and the bureaucrats take most of it before they give it away. But you don't want to hear me rant about government. Where did you attend college?"

I was born in Illinois, so I went to the greatest university of all, the University of Illinois. She smiled and said, "I'll bet you went to the University of South Carolina."

"Not hardly. I went to Clemson A & M College. You've probably never heard of it. It's the only place in the state that offers architecture and I had a little help, a partial basketball scholarship. I played basketball and was on the track team, but wasn't good enough or fast enough to make any impact. I got to eat on the training table and practicing kept me out of some of the military stuff. It was a military school like the Citadel or West Point, so it got a little brutal at times, especially the hazing. I love the place now, but my freshman year wasn't a lot of fun. But it taught me discipline, so it wasn't a total loss.

"Were you in a fraternity?" she asked.

"Sure, the cadet corps." I laughed. "We didn't have fraternities, except a few honorary ones. They may have some now since the cadet corps has been abandoned. Actually, being all male and military made it a pretty boring place, but there weren't many distractions so we had plenty of time to study. My biggest problem was missing my girlfriend. We couldn't come home until Thanksgiving so I was pretty homesick my freshman year."

"That sounds more like prison than college," she said incredulously. "Surely there was some entertainment."

"Well, once a month the girls from Anderson Junior College came over for a Saturday night dance at the YMCA. We could stay up until midnight, but the dances were pretty boring and they were very well chaperoned. I was pretty ordinary and skinny. And with a shaved head, I didn't attract much attention. Most of the girls went after the upperclassmen, anyway, and many of them already knew some of the guys."

"I can't believe you were ever skinny," she said. "Not that you're fat, but you certainly aren't thin."

"No, you're right. Uncle Sam fattened me up when I was in the service. I went into the army at 155 and came out at 175. I guess it was good German food. Apparently American food ain't so bad either. I've been gaining ever since and I'm up to 210 now. I always wanted to gain weight when I was young, especially in high school when I played football. Now I don't have any problem gaining weight. You must watch what you eat. You have a nice figure."

She blushed slightly and said, "Thank you. I'm a size 10 and being 5' 9", I think that's big enough. Pat and I play tennis and golf and that helps. We try to play golf every Sunday afternoon. I think he does that to humor me, but I enjoy it."

"Have you joined the country club?" I asked. "That's the only good golf course in town. To be truthful, that's about all we have for social life, so most of our friends are members. The food's not bad and the parties are interesting. You and Pat should try to make the fall dance. We usually have a decent band."

"We have joined, as a matter of fact, and plan to attend the dance. Pat enjoys golf and I encourage him to play. He played a lot of tennis in California. That's the national pastime there. Probably more tennis players there than any place in the world. Excuse me," she laughed, "more people there TRY to play tennis than any place in the world."

I liked her sense of humor. "Well", I laughed, "We have more shaggers than any place in the world, and you'll see some of them at the fall dance. You'll also see some of the worst, but that want stop them from trying."

"What in the world are shaggers?"

"I'm sorry. I forget you're not a native. The shag is a dance that started in the Fifties and was perfected in the Myrtle Beach area. It's a fast dance, a takeoff of the jitterbug. The music we dance by is called 'beach music'. It's a Southern thing."

"Is it hard to learn?"

"Not really. It has a basic step that's pretty easy. Good dancers create their own variations, which make it look complicated, but it's easy to learn. Right now, the big thing is the twist. You'll see some of that too."

"I can do that. That's big on the West coast. I like it but it wears me out. After I've had my limit of two cocktails, I can handle it. Two may not be enough to try the shag. I'll have to watch some and see if I can get the hang of it." She laughed. "Dancing's not one of Pat's favorites, but we ran with a group in California that had two or three good dancers, and I got plenty of opportunities."

I grinned. "W-e-l-l n o w, I'll see that you have plenty of partners, including myself. Southern boys see to it that all the ladies have a good time. As a matter of fact, I don't think you'll have any trouble finding someone to dance with."

She looked at her watch. With lips pursed and a warm smile she said, "I'm sorry. I've taken too much of your time. I know you're busy, so I'd better get out of here and let you work. You know what they say. 'Time goes by when you're having fun'. Actually, I'm still not sure who 'they' are, but I've enjoyed the conversation immensely."

"Hey, I enjoyed it, too. Don't worry about the time." I smiled. "It's part of the fee."

"Well" she said in mock disgust, "I'm not sure I appreciate that."

"No offense intended." I held up my hands in surrender.

I followed her as she walked toward the door. I hoped that she couldn't feel my eyes surveying her. I felt a little guilty, but she was certainly attractive. I opened the door for her and she lingered for a moment in the doorway.

"I appreciate your being patient with me. I can't wait to get started. I guess that's why I have to get settled in on a lot. Getting your help is the only way I'm going to get it done." I could feel some pleading in her thanks.

"Look, I really don't mind. I just don't like to get my prejudices into your decision. I'll try to keep an open mind."

"I'll accept that," she said as she turned and walked to her car. "See you," she said before speeding away. I waved and went inside. As I closed the door, the faint odor of her perfume fanned across my face. I had not noticed it before. It was pleasing.

I was troubled as I drove home. I was beginning to think about Maria in ways that I shouldn't. She was attractive and I had enjoyed our conversation. Since Jane's sexual ardor had been on the wane, I had thought about women in a general way with no particular identity. They were just amorphous creatures, sexy, waiting to please me. They were synthesized versions of Jane, as I wanted her to be. But now, I was thinking about forbidden fruit. I was thinking about someone else. I had given my imaginary lust a name and that was unforgivable. Worst of all, she was a client!! The dumb part was that Maria had done nothing intentionally to raise my libido. She just kicked up my hormones. This was one of those times when I wished I had no sex drive. Perhaps one day when I'm old, I won't think about it any more. I see that as a mixed blessing.

I saw the oaks with their plumes of Spanish moss jerking in the wind and turned the car between them onto the drive. The girls were playing ball in the front yard, but stopped and ran toward me as got out of the car.

"Well, how was school today?" I asked. "Is it better than Mrs. Green's?" I directed that to Janet because it was her first day in the first grade. That's pretty traumatic for any child. I didn't have a clue as to what she might say.

"I don't know, Daddy. We haven't done anything yet. Today, we got books and desks. I sit next to Jamie Croxton and we got called down for talking. The teacher said if we didn't behave, she would separate us. She's mean and I don't like her."

"Well, that's not a good way to start," I said. "You better start paying attention and try to learn. I don't need a dummy for a little girl. Besides, I think you want a new puppy and I might not get one if you keep misbehaving!"

"Daddy, that's not fair," Laurie shouted. "You can't punish me for something Janet does. Let me have the puppy by myself if she can't behave."

I was about to put myself between a rock and a hard place, so I sensed the need for a rapid retreat. "Well, let's wait another day and see what happens. If things are better Monday, we might try to find a puppy when I get home from work." The mouths began to turn up and the eyes were twinkling. I had hit a home run, and all was well. "OK girls, Let's see how Mama's doing. She's probably been working hard on our supper, and will appreciate hungry people". I grabbed their hands and we skipped off to the house.

I walked through the den to the kitchen to find Jane standing at the range preparing supper. She looked up at me and, in a mild state of agitation, said, "The club dance is next weekend, and I don't have anything to wear. Do you think we can afford to get me a new dress? I hate to do it, but I've worn the same dress the last two years. I'm embarrassed to wear it again."

I couldn't remember what dress she had worn or that she had worn it two years in a row, but I also knew it didn't matter what I thought. Women dress for women, not men. "Of course we can. I don't want people to think the 'great architect' can't afford to buy his wife a dress for the ball." I laughed and said, "Besides, I'll be stuck with you all night if you don't look good. Nobody'll dance with you." I stuck my lips out in a mini-pout, but she knew I was teasing her. She's a great dancer, and would have too many partners to suit me.

She didn't have time for the banter, though she did smile. "I'll have to hit all the shops early tomorrow if I'm going to find anything. I'm sure most of the nice dresses are gone by now, and it's always hard for me to find what I'm looking for. A nice dress will probably cost a hundred dollars, unless I can find a sale."

"Don't worry about the cost. Just make sure it looks good on that sexy bod," I said with a smile as I gave her a hug. I knew she wouldn't spend any more than she felt was reasonable. She was not an extravagant person, and had an innate ability to shop for bargains.

"I can charge it. That will prolong the agony. I've spent a good bit on the girls' school clothes, but I didn't charge anything. We don't have anything on our account at Belk's. Maybe I can find something there."

"Look, just find what you want. Don't buy something you don't like just so you can charge it. Go to the fancier shops and get whatever you really like. I have cash now and Martha sent out some bills this week. I've got plenty of work, so it shouldn't be a problem."

"I know..........but I hate to spend a lot on a dress I may wear only a few times. It seems like such a waste."

"So? You know I'm a member of the club primarily because it's a good place to make contacts. Just consider it as an advertisement, a business expense."

"You rat, now I don't feel bad about it at all. I'll buy the most expensive gown I can find." She stuck out her tongue. "I'm teasing, of course, but only because I know you are."

I laughed. "Don't be too sure."

"Enough," she said. "Just get cleaned up for supper. Find the girls. I'm sure they need some cleaning up. I'll have every thing on the table in about five minutes."

"OK, I'm on my way," I said as I passed her and gave her a pat on the fanny.

She laughed. "Are you going back to the office tonight?"

"Oh, I don't know. What do you have in mind? Something worth my while?"

She gave me a sexy look, licked her lips and said, "Why don't you stay home and find out?"

That was more like my baby, and it was enough for me. "I think I might just do that." I was whistling as I walked away. Maria was no longer in my thoughts.

I worked hard all day Saturday and Sunday afternoon. Monday and Tuesday, Martha and I managed to complete the Huguley residence working drawings and specifications. Martha made the few changes I wanted on the specifications and printed fourteen sets Tuesday morning. I needed thirteen sets but, being superstitious, she couldn't stop at thirteen. She managed to type the covers, punch the sheets, and put them together just after one o'clock. I was most appreciative and told her I would order some sandwiches to go as a reward, *ha, ha*!

"Thank you, but I don't think so. I've got to shop for a gift for my grandchild. It's her birthday, and I haven't had any time to find anything. You just need somebody to fetch it anyway. I know you!" She was trying to be gruff, but she couldn't. I saw the smile at the corners of her mouth.

"You've been around me too long, Martha. You know all my faults," I said jokingly. "I really appreciate your working overtime. I couldn't have finished this project on time without you. Take some time off tomorrow if you need to. Things won't be so frantic and I can hold down the fort. God knows, you certainly deserve it, having to put up with me."

"If you think you can make points with me that easy, think again," she huffed. "And you know an old warhorse like me couldn't let a deadline go by. Nobody really deserves thanks for that. That's just part of the job! Now let me get out of here before I start getting sentimental. With that, she was out the door. I knew that was vintage Martha and I had to chuckle.

Before I could pick up the telephone to order, it rang. "Terry Forte speaking."

"Of course you're Terry Forte. Who else could you be?" Maria said. "I've got some wonderful news and I need to share it with someone. Do you think you might be a worthwhile candidate?" She was laughing as she spoke.

"Depends on what it is. It must be powerful good. You sound so upbeat."

"It is, it is! I'm so excited. I spent the better part of two days with John Haskins looking at lots. What a super guy he is. I'm sure he thinks I'm some goofy lady. I made him show me everything he had. I've settled in on three lots, and they're all good. But one of them looks perfect. I know what I think is perfect may not be, but I know somebody who might help me make the right choice. Guess who?" she said in one breath.

"I can't imagine," I deadpanned. "Is it anybody I know?"

She laughed and spoke in the same moment. "It better be or you're toast. What are you doing for the next few minutes? I've just got to show you these plats and a few snapshots I took." I recognized the intensity in her voice.

"Well, to tell the truth, I was getting ready to order me some lunch when you called. I'm too lazy to go into town to eat. We finished the project we were working on, and maybe I need to celebrate. Nothing fancy of course."

"What might that be?" she asked.

"If you must know, a cheeseburger from the Blizzard shop. With everything, of course."

"How about some company? I haven't eaten yet; I've been too excited. If that's not too much of an imposition?"

"No...No, that's fine." It was kind of off the wall, and the suddenness of it made me pause. However, it seemed very appealing.

"Are you sure, now? I don't want to interrupt your work."

"Of course. It's a great idea". In fact, I was excited about her coming. But I didn't know why.

\OK, call in the order and I'll pick it up. Just get me whatever you get.

Oh...you can explain the significance of the name, you know, Blizzard Shop, when I get there. That must be a humdinger. And, by the way, this will be my treat!"

"Oh no! A dinner of this magnitude must be on the gentleman. I wouldn't have it any other way. Besides," I chuckled, "I can write it off as entertainment."

She paused. "And what if I don't entertain you?" she said provocatively.

"Well, we'll just have to see about that," I said and we both laughed.

"I'm on my way. Where is the Blizzard Shop?"

"After you turn off the Highway on Peake, it's about two blocks on the right. You can't miss it. It's pretty ratty. Don't let looks deceive you. The food is good. Not wonderful, but good."

"Good. See you shortly," she said and hung up.

In about ten minutes the phone rang. "Terry, Pat. Maria's real excited about your helping with the lot. Don't let her take up too much of your time. I really appreciate what you're doing. I would be there with you, but my plate is full right now. I'll be happy to pay you for this."

I was a bit taken aback by his call. "No, no. I'll try to steer her to the least expensive one." I regretting saying that, but it was all I could think of.

Pat laughed. "I'm counting on that. See you." He hung up abruptly. Well, at least he knew she was coming by. I had felt a bit guilty about her coming by for lunch. At least my guilt was assuaged by his knowledge of it. Somchow, that helped.

I tidied up my office and ran some prints while I waited for Maria. I was excited about her coming, and I was feeling good about getting the Hugeley residence documents completed and ready to go out for bids. I always enjoy looking at a finished set of drawings, particularly if the job went well, and I was pleased with the product. I was proud of this one, and was exited about soon getting it in the ground. I sensed that Maria's house would also be pleasing, but I've been fooled before.

I walked down stairs in time to see Maria bump the door open with her hip. She was laden down with bags and drinks.

"Anybody home?" She said as she bounced through the entrance. "I've got enough food for an army."

"Here, let me help you," I said, taking an armload. I led her to the conference room and put the bags and cups on the table. "This looks like more than I ordered."

She dug into the bags, spread the food and condiments orderly around the table and said, "Bet you don't have any ice and I didn't bring any."

"Bet I do. There's a refrigerator, sink, and a hot plate behind that folding door. Do you think this is a slack operation?"

"Since you work a lot at night and on the weekends, I should have known. Oh! The extra food is two pieces of apple pie. I thought I would reward you for being such a nice guy."

I laughed. "What makes you think I'm a nice guy? I could be Jack the Ripper for all you know."

"In this town? I don't think so. I haven't heard anything bad yet, so you must be pretty good, or you sure are fooling people. Besides, when could you misbehave? You work all the time."

"That's not true. I've had two long weekends in the last five years."

"Well, ex -c -u –s- e me," she said pointing to my place. "Sit. Let's eat before it gets cold. We can talk business while we eat. That way we won't waste your time. This can be one of those working lunches." I could see that business-like part of her personality emerging.

"Let's chat for a while first. I just wrapped up a project.... a long but gratifying project, and I need a catharsis before I start the next one. Good food and interesting conversation are a good respite. Helps clear the cobwebs out. Now I'll be ready to start my next project – your project." I smiled and watched her face for a reaction. She leaned back in the chair and started a slow-motion smile.

"I'm really excited. I'm just trying not to show it. I'm a little afraid too, because I feel so stupid about all this. I've got to make some big decisions and they must be right. Do all women get a little crazy when they start planning a home, or is it just me?" She looked genuinely perplexed and I was surprised.

"Don't feel that way. A home is arguably the largest investment you'll make in your life. That can't be taken lightly. I'm sure you'll do the right thing. After all", I gave her one of my best buddy grins, "you hired me, didn't you?" Her face changed into a smile and I could see her relax.

She picked up her burger and, after a long look at it, said, "Don't let me ruin lunch.... enjoy." She took a big bite, chewed slowly, and rolled her eyes. "Um, this really is good. You didn't lie when you said the food was good. I wasn't sure when I first walked into that place. Some of the people in there look like they've been there so long that they're part of the furnishings. That guy on the grill looks like someone in a Humphrey Bogart movie. In fact, the whole place looks like a movie set."

"But", I said, "how about that jukebox? How often do you see one of those these days? I've never been in there when *Smokey Places* wasn't playing, or some real basic country music. I screw 'em up every once in a while by playing *Stranger on the Shore*. I love that song. I don't know how it got on there."

"Well," she said, "I felt kinda uncomfortable in there. That's the kind of place you have to be member to be accepted. And, I didn't hear *Stranger on the Shore*. Sounded more like Grand Ole Opry to me. Is it safe to just walk in there off the street?"

I laughed. "Do you really think I would let you go in there if it was dangerous? Most of the people I've seen in there are not locals. In fact, most of them are migrants, and they usually disappear in a few weeks. The two story white house behind it rents rooms by the week, and most of those folks come from there. I've never seen anyone I know in there, and I stop there probably once or twice a week. I've never been harassed by anyone or heard of any problems happening there."

"I still think you have to be very hungry, very brave, or both to go in there the first time."

"Actually, my friends and I found it when we were early teenagers. They made the best thick milk shakes in about a million flavors. Only they called them 'blizzards'. That's where the name came from. They've changed hands a few times and they don't make blizzards anymore, but the name never has changed. Probably don't have enough money to change the name, or don't care."

"Well, if you say it's OK, I'll accept it. The cheeseburger is yummy. I can't deny that."

I stared at her as she took a big bite of her burger. She was very attractive and easy to engage in conversation. "Hey, let's talk about you for a while. I'm supposed to be finding out about you, but I'm not doing a very good job of it."

She laughed and said, "I was born and raised in Pekin, Illinois. Have you heard of it?"

It was my turn to laugh. "No, I'm afraid I haven't. But, I doubt if you knew much about Columbia until you moved here."

"Pekin is a small town about twelve miles southwest of Peoria. Pekin's about a third the size of Columbia. I guess Peoria is about the same size as Columbia. About the only thing going for it is it's the birthplace of Senator Everette Dirkson, and it's sometimes referred to as the Marigold Capital of the world. I attended Pekin Community High School and, believe it or not, I was a cheerleader for the Mighty Red Dragons. I lived there until I finished college, and I got married in July after I graduated. Pat and I started our married life in Atlanta, moved to San Diego, and now here. I started out working as a speech therapist, but motherhood put a stop to that. I hope to get back into it, but haven't had time. That's about it."

"Whoa...you're not getting off that easy. Tell me something about your childhood."

She thought for a minute before she started, searching for a place to begin. "My father works at Caterpillar, and my mother is a housewife. I have an older sister and brother. My sister married young, and never went to college. I think her idea of life was to start a family as soon as possible and she did. She married her high school boy friend and seems really happy. My brother finished high school and joined the navy when the war started. I think he served for three-and-a-half years. He never talked much about it, but he saw a lot of action in the South Pacific. It took him a little time to settle down, and then he went to Colorado School of Mines on the GI bill and majored in petroleum engineering. He's in the oil business and seems to do well. Phew!" she said, let's rest a minute. I'm not getting to enjoy my cheeseburger."

"Gee", I said, making a face. "Don't stop now. I feel like I'm really getting to know you, and, lowering my voice to add an air of mystery to my request, "I.... want....to....know ....MORE!"

We both started laughing and rocking in our chairs. Still smiling, I said, "I'm the architect playing psychiatrist now. I'm trying to get into your head, learn some of the intimate parts of your life. No, that's not quite right. I want to see the natural side of you."

She lowered her eyes, almost flirting, and said haltingly, "Is this included in the fee?"

I smiled and lowered my voice. "Everything is included in the fee." I knew instantly that I had crossed the line and I was sorry. She looked shocked and apprehensive and I was suddenly uncomfortable. I cleared my throat and said, "Hey! Let's look at your lot material."

She looked at me for a moment before she pushed the lunch debris across the table and grabbed her file. She seemed relieved to return to business. She handed me three real estate ads with photos attached to them and said, "I've ranked them in my mind, but I'm not going to tell you my favorite." The camaraderie was no longer in her voice and I sensed that we had better end this meeting before it got any worse.

"I can't be objective until I've looked at them. I can't do that before Friday. Hey, we'll have something to talk about at the club dance Friday night. I guess you're still going?"

"Yes, we'll be there. Pat and I are looking forward to it. I hope we have a dance or two and Pat and I can meet your wife."

I smiled. "It's as good as money in the bank. Oh my, I have an appointment at 4:00 and I almost forgot about it. That's what happens when you're having fun." That wasn't quite true, but I had promised Jane I would stop at the grocery on the way home.

She looked at her watch and said, "I've got to pick up the children at school at 3:30 so I'd better get going. I hope I didn't take up too much of your time."

"No, of course not, it goes with the territory. I really enjoyed it. Besides," I laughed, "you pack a good lunch."

She smiled faintly and said, "I'm afraid I'll have to give the Blizzard Shop credit for that." She stood up and began to pick up the lunch litter but I waved her away. "I can do that. You need to get going if you want to make it to school in time to pick up your children."

She grabbed her folder and said, "Keep the ads and photos for your file. I have copies of them."

I walked her to the entrance and held the door open for her. She moved through the door hurriedly, turning just long enough to say, "See you". I watched her turn out of the parking lot before I closed the door.

10

The girls were playing in the front yard as I drove up. It was one of those sultry days we get in the early fall, and I had all of the windows down. I smiled and said, "Is it too hot for a ball game?"

Sure to form, Janet said, "Yay! I'll get the bat and ball." Laurie looked a little undecided, but she said, "I'll play if I can bat first."

Janet quickly replied, "That's not fair. You always bat first," but she went into the house to get the ball and bat with no further words.

When Janet returned, I grabbed the ball and said, "I'll pitch and you two can take turns batting and catching. We'll play roll the bat so we want have to run as much. It's kinda warm today. I don't know how much ole dad can take." I took off my jacket, loosened my tie, rolled up my sleeves and said, "Let's play ball."

Laurie stepped up to our assumed home plate in front of the front steps and Janet stood behind her. "Don't pitch too fast Daddy," she said.

Janet said impishly, "Throw it hard, Daddy, and strike her out. She can't hit it anyway."

Laurie turned toward her. "I can hit better than you can, Dummy." I recognized the sibling rivalry and enjoyed it.

I smiled and went into my wind-up. "Get up to the plate and let's see you hit it." I lobbed the plastic ball underhanded and watched her miss it badly.

"Naa, naa, naa, who's a dummy now? I told you you couldn't hit it," Janet said as she threw the ball back to me. Laurie rolled the bat in her hands and pursed her lips into a determined look as she awaited the next pitch. I tried to pitch it smoothly into her swing plane. She banged it over my head, dropped the bat and turned toward her sister with that *I told you so* look.

"OK Smarty, let's see what you can do!"

I picked up the ball and went through the obligatory roll to hit the prone bat, but made sure I would miss it. This was their fun and I wanted to enjoy it with them. I motioned Janet to the imaginary plate and lobbed a pitch to her.

She watched the first pitch hit the ground in front of her and then smacked the next one just to my right. She laid the bat down and turned to Laurie with her tongue stuck out to convey her message. With some luck, I had satisfied both of them. I say luck because Laurie, with not much athletic ability, had managed to hit the ball, and Janet, the tomboy, had accomplished the same feat.

After a reasonable time, I called the game amid groans from the girls, who wanted to continue. The heat and humidity had extracted copious quantities of sweat that marked the underarms of my shirt and the waistband of my trousers, but I felt that the quality time with the girls vindicated my disheveled look. "Put up the bat and ball, and let's see what supper looks like."

I picked up my jacket and we walked into the house. The air-conditioning unit was working at capacity to keep the house cool and the temperature change was noticeable and welcome. We wandered into the kitchen where Jane was busily getting supper ready. I put one arm around her waist and kissed her quickly on her lips. She pushed me away. "Ugh! Look at you. You're a sweaty mess. Your clothes are ruined."

I playfully hugged her again, this time with both arms and replied, "Where did all that stuff go about honoring, loving, and cherishing until death do us part?"

"I don't remember sweaty bodies being included in that line," she said curtly. "Maybe you could honor me a little by taking a quick shower before we eat. What do you think, girls? Should Daddy get a quick shower?"

"If Dad has to, I will too!" replied Janet quickly. I realized it was her way of taking my side. I was in too good of a mood to let this escalate, so I picked her up and set her on my shoulders. "Let's go, Babe Ruth," and we started to the back of the house.

Jane chuckled. "Don't make a mess in the 'locker room'. I just cleaned the bathrooms today, and don't tarry. Supper's almost ready."

After a quick shower, I returned in a pair of shorts and a t-shirt, feeling refreshed and cooler. I could smell meat sauce with a hint of chili seasoning and basil. "Um! Smells good. Smells like spaghetti. Are you trying to entice me or something?"

"Maybe. Actually, I wanted to show you my new dress, the one for the dance Friday night. I want to be sure you're in a good mood before I tell you what it cost. Take the salad plates to the table for me, and I'll get the garlic bread from the oven. There's Italian and blue cheese dressing on the table."

After we ate, I started clearing the table. "I'll help you clean up the mess. You wash and I'll dry." We had a place in the base cabinet for a dishwasher, but I hadn't been able to pay for it, so we still washed them by hand. With both of us toiling, we finished up quickly.

I went into the den and cut the TV on. I tried both channels and settled on *The Show of Shows,* and watched Sid Caesar go through one of his German language comic routines. We had two local channels, one VHF and one UHF. Neither of them provided great reception, but if the snow was minimal, it was OK. Jane was in the back getting the girls ready for bed and checking over their homework.

The program was going off when she came into the den. "How do you like it?" she said giving me her best Loretta Young twirl. She had on a tight-fitting, low-cut blue gown with spaghetti straps. She looked gorgeous. The color was perfect with her blue eyes and blonde hair.

"You look good enough to eat. I'll have to keep my eyes on you at the dance. You'll have all the guys going crazy."

"Think so?" She turned her back to me, looked over her shoulder provocatively, and gave me a slow shimmy. "Cut off the TV and let's go to bed. The girls are already asleep."

She was amazing. One minute she was an ice cube, and the next she was a sex machine. Nevertheless, I got the message. I cut off the TV and followed her to the back of the house with visions of sugarplums dancing in my head – sexy ones at that.

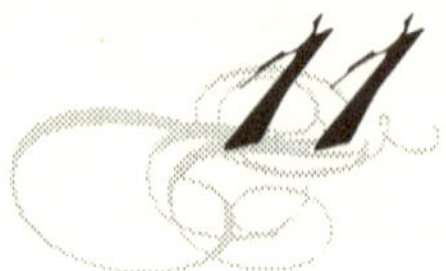

The balance of my week was routine, and I was ready for a weekend. I put up my drafting tools, covered my drawing board and took one last look around the office before leaving. I felt my party face coming alive. I was excited about the club dance tonight. I hadn't done any serious partying in a while, and I was READY! I was a little curious about how Maria would react. I hadn't heard from her since our lunch, and I thought that strange, especially with all that excitement about looking at lots. Damn, I told her I would look at them today. That wasn't good, but maybe I could regain her trust if the evening went well. I knew I wouldn't do anything to embarrass either of us. That wasn't my style. Maybe she had been too busy with other things and had no time for her house. I hoped that was the case. I really liked her, but I didn't harbor any romantic feelings for her although she was certainly an attractive woman. I guess I just let my comfort level with her get out of hand. *Oh well, I'm not going to let this make me feel uncomfortable around her, especially tonight. Jane is no dummy. She'll pick up on it even if it's not really obvious. Sometime during the evening, I'll bring Pat and Maria over to our table and introduce them around. That will be expected. I'll do my obligatory dance with Maria and encourage all the guys with us to do the same. With her looks and a little Johnny Barleycorn, they won't need much encouragement.*

I walked outside into the warm September air, whistling Chubby Checker's *Let's Twist Again, Like We Did Last Summer.* The car was very hot so I rolled the windows down and played convertible all the way home. I suspected that Jane had the girls ready for our night out. They were nowhere to be seen. It was unusual for them not to be outside when I drove up so I felt sure Jane was getting them bathed and dressed for the babysitter. Jane had that fresh scrubbed, blue-eyed, blonde, natural beauty that takes little maintenance, but she would manage to take at least two hours to get ready. *We don't go out much so I don't mind. Besides, I'm not looking forward to getting in my tuxedo, but I will admit to a little nervous excitement.*

I walked through the back door in time to see Jane scurrying into the kitchen in her bathrobe with her hair in rollers. "You've got to pick up Jessie at 7:30 so you better get moving. She couldn't get a ride. Sorry about that. We'll miss a little of the cocktail hour, but it's worth it to have Jessie. The girls like her, and she doesn't mind the late hour. I've got to fix something for the girls to eat. Then I can finish getting ready. Oh! I ironed your shirt and pressed your pants. They're in your closet."

"Thanks Honey. I forgot all about that. I'm glad you thought about it. They're clean, but they get wrinkled hanging in the closet for so long between wears. I should have taken them to the cleaners. After the dance I'll definitely take them."

"Don't tell me ole twinkle toes is going to do some high stepping," Jane said with a grin. "I was beginning to think you wouldn't get on a dance floor unless it looked like a drawing board. I guess there's hope for you yet, not to mention all those lucky women I can share you with."

"Yey? Just wait till they play some Chubby Checker number. I'll show you a thing or two."

"Sure, sure. I'll bet a dollar to a doughnut you won't dance over five times the whole night."

I stuck out my tongue and said, "You're on. Hey, I've got to get it in gear. I'm going to speak to the girls before I shower. I'll be ready in plenty of time. I'll take them with me to pick up Jessie if they want to go."

Jane and I pulled into the parking lot after a fifteen-minute drive to the country club. We went through the usual litany before we left: "You can stay up until 11:00; ice cream's in the freezer but don't be piggish; mind Jessie and don't argue. Jessie, we'll be in by 2:00. If you need us the telephone number is written down on the pad by the kitchen phone."

I jumped out and opened Jane's door. She looked great and I told her so. I grabbed her hand and we drove off for a night of bacchanalian revelry, one of a few in the course of our usual year.

"Do I detect a little more bounce in your step?" she said jauntily. She cocked her head slightly and smiled impishly, wrinkling her nose. Tight curls framed her face. She was elegant, cute, and beautiful, all at the same time.

"Ha! You noticed. I'm getting psyched up to win our bet. You'll be sorry you ever messed with me, girl!"

"Sure.......the proof's in the pudding, as they say. Talk's cheap."

I opened one of the massive double entrance doors and we entered a lobby full of people talking in small groups. The noise had reached the two-drink decibel level and was laced with various levels of laughter. We had some catching up to do. I pointed to a group of people huddled together in the center of the ballroom and said, "There's our gang. Go over there and I'll get us a drink. What's your pleasure? Scotch, bourbon, vodka or gin?"

"I think this'll be a vodka night for me. How about with orange juice and a touch of soda? Make it mostly orange juice or both of us will be sorry."

"OK," I said as I wriggled my way through the masses toward the nearest bar. I ordered Jane's vodka and got a scotch and water for myself and then I made the trek back through the crowd, protectively clutching both drinks close to my chest. I spoke to some friends and acquaintances, smiled at some I wasn't sure of, but kept walking without any small talk. I gave Jane her drink, shook hands with the fellows, and kissed the wives on the cheek.

It was good to see the gang together; we hadn't been out with them for a few months. Normally, we were six couples, but tonight, only five – Bill and Sandy Jackson, Garth and Ann Spann, Winston and Patti Gage, and Jerry and Toni Lieb. Ken and Judy Clyburn had a sick child and had had to drop out at the last minute. Bill is a general contractor, Garth is a sales rep for Westinghouse, Winston is an attorney, and Jerry is my dentist. Bill, Garth, and I attended the same schools together from the first grade through college, and Bill was my college roommate and remained my closest friend. We spend more time with the Liebs because Toni had been Jane's best friend since childhood. Actually, Jerry and I had become good friends since he came into Toni's life and he is a hoot to be around. He is a very unconventional guy and is always entertaining.

I scanned the ballroom for Maria but couldn't locate her. I turned just in time to see her coming into the ballroom with Pat and two other couples. They made their way into the crowd near one of the bars and vanished. Jane tugged at my sleeve and said, "Let's claim a table that's not too near the bandstand. I don't like too much noise." I walked behind her with the rest of the group to a table on the front row but comfortably to the left of the bandstand. The women laid their purses on the table and turned the chairs up against the table edge. They quickly turned inward and began to talk about the other women at the dance – most notably, their dresses and grooming. There were a few "oohs" and "aahs" at the jewelry on display. The men also were ogling the ladies in their finery, but their comments were lusty.

"Hey guys, take a look at Mabel" Jerry gushed. "If she bends over in that low cut, those pups'll be rolling on the floor."

"What do you mean?" Win said. Those aren't pups. They're Saint Bernards."

Bill said quietly, "Too bad her brain isn't equally as large."

"Damn Bill, lighten up!" Jerry said, chuckling. "What's brains got to do with it, anyway?"

"Come on guys," I said. "You're making me feel like I'm with a bunch of voyeurs. Let's get another drink before dinner's served." I turned and walked toward the nearest bar with the gang in lockstep. Garth caught up with me and said, "We left the girls without asking them if they want another drink. I'm going back for orders. Get me a scotch and soda."

Good ole Garth, Mr. Lancelot himself. "Sure Garth, good idea. I'll get your drink." We approached the drink line and waited our turn. As we stopped,

I saw Pat and Marie walking toward me from the bar with drinks in hand. Both of them smiled and spoke as they passed me and Marie said," I'm saving a dance for you. Don't make me wait too long." She was in a snug-fitting green gown, elegantly tailored. Her cleavage was modestly but seductively displayed, her tanned shoulders bare and her narrow waist and flat stomach accentuated by her slightly rounded hips. Her brown hair was on top of her head just as it was when we met, with soft wisps of curl in front of her ears. No question about it, she was just absolutely gorgeous.

It was with some effort that I was able to get affirmative words out as she passed. "You're first on my list." It was a stupid retort but the best I could do under the circumstances.

"WHO was that?" Jerry stammered. "Terry ole buddy, I believe you're holding out on us. How in the hell do you know her?"

"New client. They just moved here from California. Pat and Marie Champion. He's the manager of the Network America Plant," I said casually. "Nice people."

He grinned lewdly. "Didn't bring their dentist with them, did they? I'd work on her free but don't tell her that. Just give them my name and throw in some good words, like 'best in town', 'wonderful', 'reasonable', etc. Better yet, I'll do your work free if you can talk them into coming to me."

Garth walked up and I handed him his drink. "Thanks. Wasted trip. None of them wanted a drink. They're too busy talking. Say, were you talking to the Champions?"

"Damn," Jerry said. "You know them too? I can't believe it."

I smiled. "I'm designing a home for them and looking forward to it, I might add. How do you know them, Garth?"

"I've been calling on him. We manufacture some electrical items they will be using at the plant. I want to bid on them. Pat's a nice guy. I don't know his wife, but I recognize her from her picture on his desk. She's a looker."

I could hear the musicians warming up. The trilling of the various instruments was a cue that it was time to eat. I said, "We'd better head back to the table. The buffet line is open." The band always played some soft mood music during the buffet. A few adventurous souls would occasionally slip out onto the dance floor for a slow dance or two. Sort of broke the ice for the more timid ones. By the time dinner was over, most would be on the floor, or ready to be.

I walked over to the women and clutched Jane's arm. "Let's get some food. I'm ready to do some dancing!"

"I'm sure," she said rolling her eyes as she turned from the jabbering women. "If you start early, you can get your five dances over in record time. I'll get in line, and you can get me another drink. Tell the bartender less vodka and more orange juice. I don't want to be knee walking when the dance is over."

"Done deal," I said, and made my way back to the bar. I saw Maria and two ladies entering the ballroom from the lobby, clutching evening bags. I assumed they had made one of many treks to the powder room that is standard fare for women at social events. She spotted me, smiled, and pointed at me in six-shooter fashion with her index finger. I moved my feet in a quasi-dance shuffle and pointed to her and rapidly back to me. She smiled and nodded her head in the affirmative before moving away. I got Jane's drink and went back to the table. I put our drinks by her bag. I found her near the beginning of the buffet table and slid into line behind her.

" Where's my drink?" she asked.

"I thought it would get in the way going through the line, so I put it on the table." She nodded her approval and moved through the line.

"My, my," I said as I patted my stomach. "That was goooooood! I believe we finally have a chef that understands taste is more important than presentation."

I pulled out my package of Kents and lit a cigarette. "How about you?" I extended the pack toward Jane.

"No thanks. I'd kinda like to dance before the floor gets too crowded."

The overhead lights were dimmed and a few spots lit the bandstand, where a female vocalist was beginning to sing *Again*. The crystal ball was turning, sending colored raindrops through a blue-gray cloud of cigarette smoke onto the dance floor, giving the dancers a sense of anonymity and intimacy as they moved about the floor. I grabbed Jane's hand and nodded toward the dance floor. We found an empty spot and started slowly dancing to the rhythm with all the other bodies on the floor. She tensed as I pulled her close to me. "Careful," she said. Don't want to mess up my hair and dress. They have to last until the dance is over." The truth is that Jane doesn't like to slow dance. She prefers to shag or twist if the music is good, and she's good at both. I don't think she would have given me the time of day if I hadn't been a pretty fair dancer when I met her. That may have been her main criteria.

"We'll see how long you worry about the hair and dress when they play some shag music," I said with a huge grin.

I spotted Pat and Maria and guided Jane in their direction. When the music stopped, I said, "See that couple talking with John and Carla Haskell? I want you to meet them. They just moved here from California, and I'm doing a house for them." They were still talking as we approached. "Hi Pat, Maria." I turned toward John and Carla. "John, Carla, how are you doing?" I shook hands with Pat and John and Jane spoke to John and Carla.

"I want you to meet my wife, Jane. Jane, this is Maria and Pat Champion. They just moved here from California. Pat is the manager of the new Network America plant."

Jane smiled and said, "I'm so glad to meet you. Terry tells me he's working on your house."

Maria shook Jane's hand and said with a laugh, "He is, and I'm sure I'm driving him a little crazy. I can't help it. I get a bit carried away with the immensity of it. I didn't realize how complicated it would be."

"Maria's a perfectionist, and when she starts a project she really gets focused. I wish I had more of that quality, but I don't," said Pat. "Don't get too upset with her if she takes a lot of Terry's time."

"I won't. I'm accustomed to him working long hours. He's a perfectionist too, but you wouldn't know it at home. It's hard to get him to change a light bulb. Jane laughed robustly, "I guess it's that thing about bus drivers not wanting to take a trip. He's great at the office but he doesn't bring it home."

"I have great empathy with Terry, Jane," said Pat. "I think most men like to leave their work at the office at the end of the day. We have so little time to relax."

Maria brushed her hair back and spoke to Jane. "I think they protest too much, don't you Jane?"

"Maria, I think you have them dead in your sights. But for all his faults, Terry really loves architecture. I'm sure he'll do a good job for you. It's really been nice to meet both of you. We'll have to get together soon." Jane smiled demurely. "The invitation is for real, not just some of that famous Southern hospitality."

Maria smiled back and said, "I'll hold you to that, Jane. We'll have to do dinner soon. We don't know very many good places, but I'm sure you do."

"Absolutely," I said, as the band cranked up with a slow number. I put my arm around Jane and we danced away.

Jane put her head on my shoulder and whispered, "She's very nice, and very attractive. Pat's a lucky man."

"If you like tall Yankee women, but I'm kinda partial to little sweet Southern girls myself."

"Don't give me that crap. I know how you men are. Any cute woman is fair game and never safe around you ...Southern GENTLEMEN."

I laughed and rolled my eyes. "No way will I agree with that." I held her tighter and felt her familiar body press against me. The drinks were working on her inhibitions. I liked that.

The music stopped momentarily and the band broke into some beach music. The older couples stood back as the younger couples jumped on the dance floor with reckless abandon. Everyone was shagging, or trying to. Jane and I had been dancing together for a lot of years, and both of us had spent many summers at the beach. We had several routines we had developed over the years, and we both liked to dance and were pretty good at it. Some of the couples stopped dancing and formed a loose circle around us to watch. I enjoyed playing to the crowd, and Jane, though she wouldn't admit it, enjoyed it also. She is a better dancer than I am, and draws most of the attention. I led her into some of our routines and let her work her magic. I could see envy in the eyes of the women as she made some of her patented moves. She is really good and makes every move look so effortless.

I wiped my brow as the music stopped, stepped back from her, and stretched to cool off. "I believe I could stand a fresh drink. How about you?"

"Don't mind if I do," she said. "That was fun. It's been a while since we've been able to dance like that. Life really isn't over after you reach thirty, Surprise, surprise."

I walked away, looking back at her. "Hey! No telling what you might do after another vodka and orange juice."

"Don't count on it, but who knows?" she said, smiling wickedly.

As I walked toward the bar, I felt a tug on my arm. I turned to a smiling Maria.

"Did you have a chance to look at the lots today?" she asked.

"Oh my God! I completely forgot. I apologize. I had so much on my mind."

I saw her frown. "Don't..... Say, you guys are really good. What is that dance you were doing?"

"That's the shag. I told you about it when we had lunch in my office."

"It looks neat. I don't think I can do it, but I want to learn."

I gave her a serious look. "I've heard it said that learning to shag is included in the architectural fee."

Maria stared at me for a moment. Then she smiled and said, "When do we start?"

"How about the next good beach song?"

"You've got a deal," she said and we both laughed. "I've had my two prerequisite drinks and I'm about to start a third. I guess that should be enough to make an idiot out of myself."

I gave her one of those *don't kid me* looks. "Somehow, I don't believe you would ever make an idiot out of yourself. " In fact," I said as I grabbed her hand and led her toward the dance floor, "I think we should put our drinks down and dance to the next number no matter what it is."

She put her drink on the bar and said," Let's do it."

As we moved onto the dance floor the band broke into a twist melody. A tall, lanky member of the band moved into the spotlight. "Let's twist again, like we did last summer," he sang, almost in key. After the drinks, it didn't seem too bad. Maria laughed and said, "Well, at least you don't have to teach me the twist." She dropped my hand, turned to face me and began to twist her hips with the music. I got in sync with her and watched her movements. She was a good dancer, easy to dance with. She danced with the same fluid motion that I noticed when she walked. She slipped into some interesting variations, twisting on one foot, then the other, but always in perfect balance and rhythm. She was putting on a clinic, but she appeared to be oblivious to it. It was over too soon even though it lasted long enough to bring perspiration to our faces. She took a deep breath, and rubbed her brow with the back of her hand. "That was fun. I believe we must have danced together in another life."

"I had the same feeling." We stared at each other until the band started a slow instrumental, and, instead of walking off the floor, we moved together for another dance. I put my arm around her waist and she leaned against me. I felt her warm, damp forehead against my cheek and smelled the delicate scent of her perfume. I held her comfortably close and noticed that her height made us a good fit. She was three or four inches taller than Jane, probably 5'8" or 9, and with heels she was just right for me. We danced in a small area, oblivious to time and surroundings, more like lovers than new acquaintances. It was a wonderful feeling. There was no grinding together, grabbing, or lust. We danced with a quiet feeling of tenderness. Maybe it was the effect of the drinks, but whatever it was, I didn't want it to stop. I had no sense of guilt for my feelings, and didn't care who knew it. That's pretty damn dangerous. Alcohol has the ability to make me invisible. *Ha, Ha.*

Without realizing it, we danced through three more numbers and the band took a break. I was still holding Maria's hand when I saw Jane walking toward us with an unpleasant look in her eyes.

"Hey Fred Astaire, did you forget about the drink I sent you for?" She looked at Maria and said, "I hope he didn't wear you out. He just doesn't know when to stop once he gets started."

Maria laughed. "I made the mistake of asking him to explain solar heat and he made the mistake of doing it. It's my fault. You know how gallant Southern men are."

With that quick thought, Maria had given me the perfect out. "I guess I'd better apologize to both of you. I'm sorry I took so long to get your drink, Jane, and I'm sorry I got so verbose with my explanation about solar heat, Maria." I gave them both a mock bow and my best boyish smile. I hoped I didn't look too stupid. Even though I had, with Maria's help, diffused a situation that could have gotten ugly, I didn't like Jane's coming out on the dance floor to retrieve me. It wasn't her style and it didn't become her. I noticed Pat on the edge of the dance floor talking with some friends. He was keeping a close watch at what we were doing.

I turned to walk away, feeling better but wondering what Pat must be thinking.

"I'll get your drink, Jane. How about you, Maria?"

"Thanks Terry, I think I'll pass."

I walked to the bar and asked for a vodka and orange juice for Jane and a double scotch and water for myself. I felt the need for a confidence boost and some bottle bravery. I made up my mind to say little, or to play the incident down if Jane wanted to make it an issue. As I turned from the bar, Jane appeared and reached for her drink.

"Thanks," she said with a touch of sarcasm.

I refused to fall into the trap. "You're welcome."

We walked to the table and I put my drink down. "Let's dance and let the drinks cool off. That's a good shag number and they don't play many." I was really thinking *Let's you and I cool off, and dancing might do it.* She put her drink on the table, gave me one of those 'I'm still mad' smiles, and walked out on the dance floor. I noticed her failure to reach for my hand as she walked away, not a good sign. Nevertheless, her state of mind didn't affect her dancing, which was flawless, and she appeared to enjoy it. After the shag music, the band slipped into a slow piece, and Jane immediately left the floor. I assumed that she wasn't ready for any physical contact, and followed her back to the table.

In an attempt to bring things to closure and to prevent an absolute night of horror, against my better judgment and previous resolve, I offered a small apology. "Jane, I'm sorry. Let's not let this get out of hand. It's not that big a deal. I just wasn't thinking."

She took a deep breath, set her jaw and her lips were drawn into a thin line. She hesitated so she could get everything exactly right before she spoke. "Terry, I don't think it's too much to expect a husband to keep his wife foremost in his mind, especially when he's on a mission for her. To think that you could get carried away with some women who's more of an acquaintance than a friend is a little much. Oh, I'm sorry. A woman who is a **client** rather than a friend. I *expect* you to dance with *our* friends. In fact, I encourage you to. But I expect you to remember whom you came with, and that you treat me with respect. I'm not trying to read anything into this, at least not yet. I just think it's a matter of good manners and you let me down. It's embarrassing to be left unattended at a dance, and it's really embarrassing for me to have to suck up my pride and come looking for you. I felt like a fool coming out on the dance floor to get you."

"Look Jane, what's done is done. I made a mistake, but I can't change it. I'm sorry it happened, but you know how I am when someone asks me a question. If it's not a yes or no question, I'll find a way to answer it with every word in my vocabulary. Let's face it. I like to talk, particularly when it has to do with architecture." There was some truth in my argument, but in my heart, I knew I was lying and that hurt. I knew the real reason for my behavior was that I had enjoyed every single minute of it. And what's more, I would do it all over again. That troubled me and I felt bad for Jane. I felt myself being drawn to a woman I hardly knew, and I really didn't know why.

"I'm so sorry, Jane. You're absolutely right. You're my wife, lover, and best friend and you deserve better. It won't happen again." I meant what I said, but I knew that something very bad was happening to our relationship, and spending so much time dancing with Maria was just a symptom. I had never put anyone above Jane, ever, and I felt a real sense of shame at what I had done. I knew that I had to identify my problem, *our* problem, if I wanted to work this out. Maybe I was making too much over nothing. How could I possibly have even a little feeling for Maria without any provocation? She had done nothing to encourage me.

"Jane, please, I wouldn't do anything to hurt you. Maybe it was the booze. Whatever it was, it wasn't intentional." Jane was staring at me, and there was a trace of a tear in her eye. I leaned over and kissed her softly on her forehead.

When she didn't resist, I hugged her very tenderly and said, "Baby, you're the love of my life. Don't be mad." I felt her relax, and then she pulled away and walked back toward the table.

"Why don't you dance with Ann? Garth danced with me twice while you were gone," she said. It wasn't exactly an order, but close. I don't like to dance with her. She's a closet drinker and tends to get sloppy early. Worse than that, she has absolutely no rhythm in her body. She also tends to dance too close and sometimes comes on to her partners in embarrassing ways.

"OK. I guess I can handle it." The band was playing a slow piece so I figured this was the best time. I couldn't bear the thought of trying to shag with her. I walked over to her and extended my hand. "Let's show the multitudes how to really dance, Ann. Can you handle it? She looked up at me with that vacant stare drunks acquire before they lose the ability to walk. I could tell she was just sober enough to debate whether should or not.

She took a big pull on her drink, set it down and said, "Why not?" She stood with some effort and I grabbed her hand to steady her. She's a quiet, well-mannered lady ordinarily, but she's just short of being a full-fledged alcoholic. We stepped onto the dance floor and she fell into my arms. I was holding her up more than dancing, and, small as she was, she still felt like a sack of cement.

She pulled away abruptly, rolled unsteadily on her heels and toes and blurted drunkenly, "What's that you're poking me with? There's something hard in your pants, Terry." She was slurring her words but I detected real agitation in her voice. "You must still be thinking about that lady Jane had to pull you away from on the dance floor."

I realized what she felt and laughed. "Ann, it's a measuring tape. I was measuring the kitchen cabinet for a dishwasher before we left tonight. I want it to be a surprise so I stuck it in my pocket to keep Jane from seeing what I was doing." As I was giving her my explanation, I pulled it from my pocket and held it up for her to see. I could see she was embarrassed. "I won't tell anyone if you'll forget about the dishwasher. I really want to surprise Jane." She snickered and said something I couldn't understand. I took that to mean OK. We finished the dance and I guided her to her seat. "I enjoyed the dance, Ann."

She reached for her drink and gave me a smile before mumbling, "I did too. But why didn't you give me the same treatment you gave that other lady? I saw how you were holding her. Couldn't tell what was you and what was her. I may be drunk, but I'm not stupid. Jane's got a problem, lover boy."

"Don't be silly, Ann. She's a client. That's just good public relations."

"Relations all right," she mumbled. "But not the kind you do in public. Motel'd be more like it." She went into a silly giggle and I thought I'd better get her in her seat before she became a spectacle. She was just about gone.

I liked Ann. She is truly one of the most beautiful women I have ever known. When she married Garth, I thought he was a lucky man. I couldn't understand why he had resisted so. Even though he never told me anything negative about her, I have come to understand she has a dark side, which manifests itself in a need for alcohol. For all her beauty and wealth – she inherited a considerable sum when her father died – she seems to have little self-esteem. I think it comes from having a father who gave her everything but affection. Garth is a strong man and I know he loves her very much. It's too bad she can't accept it, but she probably isn't capable.

I walked back to Jane and sat down. She gave me a weak smile and patted my hand. "I'm sorry I made you do that, but you deserved to suffer a little. At least you've gotten it done. What if you'd waited? You should thank me." The hand pat was a good sign.

I shook my head. "I don't think that would have worked. One more drink and she'll be unconscious. God, I feel so sorry for her. Garth, too. She needs help and we're just enabling her to fall down the slippery slope. I wish we could help her, but I don't know how."

I could see Jane's mood changing in her eyes. She stared at me intently. "Terry, do you think it's that bad? I know she lets her hair down a lot more lately, but she always seems so intense. I think it's her way to unwind. You know, she hasn't been herself since her father died."

"Jane, I think for her he died a long time ago, and it might have been better if he had. She tried to earn his love all her life. Now she knows she'll never have it. I'm afraid she and Garth are in deep, deep trouble. Oh well.........Hey, I'm on a roll. I may as well get my obligatory dances over with."

I finished the night dancing with all our friends and a few others I felt obligated to dance with, and trying to smooth things over with Jane. As the night wore on, Jane seemed to forget about my dancing with Maria, but I didn't. The excitement that permeated the evening before I danced with Maria disappeared, and the rest of the night settled into a monotonous nothing. I caught glimpses of her from time to time. She seemed to be on the floor with a different person each time I saw her, smiling and entertaining her partner. I felt envious and wondered if all her partners were as smitten with her as I was. I wanted to dance with her again but I knew it was a bad idea. I saw her in the coat check line as we were leaving.

We spoke, smiled and waved goodbye. Pat smiled, but I could feel some anger in his demeanor. I left the club with a very uncomfortable feeling.

Saturday we slept until noon. The girls were still in bed when we got up. They had stayed up late with the babysitter. I was thankful! My head wasn't right, and my stomach was queasy. It was Alka-Seltzer time. Jane didn't look perky either, but she was in better shape than I was. I washed my face with cold water, brushed the fuzz off my teeth, dropped two Alka-Seltzers in a large glass of water, and, after watching it fizz and bubble, drank the magic elixir down in five huge gulps. Miraculously, it stayed down.

I followed Jane to the kitchen, grabbed the orange juice from the fridge, poured a small glass and offered it to her. She made a face which I took to mean no, so I drank it cautiously.

"How'd you like something easy? Pancakes, bacon, and coffee?"

I managed a smile. "Sounds perfect." Pancakes sound good after a night of partying; I have a mental picture of pancakes turning into sponges in my stomach, sucking up the night's poison.

Jane was strangely attractive after our night of revelry. Her tight curls were still in place, albeit a little off center, and her face was scrubbed clean. No matter how late we were up or how bad she felt when we got home, she always took her makeup off before going to bed. That amazed me. Watching her prepare pancake batter, setting the table, frying bacon, and brewing coffee was equally amazing.

No way could I do it. She's tougher than I am. I went to the bedroom, grabbed my bathrobe and went for the paper. I shamed myself into that after watching Jane working so hard. Right then, I decided to stay home and tackle her "honey do" list." I owed her for my breakfast and my faux pas with Maria. Besides, a little hard work and honest sweat would help get rid of the remaining poisons the pancakes didn't suck up. I could go to the office after church tomorrow.

Saturday was a tough day. I worked hard in the yard and around the house. I found some forgotten and little used muscles, and I would be sore by nightfall. I raked up pine straw, and used most of it to mulch the azalea beds. The centipede lawns were beginning to feel the approach of winter and were starting to turn brown. Not much to cut, but I did it anyway. It would probably be the last time until spring. The girls helped me rake in the morning, but they weren't too happy about it. I felt I was taking their weekend away from them, so I let them quit about lunchtime. In the afternoon, the temperature got into the seventies and I worked up a good sweat. Jane was beginning to worry about me. She brought me a glass of ice water as I was finishing the mowing.

"I haven't seen you work this hard in a long time. Not feeling guilty about anything, are you?" She smiled as she gave me the water and dabbed at my sweaty forehead with a napkin.

"Of course not. The yard needs attention and I need exercise. Best thing for the day after." I drained the glass and handed it back to her. "Thanks. Tastes better without the scotch." She looked at me as if I had said something unnecessary and turned to walk back to the house. I stopped her with a loud "Hey! I'm going to be hungry when I finish. Do we have any steaks? I'll fire up the grill if we do. If you want to."

"Sure, we've got two rib-eyes in the freezer. I'll thaw them, but it may be late before we can eat. If you'll take the girls to the drive-in for a cheeseburger, I'll bake potatoes and fix salad. They'll like that better I'm sure."

"Great! Maybe they'll get to bed early and we can have some time to ourselves."

"Is that a question or a suggestion?"

"I'd say that it's more like a comment." I gave her a sweaty smile.

"If I didn't know better," Jane said , "I'd say it might be a request of love for labor. Of course, I'm sure that never entered your mind."

I grimaced. "Of course not. Why should I get excited for nothing? I'd rather think about having a tooth pulled." Oops, that slipped out. I knew I'd said the wrong thing. I hit my forehead with the palm of my hand in frustration. I was moving our conversation into major confrontation. I could see it in her eyes. She looked as though I had slapped her face.

"Do you feel deprived? Maybe I'm missing something here. I just don't remember your complaining about it. I'm not a mind reader, you know."

"Forget it," I said softly and turned back to my work. "I shouldn't have said that." I had opened a wound that I couldn't heal. Occasionally, I let my mouth get ahead of my brain.

Jane jumped in front of me and grabbed my shoulders. "Whoa Buddy! You're not going to make a snide remark like that with no explanation."

I could feel the anger welling up inside of me, and once more I blurted out without considering the consequences. "Damn it Jane, our sex life is going down the toilet. It's never spontaneous anymore. Hell, sometimes we don't even kiss when we make love. I feel like you just want to get it over with."

She looked away and bit her lip before framing her reply. One thing about her, she was better at measuring her reply that I am. She turned back to me and said, "I guess you're right. I know I haven't been very passionate lately. I feel like I never have any free time anymore. You're right. Sometimes I do just want to get it over with. And I often feel guilty about it. But going through two pregnancies, raising two children without much help from their ever-working father and trying to run a household on a tight budget is not easy. You're never here when I need you, and when you are, you expect me to be "Miss Hot Pants." Well, I'm sorry, it just doesn't work that way. I don't have an on/off switch."

I smiled sarcastically. "I think you do have an on/off switch and it's in the *off* position all the time. When I get close to you, or touch you, I can feel you pulling away. It's frustrating as hell. Am I that repulsive? Do I have bad breath or something?"

She sighed, took a deep breath, and spoke in a whisper, "It's not you. If it makes you feel better, it wouldn't matter to me if you were Elvis. I just don't have time to think about it. It's not my first priority. Right now, the children and taking care of the house come before sex for me. My priorities may be mixed up, but do you realize that this is the first Saturday in months that you haven't gone to the office? Big deal! Is that supposed to make me all lovey dovey? If it is, then you'd better stay home more often." She had her hands on her hips and fire in her eyes as she spoke those last words. She had put the dagger in my heart and I knew she was absolutely right.

"Look, I know I should spend more time at home. Hell, I would love to spend more time with you and the girls, but I'm trying to get a business going. I wish I could hire some help but I can't afford it. I have to do all of the work myself. I hope that'll change but it's not possible now. I've got to think about clothes for you and the girls, food, house payments, car payments, college for them in the future. It goes on and on and it takes a lot of money. Unfortunately, I only have one way to do it, and that's by working long and hard. I get tired, too, but that's not going to affect my libido. That's too important to me, and for your information, it's a lot more important to me than your keeping the house clean. I'll accept that the children are your top priority; they should be. But that's the only thing I'll play second fiddle to."

"Terry, I know your work is important, but I'm afraid that what you're doing now may become a permanent way of life. I'm afraid this will never change, even if things get better. Maybe subconsciously I resent being second to your work, but have you, just once, thought that we might need you more than material things? The girls don't say much about it because they think you have to be at work all the time, but they hardly see you and they miss you. And as far as your libido – if you were on your death bed, your last words to me would be 'get in here with me and let's do it once more before I check out'."

Inappropriately, I laughed. I liked her last quip and had to agree it was probably true. Nevertheless, I thought part of me was dropping off the earth's western horizon with the afternoon sun. I could feel the tension between us, and I knew that we were not connected in this relationship called marriage. It hurt me to think that, but it was true. At some point, we had just stopped talking. We weren't friends anymore. Was it my fault? I needed an answer, but I didn't have a clue how or where to start. I swallowed hard and said slowly, "You're right, I know you're right, but what can I do? What can we do to get straightened out?"

Jane looked away vacantly and said, "I don't know. I never thought we wouldn't be able to communicate. I always thought that was the glue that kept us together. I thought having children would be our greatest achievement, and it has been to some degree. But neither of us has been able to cope with the personal sacrifices that come with it. I know sex is important to you, and I know if I don't respond, it may destroy our marriage. But I'm so tired at night I just don't think about it, in fact, I don't feel like doing it. Many times I respond because I feel it's a duty, and sometimes I don't enjoy it. Most of the time I do, but I don't have a big desire to initiate it. It's not your fault. You're still a good lover. It's just that I don't have any interest in it. For me, the sex candle burned out, and I don't know how to re-ignite it. Maybe we need to go to a marriage counselor, or spend some time together alone. I don't know; maybe we're making too much of this."

"I don't think so," I said quickly. I turned her towards me and forced her to look at me. I didn't want to let this moment go by without some meaningful closure. "We *DO* need some time alone. It's hard to accomplish much with two little sets of eyes and ears around. I know I'm more physical than you. I just have to be 'touchy feely'. That's my natural way. Sometimes I come on too strong and, judging your current mindset, I need to rein in my ardor. But when I reach out for you, it's because I love you and that creates a very special need for me. Sex doesn't mean much if love isn't the main ingredient in the mixture. I might find some physical pleasure in it, but it wouldn't be worth much if I didn't love you. It also isn't worth much to me if you don't enjoy it. I have a thing about that. We have at least two problems here, and I'm willing to work on them no matter what it takes."

Jane gave me a tired smile that looked like the corners of her mouth were lifting heavy weights. "Let's don't try to solve this now. We've made progress by recognizing we have a problem. I promise I'll try to do better. I can't set any goals or timelines. If you do the same, maybe we can put this behind us. Somebody said ' the longest journey starts with the first step'. I've just made my first step. That's the best I can do." I recognized the frustration and finality in her voice.

I dropped my shoulders in despair. "I'm sorry I acted like a jerk. I can be selfish and inconsiderate without meaning to. You've given me some things to think about that I should have already known. I'm the one who should try harder." I put on my best smile to break the somber mood we were in. "I'll get cleaned up and take the girls to Mack's for a burger, fries, and a shake. Why don't you marinate the steak and put the potatoes in the oven? I'll help with the salad when I get back. Maybe we can salvage something with the rest of the evening." I patted her on the shoulder being careful not to get dirt and sweat on her, and she walked to the house while I put away the mower and yard tools. She didn't have a lot of spring in her step.

16

Sunday morning we got up early, went to Sunday school and church, then to the Friendly for lunch. My routine was to go to the office after we ate, set up my agenda for the week, catch up on correspondence and get any grunt work – shop drawings, cross hatching plans, and details – out of the way. I knew it wasn't a good idea in light of our conversation Saturday, but routines are hard to establish and equally hard to re-establish if you vary from them. I decided it wasn't time to change my ways, at least until Jane made some positive response.

When I told her I was going to the office, she didn't object. I think she was glad I would be out of her way for a while. She wasn't ready for any more "truth or consequences" conversations, and she wasn't sure I wouldn't try to start one again.

She walked me to the door as if she were afraid I might change my mind. "I think I'll take the girls over to Mama's, but we won't stay long. Try to be home by 6:00. I'll have supper ready by then."

"Sounds good," I said before I shut the door and hopped into the car. I drove to the office in silent contemplation without the ubiquitous sounds of the radio and wrestled with thoughts of our conversation Saturday. I was not happy, but escaping to my sanctuary – and I thought of my office in those terms – gave me a fuzzy, warm feeling.

I exited the highway in what seemed like record-breaking time, turned on Peake, and came to a stop in the parking lot. I hadn't noticed the darkening skies, and I was unprepared for the rain I could see rapidly approaching. It was so oppressive and heavy I could smell it in the air. I dashed for the door, but got caught in the deluge before I could get it open. Lightning arced down from the sky followed by a clap of thunder, and a sudden gust of wind pushed the door shut as I ran into the office. I made it without getting wringing wet, but I was wet enough to be uncomfortable and my hair was damp and wind blown. I went into the toilet, grabbed a hand full of paper towels, wiped at the wet spots and vigorously rubbed my hair.

I plugged in the hot plate and put on a kettle of water for coffee. I felt cold from the dampness and needed something warm to get me started. I found a clean cup, put in some instant coffee and two sugar cubes, and waited for the boil. I switched on my desk lamp and pulled back the desk cover, uncovering five copies of the partially corrected hardware schedule for the Hugeley residence and a red marking pen. I opened the specifications to the hardware section and began to check the next hardware set on the schedule. I managed two more sets before I heard the kettle whistling. I walked to the kitchenette, poured, stirred, and sampled the coffee. Satisfied, I returned to work. I finished with the hardware schedules, and put them on Martha's desk for mailing and filing. As I turned to walk back to my desk, the phone rang. *Probably Jane wanting me to stop for something on the way home. One of her ways to check on me and get me home earlier.* I grabbed it on the third ring and said "yesssss", dragging it out in two syllables to indicate I knew it was her.

There was a period of silence. "Is this Terry Forte's office?"

I recognized Maria's voice and immediately said, "It is." I chuckled. "I'm sorry I was so flippant. I don't get calls on Sunday. I thought it was a wrong number."

She giggled. "I almost hung up, but I had to give it a chance. I'm in a phone booth and I don't have another dime. I passed by your office and saw your car. I thought I'd drop off the questionnaires you gave us." She paused. "If that's not a problem?"

"Of course not. In fact, I was having a cup of coffee when you called. I could put on another if you like?"

"I'd like that. A little cream, no sugar. I'm at the post office and I'll be about ten minutes."

"No problem. I'll unlock the door for you."

"Good, see you shortly."

I went to the bathroom while I waited, cleaned up the bar and put the kettle on the hotplate. I put a teaspoon of instant coffee and creamer in a cup and waited for the water to boil. She drove into the parking lot as the kettle started whistling. I poured the water into the cup and walked to the door to meet her with it in my hand.

Maria came through the door with a big smile on her face and wriggled out of her rain coat. "Now that's real service," she said as I handed her the coffee and hung her coat in the closet.

"We try to think of ourselves as an all-encompassing service. That way we might get some repeat clients. You have to be ahead of the pack in this business."

She took a sip of coffee. "Well, you've won me over. See how easy I am?"

I wish. "Probably the weather," I said laughing. Let's go into the conference room and spread out on the table. I'm curious to see your comments." I followed her, taking notice of her soft, cherry red sweater set and black tailored slacks. She had a flat stomach and narrow waist with ample hips and bosom that I appreciated. I hoped she didn't feel my wandering eyes on her body. Actually, I felt a little lust and the guilt that goes with it, but I didn't turn it off. I pulled out a chair for her and sat facing her. She dropped a thick file folder onto the table, pulled out the questionnaire, and pushed it toward me. Her comments were printed very concisely. All of her letters were vertical and orderly. "Uh oh! Do I detect a perfectionist here?" I was not surprised, but I pretended to be. She seemed disturbed by my question and narrowed her eyes. The wind driven rain spattering against the windows became louder in the silence as she framed her answer.

"Is this part of the psychology you referred to at our first meeting?"

"Did I hit a nerve? I didn't mean anything sinister. I rather like that characteristic in a client."

"To be truthful, I am a perfectionist. But I don't want it to be too obvious. It may give me a neurotic label, and I don't think of myself that way." She tugged at her sweater sleeves, exposing a number of silver bracelets.

"Forget it. You may think I'm neurotic and a perfectionist before we finish your house. Some of the contractors have that opinion of me, and I'm glad. It helps me intimidate them and that's important if I'm going to get the kind of workmanship I expect.

I could swear that her eyes were twinkling as she said, "Do I intimidate you… since you think I'm a perfectionist?" I do believe the lady was having fun with me.

"Wow! Now who's being the psychiatrist?" I gave her one of my best smiles. "Actually, I think you're a very bright and attractive woman. I wouldn't tell you that if I was intimidated by you. Oh, I almost forgot. You're a great dancer too."

"Thanks, but I was trying to forget about the dancing. Seems like we created some major problems. I know it upset Jane, and surprisingly even Pat made a comment about it. He knows I like to dance, and it doesn't bother him. Gives him more time to talk. We didn't do anything bad, did we?"

"No...I don't think it was anything like that. Don't take this wrong, because I don't mean it in a forward way. It was just so comfortable, like it wasn't the first time."

She looked startled. "I felt the same way and that's not like me. What's the expression? Deja vu? Have you ever done something for the first time that you felt you had done before, or been someplace that you recognized that you'd never seen before?

"No.......I don't think so". I thought for a minute. "Maybe that's what bothered our spouses. We might have a hard time convincing them that it was an innocent thing, that it hadn't happened before. I really can't explain it, but it was a pleasant feeling. It was like we were alone on the dance floor. I guess I thought we were invisible." I laughed and raised my eyebrows. "Obviously, we weren't."

"Obviously," Maria said. "I don't think I've ever seen Pat jealous. At least, not from me dancing with someone. That's not his style. He knows I'm a bit of a flirt, but he also knows it's only fun. He sensed something that wasn't there, or wasn't supposed to be."

I wasn't sure I liked her explanation. "Are you saying that I'm not worthy of your attention?" I kept my gaze very serious, then slowly smiled.

"Of course not!" she said quickly. She sensed that I was teasing and returned my smile. "It could have been anyone. You just happened to be the unlucky one."

"Now you're teasing me a little, but I understand. My theory is men don't need an excuse for sexual misbehavior. It's part of our makeup. But women, now that's a different situation. Women must be in love, or think they are, before they even consider sex. Even a one-night stand for most women is a misguided, romantic interlude. With women, it's love then sex. With men, it's sex then maybe love. We want to love our partner, but our libido keeps getting in the way. Of course there are exceptions, but I think most people fall into my theory."

She tugged at her earring as she considered what I had said. "Are you telling me that men can't distinguish between love and sex? If that's true, men are animals who've learned to talk. I'm not sure I can accept that, and I'm no Pollyanna."

"It's sad, but, I'm afraid, probably true. I know some men who have managed to overcome lust, but they're exceptions. They're the ones who have good relationships with wives or girlfriends, are more mature, and have probably worked through some bad situations before they found their nirvana. I don't want to imply that all men are evil. I just think that some are and the rest were. How else can you explain the minister, the doctor, or the respected businessman suddenly going astray? All of them know it's wrong, but sometimes their ability to procreate overcomes their ability to think. It can happen to anybody. I just hope if it ever happens to me it's just physical."

Maria looked at me quizzically. "Why in the world would you say that?"

"Because I can deal with a physical thing, and I wouldn't let it affect my family. I'd never confess, so they'd never really know. But a spiritual kind of relationship? With meaning? Now that would be a bear. That's the culprit that breaks up families, or, at the least, destroys trust forever. I hope that I'm never faced with it, but if I am, I hope I'm man enough to say no."

Maria picked some lint off her sweater. "Which situation are you talking about? Physical, or spiritual?"

"Actually, both," I said without hesitation.

She smiled and said, "In that case, have you ever been faced with either?"

I sat back in my chair, stretched, and laughed. "I'm not sure I know you well enough to answer that, but, without getting into details, I've run into the physical situation a time or two."

I sensed that she might be uncomfortable with the direction the conversation and was about to change the subject but she said, "Do you think all men run into physical situations or just attractive ones like you?"

"Ouch," I said with a big laugh. "Is my ego showing?"

She pushed her hair over her ear and smiled. Her eyes sparkled as she spoke. "No, of course not. What I meant was.... is this universal? I'd really like to know if you think all men get into physical relationships. I've never suspected that Pat's been involved with any women, but, after hearing your theory, I'm not sure. He does travel a lot and I think he's very attractive. Of course, I'm a bit prejudiced. Maybe you think I should be more diligent?"

"No, I'm not implying anything. You both seem secure in your relationship. I don't think anyone marries without thinking this is it. It's just that relationships change over a period of time without recognition. That's when marriages falter or get stronger. I'm going through a bad time now that doesn't share the same priority with Jane. I hope we can work it out, but I'm not sure."

She looked at me with a suggestion of sadness. "I'm sorry. Its none of my business so I wont ask about it. I think we have the attitude that, like in fairy tales it's love, marriage, and live happily ever after. That's a bit simplistic and it works only for Mother Goose."

I offered Maria a cigarette. She declined with a shake of her head and reached into her pocketbook. "I'm smoking menthols this week." I lit it for her, and then mine.

I dropped back into my chair and said, "Mother Goose didn't have problems. She only had good times. It's a shame life isn't like that."

She thought for a moment and asked, "Would you like it if you didn't have a few problems once and a while?"

"I like challenges, not problems," I said. "Problems are nuisances. Problems usually have people in them. Challenges usually don't. I'd much rather think about space. Have you ever considered what space is shaped like to be endless? And if it has a shape, what's on the other side of space?"

She wrinkled her nose in disgust. "Only an architect would think about that. Besides, that's not a problem or a challenge. It's a theory."

"Maybe, but I work with space every day. It's natural for me to think about it."

"OK, but you're not getting out of your other theory that easy. I'm curious about your temptations. Tell about them. I promise I want tell anyone, and I certainly won't judge you."

"I'll tell you about a situation when I was in the army. After I graduated from Clemson, I was commissioned a second lieutenant, attended Officer's basic at Fort Belvoir, Virginia, and was immediately sent to Germany. It was 1954 and Germany was still an occupied country. Shortly after I arrived, I ran into a buddy from college in the officer's club. It was good to see a familiar face. He was with an attractive blonde who was hanging on to every word he said. He introduced her as Gisela, which surprised me, because her English was not only perfect, but she also had a trace of Southern accent. He told me he had been on TDY, temporary duty for the uninitiated, for about six weeks but had just been assigned to an engineering company in Hanover. He was leaving the next day. I remembered that he was married and had a small child, so I asked him if they were coming over. Gisela looked at me, then at him. And in a state of shock, she dropped his hand and ran to the restroom. He grinned sheepishly and told me she didn't know he was married. I felt bad and told him so. I decided it was time to wish him well and get the hell out of Dodge; I didn't want to witness the shoot-out.

"The next weekend I was in my room reading and my phone rang; I was surprised to hear a female voice. It was Gisela. She asked if I remembered her. I said of course, and asked how she was doing. She said she was better but had had a rough time. She explained everything in detail about her affair with my buddy and said she had really fallen for him. She had no idea he was married, and was totally shocked when I inadvertently blew the whistle. I tried to apologize, but she cut me off. She said I had done her a favor, good riddance and all that stuff. She asked me if I would like a tour of the town. She felt she owed me for ratting on my pal and suggested I bring a camera and take some pictures to send home. She volunteered a picnic lunch and told me where to meet her. I was terribly bored and it seemed like a good idea, so I accepted and set the time for the next Sunday afternoon. She had borrowed a small car from a friend and she drove me to the few historic landmarks in town and then out into the countryside where we enjoyed the picnic she had prepared of crusty German bread, cheese, chunks of bratwurst, and a wonderful white wine. We talked a bunch and became good friends. I won't bore you with details. The bottom line was that she invited me to visit with her family Christmas weekend. I accepted with the stipulation that it would depend on my remaining at my present assignment. It worked out so I got a three-day pass, and we took a train to a small town near Stuttgart. Her mother and father treated my like visiting royalty and her brother and sister were a pleasure. The brother spoke some English but no one else did. Gisela spent a lot of time interpreting for me and I had a great time. Ate a lot of good German food and drank copious quantities of beer."

I stopped for a minute. "If I'm boring you, I'll stop. I didn't mean to be so detailed."

She pulled her chair close to the table and with receptive eyes said, "No, no, I'm enjoying it. I just can't imagine where this is headed."

"You're a good listener," I said. "I wish I were a better story teller." I stubbed out my cigarette and continued. "I returned to my base and went about my duties. Two weeks later on a Saturday afternoon, I was in my quarters and someone knocked on my door. There, to my surprise, was Gisela's 18-year-old sister with a small suitcase. She had come, unannounced, to spend a few days with me. The problem was that we couldn't communicate."

Maria gave me a sly grin. "Come on now, did you make any overtures to her when you were there? I can't believe she just came out of the blue."

"I promise you, nothing happened while I was there. I could only talk to her with Gisela's help. She didn't speak a word of English."

"Sure, sure. Then how did she know how to find you?"

"That was my fault, but innocent enough. I wrote the family a thank you note and she kept the envelope with my return address on it."

Maria chuckled. "Well, she certainly wasn't stupid. But don't leave me hanging. What happened?"

"I called Gisela and told her that her sister, Brieta, had come to visit me. She didn't believe me. But after I put Brieta on the phone, she told me she was on the way. It took her about twenty minutes to get to my billet, but it seemed like forever. Have you ever had to entertain someone for twenty minutes without being able to understand one another? Try it sometime. It ain't easy!"

Maria gave me a *do you think I'm stupid* look. "Well, I can think of some things you could have done that wouldn't have taken many words, but I guess you didn't think of that. Something tells me I may not be getting the straight story here. How did Gisela react when she got there? That might give me a clue."

"She was angry. They got into an argument, but I didn't understand any of it. I felt like an idiot, but there wasn't a lot I could do. They spoke German and Gisela wasn't giving me an interpretation. I asked her what was going on, but she wasn't having any part of that. I think she wanted to get the argument over before she offered an explanation."

I paused for a moment and Maria shook her head. "I still don't understand why she was mad if you two hadn't been getting it on. It seems to me that something was going on that both of you were hiding from Brieta. Why else would she have come without telling her sister, and why would Gisela have cared? Do you want to 'fess up? I promise I want tell."

I had to laugh. "I may have left out a little, but I don't know how well I can trust you. I hardly know you."

"Oh come on, Terry. That's a cop out if I ever heard one. Who would I tell? Certainly not your wife. She's pretty mad at me anyway, and I wouldn't tell Pat. He'd want to know how we ever got into a conversation like this. No, your story is safe and you know it. Now tell me how it really happened."

"Well, I did change a few details but, for the most part, I was ashamed and guilty about what really happened and I've tried to put it behind me."

Maria's eyes mirrored a change of attitude. "Why were you ashamed? I don't understand."

"Jane and I were engaged. Not formally, but we had an understanding. I had let her down and I was hurt that I was so weak. I couldn't help but think how I would have felt if she had done the same thing. I guess that's a good example of why men are animals who've learned to talk."

"Look, I told you I wouldn't judge you. I can understand how it could happen. You were a young man full of hormones, lonesome and probably confused. Not many men could have passed up a situation like that. At least, you were disturbed because you did it. It's not like you were looking. I think you're being a little hard on yourself. I'd still like to know what really happened, if you feel comfortable telling me."

I thought about it and decided I'd confess. "Most of what I told you is true. The part I reneged on was the location of our picnic. It took place in my room … on my bed. I didn't plan it that way; it just happened. It happened so fast, I didn't have time to think about it …. until it was over. I let it happen and I hated it. The bad thing was I didn't stop it, and I could have. I was so upset that after she left, I cried. That's not easy for a man to admit."

Maria stretched and said, "Well, at least now I understand the confrontation. Gisela had a jealous moment and decided to set Brieta straight. That's kinda what I thought, but I wanted you to tell me. Why didn't you want to come clean?"

"To tell the truth, it was not one of my proudest moments. I've always wished that it hadn't happened. Besides, I don't know you that well, and I don't know what you might think. I was trying to illustrate how men get into situations, but I ended up showing how weak men are, how weak I am. I'm afraid that story didn't have a hero."

Maria looked at her watch and stood up in one move. "Oh, my God! It's five o'clock. I can't believe it. We've talked for two hours and now I'm in trouble. I told Pat I was going to the post office, and it's difficult to spend two hours in the post office."

I had to chuckle. "Tell him the truth. You saw my car and decided to drop off the questionnaire. I've spent days talking to clients, Maria. That's hardly unusual. I admit, we strayed a little from architecture, but I'm sure Pat will understand and probably want ask any questions. If he does, tell him we talked about the questionnaire. He'll be glad he didn't have to sit through a two-hour session. I may not understand women, but I understand men. He won't give it another thought."

I let her walk ahead as we moved to the closet to get her raincoat, letting my eyes roam over her body and enjoying every minute of it. Her sexuality was overpowering, but it seemed a mystery to me. It was like looking at somebody's wrapped present and guessing what was in the box. I knew it was wonderful, but I also knew it wasn't mine. Strangely enough, it didn't seem entirely about sex. *Get over it. She's just a nice lady who enjoys people.*

The meeting deserved some kind of closing, and I searched for something clever to say. Finally I said, "You're really not getting your money's worth; you're not getting much architectural help."

She wrinkled her nose in thought. "On the contrary, I'm learning how architects think …about other things. I find it quite interesting, and I think you're pretty normal. You're not just another pretty Southern boy full of manners and chivalry. And remember, that comes from a damn Yankee."

I scratched the top of my head and rolled my eyes. "That's amusing, but I deserved it. And you're not a damn Yankee. You're a damn smart women."

"You're much too serious," she said. "Think of it as a good story among friends. Who knows, I may have one for you next time," she said grinning mischievously.

"That'll be the day," I said as I handed her raincoat to her.

She reached for the doorknob, stopped, and turned. "But you don't really know, do you?" Then she was gone.

I watched her drive off before I shut the door. Did I detect a bit of flirtation in her last remark? I had to assume it to be more of an amusing retort than flirtation.

Still, it intrigued me. The jangling ring of the phone brought me back to earth, and this time, I knew it was Jane. I let it ring without answering. I turned off the lights and headed home.

Monday morning I drove the girls to school. It was Jane's day to do carpooling, but she woke up complaining of a headache so I graciously volunteered. I was a little late and Martha was already at work. "Good morning," I said, whistling as I walked past.

"Not too good," Martha said without looking up. "You left a mess for me to clean up."

"I'm sorry Martha. I had a meeting Sunday afternoon and I was in a hurry to get home. I would have taken care of it this morning but I was late getting here, as you can see."

"I noticed the lipstick on the cigarette butt", she said slyly. "Wasn't Mrs. Champion's, was it?"

"As a matter of fact, it was. Why the interest?"

"Well," she drawled slowly, "you seem to meet with her at some odd times, and alone. You're not having any problems at home?" She left her comment hanging for my consideration.

"No, of course not." I smiled and said, "You're not jealous are you?" I thought some levity might diffuse the situation.

"If I were, it wouldn't be over some young whippersnapper like you," she harrumphed. "I'm an old woman but I'm not stupid. And neither is Jane. Just a word for the wise, that's all. It's none of my business anyway." She turned back to her typewriter.

Martha tended to be taciturn and I didn't have anything else to say. I thought it best not to protest too much, so I let it go. I knew Martha's intent was good and she always said what was on her mind. Once said, however, it was over. Nevertheless, her comments planted thoughts of Maria's visit in my mind and I couldn't think of anything else. I spent the morning pouring over the questionnaire she had left and found it to be pithy and analytical. I made a lot of notes and sorted them into bubble diagrams by function and relationship. Of course, that led to many questions I would have to ask. I wondered if I was looking for an excuse to call her. I couldn't allow that kind of thought. After all, she WAS my client, and she was paying for that privilege.

Martha came into the drafting room with some papers in her hand. "I'm leaving. I'm going into town, so I'll take these hardware schedules to W.B.'s." W.B. was short for W. B. Fields Contractors, who were the general contractors building the Huguley residence. "I'll see you tomorrow."

I looked at my watch; it was twelve ten. The morning had gotten away. "Thanks Martha. I appreciate your doing that. See you tomorrow."

I went to the fridge and took out some sliced tomatoes I had brought from home. Poppa Jim, my father, had grown them in his garden. They were the last I would get from him this year. The season was over. I put together my favorite summer meal: a tomato sandwich with cheese, lots of salt and pepper, and copious quantities of Miracle Whip. No true Southerner will use mayonnaise on a tomato sandwich. The only thing missing was two slices of bacon. I grabbed an ice-cold Coke and returned to my drafting board. The phone rang and I got it on the second ring.

"Terry Forte speaking."

It was Maria. She laughed and said, "Of course it is, but you're much too serious."

Her laugh was contagious. It was a happy sound. "Had I known it was you, I would have risen to the occasion."

"Don't get too carried away. I'm beginning to like your seriousness. Are you working on my house?"

"As a matter of fact, I am. In fact, I've been working on it all morning."

"In that case, I probably shouldn't have called. Ha! Ha! But, I have an ulterior motive. I know you don't usually work on Monday nights, but I thought I would ask if, by chance, you're planning to work tonight?"

"That doesn't sound to ulterior to me, but why do you ask?"

"I've been asked to serve on the Greater United Fund Drive committee this year and I've accepted. You know how new arrivals are recruited to serve on all the "do good" drives. Makes us feel important. Besides, I'll meet a lot of important citizens. What I'm trying to get to is we're having a kick-off meeting in town at six o' clock that is guaranteed to adjourn by seven, and I baked a beautiful pound cake I wanted to bring you for letting me mess up your day Sunday. It's really good, my mother's recipe. I want to make amends. I promise, if you're working, I'll just stop by and hand it to you at the door."

The decision took two seconds. "Yes, I am planning to work, and I would love to have your cake. That's very thoughtful of you, but it's not necessary. I enjoyed your being here." I thought for a minute and said, "We'll spend a lot of time together before we finish with your house, so don't feel badly. Besides, I've got some questions that you can probably answer in fifteen or twenty minutes. It'll help me get started." I thought to myself, *That was a masterstroke.*

"OK, it's a done deal. I'll see you about seven thirty."

The phone went dead but I was exhilarated. I didn't understand it, but I felt like a kid waiting for Santa Claus. This dichotomy of right and wrong was wearing on me, and I knew I must come to grips with it. But how? I knew I would rush home early with some cock and bull story that would bring me back to the office. I would be telling Jane a lie, and that was bad, really bad. How could I look her in the eyes and lie to her? I knew I would and that hurt.

18

I was back in the office before six. I felt guilty, but not enough to take the edge off my excitement. Maybe I was losing my mind. I busied myself straightening up the office. That didn't require much effort. I had no desire to work. I just wanted to kill time until Maria came.

Seven o'clock came, then seven thirty. I was beginning to think she wasn't coming when I saw the car lights reflect on the pavement as it glided to a stop. She popped out of the car and moved quickly to the door. I opened it, and she stood there with a cake pan in her hands.

Maria had a big smile on her face. She said, "Beware of strangers bearing gifts," and handed me the cake pan.

I took it, shoved the door open and invited her inside with a bow. "If you come in, you certainly won't be a stranger long."

She followed me to the kitchenette. "I'll have to have a bite of this. It looks too good not to sample. Would you like some?"

She waved me off and said, "I ate some finger food at our meeting, and I don't have the appetite for it. If you need a poison test, I'll take a bite," she said playfully.

I cut a small slice and popped it in my mouth. "Now that's a real cake," I said, rolling my eyes in mock ecstasy. "My compliments to your mother… and to the chef. It's marvelous."

"Will you accept that in as an act of contrition for my messing up your Sunday?"

"You didn't mess up my Sunday. I think it was the other way around. I was the one with the stupid story and you just felt obligated to listen to it, or you would have left. You didn't want to hurt my feelings."

"Not so, not so," she said emphatically. "I always enjoy our talks no matter what the subjects are."

"OK, let's put it to the test then. I have a few questions about some of the information on the questionnaire." She followed me into the conference room. I had stacked some papers and pads on the table anticipating that I could entice her to come in. "You look very nice tonight. I like your dress." She had on a simple black dress, black pumps, and a single strand of pearls on her neck. Her hair was on top of her head as it was at the club dance. Her dress followed the form of her body but was not snugly fitted. She was conservatively dressed and looked very elegant. "I'm impressed," I added.

"Thanks, I wanted to impress the natives," she said simply. She laughed and continued, "I really did it to impress my architect." Her laughter filled the room.

"I'd like to believe that," I said with a big smile.

I pulled out a chair for her and sat down beside her. "Tell me which room is more important to you. I couldn't tell for sure, but it seemed to be the den."

"That's probably misleading. I have lots of hobbies, and I use the den for them, mostly out of having no other space to work. I don't like to use the kitchen, because I'd have to stop and clean up to prepare meals. Not very functional. I probably need a private space of my own with a sink and a small cabinet - like a kitchen base cabinet."

"How about Pat?" I asked. "Does he have any hobbies?"

"Not really. He could use a desk and telephone. He works at home sometimes, but not often. Not enough to justify an office. We have a lot of books and we like to read. Perhaps a small library with a space for a desk would suffice."

"Do you have any strong feelings about any particular rooms?"

"I sure do! Men and women should never share bathrooms. I need a well-lighted space for makeup with a large mirror and lots of counter space. A full-length mirror would be nice, maybe on a door. Frankly, I don't like to share dressing space. The shower and water closet can be contiguous, but I need a separate dressing room, preferably with a connecting walk-in closet. It would be nice if you could enter the closet from the bedroom also."

"Do you like bathtubs?"

"I do, but I take showers most of the time. I enjoy a bathtub in the winter, you know, a bubble bath with a good book occasionally. I prefer the tub and shower to be separate. I've never liked those silly little sliding doors on the tub. They never work well and the space is too confining."

"How about your kitchen?"

"Well, I like to cook and entertain. Good circulation that combines the kitchen, dining room, living room, and den are desirable. We also eat many of evening meals as a family, and I like to do that in the dining room. I know I'm in the sunny South, but I sure would like a fireplace in the den. It defines a room and gives it warmth, also helps in furniture groupings. I'm still a Northern girl at heart, accustomed to snow and ice, and a fireplace gives me a sense of shelter."

"Hey, you're beginning to sound like an architect. How about bedrooms?"

"I want four bedrooms: one for Patricia, one for Mathew, one for us, and a spare. Patricia needs privacy. Mathew couldn't care less. We need to be away from the children so we don't disturb them. I'm a night person, and I read a good bit before I fall asleep. Pat watches television or reads and is usually in bed before me. That's good because I'm a light sleeper and don't like television in the bedroom. We don't have any special needs. Mathew's a pig and Patricia is very neat. If we can afford the luxury of separate bathrooms for them, I want them. I also have strong opinions about keeping everything on one floor. I want a lot that is big enough to accomplish that. That's why I want you to look at lots with me. I might make a mistake without knowing it. Hint, hint!"

"Let's don't ride that horse again. I promised I would help if you're not too vocal about it. My tastes aren't always in agreement with my clients, and that's too early in the game to get at loggerheads with them."

Maria responded quickly, "I agree with all that, and I won't accept your opinion unless I'm in agreement."

"OK, but I can't do much more until you settle on a site. You really need to get going on that. Didn't you tell me you had three sites you liked? We need to take a look at them as soon as possible. I could check them out this week if you tell me where they are."

"Oh no you don't! I'm going to be with you when you look. I want to know what you think as soon as you see them. I may have a question or two that I'll forget about if I'm not with you. You can call me before you go and I'll meet you. I promise I won't hold you up. If I'm not available, I won't make you wait, but I prefer to be there when you go."

"What about tomorrow? I could pick up something from the Blizzard Shop for lunch and meet you at the first site. That would save me some time."

"Let me call you tomorrow after I see how my day is going. I think that will work, but I need to be sure. I'll call early if I don't have any problems."

I stood up and extended my hand to help her up. "I promised you my questions wouldn't take long." She took my hand and smiled. She stood close to me and I could smell her perfume. I fought the urge to take her in my arms. I knew that would be stupid.

Maria squeezed my hand lightly and sent a tremor through my body. I was in the sixth grade again, in a dark movie theater groping for my girlfriend's hand for the first time. She broke my magic moment saying, "I appreciate all you are doing. I'll try not to be a difficult client." She was smiling, oblivious to my childish thoughts. The only thing difficult, I thought, was restraining myself. Maybe I WAS ready for one of those long, white straight jackets.

I looked into her eyes. They were glittering opals, fiery green. I forced myself to move away. "You won't be difficult. Besides, you bake a mean cake." The forced levity helped me regain my composure. The dichotomy of the situation was ridiculous. She was talking business and I was thinking about things I shouldn't be. I felt a sense of shame. Without any overt actions, Maria attracted me like a magnet. I couldn't remember feeling like this about a woman; I don't think Jane had ever had this kind of effect on me, and I felt that I loved Jane very much.

I opened the door for her and walked with her. "I know it's safe here, but I'll feel better walking you to your car." Truth was, I wasn't ready to see her leave. I did, however, feel a need to be protective.

"That's nice; I like that," she said quietly. "Tomorrow, then?"

"Let's plan on it. If you can manage it." I closed the door and she drove away.

The next three days we looked at lots. We talked about all the necessary things - location, schools, utilities, physical properties and price - and enjoyed a lot of small talk about each other. We managed to eat lunch together each day, and, except for the first day, we met at the Blizzard Shop to eat. We made it a practice to sit in the last booth to afford us some privacy. With the sparse crowd at lunch, it was quite intimate. Occasionally, we played the jukebox. *Smokey Places* and *Stranger on the Shore* became our favorites.

We agreed on a first choice, a wooded lot with abundant pines, three large oak trees and a gentle, rolling topography. It was located in a good school district near my house, but not quite as far from town. All of the houses in the subdivision were new, large, and expensive. I had designed two of them, and most of the others were architecturally designed. Pat agreed with Maria's choice and bought the lot a week later. I had a survey done and I started working on preliminary drawings.

Maria and I talked on the telephone every day. Once and a while we met for lunch. We also met in the office about every two weeks to look over the newest drawings. We began to find excuses to meet for lunch two or three times a week – always in the back booth at the Blizzard Shop. It was a safe place to meet without much fear of being seen, but we were beginning to feel twinges of guilt. We talked about everything: religion, politics, people and, finally, sex. We became comfortable with each other and began to open up about our personal lives. Nothing was ever said about our spouses in a personal or negative way. We managed to keep that to ourselves. Even though nothing serious happened or was ever discussed, we often held hands under the table like high school kids on a date. I knew I was in trouble emotionally, even though I tried to deny it. But I really wasn't sure how Maria felt. I was beginning to miss her terribly when I didn't see her, and the weekends seemed intolerably long unless she managed to call me at the office.

On a cold Thursday evening in November (the twenty-ninth to be exact) Maria called me at the office after she had attended a United Fund meeting. "What are you doing?" she asked.

"I'm trying to finish up a job for my favorite client, but I keep getting interrupted," I joked.

"Got time for a cup of coffee with and old friend? I won't stay long."

"Absolutely, I need a break. All work and no play make Terry a dull boy."

"I've got to make a quick stop at Taylor Street Pharmacy but I should be there in about fifteen minutes."

"Good, I'll have coffee ready when you get here." She hung up abruptly after a short goodbye and I put the water on. By the time the kettle boiled, I heard her soft knock on the door. I opened the door quickly and felt the cool night air as she stepped inside. She was wearing a full-length London fog coat, and she turned so I could help her take it off. I slipped it off her shoulders and hung it in the closet. I poured coffee and carried it into the conference room. She was looking at ceramic tile samples and said, "Is this expensive?"

I laughed. "Not for a rich client like you."

She seemed distracted and not interested in small talk. She looked at me for a long time without speaking. Then she nervously blurted, "I'm going to the beach this weekend with some girls in my bridge club. Garden City, near Myrtle Beach. Do you know where it is?"

"Sure, I've been there many times. It's a nice family beach, but it's pretty quiet this time of year. Good time for fishing, but not much else. Who's going?"

She rattled off seven or eight names. I knew one of them, but I didn't comment. "Is it a special occasion, or just for fun?"

"Nothing special. Just a quiet weekend with the girls. We'll probably eat a lot, sleep a lot, and maybe do some shopping." She put her cup down and walked over to me. She was looking at me in a strange way, as though she expected some comment from me. I moved toward her, waiting for her to speak, but she didn't make a sound. With nervous trepidation, I put my arm around her waist and gently pulled her toward me. As she tilted her head up to meet me, I kissed her lightly on the lips, letting my tongue tease her. Then, in a moment of absolute surrender and tenderness, her lips parted and we kissed as though we had done it many times before. I was totally swept away and hoped it would never stop. She made some low mewing sounds as I kissed her eyes, her earlobes, her cheeks, and her neck. I was covering as much of her as I could, afraid she would stop me. Our first kiss was everything I had imagined it would be. She pulled away from me and mumbled something I couldn't make out.

"What?" I said huskily, "I can't understand you."

She shook her head in disbelief and pushed a fallen lock of hair from her forehead. "I can't believe I'm doing this."

She handed me a piece of paper that was dog-eared from being folded and unfolded, kissed her finger and pressed it on my lips, and sped out of the office taking her coat with her. She was gone before I could make a move, and when I got to the door her car was turning out of the parking lot.

I returned to the conference room and unfolded the paper. Written on it in her meticulous handwriting was, "The Conch Shell on Second Avenue. Just in case." She had thrown down the gauntlet. The invitation was plain and I knew I had to find a way to be there no matter what. The question was how could I justify it, especially on a weekend? I had two days to come up with a plausible excuse.

I was exhilarated but very nervous. Worse, I was feeling the first twinges of guilt. I was not comfortable with this, but none of those feelings would deter me.

I went into the toilet and rinsed my face with cold water. I saw the traces of her lipstick on my mouth and realized the enormity of what we had done. I blotted the evidence off my lips, walked back to my office, and sat down. I remained for a long time waiting for some sense of normalcy to return. I felt that I had been marked with some symbol that Jane could see and know that I had betrayed her. I had climbed Mt. Everest only to fall off the precipice like a modern-day Sisyphus.

I closed the office and drove home full of fear, elation, and guilt.

I got home a little after 10:00 and Jane was in the den watching television. She looked up and said, "I left you a piece of pie in the fridge" and returned to her program. I thought it best that I tell her I would be out of town Saturday night while she was busy and I still had my nerve. I was running through a kaleidoscope of excuses in my mind and blurted out, "Did you get a call from Johnny Boyle and tell him I was at the office?"

"No, I don't think the phone has rung at all tonight. Why?"

"He called me at the office and wants me to come to Myrtle Beach to look at some property he's developing. He has some interested investors coming in Saturday and wants me to meet them. It could be a big project for me. He plans to wine and dine them Saturday night and take them fishing Sunday morning on his boat. I told him I could be there. I didn't have much choice."

"Well, you work all week anyway. I don't guess it matters if you work at the beach. I've gotten accustomed to you not being here. You told me you were going to spend more time with us, but I guess we're still second to your work." She looked disgusted.

"I'm not crazy about it and I know it's short notice, but I have to go after jobs when they're available." My insides were churning and I felt like a total jerk. I was lying and it was eating me up. Worse, I knew meeting Maria was more important to me than anything else in the world, even my family. My values had flown out the window. *What was happening to me?*

"Terry, you hardly have time for us anymore. It's getting old. We're about to lose all our friends. Do you realize that we haven't done anything socially except the club dance? I thought after our last heart-to-heart that you were going to make some effort to be a better husband and father. That might help me solve some of my problems, my lack of ARDOR. You do-o-o-o have to be here sometimes, if you really want me to do something about that!" Her sarcasm and anger was biting, and it was right on target.

"I'm sorry. I know I need to improve. I know the kids think I'm their uncle and it's obvious how you feel. I promise I'll temper the weekend work; in fact, let's invite the gang over next Saturday night for steaks. I'll get some T-bones from Shorty's, buy some beer, and cook on the grill. That'll be fun, like old times."

I could tell she was thinking about it. "You know that'll cut into our grocery money, Big Shot. I'm not sure we need to jump into that," she said.

I couldn't let the opportunity drop. "We can handle it. I'll write a company check and expense it as entertainment." She nodded her head acceptance.

"If you can pay for it, I'll start planning. I just can't stretch our grocery budget for that much food," she said with excitement.

"No problem. I'll cash a check tomorrow and you can call everybody next week. I'm sure we can get at least four couples. If you'll pick everything up, I'll help with the cooking." I was really into it now; I felt like a con man deluxe… if I could only dodge the lightning.

Jane was deep in thought. "It's not that easy," she said. "I'll have to get a menu together. Something simple like baked potatoes, salad, rolls, iced tea maybe, desert and coffee. I'll need to get the house straight, and you need to cut the grass and get the yard neat. Some cut flowers would be nice for the dining room. It's probably going to be too cold to eat outside. You need to check the liquor; we're probably low."

The weight was suddenly off my shoulders and my stomach stopped churning. Too bad it didn't do much for my conscience. The guilt remained and I still felt like a bum. "I'll cut the grass and mulch the front yard. It looks bad, especially since I've mulched the back. Maybe I can touch up the ball mark on the front door from our last ball game." I didn't want to get too carried away but some of it slipped out in my moment of angst.

Jane made a face. "I think I can live with just the grass cut and the trash raked. What's the matter? Are you feeling guilty?"

"No, I know you've wanted some things done around the house, and I haven't been responsive. Just trying to set some goals." It was time get back to normal before I got into trouble again. I decided to stop while I was ahead. "I'm tired. I'm going to turn in." I stretched and yawned for emphasis and started to the bedroom.

"I'll be there in a minute. I want to see the end of this program. It's almost over," she said as she turned back to the TV once more.

I woke up Friday morning feeling like I had gone fifteen rounds and lost. I was worn out from bad dreams, turning and tossing, and waking up during the night. My mood was one of total ambivalence, shifting from excitement to foreboding. I wasn't sure I was doing the right thing, but I knew that no matter what, I wouldn't change my mind. I assumed Maria was having some of the same problems, but she had the luxury of not having to lie about anything. That was a big plus in my book.

I got out of bed and went through my routine like a robot. I just couldn't face Jane and the children. I left without breakfast and hurried to my automobile. The temperature had dropped about twenty degrees overnight and frost was scattered over the grass. A front was moving in and a lot of low, scudding clouds were racing across the sky. I started the engine and defroster, and got out of the car to scrape frost off the windshield, watching my breath vaporize in the air. I was not dressed for the cold and shivered uncomfortably until I got back into the warm interior of my car.

As I turned onto the highway, I looked back at my house and was filled with nostalgia. I knew my life would never be the same. I had made a choice without considering the consequences of my action. Jane, the children, my career – all seemed unimportant.

Had I become like Icarus, only to find that my means of escape might be my end? I wondered if Maria was going through the same kind of mental agony. I was the proverbial moth busting my chops to dive right into the burning candle. How in the hell could anything be worth all this anguish? I didn't know. But I damn well knew I had to find out.

A light rain was falling as I drove in, and the wind from the front plucked fall leaves from the roadside trees and hurled them through the air. They danced across the road like cats trying to keep their feet dry. It was not a pretty day and the inclement weather dampened my thoughts. I pulled into the parking lot, parked as close to the door as possible, and hurried to the entrance.

Inside my sanctuary at last, I sat at my desk and went to work. I was determined to cleanse my mind of all superfluous thought. It would be a long day!

22

If Thursday night was tough, Friday night was Dante's *Inferno*. I slept little and worried a lot. I couldn't wait to get up and get going. I had managed to create my own hell.

Jane didn't notice my anguish, which seemed impossible. But she hadn't departed from her usual Friday night routine of television and more television. I got my fishing gear together and packed my overnight bag. I packed like I planned to fish – whatever that is – and put a pair of slacks and a sport coat in a hang-up bag. I finished my packing with a turtleneck shirt, a heavy sweater, and a windbreaker. After a quick breakfast, I kissed the girls goodbye, hugged Jane, told them I would miss them. I marched away like Benedict Arnold.

Strangely enough, my fit of guilt diminished as I drove away. Maybe guilt is inversely proportional to distance. Made sense to me, but it was a bit too cynical to accept.

I drove through town and headed east on Devine Street. There wasn't much traffic at 7:30, but that was normal. Columbia isn't exactly a metropolis. Soon I was on the Sumter highway, Highway 378, watching the city diminish, and approaching farmland. The houses became sparse and they were parts of enclaves of pasture land, barns, and cultivated fields without crops. Some of the houses retained the glory of former days, and true to their heritage, even the run-down ones had tree-lined approaches from the highway.

It was dark but I could see a thin band of light creeping over the horizon behind me, probably the end of the cold front. I was chasing bad weather but the wind would keep it in front of me and take it out to sea before I reached the coast. Wisps of fog settled in low-lying areas and perched on the treetops. The pines punched through the fog top, but the deciduous hardwoods carried it on their bony limbs. When I crossed the Wateree River, the dense fog clung to the surface of the water. I felt cold, and turned up the heater.

I had the highway to myself and enjoyed the solitude. I turned at Highway 261 and drove through Manchester State Forest. It was a quiet drive with a few small towns, dense woodlands, and large farms. It was out of the way but, what the hell? I had lots of time and needed it to calm my nerves. An hour and a half later, with Wedgefield, Pinewood, and Paxville behind me, I stopped for the only red light in Manning. I was halfway to Garden City and absolutely without a plan. I had no idea what I would do when I arrived. I had to find a way to contact Maria without doing anything stupid. I couldn't just drive up and knock on the door, and I didn't have a telephone number. At least the weather was improving. The sun, having burned off the fog, was a bright orange ball in front of me as I left Manning on 521 heading to Georgetown.

I drove through Andrews, a sleepy little town with dark, lagoon-like ponds in the midst of a few nice homes just off the highway. I made Georgetown before 10:00 AM. I had about thirty minutes to decide what I would do. I opted to look for a motel somewhere before Garden City. At least I would have a base of operations. And if I could make contact with Maria, she would know where to find me.

I was enjoying the drive. The sides of the highway were laden with magnificent, ageless live oaks laced with Spanish moss that canopied the entire width of the road in some places, and wind sculptured wax myrtles that put man's artwork to shame. The coast was beautiful, even in winter, and it put me in a positive and buoyant frame of mind. I certainly needed that. I passed Pawleys Island turn off and spotted a few familiar places –

Lachicotte's store and the post office – and began to look for a motel as I approached Murrells Inlet. I was five miles from Garden City.

I spotted a small motel on the left side off the highway identified by a sign with a seahorse on a white background, named appropriately "Seahorse Motel". The office was part of the first building and the rooms were spread over the site in five buildings of four units each. It wasn't the Ritz, but it was attractive and well maintained. I turned in, drove through the complex, and decided it would do.

I parked and walked into the office, which was really more like a den, and was greeted by a smiling, middle-aged woman in brown slacks and a baggy yellow sweater. She stood behind the usual counter with a cabinet of two rows of pigeon-hole shelving mounted on the wall behind it, a spiral bound guest book open on the counter, and a bell to summon the desk clerk if you came in while it was unmanned.

"Hi. I need a room but I don't have a reservation," I said without smiling too much.

"Don't reckon that's a problem," she said, still smiling. "Not much going on this time of year. You here for the bill fishing tournament?"

"No Ma'am. Not really. I plan to do some fishing off the Garden City pier, but I have some work to do first."

"You a salesman?"

"Yes Ma'am. I sell construction products to building contractors," I lied without any feeling of guilt. I was carrying a bigger burden and one more lie couldn't hurt. I knew this lady was curious and would probably continue with the third degree. I didn't feel like giving her too much information.

"How long you plan to stay?" she said as she pulled out a check-in card.

"I'll probably be here till Sunday checkout." I reached for the card.

"I can give you a better rate then. Ten dollars a night. We usually get fifteen dollars for one night."

"Guess it's my lucky day." I smiled broadly.

"Put your license number on the card. We keep track of our guests. Make sure they have a place to park. We don't have many spare spaces."

I nodded, wrote in my auto license number, and reached for the key.

"Put you in the third building; that'd be unit C-4. It's got a new TV."

"Thanks. I appreciate that. Can I check in now, or must I wait for 12 o'clock?"

"Naw," she drawled. "Would'na given you the key if it weren't ready."

"Just kidding. See you later." I turned and walked away, thankful she didn't ask any more questions.

No cars were in the parking area of loose, crushed shells carefully marked and terminated with cross ties. I turned at the third building. There was a neat *C-4* incised into a wooden square of cypress inlaid in the vertical stained wood siding. Wax myrtles identified the entrances and gave each unit privacy. The live oaks, laden with Spanish moss and elegantly maintained with surgical care to protect their antiquity, provided shade and shelter. Not bad, I thought as I guided the car into the last space.

I left my luggage in the car, opting to inspect my new temporary digs before unpacking. The lock was difficult to turn unless the door was lifted slightly. Once I was inside, I discovered that the room was tidy and spacious. A double bed on the right, a sitting area on the left with a comfortable, stuffed chair, straight backed ladder chair, coffee table, floor lamp, that new TV, and a small kitchenette with an under counter fridge. A roomy closet separated the kitchenette from the bathroom. Surprisingly, the bathroom had a large walk-in shower, adequate vanity with lavatory, and the floors and walls were ceramic tile. I had hit a home run.

I went back to the car, retrieved my luggage, put everything away, and turned on the TV. It was tuned to the local news from Myrtle Beach. The reception wasn't good, but I could live with it. I found a telephone on the bedside table with instructions for dialing out and room-to-room. That wasn't going to do me much good.

My mind turned to the problem at hand – namely, to find and make contact with Maria. I decided to ride to Garden City and locate the Conch Shell. That shouldn't be too hard this time of year. I turned out the lights, locked the door and drove away. I stopped at the first liquor store I came to and got a fifth of scotch. I figured we might need that before the night was over. Maybe before, if I couldn't get my nerves in order. I asked the proprietor where I could get packaged ice. He directed me to a Red and White about a mile from Garden City. A bottle of distilled water would be a good idea too. The local water had a distinct sulfur taste.

I went a mile past the Garden City exit to Surfside Beach, took Ocean Boulevard, and drove south looking for Second Avenue. The beach was deserted, except for a few die-hard fishermen on the pier hanging over the guardrails waiting for a spot or drum to grab their lines. I drove on and counted down the avenues. I had three blocks to go. With a churning stomach and shifting eyes I turned right on Second looking for the house. I spotted three cars at the fourth house on the right. It was a typically square, shingled house on creosote pilings with a screen porch across the front. The white rental sign on the front had a red conch shell and the owner's name. I went by slowly looking for signs of life and wondering what in the hell I was going to do. I turned at the next street, went around the block and drove past again, stopped two houses down, and pulled into the yard of a house that looked deserted. I sat there for a few minutes, adjusting the rearview mirror to give me a good view of the Conch Shell. I got out carrying a legal pad pretending to make notes as I stared at the house. I walked around it slowly, and peered in all the windows. All the while, I was positioned to watch the Conch Shell for any sign of Maria.

Suddenly, a woman came out of the front door, got into one of the cars, and drove off slowly. As the car approached, I recognized Maria. She made a follow me motion with a nod of her head. With my heart in my throat, I jumped into my car, pulled in behind her, and followed. She drove to the highway with me a discreet distance behind and pulled into a Gulf station.

I stopped behind her and got out. As I approached the car, she rolled down the window. She had a startled look on her face. "Oh my God," she said. "I can't believe it! I didn't expect you to come."

I smiled. "You shouldn't have given me the note. I never had a choice."

"Don't misunderstand me. I'm just shocked...and pleased that you came. I just don't know what to do. I've never been in this situation before."

"Don't feel like the Lone Ranger. If you're confused, so am I. If you don't know what to do, neither do I." I thought a little humor might calm the nerves. "I checked into a motel called the Seahorse, this side of Murrells Inlet. Follow me; I'll show it to you. I'm in room C-4. It's the last room in the third building."

She bit her lip and shook her head before she spoke. "I'll follow you, but I can't come in. I don't have much time. I volunteered to go the grocery so I could leave, and I was lucky no one wanted to go. I promise I'll come back as soon as I can. I don't know how or when, but I will. Even if I have to walk. Trust me."

I leaned in the window and kissed her lightly; the magic was still there. "I know you'll come. I'll wait. There's a Red and White near the motel. It'll be on your right. You can shop there on the way back. See you," I said before returning to my car.

I pulled ahead of her and she followed me the few miles to the Seahorse. I turned in and parked, pointing to my room. She nodded in acknowledgement and sped back to the highway. I watched her until she was out of sight. I went into my room and prepared for my vigil.

I woke up after a nap at five thirty, bright-eyed and bushy-tailed. I had slept hard and had to think for a minute where I was. I was startled by the unfamiliarity of my new quarters, but I came back to earth in a flash. She was coming, but when? I hated to wait, a lifelong obsession. I wasn't prepared for the ambiguity, but logic dictated my choice. I was at the mercy and whim of a woman I really didn't know well. And yet, I felt like I had known her forever and was destined to be here. I felt like my entire life was distilled and focused into this one moment. Intellectually, I knew this was silly, but my heart said otherwise.

I stripped and headed for the shower; I needed a clear head. I shaved quickly, brushed the sleepy taste out of my mouth, and turned on the hot water, letting it warm to steam. The mirror fogged over before I opened the shower door and adjusted the water, testing it with my hand. I wanted it as hot as I could stand. I stepped into the shower and felt the water, hot little needles on my back. It was luxurious and sensuous, just what I needed. I took my time, soaping up twice and shampooing my hair. I wasn't in a hurry, so I rinsed a long time. I toweled off in the shower, and when I stepped out I was cold. I hadn't activated the heat when I came back to the room. I tiptoed, wrapped in the towel, to the thermostat and set it on 90 degrees. I heard the heat pump come to life, and in a few minutes the fan was blasting hot air from the ceiling grills. After I toweled my hair dry, I felt like I was in a sauna. I re-set the thermostat to 70 degrees. At least I knew the heat was working.

I slipped on a white, v-necked tee shirt and a pair of blue boxer shorts, grabbed a paperback from my bag and fell on the bed. I piled all the pillows up and turned the bed lamp on. Maybe I could spend some time reading. Didn't work; I couldn't concentrate. My mind was 600 volts ready to light up the world. I was waiting for something I had never experienced, and I wanted it to be perfect. It had to be! We had waited so long; it would be wonderful. *Of course it would, idiot.* I was a fool to think otherwise.

I got up, dropped to the floor; whipped off 30 push-ups, turned over, and did 50 quick sit-ups. Activity helped. I tried running in place for a few minutes. I cut on the TV, adjusted as much snow out of it as I could, and watched the news. It was six thirty. God help me, I was going absolutely nuts. My clothing was soaked with sweat from exercise. I decided to rinse off in the shower again. I had to relax.

24

At 9:30 a car pulled into the parking lot, and I heard a door shut. There was a soft knock as I reached for the door. Maria stood there in slacks, sweater, and jacket. She stepped inside quickly. "I'm not sure you're going to like this," she said, "but my friend, Ricky, is with me. That's the only way I could get out. We're with a guy who lived next door to her for a few years, got a divorce and moved here. You might know him; his name is Robby Wilson. If it's a problem, and you think you better not come, I'll understand. I didn't know what else to do."

I met her grin with half a grin. "I didn't come this far to be a no show. You've got as much to lose as I have. I know him, but what the hell? I'm game if you are."

Maria reached for my hand and kissed me. "Let's give it a go. Ricky says he's OK and that's good enough for me. I trust her. Besides, she's not supposed to be with him; she's a married lady. We're all carrying baggage."

I put on my turtleneck and grabbed my windbreaker and the bottle of Johnny Walker Red. "We'll need this. This is brown bag country."

Maria grimaced. "I forgot, and I could do with some of that. We're not as cosmopolitan as we'd like to think, are we?"

I smiled. "No, but we've got a lot of hours to get over it. Just a little case of nerves. Like a first date."

"Don't be so naïve. That's like comparing lung cancer to a cold."

I shrugged, put my arm around her waist and led her to the door. I stopped and kissed her gently. Her response was guarded. I felt her tenseness.

She looked at me and said, "This is stupid," and kissed me like she meant it. "We wanted this; let's not waste it." We walked to the car.

We got in the back seat and I spoke to Robby. "How you doing Robby? It's been a while since I've seen you, maybe two or three years. Maria tells me you live here now."

He reached over the seat and shook my hand. "Yep, been in Myrtle Beach almost two years and really like it. It's more fun after September; the tourist's are a pain in the butt." He laughed. "Can't get along with out them though; after all, they ARE the economy."

I shook my head in agreement and said, "A necessary evil." I turned to Ricky. "Good to see you Ricky; how's Harry?" Harry is Ricky's husband and I've known him since high school. Maria looked surprised. She wasn't aware I knew Ricky, and obviously Ricky hadn't told her.

Ricky was a thin, small woman with large protruding eyes and a sharp nose. She wasn't the type to gather stares, but she was garrulous and fun to be with. Jane and I had been to parties with her and Harry, and I liked both of them. "Hi Terry", she said. "I hope you brought some liquor. I was afraid some of the other girls would want to come with us if I tried to sneak any out."

I smiled. "Of course I did. I figured this would be a BYOB party. I have enough for all if you can tolerate scotch with this beach water."

Her laugh filled the car. "You got that right; this water's for the birds. Mixing it with adult beverage is the only way I can get it down."

I turned toward Robby. "What's our destination, Robby?"

"Pete's Beach Bar is about the only close place open this time of year. It's about six or seven miles north of Surfside. It's bona fide redneck, but it's got good music on the juke, and you won't see anybody you know."

"Sounds like a winner," I said. "How about it, Girls?"

Maria snuggled against me, giggling and she whispered, "Sounds a lot like the Blizzard Shop." Her giggles caught Ricky's attention.

"What Maria?" Ricky asked.

"Private joke," I said. "But we don't need to get into that. She's satisfied with Pete's."

We walked into Pete's and Robby had described it perfectly. Two feet of thick, gray smoke hung over a small rectangular room with a juke box and dance floor at one end and a bar straight out of a B-grade Western movie at the other end. Seven four seated booths lined the windowless street wall and a few round tables with four chairs completed the space between the bar and the dance floor. Bare bulbs suspended through the smoke layer provided just enough light to make walking and dancing safe. People were everywhere, but we had our choice of one table or the last booth. We opted for the privacy of the booth, and I took my bottle to the bar and gave it to the bartender while the others settled in. I looked around the room casually as I walked to the bar. I didn't recognize anyone, just as Robby had promised. I noted that the drink of choice was Blue Ribbon beer. Five couples locked together in a four-armed embrace danced to a slow number. It would take a while to decide if their demeanor was a statement of passion, or an attempt to hold each other up. Everyone else was standing around talking with a can of beer in one hand and a cigarette in the other. We had found redneck heaven. White socks and tee-shirts with cigarette packages rolled up in the sleeves were everywhere.

When I returned to the booth, the waitress was taking orders. She was slender and tall and had wet, red hair tucked behind her ears. Her skirt was too short, her sweater too tight, and she wore the worst looking white boots I had ever seen. As a matter of fact, I don't think I've ever seen boots like that anywhere. But they seemed perfect for Pete's. With little small talk and a look of absolute boredom, she wrote down our order, stuck the pencil behind her ear, and left.

I smiled as she walked away. "Obviously Miss Congeniality of her senior class."

The girls tried hard to suppress giggles but couldn't. "I've got to find some boots like that," said Ricky, and she and Maria cackled with laughter.

"Don't get too carried away, ladies. She's all we've got and she's the best of the lot," said Robby. "We don't want to make her mad."

In a matter of minutes, Miss Congeniality returned with our drinks, put them on the table, and left without a word. I thanked her as she walked away in her white boots, but she didn't acknowledge my gratitude. "I guess we're running a tab," I said to no one in particular, as I took a big swig of my drink. With a clinking together of our glasses, and a chorus of "Cheers," we began this momentous evening.

We chatted aimlessly for a few minutes and savored our drinks. I grabbed Maria's hand and ushered her toward the dance floor. I wanted her in my arms. I had weathered enough of the foreplay, so to speak. We took our place among the locked together couples and she slid into my waiting arms. She moved against me as she had at the club dance, and I could feel her entire body. Her hair brushed my cheek, and the wonderful fragrance of her perfume sent me a message of pleasure. I kissed her gently on her cheek, and she turned her face upward to meet my lips. We kissed. It seemed we were alone, and neither of us cared that we weren't.

The music stopped and Doug Clark and the Hot Nuts came on the jukebox. Some of the dancers continued locked together as though mesmerized by their passions. The rest went into the shag as though they were programmed. We tried to shag, but it wasn't our thing. I laughed and put my arms around Maria, turned and led her off the floor. I hadn't realized how hot it was as I wiped the perspiration off my brow. "Damn, it's hot," I said. "I think it's time for a drink."

She looked at me with her luminous green eyes, smiled and said, "I couldn't have said it better myself."

We sat down and sipped our drinks. Ricky and Robby were deep in conversation and ignored our return. Finally, Ricky turned toward Maria and said, "You were the best dancers on the floor," and they laughed heartily.

I said, "We did good until they played 'Hot Nuts'. I couldn't do them justice."

"I'm not sure I've heard them before," Maria said. "Where did they come from?"

"That's a Southern thing. Our attempt to be risqué. They're big at the beach, but not too much at home," I said.

Maria arched her eyebrows. "I should have paid more attention to the lyrics. I must have missed something."

"I ordered another round," Robby said. I hope you don't mind Terry, but it's Sunday and drinks are cut off at midnight. Ricky said she wanted another, so

I ordered for everybody."

"No problem," I replied. "After that mash on the dance floor I could use another one. I bet its twenty degrees warmer out there." I noticed Maria was lifting her hair off her neck to cool down and wet ringlets had formed on her forehead from perspiration. "Too hot for you?" I asked.

Maria gave me an evil smile. "Not as hot as I'd like," she said, just quietly enough for me to hear.

I patted her leg under the table. "That's either passion or alcohol."

"A little of both," she said. "I think I'm just trying to keep my nerve up. We both know where this is heading and I'm nervous. Big time. I've never done this before, but I want to....with you. I knew what I was setting in motion when I asked you to come."

I grinned. "Perhaps my lady is beginning to feel the early pangs of guilt."

"Actually I don't. Maybe I should, and I can't explain why, but I don't. I've never felt much guilt with our relationship...well a little. I will admit that I never thought it would get this far, but I didn't discourage it. Ever."

I looked steadily into her eyes and noticed the glitter, or perhaps a hint of tears. "I never felt much guilt either, until I had to look Jane in the face and lie about coming here. That was tough, but there never was a moment when I considered not coming. It just gets hard when you bring third parties into the equation and one of them is a spouse."

Miss Congeniality arrived with our drinks and placed them on the table. She retrieved our empty glasses and laid the bill on the table in front of me. "That's last call. You can play the juke and dance if you want until one. That's when we lock the doors. If you want to pay now, I'll bring you your bottle.

I picked up the bill. It was seven dollars. I handed her ten. "Keep it," I said.

"Thanks" she said and smiled. I couldn't believe it. She actually smiled. I settled back and took a sip of my drink. I put my hand back on Maria's leg and gently pulled her closer to me. I could feel her warmth through my pants leg. Some gentle soul played a slow piece, and calm pervaded hillbilly heaven. I nodded to Maria. "Let's try it one more time before they slam the door."

We walked onto the floor and started swaying with the music. I heard the lyrics in the background. "Again.......this couldn't happen again. This is that once in a lifetime......"

"I like this song," I said. "Maybe it's appropriate."

"I do, too," Maria said. I could hear her breathing in my ear. "I feel so good, so warm. Terry, tell me this is right for us. I feel at peace being together, and I honestly don't feel any guilt. In my mind, I know I should, but my heart tells me it's good. Is this the way all affairs start? God, I hope not. I don't want to feel like everybody else. I want this to be special. Is that so wrong?"

"No, it's not. All I know is, since the day you walked into my office, I've never stopped thinking about you. There's not a minute during the day when I don't want you. I've never felt like this before. I hardly know you, but I feel like I always have. Like I've been marking time, waiting for you."

She looked at me, serene and sparkly eyed. "Don't say any more, Terry. I'm afraid we'll ruin the moment. If it's right or wrong, we'll know soon enough."

She slid her head across my shoulder and held me close. I dropped my hand down her back and pulled her against me. We stopped dancing and just swayed together. I didn't want to leave the dance floor, but I realized the music had stopped. I hugged her and led her back to the booth. I looked at my watch; it was a few minutes before one.

"We'd better shake this place before the fights start," Robby said. "I can't stand the carnage." The girls stood up quickly. They weren't sure if he was serious.

Ricky turned toward Maria. "I think it's time to leave. The girls will worry about us if we don't make bed time. They don't need anything to speculate about. You know how women like to talk. Last one in bed is the only safe one."

"Damn Ricky," I said as I reached for my bottle. "You're not giving your friends much credit."

"Oh come on, Terry. Women like to gossip, and fact is no prerequisite for gossip, especially not with a bunch of women partying at the beach."

I stood up and slid away from the booth. "Well, let's get out of Dodge and get you ladies home."

Maria and I waited until Robby and Ricky were up and we let them lead the way. "Well," I whispered, "where do we go from here?" I could tell Maria was thinking very hard as we got into the back seat.

"I'll find a way to get to the motel. I'll borrow Ricky's car, and when all the girls are asleep, I'll slip away. Ricky and I are sharing a bedroom so it shouldn't be hard to get away."

"I guess that'll have to do. I sure don't have any suggestions. Just don't fall asleep."

"Don't be funny. I'm so nervous; I could never go to sleep."

I chuckled. "Well, I might, so I'll leave the door unlocked."

"I don't believe you … but leave it unlocked, just in case." She leaned over and kissed me lightly on the lips. "Think about better things. It may be a long night".

I leaned over the seat and tapped Robby's shoulder. "Robby, how about dropping me off first, if you don't mind? I'm meeting a friend for an early breakfast at the Garden City pier and then do a little fishing. I've got to get some sleep or I'll be dead." The truth was I was afraid someone might see Maria and me together, and I knew that would be bad.

"Sure, no problem."

I was beginning to feel the chill of the night air as my clothes, damp from the heat of dancing at Pete's, turned from warm to cold. I moved closer to Maria, trying to siphon of some of her body heat. A full moon hung in the eastern sky, looking cold and ominous. It was an icy ball without the sense of romance it normally generated. We rode with little conversation, and soon reached the Seahorse. As Robby pulled into the parking space, I could see the frost on my car reflecting from the headlights. I patted Maria's hand as I reached for the door handle and whispered, "See you soon … I hope." She gave me a sheepish smile, but said nothing. "Well guys, I really enjoyed it. I just hope when I get up at six o'clock I can still say that. Good to see you, Robby. When you get back to Columbia, stop by the office. I'll buy you a drink."

"It might be a while, Terry, but I'll take you up on that. I hope you catch some fish, but I don't envy you having to get up so early. If it were me, I'd stay in bed."

"You're right Robby, but I made a promise and I'll have to honor it." I moved away from the car and waved as they drove off. I put the key in the lock and remembered to pull up on the door so the key would turn the lock pins. It was good to get in a warm room again. I was relieved to be in safe confines, but I felt the stirrings of apprehension, nervousness and excitement coming on. It was a mixed bag, and one that I wasn't sure how to handle. Why was I hung up with all this ambiguity? Was guilt a factor, or was it a game my head was playing? Like all men, I had imagined a situation like this many times, but imagination was one thing. Reality was another. Nevertheless, I was here, the field was chalked off and the lights were about to come on. It was too late for second guesses.

I walked into the bathroom and brushed my teeth. It felt good to get the party breath out of my mouth. I rinsed and drank a full glass of water. I was thirsty after all the dehydration from the alcohol. Now all I could do was wait. Same old story. I left the bathroom light on and turned off all the other lights. I stripped down to my shorts, hung my clothes over the straight chair, put on a clean t-shirt and lay on the bed.

I was surprised a few minutes later when I saw car lights through my windows. As the car angled into the parking place, the lights moved slowly across the walls like a shooting star and faded into blackness. The door slammed shut with a hollow thump and Maria, a ghostly apparition, met me at the door and put her arms around my waist. I kissed her ever so gently, taking my time and touching every part of her lips. Slowly, I worked my way around her face, kissing her eyes, the tip of her nose and her neck. Her perfume, a sexual pheromone with just a hint of sweat from our night of dancing, was a gossamer vapor clinging to her hair.

She had changed from slacks to a skirt, and for the first time, my hands wandered to her mons pubis area and felt that mysterious, rounded profile of her body. I was entering a sacred place and I heard my heart pounding in my ears. She moved against me and pulled my face down to meet her lips, kissing me passionately and letting her tongue probe my mouth. I was on fire, and I knew that whatever it cost me in human terms to be here, it was not nearly enough for the value I was receiving.

She backed away, smiled, and pulled her sweater over her head. She unclasped her bra and let it fall away to the floor, exposing her ample breasts, and reached for the zipper on the side of her skirt. I dropped my shorts to the floor, kicked then to one side, threw my tee-shirt on top of them, and watched Maria's transformation to nudity.

The light of the full moon through the windows cast a silver glow over her body. I could make out the contrasting shades at her stomach and breasts, products of last summer's tan, and the dark, triangular shape of her bush at the bottom of her belly. I held her in my arms and felt the secret places and heat of her body against me. Heaven, or what I thought it might be, was suddenly defined, and I entered a state of rapture I had never known before. I kissed each breast, lingering over her nipples, and slid my hand between her thighs. She was warm, wet, and lubricated.

Maria lay on the bed as I fumbled for a prophylactic left discretely under an ashtray on the coffee table. I tore the wrapper off and began the arduous and unromantic task of rolling it onto my erect penis. As I attempted to enter her, uncontrollably and unexpectedly, I ejaculated. As quickly as it had started, it was over. I couldn't believe it.

"I'm sorry. I don't know what happened," I said perplexed, and with heavy heart. Those were the first words spoken since Maria had arrived. The second words came from Maria and were a dagger to my heart.

She pushed me away, stood up and, in one motion, reached for my shorts on the floor and threw them to me. "Put on your pinkies, I've got to go."

Humiliation was not a strong enough word for what I was feeling. I couldn't think of one thing to say. I got up from the bed with a wet condom hanging on

my limp member, and watched Maria, without a word, dress and bolt from my room. Without a shot being fired, except for my one dastardly exception, I had become a romantic casualty. Somewhere in the catacombs of my mind, I could hear those fateful words that articulately emerge from my minister's mouth every Sunday at midday service: "Here endeth the first lesson."

I left the beach like a thief in the night just before the first light of day. Sleep had been a no-show. Strangely enough, I wasn't tired. After Maria left, I spent the remaining hours of the night trying to figure out what had happened. I thought sex was automatic and it always had been. I was baffled. I remembered reading about the German poet Goethe who, while on a business trip, stopped at an inn and enticed a young waitress to spend the night with him. He was unable to perform the sexual act because of guilt and never attempted it again. Could guilt be my culprit? I don't recall any thoughts of Jane, but who knows what lurks in the minds of men? Maybe I was too tired, too eager, or too anything. Hell, I had no clue. I ran ideas through my mind like an ad salesman, but to no avail.

I decided to get to Columbia as fast as I could. I drove like a maniac, making only one stop for coffee and to relieve myself. The outskirts looked warm and inviting as I approached the city. I drove through light Sunday morning traffic to my office. It was nearly eight o'clock and too early to go home; I was supposed to be fishing, and I didn't relish the idea of explaining to Jane why I wasn't. Besides, a few hours of rest in the office would do wonders for me. Fatigue was coming on big time.

I pulled in behind my office and parked as close to the door as I could. I didn't want anyone to see me or my car. Once inside, I dropped a pillow on the conference room carpet and fell into a deep sleep.

I woke up at one thirty; it was a long trip back to reality. I was still tired, and coming back from sleep was like climbing a long ladder one rung at a time. I was instantly hungry, and I realized I hadn't eaten since lunchtime Saturday. I found some cookies and boiled some water for coffee. It wasn't much, but my stomach didn't know the difference.

I couldn't think about Maria without feeling betrayed, unloved and humiliated. I couldn't understand her reaction and had seen a side of her that seemed totally incongruous. Although we had never spoken the I love you words, our actions had spoken them for us. This was no one-night stand, and two people just don't come together like we did without deep feeling. My thoughts were muddled and they turned to Jane and my children. In my confusion and pain, I sought refuge in them, knowing they loved me unconditionally, albeit without passion in Jane's case. Suddenly I yearned for them and the comfort they offered. I wanted to rush to them and confess all, to tell them how sorry I was for lying to them and doing what I had, but I knew this would never happen. I would never tell Jane. She was too fragile and trusting to ever hear this and I knew what it would do to our marriage, which was not on firm footing as it was. No, I would take this secret to my grave. I would show my contrition in other ways. But before I could wear my new found halo, I had one more lie to tell. They would want to know the details of my fishing trip.

Monday morning I awoke refreshed, partly because I had felt brain dead and fatigued when I went to bed, and partly because I was in the friendly confines of my own bed. Few questions had been asked about my trip so my prevarications were limited. The children were happy to see me back, and a game of roll the bat was enough to get me back in their good graces. As tired and guilty as I was, I managed to make love to Jane, partly out of desire and partly to find out if I could still perform after my fiasco with Maria. Jane seemed interested for a change, which only served to add to my guilt.

After breakfast, I kissed Jane and the girls goodbye and drove to the office. I tried not to think of Maria as I drove in, but that was like sticking my hand into a fire and not feeling pain. I knew that sooner or later I would have to face her, and somehow manage to repair the damage enough to return to my architectural duties. She could choose to pay me off and take her work to some other architect, but that would be hard to explain, especially to Pat. *Do I call her or wait for her to call me?* I didn't relish the thought of either.

Martha's car was in the lot when I arrived. I hoped she hadn't found any signs that I'd been there Sunday. Actually, I wasn't sure if I'd told her about my trip, so I walked in without much fanfare.

"Morning Martha. How was your weekend?"

"The usual," she said. "Seems like all I do anymore is babysit."

I smiled. "If you have to work that hard, you may as well find you a new husband and have some more of your own."

"I'd rather have a root canal," she muttered and turned back to her typewriter.

Good old crusty Martha, I thought, as I moved into the drafting room. At least she hadn't changed.

"Oh, Mrs. Champion called. She wants you to call her, as soon after nine as you can. She sounded so urgent about it that I told her to call you at home, but she said that wasn't necessary."

I was startled. Why would she be calling this early? Maybe an apology for her actions at the beach? I was excited at the prospect of talking to her. Damn it, it was starting all over again. I was either a fool or masochistic. What a choice.

"Thanks Martha. I'll call her later, after I've had a chance to get my day lined up. She probably wants a progress report and I'm not in the mood for that." My stomach was churning. I wanted to call her in the worst way, but I was apprehensive. What would I say to her?

I made my way up the spiral stairs to my loft office and busied myself cleaning up my desk. I needed some grunt work to do to keep me occupied and keep my mind off Maria. (That was akin to putting my feet in a roaring fire and sucking on ice cubes to cool them off.) I succeeded in neurotically stacking all the paper neatly in same sized groups, laying my pencils in descending order and pushing other items around to make my desk appear neat. I was a real nut case. I glanced at my watch. It was eight forty-five and I knew I wouldn't make it to nine before I'd call her. I felt powerless … a moth going for the candle flame.

I couldn't stand it any longer. I reached for the phone and dialed her number. She answered on the fifth ring. "Hello" she said pleasantly.

"It's me. How are you?"

She was quiet for a minute. "I need an answer to a question before I can say," she said gruffly. "Is there any chance I could be pregnant?"

I was stunned. "I can't believe you asked me that. Of course not. I almost wish I could say yes. Is this your idea of a cruelty joke?"

"No, it's not. I just had to know. I don't have anything else to say. Goodbye."

She was gone and all that was left was the monotonous drone of the disconnect. I held the phone hoping she hadn't hung up and then I put it into the cradle. This was worse than the episode in the motel. I couldn't believe she could be so heartless. Everything seemed to be closing in on me. I couldn't stand it. I had to get away, go somewhere, do something, anything. I had to leave. I grabbed my coat and passed Martha in a flash. I stopped at the door long enough to say, "I forgot. I have to meet John Wicker to select face brick for the Hugeley job. I'll be back as soon as I can. Lock up if I'm not back when you leave."

I jumped into my car and headed out of the parking lot. I didn't have anyplace in mind, but somehow drove to one of the lots Maria and I had looked at for her house. I felt a strange need to go somewhere we had been together. It didn't make any sense, but it made me feel better. It was the most remote lot of the three we had surveyed, surrounded by wooded areas and devoid of housing. I pulled off the road and parked near a grove of hardwoods. Dark, puffy gray clouds hiding impending raindrops were building up in the west. If you could substitute tears for the rain, I could equate with it. I was really down.

Talking to her was out of the question, so I did the next best thing. I grabbed a legal pad and wrote her a single-spaced note filling both sides of the page. I poured out my heart to her, telling her I was sorry for what had happened at the beach, but didn't attempt to offer an explanation. I really had none and told her so, but emphasized that it had nothing to do with her or how I felt about her. I pleaded with her not to shut me out of her life, and asked her to meet me for lunch at the Blizzard Shop next Thursday at one o'clock. *Just think about it*, I wrote. I would be there, and if she didn't show up, I would understand. It wasn't necessary for her to tell me beforehand. I would wait until 1:30 for her, and if she decided not to come, so be it. I folded the note and drove to her house. Pat's car wasn't in the drive, so I pulled up to the mailbox and shoved the note to the back so it couldn't fall out. I drove away, feeling a little stupid and high school-ish, hoping no one saw me, and returned to my office. I called her when I got inside and she answered on the third ring. "Please don't hang up. I left you a note in your mailbox. I don't want to talk about it. Just read it and think about it. Bye."

I hung up before she could reply. I knew she would hurry to the mailbox to retrieve it before it fell into the wrong hands, and I felt she was curious enough to read it. Now I could only wait. I'd had plenty of practice waiting at the beach.

28

An eternity would have been an apt description of my next few days. I tried to stay busy, but knew I was merely marking time for Thursday to come around. I played golf Wednesday afternoon with Bill, Garth, and Jerry. We hadn't played much during the summer because of the heat and the difficulty of getting all of us together on the same day. I hadn't seen any of them since the country club dance. I enjoyed being with them, and it helped me forget about Maria. At least for the afternoon. Remembering my guilt-ridden promise to Jane, I invited them come over Saturday night for dinner. Jerry was my playing partner and he quipped, "If you have ham, I'm not coming."

"Of course not, I'm having grilled pork chops, but the rabbi promised to bless them just so you could eat one."

Jerry grinned. "Is it going to be BYOB?"

I took my putter out of my bag and pretended to swing it at him. "I've had about enough of you for one day. Now try to hit a few good shots so we can win this match. I've got cleat marks all over my back from carrying you."

He danced a little jig to his ball, lined up his shot and hit a five iron to the center of the green. "How'd you like that, Smart Ass? Are you happy now?"

"Damn right. Why can't you hit every shot like that?" Jerry was always up, and I could count on him to entertain me. He was tonic for my soul.

We finished our round, had a few drinks at the bar, and went our separate ways. I reminded them about dinner Saturday, and told them Jane would be calling their wives.

The days were getting noticeably shorter with winter approaching, and as I walked to my car I noticed how much colder it had gotten. With no clouds in the sky, the temperature dropped rapidly, as soon as the sun signaled the end of the day. My damp shirt felt like ice on my bare skin and added speed to my stride.

I was thinking about Thursday as I drove out of the parking lot, but I knew it was more important to tell Jane about dinner Saturday night. I was going to deliver on my promise. I suddenly felt good about something for a change.

Thursday came in with a whimper, promising rain and below average temperatures. A brisk wind made it seem colder, and the inclement weather served to intensify the anxiety I felt. I left the house with little conversation – trying to be normal – but unable to pull it off. I had managed to keep my mouth shut, but smiled a lot whenever the girls asked their usual ration of morning questions. That kept my answers civil.

I drove without the usual urgency, but my mind was racing with thoughts of what I might say to Maria if she showed up. I felt like a jilted lover begging my way back into a love affair that may have existed only in my mind. Perhaps I was assuming too much. Maybe we were just two ships passing in the night; but in my heart, I knew it was much more than a tawdry sexual union. That certainly was a joke based on my lusty performance at Garden City.

In retrospect, Maria never came on to me in a physical sense until the night of the note. We had become friends first. We truly enjoyed our time together and our conversations were always interesting and cordial, even if we disagreed. We valued each other's opinions and counsel, and, when we were together, there was never enough time. Our conversations weren't littered with sexual innuendo or flirting. We had discussed some pretty weighty things. I remembered that once in the stimulating background of the Blizzard Shop, we had had a lengthy discussion of why God had to exist, and what was on the other side of space. That's certainly not the stuff affairs are made of. That doesn't mean that her animal magnetism ever escaped me. It didn't, but I was more impressed with her mind. That was the part of her that had become a cardinal point in the compass of my life, and I couldn't bear the thought of giving that up.

I pulled into the parking lot and parked away from the hoary live oak whose knobby limbs were shadow boxing with the wind. I didn't want to chance having one of those thick limbs crushing the top of my car. Martha's car wasn't in the lot. That surprised me because she almost always got to the office before me. I hoped she wasn't ill. I hated days she was out. She had a way of shielding me from unwanted calls, and today that would be important. I zipped my jacket up, pulled it around my neck, and jammed my hands into my pockets as I bolted for the door. The cold air was brutal.

The office was dark, mirroring the overcast sky, and the inside was cold. I flipped the light switch on and adjusted the thermostat. Coffee seemed appropriate, so I filled the kettle, set it on the hotplate, spooned some instant Maxwell house into my cup and dropped in four cubes of sugar. I like sugar. As soon as the kettle started steaming, I filled my cup and headed to the loft. The office was quiet as a tomb and heavy on solitude, and I felt the need for both.

A pile of mail and a note from Martha lay on my desk. She had written in her carefully crafted handwriting, "I forgot to tell you before you left on Wednesday that I had a dental appointment Thursday morning. I'll be late." Martha didn't waste many words.

I sipped on my coffee and started thinking about Maria and the odds of her showing. I figured it was about fifty-fifty. Thinking about her, in my present state of mind, was not a good move, and sitting on my butt wasn't any better. I decided I'd find some work to do that wouldn't take much thought or talent; maybe that would keep me busy until lunchtime. I went downstairs, found some framing shop drawings for the Huguley house and went to work. I managed to spend over two hours on that before Martha came in.

"How're the teeth, Martha?" I asked as she made her way to her desk.

"How do you expect them to feel? They're sixty years old and feel just like the rest of me. I'm full of Novocaine and can't talk, so leave me alone and let me do my work."

"Sorry I bothered to ask." I said with a big grin, and went back to work. Martha's not very pleasant when she goes to the dentist.

At 12:45 I decided to make my move to the Blizzard Shop. "Martha, I'm going to lunch. Lock up if you leave before I get back." She mumbled an answer and kept on typing. I assumed she understood what I had said, and I grabbed my jacket before going out the door. The same cold wind greeted me, but now it also propelled a drizzling rain with the force of small needles into my unprotected face. Instinctively, I shrunk into the lapels of my jacket and bent my head to avoid it.

I hopped into the car and started the engine. It responded sluggishly, and took a few minutes to slip into a smooth idle. As unpleasant as the air felt, it wasn't cold enough for rain to freeze on the windshield. My warm breath produced a cloud of fog on the glass that I had to wipe away. With the wipers in motion and the heater on full blast, I rolled the car onto the street and drove toward the Blizzard Shop. I was full of apprehension and hope.

I parked in the front as close to the door as possible, and hurried inside. Cigarette smoke hung over the counter, which was filled with a mélange of construction workers who couldn't work outside in the weather, and street people who wouldn't work regardless of the weather. Each of them held a cup of coffee or a bottle of beer in one hand and a cigarette in the other and were engaged in conversation or staring vacantly into space. *Amazing how emaciated men with few teeth, dressed in tattered dirty clothes, can make a cigarette and a bottle of beer look so good.* I walked past and eased into my regular booth in the rear, sitting so I could see the front door.

Angie, who waited tables and owned the restaurant with her sister, Agnes, must have seen me when I came in. She ambled over with a sliding motion that reminded me of a hermit crab. She had been victim of a stroke some years ago and her left side was affected. She greeted me pleasantly. "Where've you been Mr. T? I haven't seen you in a while."

"Hi Angie, working hard and chained to my desk, but I've missed your cheeseburgers so much, I decided I'd get out in the rain and get one."

"Sure Mr. T, I believe that like I believe you're the pope. I'd bet a dollar to a dime that pretty lady who meets you here will be having a hankering for a burger, too."

"I hope you're right Angie, but I think I'd better order a Coke and a large cheeseburger with lots of onions. Hold it for about 15 minutes just in case I have company. I'll give you a wave when I'm ready for it."

"OK, but why don't you order two now and save me the trouble of coming back?"

I smiled at her optimism. "I don't think so Angie. I like your burgers, but I can't eat two."

She wrote down my order and walked away. I watched her for a moment and felt sorry for her. Even with her impairment, though, she always seemed happy. Maybe she was better off than I was. I was a wreck.

In a few minutes, much to my surprise, Maria came racing through the door. She saw me and smiled as she walked quickly to the booth. She dropped her coat on the seat, sat down with a flourish, put her elbows on the table cradling her head in her hands and said simply, "Hi." She was dressed in a form-fitting gray skirt and a pink angora sweater.

I couldn't believe her nonchalance. It was as though the trip didn't exist and nothing had changed. I had to push my mouth open with my tongue to get a word out. "Hi. Long time no see." I tried to smile.

"You can do better than that," she said. "How about getting Angie over here? I'm hungry."

"If you want what I ordered, I'll just hold up two fingers and save her the trip."

"What did you order?"

"Large cheeseburger smothered in onions and a coke."

She made a face. "Onions?"

Her comment encouraged me. "Well, I could cancel the onions."

"Please do, and get me coffee instead of Coke. I need something warm." She brushed my cheek with her cold hand to emphasize the point. It was a simple gesture, but it gave me the same feeling I had when I was in the sixth grade and held my girlfriend's hand for the first time in the darkness of the Saturday morning movie at the Palmetto Theater. Do miracles ever stop? I was galvanized into action.

"I'll go tell Angie. I need some change for the juke box." I went to the bar, located Angie in the ever present cloud of smoke and gave her the new order. She gave me a knowing look when I cancelled the onions. "I need some change for the juke box," I said, handing her a fifty-cent piece. I grabbed the change, and returned to the booth. Two dimes later, *In Smokey Places* was playing with *Stranger on the Shore* in reserve.

"I see you haven't forgotten," she said. I thought she would like the sentimental effort, or at least I was hoping she would.

I pouted at her suggestion. "Of course not. How could you think that?"

She patted my hand. "Just kidding. Don't be so serious. How's my house coming along?"

That was a question I wasn't prepared for, although I should have been. "It's moving along," I said quickly, "but I could use some input from you." That wasn't true, but I wanted her back in the equation. That would give me a legitimate reason to be with her.

"Any time. You know how excited I am. I'm always available while the children are in school and in the evening after I get them down. Don't let me slow the process."

Without exposing my excitement and choosing my words with care, I said, "I have some appointments today, but we could get together in the evening. I'm planning on working till about ten." With all the mental turmoil I'd put myself through since the beach trip, creative work was impossible. But with this bit of encouragement, I could see some light at the end of the tunnel. I'd have to work fast, but I could get some sketches ready by evening.

"That just might work. I'll call you after I get the children down for the night. If I don't have any problems, I'll come over."

Angie walked up with our order just as Acker Bilk was finishing the last chords of *Stranger on the Shore*. She set the food on the table and asked, "Can I bring you anything else?"

"Thanks Angie, I think that'll do it."

"OK," she said, dropping the check in front of me and discretely walking away with her peculiar gait.

The aroma of the cheeseburger was wonderful. I realized how hungry I was and took a big bite. Maria's attitude was the catalyst for my appetite. A good cheeseburger's hard to beat when you're hungry.

Maria's look mirrored her satisfaction. "Um, this is good! The best! I'm glad you introduced me to this place." She set the burger down and stirred some sugar into her coffee. "The company's not bad either."

"You probably say that to everyone who takes you to lunch."

"No, just the important ones." She teased me with her eyes.

We finished our lunch without further conversation. We were hungry. I offered her a Kent, lighting hers and watching the smoke curl around her face before lighting mine. *Nothing like a cigarette after good food ... and good sex,* I thought slyly. I was sorry I had thought about that. I certainly hadn't proved it at Garden City.

Maria slid over in the booth and patted the empty seat. "Come over here. I'm tired of looking at you way over there."

The invitation confused me, but it was more than welcome. I wasted little time moving and slid in close to her. I reached for her hand, kneading her delicate fingers gently, and entwined them sensuously. Her eyes were sparkling emerald green, and my impulse suddenly took control of better judgment. I kissed her, not in passion, but as though I were drinking fine wine from a sacred vessel. She did nothing to discourage me, and she made a soft sound before our lips parted. What had started out for me as a mundane meeting had turned into a communion of spirits, or as close to it as I would ever wish. I began to wonder if the beach trip had really happened.

"Maria, I know this is a stupid thing to say, but I love you. I wish with all my heart I didn't. I've witnessed the misery in it, but I'd sure as hell rather be miserable with you than without you."

She put her finger across my lips to hush me. "Terry, I can never love you. I'm sorry. I know that's not what you want to hear."

I wasn't shocked or hurt. I had expected her to say that. "You don't have to love me. How I feel about you isn't based on your feelings. I'm not even sure why I love you, but it's not important except to me. I don't need to examine it to feel it. It's like a flower. I know it's beautiful, but I'm not going to pull all its petals off to see why."

"You don't understand Terry. It's not about how I feel. It's about what must be." She took a deep breath and continued. "We're not allowed to love each other. We're married and we have children. Those are obligations that we chose. They weren't forced on us. I care very deeply for you, but not enough to sacrifice my children. I'm sure you feel the same. Let's not mess up a wonderful relationship. Be satisfied with what we have. Just love me when we're together. That's how it must be. This is new and frightening to me. I've never been unfaithful, and it bothers me that I can be so cavalier about it. Everything is happening so fast. Honestly, I'm not sure I can cope with it." She spoke in a measured cadence, just above a whisper, and wiped tears from her eyes with her free hand.

"I'm sorry Maria. I shouldn't talk to you this way. I don't have the right. Forgive me."

"No Terry; don't apologize. It means a lot to know you really care about me. I believe your motivation is good and I need to know that. If I thought I was just another notch on your belt, it would destroy me."

"Maria, Maria...I couldn't touch you if I had any evil thoughts. That's the problem. I know what I'm doing is wrong, but I don't feel it's evil. You came into my life as though it was meant to be. When you come into my space, you light it up, and, when you leave, I'm not sad. I just can't wait for you to return. It's gotten so that I mark time until I'm with you again. God knows, it's not sex. I failed at that when I had the chance, and I'm not sure it wouldn't happen again."

She looked away. I could tell she was deep in thought. "Terry," she said slowly, "just what do you want from me?"

I monitored my thoughts and chose my answer carefully. "I don't want our relationship to jeopardize you or your family...... or mine. Our families have to be our first priority, and we must be careful not to be seen together in a compromising position. I'll never ask you to leave your family for me, and I know that sounds presumptuous considering where we are in this relationship. I want you to be part of my life, whatever you can give me for however long you can. If it's a year, a month, or a day, I'll accept it on your terms. Just give it a chance. If it gets out of hand, or you get uncomfortable with it, I'll leave you alone."

She bit her lip. "Don't press too much." She looked directly into my eyes. "I need some time to think. This isn't like asking me out for a date." She smiled. "In my heart and mind, I need to have a feeling that you may not understand. It's a woman thing, but I can't be comfortable without it. This isn't about sex. I can have sex with lots of men. Any woman can. But I would never do that. Sex is important, but only when it's not the most important thing in a meaningful relationship. It's a very special way to communicate, but so are smiles, touches, and conversation. I won't say that sex is at the bottom of the list. That would be foolish. But without all the other things, it would be meaningless for me." She kissed me lightly on the side of my mouth. "It's been a lovely day, but I've got to go."

I slid out of the booth and helped her with her coat. "I guess I did come on a little strong. I apologize if I upset you, but dammit I meant everything I said."

"Don't apologize. What could be better than hearing a wonderful man saying he loves me?" She pulled her coat tightly around herself and walked away. She turned around, as though she had forgotten something. "I'll call you about tonight."

I watched her disappear through the door before I sat down. "Well," I thought, "I'd better get my butt in gear and get some lines on paper or I'm going to fail the first test." I paid the bill to a smiling Angie and left.

I worked hard all afternoon, and at four o'clock I had a preliminary floor plan worked out. I wasn't totally satisfied with it, but it was headed in the right direction. I wanted to open it up more, get a more flow in it and take advantage of the vistas. It was good enough to show Maria and I knew she would be excited with it. I called Jane to tell her I'd be late coming home. "Honey, I've got to finish a sketch for a meeting tomorrow, so I'll be late. Don't wait supper on me; I'll pick up something on the way home. No use to get out in this weather to come home to eat and come back out. I'd rather get finished and then come home."

"So, what else is new?"

"Come on now. If I didn't have to get this done, I'd come home now. I don't have any choice. Staying here until I finish will get me home an hour or two earlier. Besides, you need to call all the girls about our cookout Saturday night. They need to know all the details."

"Will you be home in time for the party? Oh, never mind. Just be careful driving home. The roads will be getting slick with this rain and cold."

I ignored the sarcasm. "I'll be careful. I'll call you when I leave."

"OK. Goodbye."

"Bye."

With that unpleasant task out of the way, I returned to my drawing board with a vengeance. I polished up the floor plan until I had the area under three thousand square feet and had eliminated some of the functional problems. I started some elevations and did a few freehand perspectives before the phone rang.

I put on my best professional voice. "Design Concepts, Terry Forte speaking."

As expected, it was Maria. "There you go trying to impress me again. Don't you ever give up?"

"Of course not. That's my mission in life."

"Well, you'd better find a new one. I think you've succeeded with me."

"That's the best news I've had today. How's your evening looking? I've got some great stuff to show you." Of course I left out telling her how much of it I had managed to do after our lunch.

She chuckled. "You'd better have if you expect me to come out in this mess. I just got the kids down but Pat's in Savannah tonight so I can't stay very long."

"I understand. We can get through most of this in an hour or so. When do you think you'll be here?"

"Not more than twenty minutes. I'm ready to walk out of the door."

"I'll leave the lights on and the door unlocked."

"Gee, thanks. How about some coffee? I'll need something warm."

"The pot's on. See you shortly. Bye."

I picked up all my drawings and sketches, took them into the conference room and spread them neatly on the table. In minutes I had a pot of water on the hot plate and two cups on the counter with all the necessary ingredients – instant coffee and sugar. Now all I had to do was wait, something I was becoming a master at, *and* contain my excitement.

I turned the outside entrance light on, and watched the approach to the parking lot from a darkened reception room window. In a few minutes I was rewarded with a wash of light across the wet tarmac from Maria's auto as she turned into the lot and parked. I watched her walking gingerly under a wind blown umbrella across the wet pavement, avoiding standing water, and I held the door open for her. She lowered the umbrella, shook it vigorously, and stood it against the wall. I helped her with her coat and hung it in the closet. She was still wearing the pink angora sweater and gray skirt.

"Pretty bad weather, huh?" I said.

She laughed. "That's an understatement or an oxymoron. Take your choice."

"Just proves that women will do anything to see architectural drawings. That's a better line than, 'Come by to see my etchings'." I was proud of my retort.

"I think it was the coffee you promised," she said seriously, but then she broke into a wide grin. "And where is it?"

"Never promise a lady something you can't deliver." I said with a bow. For a moment, Garden City crossed my mind and my comment seemed hollow.

"One lump or two?"

"One's fine."

"At your service, Madame. I'll serve you in the conference room."

"You're a dangerous man when you do that Southern gentleman thing." She walked to the conference room and sat down in front of the drawings. "This looks interesting, but you'll have to explain it to me."

I set the hot coffee on the table and stood behind her. The faint scent of her perfume reached out to me. "Let's look at the floor plans first. My first thought was to segregate night spaces from day spaces. Night spaces are for sleeping and day spaces are for dining, entertaining, and for you and Pat when the children are sleeping. I tend to open day spaces to the most attractive views and to the south where possible to provide the best orientation. I can use the sun to heat glassed areas and control it in the summer with overhangs and face the prevailing breeze. You know … the passive solar thing we talked about at our first meeting. Am I going too fast for you?"

"Look, it's me, Maria. Don't be so professional with me. I like to ask questions, and you make me feel stupid when you get too technical."

"Ask away. I'm sorry. I'm just being Terry Architect." I put my hand on her shoulder and laughed. "You DO want to get your money's worth, don't you?"

"Of course, but we're not exactly strangers."

"Touche! I stand corrected." I took a seat beside her. "This plan is really preliminary; it's just a starting point. We'll change it a million times before we get it right. Well, maybe not a million, but a lot. It's a tool to make us both think. It's more about function than anything else. You and Pat need to look it over and write down your comments. I want it to fit you like a glove when it's built."

She leaned back into her chair and pushed her hair from her face with both hands. "This is hard work, isn't it? Almost like giving birth."

I had to smile. "Not quite that difficult, but it certainly requires a gestation period. That's a reasonable assessment."

"Don't you ever get tired of it?"

"No, I don't." I thought for a minute. "It brought us together. How could I ever be tired of something that makes me happy?"

"That's not what I mean. Be serious."

"I am being serious. I've never been more serious in my life." I stood up and reached for her hand.

She stood beside me and gave me a shy look. "Are we through with architecture for the night?"

I pulled her to me and put my arms around her waist. "I think so." I kissed her tenderly on each eyelid. Then, I found her warm lips and felt the wonder of her in my arms. My arms dropped to her buttocks and pulled her closer as I covered her face with kisses. My hands moved over her body, touching her breasts and the perfect "Y" where her legs came together. She clasped me around the neck and turned her face upward to meet me. She kissed me lightly, then moved away.

"Whoa," she said. "Let me get my breath." She laughed heartily and patted my hips.

I loved her laugh. It was effortless and lyrical, sometimes lusty. Whenever I evoked it, by word or deed, I felt a rush not unlike what a stage actor must feel when he is rewarded by the audience's applause. Even as she moved away, I couldn't let her go. My hands slipped down her arms to her wrists.

"I've got to go", she said. She looked as though she didn't want to. "The kids are OK if I'm not gone too long, but I don't like to leave them alone for more than an hour."

"I understand. I'm just glad you were able to come. We got a little bit accomplished."

She paused. "I know I shouldn't say this, but I liked the contact part better than the plan review." I noticed a blush on her face.

I put my arms around her and pulled her against me. "Are you blushing?" I couldn't suppress a chuckle.

"I might be, but I won't admit it." She brushed my lips with a quick kiss. "I've really got to go. If I had a choice, I wouldn't."

I walked her to the door, retrieved her coat from the closet, and helped her put it on. "You'd better button up; it's cold out there."

"You're right," she said. "I wish I could take some of the warmth in here with me, and I don't mean what's coming through the ductwork."

I held her close and she felt good, even in the bulky confines of her coat. I kissed her goodbye and forced myself to let her go. "God, you're gorgeous, even all wrapped up." I joked. "Come to think of it, it sure would be fun to unwrap you. I probably shouldn't have said that, but I meant it in a good way."

"No offense taken. I'd kinda enjoy that myself." She planted a quick kiss on my cheek, smiled, and disappeared into the cold rain.

I heard her open and shut the car door, start the engine, and drive out of the lot before I closed the door. The cold air was brutal. The temperature was close to freezing.

As I cleaned up the conference room and put the drawings away, it struck me that, through all the foreplay, I hadn't been noticeably aroused physically. I was certainly emotionally and mentally moved, but I didn't recall any semblance of an erection. That frightened me, especially since I was such a failure at the beach. Was there something wrong here? Surely that wouldn't be a problem, given another chance. I decided to chalk it off to knowing nothing was going to happen tonight. Nevertheless, I couldn't help thinking I was a little relieved that things didn't progress any further. I hadn't failed at anything, BUT I hadn't been put to the test. It was not something I cared or needed to dwell on, so I excised it from my mind. It could wait.

I called Jane, told her I was leaving and asked her if she wanted me to bring her anything. She said she had just eaten and suggested I pick up something if I was hungry. I called Angie and asked her to fix me a large cheeseburger with lots of onions to go. I heard her laughter. "Onions, eh? Must be going home. It'll be ready by the time you get here, Mr. T."

"Thanks Angie. How about a piece of that famous apple pie, too?"

"Sure thing. Bye."

The smile on my face was a mile wide. The day had ended pleasantly, a far cry from the way it started. I was a happy man, at least for now.

I woke up Friday refreshed and ready for a new day. I went through my usual routine – shaving, showering and dressing – and went outside to pick up the newspaper. It was early and the stars were still bright in the dark sky. A front pushed through during the night, bringing warmer, more seasonal weather and clear skies. The moon was large and full in the west and Venus was still prominent. All of this forecast a beautiful day in the offing and lifted my spirits.

When I returned, I heard Jane in the kitchen preparing breakfast. As I walked into the kitchen, Jane dropped some bacon into the pan. "Fried or scrambled?" she chirped. "I'm going to scramble the girls' eggs." She had a pink robe on with the sash tight around her waist. Her face, scrubbed free of makeup, was framed with three long curlers in the front of her hair. Without thinking, I pinched her bottom and she moved away quickly.

"Stop it! You want me to spill grease on the floor?" She grimaced, and I knew she meant it.

"Of course not. I'm sorry. I wasn't thinking." I sure was sorry. Sorry I had made the effort. I should have known she would respond in that manner. The old Jane, the one in years gone by, would have wiggled her bottom in a suggestive way and made some ribald comment. This Jane was serious about eggs and didn't have time for fun. Sex was definitely not on her fun list. Strangely, I wasn't upset with her rebuff. "Scramble mine too. No sense in making two operations."

"I don't mind frying yours. I know you like them better fried."

"Nah, that'll take too much time. I'll read the paper and wait for the girls. We can all eat at the same time."

"Have you ever thought about talking to me instead of reading that damn paper?" Jane was doing her best to ruin my happy mood. She had a valid complaint, but she could have framed her question more adroitly. Naturally, I fell into her trap.

I looked up at her over the top of the paper. "OK, what do you want to talk about.... yard work?" She was biting her lip and I could see the mercury rising.

I had given her just the entrance she needed.

"We COULD talk about the party tomorrow night. You seem to have forgotten about all the things YOU were going to do. Remember the company check you were going to cash so I wouldn't have to use grocery money? I suggest since you forgot it, that you make a list of things we need – steaks, potatoes, beer, and liquor – and get busy getting them. I'm sure we're short on scotch and probably vodka. I don't want to be flying around Saturday taking care of those things."

Damn! I had forgotten, but I wasn't about to admit it. A little prevarication seemed appropriate. I was getting good at that. "I've got the liquor at the office. I'll bring it home tonight and I'll call Shorty's and order the steaks. How many do we need?"

"Ten at last count; Judy and Ken can't come. They're leaving today for a convention."

"Damn, that's too bad. They didn't make the club dance either." I reached into my pocket. "Here's forty dollars. You pick up the potatoes and salad, and whatever else you think we need. I'll take care of the steaks and beer."

"That should be plenty," she said folding the cash and laying it on the cabinet top. She was over her tantrum. "I may stop by the bakery and get some pies; we need something sweet for desert." She slipped the frying pan off the stove and dumped the eggs onto a platter with the bacon. "How about getting the girls while I make toast?"

I folded the unread paper, dropped it on the floor and walked into the girls' bedroom. As usual, their room was a mess reflecting their morning routine of trying to stay in bed till the last minute, but Janet looked scrubbed and presentable. Her hair could use some more brushing, but Jane would correct that. I didn't see Laurie.

"OK girls, it's time for breakfast. Let's get moving," I bellowed, doing my best imitation of a drill sergeant.

Janet grabbed my shirt as I was walking away. "Are you taking us to school, Daddy?"

"Sure, if you want me too." I hadn't spent much time with them lately and it was beginning to show. My newfound guilt prompted me to ask, "How about a walk in the woods when I get home?"

Janet hopped along with me as I walked and looked up at me with her large, animated eyes. "Can we try to find the rabbit?"

"Sure, if it's still around." She held on to my belt as we walked. "Where's Laurie?"

"She's in the bathroom, Daddy. I think she's mad at you."

"Why, Jumper?"

"She said you forgot about the puppy you promised us. She begged Mama all week before she finally said it was OK, and now she thinks you don't want to get one."

Vintage Laurie, I thought. Never confrontational and tends to become quiet and introspective when she's not happy. I hadn't picked up on it because I hadn't spent any time with her for the last few weeks. I was ashamed, and knew it was time to make amends. "Well, let's go check the want ads and see what's available. Maybe somebody might have some cockers for sale."

"She wants a black one," Janet reminded me.

We sat down at the table and I picked up the dreaded newspaper. I turned to the want ads and looked for 'dogs for sale' and said to no one in particular, "Laurie's coming." The fourth ad had a listing for AKC registered cocker spaniels, sixty dollars for males and fifty for females. I wrote the phone number on my pocket calendar and stuck it back into my coat pocket. I felt better. I would have a surprise for Laurie tonight.

Jane put the food on the table just as Laurie came in and sat down. "Morning Daddy," she said quietly. "Do we have any juice, Mama?"

"We've got orange and tomato. Which would you like?"

"Yuk, not tomato."

"I take that to mean you want Orange. Anybody else?" asked Jane as she pulled a pitcher of fresh orange juice from the fridge.

"That'd be nice," I said, just before Janet's "me too." "How about some jelly while you're in the fridge?"

Jane poured the orange juice, put a jar of grape jelly on the table, and sat down. "Who's going to say the blessing?" she asked.

I pointed at Janet. "It's your turn."

She went into one of those "God is great, God is good" things, bringing a smile to my face, and we launched into our food. It was nice to eat with the children for a change.

When we finished eating, I told the girls I was taking them to school. They went to their room to get books and coats with Jane tagging along to put final touches to their hair. I was waiting for them at the door and gave a pleased Jane an obligatory hug before heading for the car. "I'll be home early" I said, but got no response from Jane. She'd heard that number before. She did wave as we pulled out of the drive.

Janet and I engaged in some mindless chatter on the way to school, but Laurie didn't have much to say. I didn't bug her. I knew my stock would be going up tonight if I could find a black cocker puppy, and I intended to do just that! I turned off the road into the school entrance and fell in behind the line of cars.

"We can get out here, Daddy," Laurie said reaching for the door handle. "Then you want have to wait." Janet jumped out behind her.

"OK, but I don't mind taking you to the door." It was too late. They were gone, skipping hand in hand down the sidewalk. I watched them for a moment before pulling back into the roadway. They were growing up so quickly. It seemed like such a short time ago when Janet was born, and now both of them were in school. I realized what a wonderful job Jane was doing nurturing and raising them without much help from me. I vowed to do better. But if that were anything like my new year's resolutions, not much would be done.

I drove the rest of the way to my office giving myself a voracious helping of mental flagellation for being a poor excuse of a dad and pulled into the parking lot beside Martha's car. She would be pleased that I had taken the girls to school, but I wouldn't tell her unless she asked why I was late. In my present state of mind, I didn't feel like soliciting admiration.

A large poinsettia was on Martha's desk in lieu of the ubiquitous table flowers. That was her signal that Christmas was just around the corner. The year was flying by. Perhaps she was telling me I'd better be a good boy or Santa wouldn't stop at my house.

"Lovely poinsettia," I said as I passed her desk.

"I just put it on my desk; it's not mine. Wilson Steel left it at the door with a Christmas card." I could almost hear the "bah humbug" in her voice. With the passing of her husband, Christmas had lost some of its meaning. I was completely wrong about the Christmas signal. I should have known better.

"Well, it's yours now," I said as I moved toward my office.

"Mrs. Champion called. She said she had a question about the preliminary drawings. She wants you to call her when you have a moment. And thanks for the poinsettia." Martha's crusty demeanor was softening.

She didn't look up, but offered another comment. "I don't suppose Mrs. Champion was here last night. I noticed two coffee cups out and one had lipstick on it. I'm beginning to think all might not be kosher with this architect-client relationship." Her squint at me over the top of her glasses was not jocular and her comment caught me unprepared.

For once, I stopped before I spoke and phrased my answer in a question. "Why in the world do you think that?"

"Two reasons. I have eyes and the experience to know you've never had women in here alone at night. I'm old and stupid, but there's something going on. It's none of my business, but I think enough of you to warn you. I'm not suggesting an affair....not yet, but I can tell you it's bad if you let it happen. You have a wife, children, and a wonderful career ahead of you. Remember what happened to Frank Lloyd Wright? He never was able to overcome his mistakes."

I laughed nervously. "I'm no Frank Lloyd Wright and I'm not having an affair. My client is excited and in a hurry to get a house. I'm trying my best to get it done. And when I do, it will all be over. She'll just be another former client with a job file."

"OK. Like I say, it's none of my business, but if I can get wind of it others will too. And if they do, you won't like it. Talk like that spreads like wildfire in this town. Let's just say I told you what I thought and leave it at that. Now get on about your work and leave me alone."

"I'll do that," I said with just enough annoyance in my tone to make her think I was telling the truth. Even with that, I didn't have my heart in it. She was a wily old gal and I knew she was only telling me for my own good.

I retrieved Maria's drawings from the flat file, took them into the conference room and spread them out on the table. I could visualize mentally the happenings of the night before and detect the faint smell of her perfume lingering in the room, a pleasant figment of my very overactive imagination. I reached for the phone and dialed her number. Martha's comments had failed to dim my enthusiasm.

"Good morning," I said after her cheerful answer. "It's your faithful architect returning your call."

"Guess what? My traveling husband was home when I got back last night. Fortunately, he was asleep in the chair, so I drove back to the Gulf Station on the highway and used the restroom to repair my makeup and hair. I was really a mess when I left your office."

"Oh my God! Was he suspicious?"

"No. I told him I had gone to the drugstore for a few things and he seemed to accept it. He did comment on the fuzz balls on my sweater, but didn't make an issue of it. I almost choked when I saw it in the mirror and I got them off as quickly as I could. I had forgotten how angora balls up when it's rubbed. I won't wear that anymore when I come to see you.

"Gee, I'm sorry."

"Not to worry. I didn't realize how quickly one reacts when they're caught. I lied when I probably didn't need to. I don't think he would have been upset if I had told him I had stopped by your office to look at drawings. I guess I was a victim of guilt. I shouldn't say it, but I don't feel any guilt today."

"Listen, I think you reacted like anyone else would have, but I have a suggestion."

"And what might that be, great genius?"

"If you wear it again, I'll take it off before I touch you." We both laughed.

"There won't be a next time," she said. "You'll never see that sweater again." She paused and said softly, "That's not meant to discourage you. I'll be more selective with my sweaters."

"Aha! I like that answer."

"Enough of this. Are you working this weekend?"

"Actually, I'm not. We're having three couples over for a cookout Saturday night, and I probably won't feel much like working Sunday. That's part of my penance for going to the beach on that ill fated weekend."

"Why do you call it 'ill fated'? It was a wonderful weekend. Certainly one I'll never forget."

"That was a bad choice of words. It WAS a wonderful weekend…except for the way it ended. I just felt that I failed you, and I can't forget that. It's a male thing. I don't expect you to understand."

"That was my fault," she said slowly. "That was our first time together, and we weren't exactly comfortable. I was nervous and a little drunk. Whatever I did doesn't reflect on how I feel about you. It won't happen again."

"What do you mean, it won't happen again?"

"Silly, what do you think I mean? I'm telling you I won't respond that way again. If we ever have another chance."

That was the explanation I was hoping for. "We'll have another chance if I have anything to do with it," I said with conviction.

"OK, that's out of the way. Tell me about your party."

I could sense her relief. "Same group we were with at the dance. We'll drink a little and cook some steaks on the grill. Lots of male stories and the women will talk about whatever women talk about. Guys in one corner and girls in another. Know a better way to spend a Saturday night? You don't have to answer that."

"I know the deal. Men talking about sex and women talking about shopping. Men are just oversexed children and women are shallow."

I laughed. "If I implied that, I didn't mean to. I don't think women are shallow. I'm so busy listening to war stories that I don't hear what they're talking about. But you're right. Men are oversexed children. Remember, that's my theory."

"I think I do remember your telling me that somewhere between 'glass and deciduous trees on the south and no glass on the west'. One of your more profound statements." Her laugh resonated in my ear. "Who says I can't remember important things?"

"Certainly not me. I'm impressed."

"Well, don't get too carried away," she said. "What have you got to do today besides work on my house, of course?"

I went through a litany of things I hoped to accomplish and told her about trying to find a puppy for Laurie. She agreed that was the proper thing to do, but reminded me to be patient with the puppy. She never relished the idea of having to housebreak one. We tossed around a few ideas about that before we ended our conversation. I asked her to call me Monday and she said she would. We had talked for thirty minutes.

I worked hard until Martha left, and during lunch I picked up liquor and beer. I didn't want to have to do everything at five o'clock. I had to drive out into the country to get the puppy, and that could take an hour. I called Shorty and asked him to cut me ten T-bones about an inch thick for pickup Saturday afternoon, but he convinced me that his rib eyes were better. I told him I'd see him about five Saturday afternoon.

I called the number on the want ad and found out that only two puppies were left, both black. The ad had been running for the entire week and three of the puppies had been sold. I implored Mrs. Hardy, who answered the phone, to save the male for me. I told her I'd be there by five o'clock. She gave me directions and I thanked her. I asked her if she would take a check and she said she would. Everything was in place. Now I could go back to work. I felt like Mr. Dad again.

I left the office a little after four. I figured it would take me about thirty minutes to get to Mrs. Hardy's farm if I didn't have any problems with her directions. Fortunately, they were good and I arrived before five. The Hardy home was a typical two-story farmhouse, probably built in the late 1880s with spacious porches on the front and back. The wood siding and tin roof was well maintained and it appeared to have been painted recently. Shrubbery was sparse but the yard contained a number of mature pecan and oak trees.

Mrs. Hardy had seen me driving up the unpaved road to her house and met me at the front door. She was a large woman with a round, friendly face and was dressed in a house frock that hung formlessly on her large frame. Her brown hair was peppered with gray and was twisted into a neat bun in back. She smiled and offered me her hand that I obligingly shook.

"I'm Sarah Hardy," she said with a smile. "I expect you're Mr. Forte."

"Yes Ma'am," I answered with a smile larger than hers. "But I prefer Terry."

She said she had to get a jacket and directed me to meet her at the back door. She was obviously preparing supper for some lucky people. I could smell the delicious aroma of country cooking through the open door.

Mrs. Hardy, with a man's corduroy jacket wrapped around her, met me in back. With the sun fading and lighting up the faint stratus clouds on the horizon into long pink strips, the night air was taking on a chill. Mrs. Hardy took me to a fenced-in kennel and whistled loudly. The pups bounded from the enclosure, bumping into each other and tumbling on the ground. They were so cute. I think I would have taken both of them if I hadn't returned to my senses quickly. Both of them were black, as Mrs. Hardy had said when I called, and their tails were bobbed.

"Mr. Forte......uh, Terry, both of them have had distemper shots, but it's too early for a rabies vaccination. That comes at three to four months of age. I don't have papers on them, but I have the records on their mother and father, so they can be registered easily. I have copies for you. I think it costs about fifteen dollars to get it done. They were born October 26. That's indicated on the records."

"Thanks, Mrs. Hardy, I may do it, but, frankly, I just want him to be part of our family. I don't want to breed him. I have two little girls who will fall in love with him as soon as they see him."

"That's fine, Terry. It's your decision to make. I'm particular who I sell my dogs to, but, when I talked to you today, I knew you would give him a good home. I'll warn you, though. I may call you from time to time to check up on him."

I chuckled. "Anytime, Sarah."

She went into the kennel and picked up the male puppy, but not before rubbing both of them. She walked me to my car, holding him gently in her big arms, and kissed him on top of his head before handing him to me. I could see the beginning of a tear down her cheek. I put him in the car and wrote her a check, which she stuffed into her jacket pocket.

"Just a minute," she said, almost as an afterthought. "You'll need some newspaper to put under him, or he'll wet all over your car. He's never been in a car, so he'll be frightened. Just try to hold him close to you and he'll be OK." She walked back to the house and quickly returned with an armload of newspapers. "This should do it," she said.

"I almost forgot! What does he eat?"

"He's been weaned, but I'd try him on dry food for a while. Don't give him anything off the table. His tummy can't take that yet. Give him canned meat about twice a week. In two or three weeks, he'll be able to eat most anything."

"Thanks, Sarah. I really appreciate this." I waved and drove off with Laurie's precious cargo in hand.

It was dark when I pulled into the drive, and the house was lit up like we were trying to win the power company award of the month. I surmised much of that had to do with preparations for Saturday night's cookout. The puppy was asleep on the pile of newspapers and was snuggled against my leg. Much to my amazement, he had responded like a seasoned passenger. My devious plan was to request Laurie's help in unloading the car, and let her discover the puppy. I was just selfish enough to want to see her reaction all by myself. Trying hard not to arouse the pup, I slid out of the car with an armload of liquor and headed for the back door. Jane was at the sink chopping up something for salad as I entered the kitchen and placed the liquor in the pantry.

"Where's Laurie?" I asked with a stupid grin on my face. If she had looked up, I might have had to explain why it was there.

"She's watching TV in the den," she answered, still chopping away.

"Laurie!" I called loudly. "I need some help. Come here a minute."

"Oh Daddy, do I have to? I'm watching 'Andy Griffith'."

"Yes you do. Now hurry up. It won't take but a minute." I could see this might be a battle.

She came grudgingly, looking back at the TV. When she turned, she gave me a look that would curdle milk. I pushed her ahead of me and we walked toward the car.

"Get the package in the front seat," I requested. "That's all I want you to carry. I'll get the rest."

Laurie grabbed the front door and opened it like she wanted to destroy it. The startled pup jumped up and greeted her with a staccato of squeals and barks, and then backed away from her. Laurie froze in her tracks. She was as surprised as the pup.

"Daddy, Daddy! It's a puppy!! I can't believe it!" she squealed as she reached inside the car for him. She cuddled him in both arms and stroked his head. "Thank you! Thank you, Daddy." She held him in one arm, wrapped her free arm around my waist and uttered the words I would kill for. "I knew you wouldn't forget. I love you Daddy." It took a lot of effort to fight back my tears.

"Let's show him to Mom and Janet," I said, but she was running ahead of me toward the house. I wiped my eyes and took the beer from the trunk. By the time I got in the house, the girls had the happy puppy on the kitchen floor taking turns playing with him. Jane was standing by them with her hands on her hips and a scowl on her face. I knew something bad was about to happen. She nodded toward the den and motioned for me to follow her.

"Are you crazy?!" she hissed. "Don't you realize that I have enough to do trying to get ready for tomorrow without having to take care of a puppy? For God's sake, Terry! Don't you ever think? Your timing is terrible. Couldn't this have waited until next week?"

She was right, of course, and her tirade had let all the air out of my *feel-good* balloon. "I'm sorry," I said apologetically. That was all I could muster.

"Of course you're sorry. You're always sorry. You could have discussed this with me before you did it."

"I know, but Laurie's been so withdrawn lately. I thought it would be good for her. Janet told me you said it was OK. It was a spur-of-the-moment thing. That's why I didn't tell you."

"You don't understand, Terry. Getting the puppy is a good thing. I just think the timing is truly unforgivable. You do have a telephone. You could have called.

It's that same old thing, we just don't communicate. We'll talk about this later," she said curtly. With that, she headed back to the kitchen. She had fired the last shot with deadly precision.

Mother Nature was kind. Saturday was sunny and mild, but that was about all that was kind between the adults in our house. Conversation was a bit icy, but due to the impending cookout, things were at least civil. Not many words were wasted. In fact, if words had been pearls, there wouldn't have been enough to make a pair of earrings.

Laurie and Janet were busy teaching Inky, an original name by Laurie, how to do doggy tricks. I hope that included not using the carpet for his personal toilet. He seemed to have little fondness for newspaper. He didn't respond to my smacking him over the head with rolled up newspaper. That was about all I could remember to do, other than rub his nose in his own excrement. But that was just too barbaric for my taste. I decided to leave all that up to the children.

I busied myself doing outdoor things like cleaning the grille, washing down the outside furniture, and raking leaves. I managed to stay outside until it was time to make the run to Shorty's for steaks. I cajoled my parents into letting the girls spend the night with them and they agreed to let them bring Inky, so I took all of them with me to get the steaks and dropped them off on the way. Of course I had conveniently forgotten to tell my parents that the pup wasn't potty trained. I assumed they would find out soon enough. I had finally done something that Jane liked, regardless of the lack of communication. I didn't discuss it with her before I called Mother.

When I returned, Jane was in the kitchen finishing all the final preparations, but she had little to say. That was my cue to take a shower and get dressed. If I were quick enough, I could finish before Jane started her routine, and avoid further rancor. Our pals were to arrive at seven, and that would give me time to have a few clandestine drinks and improve my personality before they got there. I figured I owed them and myself that much. I slipped into a pair of light blue chinos, a white shirt, and a gray V-neck sweater. I was ready to cook steaks and party.

While Jane was doing her thing, I went outside to get the charcoal burning. It was a pain to get started and I liked to have it ready ahead of time. I managed to mix a most wanted Johnny Walker Red and water on the way. Now I wouldn't give a damn what Jane thought or how difficult it was to ignite the charcoal.

I had another drink in my hand when the first couple, Jerry and Toni Lieb, arrived. That suited me fine. Jerry was fun and he liked his scotch. He had better taste than I. He had on blue wool slacks, a white dress shirt, and a gray blazer. Toni was dressed in a matching tan sweater and skirt. The outfit was tight, but she had the body for it. I told her she looked great, unlike her husband, and sent her to Jane's bedroom.

I mixed Jerry a drink and handed it to him. "This one's on the house." I laughed. "You'll have to fix your own from here on."

He winked. "I thought this was a BYOB, but I left my bottle in the car. I figured I could slip out there and mix my own if you give out. I don't want to embarrass you."

I drew my arm back and feigned a punch. "Asshole." We both laughed. "Let's go check the grill."

We stood around the grill talking and telling jokes until the others arrived. It had been a mild day with the temperature reaching seventy degrees, but the air was beginning to cool and my sweater felt good. It didn't hurt to be near the grill. The heat radiated and kept my hands warm, which was a plus when holding a cold glass of scotch and water. Jerry's chatter, always imaginative and full of crudeness, kept me laughing so hard that I never thought much about my discomfort.

We saw the group gathering in the kitchen and decided it would be more comfortable inside. The charcoal didn't need any more attention. It would manage on its own. Bill and Sandy Jackson and Garth and Ann Spann were with our wives chatting away. The men were mostly listening. When we walked in the men edged over to us and we left the women to themselves.

After a round of handshakes, Bill asked, "When are we going to play golf again? I need some spending money."

"Geez, Bill," Jerry said. "You must be brain dead. We got you for twenty-two dollars last week. If I hadn't had to carry my partner the whole day, we'd have killed you." He was choking back a serious guffaw.

I looked at Jerry in mock disbelief. "What do you mean? I had to throw my shirt away because it was full of cleat marks from you riding on my shoulders.

You *did* manage to win the last hole, but that was the only time you hit a green in regulation all day."

"Hey, man," Jerry said, running his fingers through his curly black hair. "We won the front and were tied for the back. That hole was for three presses, the back and the match. I don't start playing until nut cutting time. I always come through when it's time to pick up the marbles. Anybody can win a hole when it doesn't mean anything, even Bill." He was trying to keep a straight face.

Bill knew better, but he was beginning to let Jerry put a burr under his blanket. "OK big Shot, let's play next week and double the stakes. I'll even give you a stroke on the par fives."

Jerry had accomplished his mission. His gaunt face broke into a wide grin. "You're on and I've got witnesses!" He had reeled in his fish.

"Who needs another drink?" I nodded toward Garth. "I don't see anything in your hand. Is it broken?"

"I'm not drinking tonight. Ann and I are on a diet and we're not wasting any calories. I'm saving mine for that pie Jane got at the Éclair Shop." He spoke with little enthusiasm, but forced a smile. I assumed that meant that Ann was trying to stop drinking and he was helping the only way he knew how – by joining her abstinence. Garth is a good man.

I chose not to make a big deal about it. "Well, how about a glass of water, or soda with a twist?"

"Soda sounds like a winner. Same for Ann, too, if you don't mind."

"No sweat." I grabbed two glasses, ice and lemon, and filled them to the top with soda. "Want me to take it to Ann?"

"No, no. I'll do it." He reached for the glasses and seemed to relax. I think he was glad to get through the conversation. I don't know how I would have handled his situation. *I guess if you have a ten-year investment in a partnership and three children, it's hard to walk away.* I'm *glad it's his problem and not mine.* I seemed to be having enough of my own lately.

"Hey Bill, you need a freshener? You look a little dry over there."

"I'm OK, Terry. I'll get mine next time. Your hand's not heavy enough for me." He laughed and rolled his eyes. I'm trying to get even for the golf match. I figure I can get my money back in free booze." He lifted his glass high and said, "Here's to bourbon and branch, a tribute to Southern culture."

"And don't forget the steaks," I reminded him, giving him a snappy salute. "And speaking of steaks, I'd better get them on. How about checking with everybody to see how they want theirs cooked while I get everything together? Here, take this pad and write it down. Two more drinks and I won't be able to remember. Hell, by the time I get them cooked, nobody'll know the difference anyway."

In a few minutes Jane rushed into the kitchen. Whoa, Big Boy, you can't start the steaks yet. The potatoes won't be ready for forty-five minutes."

"Whoops!" I said, slapping my head with my palm. "There's that communication thing again." I gave her a sarcastic grin.

Her eyes turned to ice. "You know, you really can be a jerk. I'm going to let this one pass because you've had too much to drink, but don't provoke me. You're treading water. I haven't forgotten your Fred Astaire imitation with Mrs. Champion."

I was sober enough to know I had blundered. "I was trying to be funny. I guess I blew it, but lay off the dance thing. She's just a client, nothing more."

"Don't quit your day job. You'll never make it as a comedian."

Bill returned with the pad and saved the day. "Here's the orders, boss man. Five rare, three medium, and one ruined – that's well done to you." Jane walked away while Bill was talking.

"I'm going to marinate them a little longer," I said, sipping my drink. "Jane says the potatoes need more time. I'm not real good at scheduling. Besides, I forgot that Winston and Patti aren't here yet."

Bill hiked his pants up and grimaced. "Lawyers can fuck up a one-car parade."

"Careful, you're talking about your golf partner." I laughed.

"I know," Bill said. I love him, but why did he have to be a lawyer? I should pick my friends and golf partners more carefully. He does all my home closings and he's always late." He paused and looked over his shoulder to see if we were alone. "I know it's none of my business, but do I detect some animosity between you and Jane?"

"Yep, you do. I don't know what the problem is, but we can't seem to get on the same page. Jane says we don't communicate, and maybe she's right. But she punishes me by cutting me off. That just adds gasoline to the fire."

Bill smiled. "I guess you mean sexually."

"You got it. I feel like the only way I can get in her good graces is do some chore for her. It borders on prostitution. Our lovemaking used to be spontaneous. Now it's come to begging or bartering."

"Well, Buddy, you need to do something about that. I did. This is tombstone talk. Something I've never told anyone. So you can't tell anybody, especially Jane. I wouldn't tell you, except I'm a little drunk and you're my best friend." He looked at me waiting, I surmised, for my solemn promise.

I stepped closer to Bill. "For God's sake, don't keep me in suspense. I'm not going to tell anybody." I raised three fingers. "Scout's honor."

He looked around, checking the area, and stepped closer. "Two years ago, when Bill, Jr. was born, Sandy lost all interest in sex. She was honest about it, but that didn't make it any better. I felt like my life was over. I considered leaving her. But I love her, so that wasn't an option. I really didn't know what to do. Remember my old secretary, Susie? I always thought she had a thing for me, and I knew she was lonesome after her divorce. So I started stopping by to see her under various pretenses, all legitimate of course, and things just fell into place. Her daughter being at home was a problem, so I bought a large parcel of land with a small cabin on it near the country club. It's heavily wooded. Nobody could ever find it if you didn't know about it. One road in, and one road out. We meet every Tuesday afternoon and do our thing. She saved my life, and probably my marriage."

I was incredulous. "Does Sandy suspect anything? Don't you feel guilty?"

Bill snickered. "Of course she doesn't suspect. She'd kill me if she knew. But, you know, sometimes I think deep down she maybe does know and just chooses not to believe it. I feel a little guilty about it occasionally, like after I do it, but never before. I don't have time to feel guilty when the hormones start raging on Tuesday morning. Susie understands that she's a distant third behind Sandy and little Bill, but she seems to handle it. I know it'll come to an end sooner or later – either my doing or hers – but I'll ride the horse as long as the race lasts." He pulled something from his pocket and pressed it into my hand. "This is a key to the place. You sound like you might need it sometime. Turn right on the first dirt-logging road after the country club and drive to the end. The electric panel is in the closet. There's hot water, but no heat. I have two electric heaters in the closet that will do except on the coldest days. It's pretty bare but it has all the essentials." He chuckled and added, "If you know what I mean. But just remember: **Never on Tuesday afternoon**." He drank from his glass and smiled. "Never thought I'd ever tell anybody that."

"Damn Bill, I don't know if I've been honored or cursed, but I'll take this conversation to my grave. I think it's remarkable that you've been doing this for two years and nobody knows."

Bill's voice dropped to a whisper. "Nobody knows because we're very careful. We go there in separate cars and we *never* go anywhere together. All our communication is by telephone and when we talk we never call each other by name. No cards, no presents, unless it's something that we can eat or would buy ourselves. We don't leave tracks."

I laughed. "Well, now you've told me, so you've broken one of your cardinal rules."

Bill looked me straight in the eyes. "I guess I'll have to kill you." He let out a cackle. "Let's get another drink."

We replenished our drinks and wandered into the den with the rest of the revelers. Winston and Patti Gage had come in while Bill and I were talking. Now our group was complete, and it was time for me to cook the steaks. I made my way over to Jane and asked, "Is it time to start the steaks?"

"You asked. I can't believe it." She was smiling. Either the ice was thawing or the liquor was promoting a change in attitude. Either way, it was at least a momentary win-win situation for me, and I decided to take advantage of it. I planted a quick kiss on her cheek. I didn't want it to look too obvious. "Good, I'm going to the grill."

I grabbed the steaks from the fridge and went outside. The coals had reached a perfect ashy gray. I felt the intense heat radiating from the coals on my hands as I placed a few more pieces of charcoal on the fire to be sure I had enough to finish the task. The rib eyes were at least an inch thick, so I needed about twenty-five minutes to cook them from well done to rare and finish them at the same time. (What else would you expect from an architect but logical planning?)

Bill appeared from the half-light and moved close the grill extending his hands toward the warmth of the fire. "Need any help?" he asked.

"Naw, but I can use the company, and you could freshen my drink every once and a while. I can't leave the steaks once I get started. I'm always afraid they'll burn."

"Hey, that's what friends are for;" he said. He looked away, deep in thought. He was searching for his next words. "Terry, what I said about Susie, I don't want you to get the wrong idea."

I cut him off with a wave of my hand. "Whoa, Bill. I'm not making any moral judgment. I've got plenty of faults. I'm no 'goody two shoes'. Our decisions, good or bad, are private."

"That's not what I mean," he said. I don't want you to think I'm some hypocritical bastard because I'm a big church worker and wouldn't condone this conduct in a public forum. Ninety-nine percent of me wouldn't do anything to hurt Sandy. It's my libido, the other one percent, that I can't control. I'm not a womanizer. Sandy and I will always be together."

"Look, Bill, you're my best friend. That's not going to change. I know you'll do right by Sandy. It's you I'm worried about. What about Susie? What if she gets serious? That could be ugly. Are you prepared for that?"

"That won't happen," he snapped. I've explained exactly how I feel about her. I've even encouraged her to date. I want her to have a happy life, and I'm sure she'll find a guy someday. If she gets serious, I'll cut it off."

"I know that's how you feel, but what about Susie? She's divorced and has a child to raise. Is she stable enough to ride that kind of emotional roller coaster?"

Bill bit his bottom lip. "That's a good question. Truth is, I don't know. Never thought about it."

"Well, you better," I said. "I've never known a woman who didn't expect something from a relationship. Usually, it's love, but they don't give sex away without motivation. Men can be motivated by pleasure, but women invariably add emotion to the mix. I know it's coarse to say, but even prostitutes demand money. That's apples and oranges, but you get the picture."

"You're right, Terry, but I'll cross that bridge when I get there. Know what, you talk like you've been there yourself?"

It was my turn to laugh. "Not hardly. I just read a lot."

Bill grinned and looked into his glass. "Looks dry. It's time for Gunga Din to head back to the water hole. How's yours?"

I handed him my glass. "I could use some sweetening." I flipped the medium steaks and put on the rare ones. "Go easy on the scotch and heavy up on the water. I think I've about reached my limit."

He bowed. "What self control. No Susie for you."

As Bill walked away I thought, *You're right, it's much worse than that. My emotions* ***are*** *my motivation.* I shivered in the night air.

When Bill came back with my drink, I had already flipped the rare steaks and moved the rest away from the fire. We chatted for a few minutes before I took all the steaks off the grill, and we walked to the house. Bill must have told Jane I was nearly through. She had removed the potatoes from the oven and put them on the plates. She was busy with a large pair of tongs loading up salad plates. I put the steak pan on the kitchen counter, and in my best bunkhouse voice said, "Come and get it!"

Hunger took over the party, and the merrymaking became a victim of satisfied palates. Drinking ceased, conversation became yawning contests, and the participants began to search for their coats. It had been fun, but fatigue had become a factor. As our guests filed through the front door, the men agreed to play golf the following Thursday. Jerry gave me a wink as he left, and said, "OK partner. I did my part. We've got 'em where we want 'em."

"I'm not so sure. You made Bill pretty mad. We'll have a hard time beating them. I hope we don't lose the farm!"

Jerry grinned. "I've got faith; you can do it."

"Not without some help," I pleaded. He laughed all the way to his car. I shut the door and put my arm around Jane. She shrugged it off and said, "Let's clean up the mess." So much for the thaw.

Sunday came, but we didn't rush to embrace it. Half the day was gone before we got up. I kept my eyes closed for a long time after I woke up and when I did open them, I did so one at a time. I was checking for the inevitable headache I richly deserved, but I was relatively free of pain. I heard Jane in the bathroom, but had no idea what stage of morning routine she was in. My bladder was sending me signals to get up that were too intense to ignore. Jane came out of the bathroom in her robe as I made my entrance. She nodded, but said nothing. I wasn't disturbed by her silence. She's not a morning person, and is best left alone until she's had coffee.

I completed my primary task, washed my hands, and made the mistake of looking into the mirror at a very unkempt male with watery, red eyes embedded in dark, baggy lids. *Where was that handsome, intelligent young man who shared this body with me last night?*

I smoothed my wavy, wild blond down with a damp hand and brushed my teeth. That wasn't enough, so I tried some mouthwash. It helped but didn't mask the lingering taste of day-old Johnny Walker and cigarettes. It was obvious that only time would heal my morning blahs. I put a robe on over my shorts and t-shirt and dragged my hung-over body to the kitchen.

Jane was standing at the sink with a cup of coffee, looking at a box of corn flakes and a carton of eggs. She was trying to make a choice. *I'm betting on the eggs because she doesn't like milk.*

She saw me. "I'm scrambling some eggs. Do you want any?"

"Sure," I said. My first words came out grudgingly and nasally. "Don't cook many; I'm not very hungry. I think I'll toast some bread. You want any?" Dry bread seemed more appealing than eggs.

"Um-huh, one piece."

I reached into the fridge and poured myself a small glass of orange juice. The first swallow was great, but the rest was tough going. I poured half of it down the drain. I wasn't at my best, but I tried to make conversation. "How'd you think the party went?" A question is always the best way to start a conversation when you're trying to work through the silent treatment and you don't feel good.

Jane gazed at me as though I had tossed her a rotting fish. "Are you asking me that because you can't remember, or do you want an opinion?" She returned to her eggs.

I made an effort to pick up the fumbled ball. "You were with everybody. I was outside cooking."

"Huh! You spent more time drinking than cooking. That's why you don't know."

I decided to be humble. "You're right. I drank more than I should have, but I'd still like your opinion. You looked like you were having fun."

"I was. It's nice to be around adults for a change. My world gets pretty small sometimes."

I didn't have an answer for Jane's remark, and I knew she intended it to irritate me. I wriggled off the hook by changing the subject. "Would you like to do anything special today? We don't have to pick up the children until nightfall." I was working hard to make amends.

How about a movie?" she said quickly. "We haven't been to a movie in months and I'd like to see *To Kill a Mockingbird.* It's playing at the Carolina. It starts at three o'clock."

"Sounds good to me, but we need to get moving to make it by three." I remembered reading Harper Lee's book and thought it would make a good movie. We managed to get dressed in time to make the three o'clock movie, and after a quick phone call to Mother to alert her that we would be there about five thirty to pick up the girls, we took off. We missed part of the cartoon, but were there in plenty of time to pick up two candy bars at the concession stand, find seats, and see the entire feature.

It was a great movie about a Southern country lawyer and his children and racial injustice. The movie was true to the book and depicted life in a small Southern town accurately. The movie ended on an uplifting note despite some tear-jerking scenes. I liked that. It didn't give the impression that it was trying to make a social statement, but it left much to think about and most of the patrons exited silently from the semi-darkness of the theater.

We arrived at Mother's at five thirty as I had promised to pick up the children, and we wrangled an invitation to supper. That saved Jane from having to cook for us, and if she felt like I did, she had to have viewed it as manna from heaven. Mother had a few words to say about Inky and his ability to chew everything in sight, especially shoes and furniture, and suggested we get him some toys to destroy instead of things of value. I apologized for his lack of manners and swore to work on his behavior. Then and there, I vowed never to bring him to their house again. Her comments weren't exactly veiled threats, but I got the message.

After a delightful repast of fried chicken, rice and milk gravy, sliced tomatoes, English peas (my personal favorite), and the best biscuits in the world, I pushed my corpulent body (hopefully just momentarily) away from the table, gathered up my brood, thanked my mother and father for their kindness and courtesy, and headed home. Keeping my eyes open as I drove took some supreme will. An hour and a half later, after getting the children down, I fell into a deep and well-deserved sleep. The weekend had reached its climax. Thank God, something had.

I woke up earlier than usual Monday morning. I had slept for almost nine hours. I had overcome all the deleterious effects of excessive alcohol consumption and felt wonderful. After a hearty breakfast, I went to the bedroom to get my sport coat and noticed a foreign-looking key among the loose change on top of my chest of drawers. *Oh my God, that was the key Bill gave me Saturday night when he made his confession about Susie.* I had forgotten about it. I shoved it into my pocket quickly, hoping that Jane hadn't noticed it. I was overreacting from guilt. Jane wouldn't have questioned it if she had seen it.

I kissed the girls goodbye, hugged Jane, and went to the office. I had a lot to tell Maria when she called me. The parking lot was empty when I arrived. Martha wouldn't be there for another hour, so I had time to prepare some work for her. That suited me. I wasn't ready for more of her preaching. I made out my agenda for the day, assigned priorities, and started on my first task, checking cabinet shop drawings for the Hugeley House. One of my agenda items, unobtrusively penciled in, was to *inspect Bill's property*. I was curious to see what that cabin looked like. I preferred to see it before I told Maria about it, but I knew I couldn't refrain from telling her if she called this morning. I was excited about the possibility of taking her there if she would go, but I felt like I shouldn't be too hasty with an invitation. She might be offended. I would have to play that one by ear.

Martha came in about nine and asked me a few questions about a change order I had for her to type and plunged into her work with her usual robustness. She worked hard and never wasted a second when she had something to do. She was worth every cent I paid her. If fact, I was damn lucky to have her. I put a note on my office calendar to give her a substantial Christmas bonus. Profits were up for the year and she deserved a share of it.

Shortly after ten, the phone rang and Martha didn't answer it. She must be in the bathroom, I thought. I picked it up on the sixth ring. "Design Concepts, Terry Forte speaking". It was a good thing. It was Maria.

"I want to hear about the party," Maria said.

"Man, you really cut to the chase. Not so much as a good morning," I responded.

"I don't have time to be polite. I want to hear all the gossip."

Well, I've got some for you, but it didn't come from the women. It may disappoint you."

"Tell me anyway. I need some excitement. Housewives lead dull lives."

"I wouldn't know about that, but one of the guys confessed to a long-running affair. It caught me totally by surprise. I would never have believed it if I hadn't heard it from his lips. I still can't figure why he told me."

Maria laughed. "Sounds like too much alcohol. Was he serious?"

"Deadly serious, and I have proof in my pocket."

"Not a five-by-seven glossy?"

I laughed. "Don't be funny. It's a key."

"A key? I'm sorry," Maria said, mystified. "But you'll have to explain that to me."

"It's a key to his cabin," I whispered. Then I gave her a play by play of Bill's conversation with me, leaving out all the names. She listened to every word without comment. When I finished, I heard her take a deep breath.

"Whoo, that's some story. Do you believe it?" she asked.

"Absolutely. I'd bet my life on it. He's not the type to lie about something like that, or anything else."

"What are you going to do?"

"First, I'm forgetting everything he told me. Then, at lunch time, I'm going to drive to the cabin and see what it looks like. I'm curious as hell."

"Can I go?" Maria's statement was direct and one I wasn't expecting.

"I was silent for a time. My mind was racing and she knew I was considering it. "I don't think that would be wise. I'd like to check it out before I take you. It might not be safe, or a place I'd want to take you." I hoped she understood my concern.

"OK, but I'm calling you this afternoon and I want a full report," she said with conviction.

"Call me at two o'clock. That should give me enough time."

"Doesn't Martha leave at one?" she asked.

"Yeah, why?"

"I may not be able to wait till two, so I may start calling earlier."

I had to laugh. "When I get back, I'll dial your number and let the phone ring once and hang up. Then you can call me." We hung up on that note and I went back to work.

37

At noon I told Martha I was going to lunch and drove to the club, then headed east on the highway. I hoped the directions were as easy as I remembered them. I turned right on the first dirt road, which was a bit better than the normal logging road, but still little more than two ruts for tires. It had a few wash outs that took some time to negotiate, but nothing that scraped the bottom of my car. After about a quarter of a mile, the woods became thicker and the field of vision diminished. Bill was a good businessman and probably purchased the property for its abundance of timber. Most of the trees were pine, standing like sentinels among a spattering of deciduous trees: oaks, sweet gum, and dogwood. The cabin appeared suddenly in a thicket of wild privet of various sizes. Just as Bill had said, the road terminated at the cabin. It was larger than I expected and had a small, screened porch at one end. The wood siding was left natural and had the gray patina of weathered cedar. It was capped with a simple, gable roof of dark green shingles. The cabin, camouflaged by the canopy of trees and devoid of color, would be impossible to spot from the air, and wasn't easy to see approaching it on the ground. It was certainly secure.

I parked the car and turned off the engine. The silence was eerie. I climbed up three steps and unlocked the door. There was no landing so I backed down the steps to pull the door open. The inside of the cabin was dark and I cursed myself for not bringing a flashlight. I shut my eyes for a minute to hasten acclimation to the dark, and made my way to a door I assumed to be the closet with the electric panel. I was in luck. I struck a match and located the panel. In a flash, I activated the main circuit switch, retraced my steps to the door, and rubbed the wall with my hand until I felt a light switch. Two table lamps on each side of a red naugahyde sofa of dubious age lit up, exposing a room about fifteen feet by twenty feet with three large windows covered with Venetian blinds. I opened the blinds and darts of light, heavy with dust motes, fell on a worn carpet that had been green in better days.

I moved around the cabin, inventorying the rooms, and was pleasantly surprised to find a small bedroom, adequate bathroom, and a small kitchenette at the end of the large room. The double bed was new and overpowered the bedroom; it was obvious what this place was used for. Though austere, the cabin was far better than I had hoped. It seemed very comfortable and clean.

I rummaged through the kitchenette and found a few dishes, glasses, and eating utensils. I helped myself to a Coke in the fridge and drank it from the bottle to keep from making a mess. I took one last look around, closed the blinds, and opened the front door. That would provide enough light to keep me from stumbling on the way out after I tripped the power breaker. The cabin was A-OK as far as I was concerned, and I couldn't wait to tell Maria.

I returned to the office at one thirty and immediately phoned Maria. I let it ring once and hung up. She must have been waiting. My phone rang as soon as I put it back in the cradle.

"Tell me about it," she said quickly after I answered.

"Frankly I was surprised. I was expecting early Boy Scout camp, but it's really not bad. It's secluded and deathly quiet. I didn't hear anything while I was there, not even a mourning dove."

She giggled. "I'm not interested in the wildlife. What does the cabin look like?"

"Well," I explained, "It's not the Ritz, but it's comfortable. Small bedroom with a very large bed, compact bathroom, living room or den, take your choice, a screened porch and a kitchenette. It's not the kind of place you'd go for a vacation. Except for the bed, the furnishings are pretty meager. It could use a woman's touch."

"Did you expect any more? He told you what he used it for. Sounds like it meets his needs."

I had to agree. "I didn't know what to expect, but for a shack in the woods, I'd give it an A plus."

She hesitated and said, "I'm taking the children to a birthday party at four and don't have to pick them up until six.. Could you take me to see it and get me back before six? My curiosity is getting the best of me."

My mind went into overload. I hadn't expected her request and didn't know how to answer. "Are you sure?"

"Of course I'm sure, but if it doesn't suit we can do it another time." She paused to let me think. "I just hate to waste a good opportunity."

"Hey, I can't think of anything I'd rather do on Monday afternoon. It's great timing. Let's give it a go."

"OK, I'll be at your office a little after four."

"No, that's a bad idea. It wouldn't look good for your car to be in my lot if I'm not working. Meet me at the city park near the Governor's mansion. Park anywhere on Richland Street and I'll pick you up. If I get there before you, I'll keep circling the block."

"How'd you get so smart? I'd swear you've had some experience at this."

There was some nervousness in my laugh. "No, but I remember Bill saying not to leave any clues."

"I guess we're two babes in the woods. I'll see you a little after four. Bye."

I hung up the phone and for some unexplainable reason I felt trapped somewhere between elation and dread, exactly like the ill-fated beach trip. What in the hell was wrong with me? I should be overjoyed. I couldn't get past the thought that, given the opportunity, I might fail again, but I realized that I was exacerbating an old wound by dwelling on my earlier misfortune. Once again, I was putting the cart before the horse, projecting my passion into Maria's desire, which was perfectly justified, to see the cabin. She was just curious, and for me to worry about *what if* and *what might be* was incongruous and stupid. I put those thoughts out of my mind and relaxed. This would be an inspection trip and nothing more. With that tiger caged, I fixed a cup of coffee and went upstairs to the loft. I had plenty of work that needed my attention, and it would be a welcome diversion.

At three thirty, I brushed my teeth, grabbed a bottle of Johnny Walker Red from my credenza and left the office. I left the lights on to give the impression I was working. I don't know what that proved, but it made me feel better. I stopped at the Friendly Florist and bought some cut flowers for Maria. It was a last-minute thought but seemed appropriate for our adventure. I selected a dozen mixed flowers and laid them carefully on the floor behind my seat where she wouldn't see them.

I drove west on Laurel Street and turned in front of the Governor's mansion. Her car was directly in front of the park. I passed her, made a U-turn, and stopped beside her car. She popped out quickly; I had the door open for her.

"What's with the scarf over your head?" I was smiling like a hyena trying to hide my nervousness.

She whipped the scarf off her head. "Ta da! I'm just being careful. You know what Bill said." She folded the scarf and put it into her coat pocket, and knocked me dead with her infectious laugh. "Did I look like Mata Hair?"

She was so natural and jovial. Her mood captured me. All my nervousness fell away and I relaxed. "You looked more like a married women being picked up by her lover. I'll just leave it at that."

She made a face like a perplexed child and poked me on my shoulder. Her green eyes lit up and she said, "I'll bet you say that to all your girlfriends." Her lips slowly turned up into a soft smile and I turned into putty.

"I do believe you're flirting with me Madame, and if you keep it up, I may wreck my car." I was enjoying our playful repartee.

"Don't fool yourself, Big Boy. I just needed a ride."

"Well, I'm just glad for you that it was me driving by. No telling what kind of horrible fate I may have saved you from."

"That remains to be seen," she said playfully. She settled back in the seat and studiously stared at the road. "How far is it from the club to the turn?" She had become serious.

"It's not far, probably less than a mile. The road is almost parallel to the twelfth fairway."

"That's architect's directions. You know I don't understand that. Maybe, by the time you finish my house, I will. After all, I've got a good teacher."

"When we get to the club entrance, I'll clock it on the speedometer. It's really not hard to spot, but it's not much more than two ruts."

"Would I have trouble driving there alone?" she asked.

"It wouldn't be a problem in daylight, but I wouldn't want you to try it at night. If we ever come at night, I'll bring you." I reached for the dash. "There's the club entrance. Let me set the speedometer. It's on 42. Help me remember." Maria set forward in the seat, watching the terrain intently. "There's the road," I said as I braked the car to turn. "What's the speedometer reading?" I eased the car onto the ruts and slowed to ten miles per hour to soften the bumps.

"It's was forty-two and eight tenths when you turned in. Are you sure this is a road?"

"It gets better in a minute. There's not as much erosion when we get into the trees." We both became quiet until we approached the forest. "We're through the worst part," I said as we entered the pine forest and watched civilization disappear.

Maria whistled. "Wow, this really is a jungle, but it's beautiful. You're right. It's quiet as a tomb. Once you reach the trees, it's like another world. It's hard to believe that this is so close to the highway."

"If you think it looks like a jungle now, imagine how it looks in the summer when the trees are full of leaves. Sunlight probably never touches the ground. Look, there's the cabin."

Maria moved closer to the dash. "I see it. It's bigger than I imagined." She put her hand on my leg. "Hurry! I want to see the inside."

I pulled the car up close to the steps and shut down the engine. I laughed. "It's not much, but it's all I have."

"Silly, it's adorable, just like I imagined the gingerbread house looked when I was a child. Let's go inside," she said, reaching for the door.

"Let me unlock the door and get the power on first. Just sit still a minute." I knew it would be hard for her to stay in the car. She was very excited. I took my flashlight with me this time and I was in and had the lights on in seconds. When I got back to the door she was at the foot of the stairs. "Whoa, I've got something for you." I went back to the car and got the flowers from the back seat. "This is for you," I said bowing as I handed them to her.

Maria looked startled. "Terry, I don't know what to say. They're so beautiful." She moved toward me, admiring them, and encircled me with her free arm. "I love them," she said as she kissed me lightly on my lips. "What a wonderful surprise."

I was overjoyed with her response and inspired to move to greater heights. "If I may be so bold," I said picking her up quickly. "I always wanted to do this." I carried her up the steps and through the door before she could object. "I just carried you over the threshold," I said with a big smile.

"Terry, Terry…what am I going to do with you? Put me down before you break your back." She was rubbing the back of my neck.

I put her down and bowed again with a flourish of my hand. "It was an honor and privilege, Fair Lady. I have a bottle of scotch in the car. Would you like to toast this wonderful occasion?"

Maria smiled. "When will miracles ever end? That would be most appropriate. I'll find something to put the flowers in while you mix drinks."

"Good deal. I'll just be a minute," I said hustling off to the car. When I returned, Maria had found a large mason jar and was busy putting the flowers in it.

"There," she said, backing away to appraise her handiwork. "It's not the best I've ever seen, but it's noble."

"It's a big improvement. This place needs some color." I set the bottle on the cabinet top, grabbed two glasses, and opened the fridge. "I know there's ice in here somewhere. Ah, here it is." I pulled the ice tray out and rinsed it in the sink. I wiggled out four ice cubes and put two in each glass. "How do you want it – straight up or with some water?"

She frowned. "Please, a lady never drinks anything straight. Put a tablespoon of water in it." She laughed. "Just kidding. Put a lot of water in it. Don't make it strong."

I poured an inch of scotch in the glasses and filled them with water. "How's that?" I handed her a glass and took a sip from mine. "Nice," I said and licked my lips.

"Wait," she said extending her glass. "Here's to wonderful and exciting times."

I looked into her eyes and thought how beautiful she looked. I clinked my glass against hers and quickly kissed her. "What a wonderful thought. I'll certainly drink to that." We terminated our toast with a sip of scotch. "Are you ready for a tour? It won't take long." She took her coat off and laid it on the sofa. She was wearing a tight yellow sweater and a loose gray skirt with faint pin stripes of indeterminate color. She grabbed my hand and we walked toward the bedroom. I let her walk in front of me so I could admire her. Some of that admiration could, at any minute, turn into lust. She had that graceful, almost cat-like glide, and her legs were perfect with small ankles and well-muscled calves. Her hips rolled in rhythm with her stride. It was hard for me to turn my attention from her. Sweat was forming under my shirt and it wasn't from room temperature. She walked around the bed which swallowed up the room and stopped at the sliding door to the screened porch.

"This porch is perfect. You couldn't ask for a better view. I'm really impressed. I hadn't expected this." She turned and took a sip from her glass. "Bill's got a winner."

Without a word I reached for her glass. She looked a bit quizzical as I set both glasses on the floor. I reached out for her and looked at her face for a time. Then I kissed her slowly, letting my passion build until she pulled away. I didn't want to stop.

"Are you sure this is what you want?" she said, holding me away at arm's length.

"More than anything I could possibly wish for." I could feel my desire for her pulling me over the edge.

"Do we have enough time?" She was whispering.

"We'll find time." We came out of our clothes as though we had done it many times before. There was no attempt at modesty even though we'd never seen each other nude in the light. She folded her clothes and laid them away much better than I did, but the result was the same. We moved across the cramped floor and came together flesh to flesh. I held her close and kissed her, my tongue searching for hers. My hand found the swell of her buttocks and I pulled her to me. There was no timidity on my part. This time my erection was instant and powerful. I kissed her again and let my lips explore her upturned breasts. Her nipples were large and firm, and I rolled my tongue around them, taking my time finding each of them. I felt like a violinist caressing an original Stradivarius for the first time, capturing the mystery and rapture of holding such a priceless instrument in my hands. It was a moving experience, a feast of emotions.

I guided her toward the bed and she lay across it, watching my eyes as they moved over her body, surveying every curve and contour. I was standing on the floor bending over between her parted legs. My hands cupped her breasts and I traced a meandering pattern down her flat stomach to her navel with my tongue, feeling her soft down on my chin as I continued. She shivered and moved up to meet my inquisitive tongue, caressing my head in her hands. Her soft moan filtered down to me. It was a magic moment.

I stood up and searched my trouser pocket for a condom and she positioned herself along the length of the bed. "Don't," she said as I pulled it out. "You don't need it." She held her arms out for me. I dropped the condom on the floor and lay beside her. I kissed her and rolled over on her with my weight on my arms. As I entered her, she moved to meet me. We made love for a long time, stopping and starting often to maintain the ecstasy of the moment. It was crazy to say, but we were an absolute fit, like two matched spoons, working through a symphony to a resounding climax. We held each other in that moment like there was no tomorrow, and when it was over, we stayed together until we were totally relaxed and normal breathing returned.

We had not spoken, but there was something I had to say. "That was the most incredible experience I've ever had. I didn't realize sex could be so consuming."

"Shush," she said. She touched my lips to close them. "Don't say anymore. Let's enjoy this moment. It was a long time coming." Even though her eyes were closed, her face suggested a smile.

That was enough for me. There was no need for words. I was overwhelmed. I kissed her closed eyes and reached for my cigarettes.

"Me too," she said.

I lit two and handed her one. We lay on our backs, watching the smoke rising lazily over the bed, forming a faint gray haze. After a few languid puffs I said, "I never knew scotch, sex, and a cigarette could be so wonderful."

Maria laughed. "And only in that order."

I chuckled. "Maybe, but if any other combination could possibly be better, I wouldn't want to know. My heart couldn't take it."

"I can't argue with that," she said. After a moment she sat up in the bed. "I hate to break this spell, but I must. It's getting late and I have to pick up my children by six." She got up, picked up her handbag and walked into the bathroom, turning and giving me a playful wink before shutting the door.

I finished my cigarette, then stood up and stretched. I put on my shirt, socks, and shoes and waited for my turn to use the bathroom. I had some cleaning up to do before I could finish dressing. I grabbed the glasses and ashtray, took them to the kitchenette and washed them. I put them back where I found them. I felt it would be better if Bill didn't know I had been there.

When I returned to the bedroom, Maria was almost dressed. Her makeup was fresh and she had combed her hair.

"You look nice," I said. I need to do some repair work myself, so we can go. I don't need much time."

"I'll be ready in a few minutes," she said. "It's twenty till six. That's plenty of time for me to get the children by six, isn't it?"

"Sure. I'll have you back at your car in ten minutes, once we leave." I went into the bathroom, cleaned up and combed my hair. I didn't see any lipstick or makeup on my face. I came out and slipped my trousers on. "I'm ready."

We took one last look around and were satisfied everything was just like it was when we arrived. Maria took the flowers out of the mason jar and shook them over the sink. "I want you to take them back to your office. I can't bear to throw them away and we can't leave them."

"That's fine. Open the door while I trip the power breaker." We left the cabin and made our way to the car. It was dark as we drove away.

When we got back the highway, I said, "That was a wonderful day for me, couldn't have been any better. Have any regrets?"

"No, I don't. I wish it could have lasted longer. I would be dishonest if I said it wasn't on my mind when we came to the cabin, but my main motivation was to see it. I'm happy that it went the way it did. I should have guilt feelings about it, but I don't. It seemed so right, like it was predestined."

Maria's comments mirrored my thoughts and I said," It's a trite thing to say, but today had a sense of deja vu for me. Maybe we've met in some other life and been brought together again. I can't accept this as evil or immoral. There's something eternal about it that no one could understand. I'm not sure I understand it and I don't care. I do know you've changed my life and it'll never be the same. I knew you were special the first time I saw you, and, after I was around you, I sensed we could be the most compatible people in the world. That's a lot to say, but I mean it."

Maria pushed her hair from her forehead. She was sitting very relaxed, facing me and leaning against the door. "That's why I hate that we had so little time." She paused. "I would have loved to lay there and just talk. I never tire of talking with you. It's always interesting. We have so much to say and so little time. We may never have time. I'm sorry, I shouldn't have said that. Today is the first time I've felt a sense of completeness when we've been together. Usually, when we part, I feel like we need a little more, like I'm being robbed of something. Maybe a word, a smile, or some little action that would make parting easier. Now, I'm not sure I can ever be complete again without you. I don't mean to scare you; I know we're in an impossible situation."

"Wait a minute. I feel the same, but let's not get into something now that we can't talk out. We don't have enough time and today is too good to dump on a lot of serious rhetoric. I don't want to diminish it in any way. This is a conversation I'd like to continue another time. I know we've hardly mentioned the *love* word. We both have been too smart for that, but now's the time I want to tell you. **I love you**. Don't say anything. I'm not looking for a quid pro quo. I know how you feel. If you didn't care about me, you would never have gotten in to this. We just don't need to say any more. Let it take its own good time sinking in." I patted her hand. "Let's have good thoughts for now." I smiled. "Who knows? Tomorrow you might not want to give me the time of day."

"I'm afraid I want to give you a lot more than that," she said quietly. As I pulled up to her car, she turned and gave me a lingering kiss. "I think I can bask in the afterglow for a while." I caught a glimpse of her smile as she hopped out of the car.

I pulled up to give her room to get out of her parking space, and watched her drive away. It was not a good feeling. Driving back to the office, I conjured up many visions of her and mental pictures of our lovemaking. That part **was** a good feeling.

The lights were still on when I pulled into the parking lot. For an empty building, it looked bright and inviting. I took the flowers in, placed them in one of Martha's vases and set it on her desk. *I hope she won't ask me about them.* But I knew I'd get a question, so I decided to give my mother the credit. She had a flower garden and occasionally dropped some off.

I called Jane to tell her I was leaving and she was in a cheerful mood. That fact immediately let me know that she had not been looking for me. One less lie I would have to invent a story for. "Do you need anything?" I asked.

"No, but don't tarry. Supper will be ready by the time you get here."

"OK, I'll be there in a few minutes." I hung up and took one last look at myself in the bathroom mirror. After such a momentous day, I was expecting to see something more than a smiling, happy face, but it was not to be. Nothing different. Same old Terry.

I moved through the office, turning off lights, locked the door and headed home. As I drove along, my mind was totally at ease, free of any guilt, but I recognized the magnitude of my actions. I had been in a few sexual encounters in my bachelor days, but nothing like this had happened before. This was no groping encounter between two adults seeking the mutual satisfaction of orgasm. That wasn't our guidepost. It was more like two atoms coming together to form a precious new compound, like hydrogen finding oxygen to form water. The sexual part was a reward, not an end. It was the perfect blending of sexual and spiritual, a delicate balance that would be diminished if either were dominant, but each complimented the other. There was no doubt in my mind that I loved this woman, that she was meant to be mine. There was a serious price to pay here, given our marital and familial status, but I was determined to find a way for us to be together.

When I turned into the drive, I saw my girls through the living room windows. Janet saw the car lights and ran towards the front door. My heart was filled suddenly with affection for them. Maria had given me the knowledge and ability to love them more.

I got to work early, eager to make progress on Maria's house. I had worked through most of my backlog and needed something in the pipeline to generate some cash flow. I had been trying hard to get some small commercial work for the past two years and had been marketing my talents with a few realtors who developed small projects for investors. Residential work, though interesting and challenging, is not where the money is. An architectural practice that relies on residential work will always be small and always be awash with cash flow problems. If I could find a few good commercial projects with more lucrative commissions, I could hire a draftsman or two and have more time to market my services. One-man firms are back breakers and are too time consuming. I couldn't remember the last time I had taken a week off.

When I walked into the office, Maria's flowers caught my eye. They looked a little droopy so I watered them immediately. They were still very pretty and their presence reminded me of yesterday afternoon. My thoughts were of Maria and I wondered what she was doing. It was only seven-thirty, so I knew she was busy, probably in the midst of getting her household up and running.

I made a cup of coffee and went to my drawing board, pulling all the sketches I had in Maria's file. I lit a cigarette as I studied them and laid it in an ashtray. The early morning sun, low on the horizon, cast long, rectangular beams of light through the frosty windows and picked up hidden dust motes mingling with a column of gray smoke from my cigarette. I finished my coffee and without another moment's thought, balled up all of the sketches and pitched them into the trashcan. After yesterday, I realized my original concepts just weren't Maria. I knew I would have to start over if I were to capture her spirit and personality in this design. The lack of creativity in my early sketches was due to hurrying the design process. It provided me with more opportunities to see her. Now my mission was to build her a monument.

I went back to bubble charts and information I had collected and set them on my drafting board. I spread snapshots we had taken of the site over a topographical survey of the property and began making notes about obvious and subjective qualities of the site. The property Pat and Maria had selected had a number of mature trees that I wanted to save and it terminated in the rear on a lake of about fifteen acres. Fortunately, the view to the lake was southerly and would support large glass areas. It was a wonderful lot and offered much flexibility. It sloped gently to the lake and, with good planning and judicious use of the topography, it should be an economical site to develop. I was heavy into revising my bubble chart when I heard Martha coming in. I had been working for an hour and a half.

"What's with the flowers? Did you think it was my birthday?" she asked.

Good old Martha. "I know your birthday is July 3, Martha. Mother cut those from her garden, and I thought you'd enjoy them more than me. She dropped them off yesterday afternoon."

"Sure." she said. "I knew she was good, but she must be a magician to get roses to bloom this time of year."

I could hear her cackling. Damn, she had me, but I was going to end this before I got into trouble. "Don't look a gift horse in the mouth. Maybe I just wanted to do something nice for you."

She didn't make any further comment, but I could still hear her laughing. I was ashamed that she had caught me in a lie, but I decided to let it rest. I hoped she wouldn't explore it anymore, and went back to work. I was too engrossed in my work to get sidetracked by Martha.

There was one large oak, maybe four feet in diameter and spanning eighty feet or more near the rear of the site. I would have to bend the house around it if I wanted to save it. Nevertheless, I would never cut it and it would lend character to the house. A long arc might be interesting, but my philosophy of form follows function kept getting in the way of my imagination. The idea was too pre-conceived, but, if the space worked into it, it might be interesting.

I wanted the roof to have strong horizontal lines and hug the terrain. Wide overhangs would provide shade and drop the roof lower to the ground without diminishing room heights. Perhaps I could work the oak tree into a patio and use it to provide shade in the hot summer months. It would be a wonderful place to sit in the afternoon and watch the sunset and blue martins feasting on insects over the lake.

I worked steadily all morning with little interruption. By the time Martha told me she was leaving, I had created an impressive number of sketches taped on my drafting board in haphazard fashion. I had been working without stopping for about six hours and was really having fun, but my stomach was beginning to rumble. My thoughts turned to my favorite quick meal, a cheeseburger from the Blizzard Shop. I decided on a takeout and reached for the phone to place my order, but it rang before I got my hand on it.

"Terry Forte speaking," I said, a little annoyed.

"Umm.....you don't sound as nice as you did yesterday." I could almost imagine Maria pouting as she spoke, but I knew she was probably stifling a laugh.

"Well, I've been working hard and haven't had lunch. That's enough to be angry about. Of course, after yesterday, nothing else compares. Maybe that's what I need instead of food."

"There you go, slathering me with that magnolia marmalade. Southern gentlemen never give up, do they? Well, you're not fooling me with that. I'm catching on to your tricks. What are you planning to do to satisfy that hunger?"

"To tell the truth, I was thinking about a cheeseburger from the Blizzard. I haven't had one in a while."

"By my count, it's been about five days since you've had one, unless you've been holding out on me. I'll bet you're planning to get it with onions, too."

I laughed. "Not if I were seeing you today."

"Well, have at it; there's no way. It's dance lesson day at my house, so I'll be chauffeuring children. That's how moms who push their children to excel spend their afternoons."

"Where are you taking them that's so excelling?"

"Mrs. Sloan's Dance Studio on Gervais Street. She teaches them social graces as well as dance. It's ballroom, and the little dears have to dress up. It was recommended by one of my friends. Have you heard of it?"

"Sure have. And you're not going to believe this, but I went to Sloan's when I was thirteen years old. My mother was a pushy mom, too. I guess you've seen how it improved my social graces. Last time I went to a dance, I embarrassed everyone and created a scene on the dance floor dancing with some strange lady all night. What do you think about that?"

Maria laughed. "I didn't go to Mrs. Sloan's, so I guess it was my fault."

"What a lady you are to take the blame."

"Enough, enough. What I really called about, other than to hear your voice, was to invite you to a picnic tomorrow. I want to look at my lot again, and I thought it would be a good way to entertain you at the same time. It won't be much, some sandwiches, fruit and cheese. Oh, and some cake I baked yesterday."

"Aha! That's the best invitation I've had lately, and of course I accept. Sounds like a working lunch. Should I pencil it onto my calendar?"

Maria replied curtly. "Don't be flippant with me. I'd just like to spend some time alone with you. Yesterday was such a momentous time for me, but I felt like it ended too abruptly. I had a lot of things on my mind, things that I wanted to talk about, but there wasn't enough time."

I was quiet for a moment. "Are you having second thoughts?" I was beginning to feel uncomfortable.

"**NO,** I have a lot of first thoughts, but no second thoughts. Why are you so defensive?"

"I'm sorry," I said softly. "I guess I'm having a hard time accepting good fortune."

Maria said. "I don't know how I got into this situation, but I didn't walk into it, I ran. Now it's history. And guess what? I have no guilt or sorrow. In fact, I feel just fine, thank you. Now, for heaven's sake, do you want to have a picnic or not?"

"Of course," I said. "Put down the whip; I surrender. Is there anything I can bring?"

"Just you. I have everything else under control. I'll come by after Martha leaves, about one o'clock. I'll drive up to the door. Watch for me."

"OK, but you better wear something warm. It won't be pleasant outside."

Maria laughed. "I don't plan to eat outside. I thought we could sit in the car. I'm not much on pain."

I didn't sense anything hidden in any of this, but my analytical mind didn't want to accept the picnic thing. I decided to take it at face value and said, "It's in my calendar......Wednesday, December 10, 1962, at one o'clock. Now, are you satisfied?"

"You amaze me. We had such a wonderful day, and I ask you to meet me for lunch, and you start acting weird. Did I do something to make you mad? I must be missing something here."

Maria was right; I **was** acting weird. "You didn't do anything wrong. I did and I apologize. Would you like it better if I told you I wish it were Wednesday now, and that I miss you terribly? Because I do."

Maria giggled and said, "I like that much better. In fact, if we're going to wish, I wish it were yesterday so I could have it all over again."

That did it for me. With those few words, my sinister thoughts were gone. "Me too, but I was hoping that yesterday was only the first of many."

Maria was quiet for a minute and said, "I'm confident it was, but I can't think about that now. I've got groceries to buy and kids to get to Mrs. Sloan's. First things first."

"OK, but beware of those little boys. They're pretty precocious."

She laughed. "I'll remember that. See you tomorrow. Bye."

I hung the phone up and thought about our conversation. I wasn't happy with much of what I had said. Maria was lighthearted and just wanted to spend some time together, and I was trying to see disaster in it. I was going to have to find a way to be comfortable with this relationship. I made up my mind to do just that tomorrow.

In fifteen minutes, I was back in the middle of Maria's house, our telephone conversation forgotten. The floor plan was coming together and I was beginning to see it in three dimensions. In my mind's eye, I watched volumes of space interacting, creating drama, and molding it like sculpture. This was the excitement of architecture. Moving through areas of low ceilings and soffits into expanding volumes created surprise and defined the sculptural shapes I was looking for. I separated the living area from the den with a large fireplace and tucked a sitting area into a parallel wall under high ribbon windows, giving it a measured sense of shelter, and exposing it from floor to ceiling to the winter sun and views of the lake. Sketches were littering my desk and falling to the floor. I couldn't keep up with all the ideas going through my head. The cheeseburger from the Blizzard Shop never entered my mind again.

It was dark when I completed a fifth freehand perspective of the house. I looked at my watch. It was after six and I was famished. I had been working for almost eleven hours.

I picked up the telephone and dialed home. Janet answered.

"Hi Jumper, what's for supper?" (For the uninitiated, that's Southern for dinner.)

"I don't know, Daddy. I've been outside playing. Mommy's been on the sewing machine all day and I don't think she's been cooking. I'll get her."

"That's all right," I said, but it was too late. I could hear her running from the phone. In a minute she was back.

"She said she couldn't stop what she's doing, and maybe you should treat us tonight. Could you bring some cheeseburgers and French fries home? Please, Daddy?"

Looks like I was going to get that cheeseburger, after all. "Sure Jumper. Look in the fridge and see if we have any Cokes."

"Hold on, Daddy." In a minute she returned and said, "We've got enough. I'll tell Mom you're bringing cheeseburgers home."

"Wait a minute Jumper. Ask Mom if that's OK."

This time, she didn't say anything, but I heard her running. "She said that's OK with her. Hurry home, Daddy." The line went dead.

I called the Blizzard Shop and ordered supper. I was tired and hungry. It was time to go home.

I was up early and my first thoughts were of Maria and our scheduled picnic. I caught myself whistling in the shower, but stopped before I got too exuberant. Jane stayed up late sewing and was still sleeping. I didn't want to awaken her. Also, I didn't want to answer any questions about my merry demeanor.

Bringing home supper was a big hit with Laura and Janet. I made a mental note to do that more often. Jane was pleased, maybe even more so because she had more time to sew. When she gets on one of those sewing jags, she doesn't stop until she finishes what she's working on. She has great powers of concentration and determination. After supper, I played Monopoly with the girls and they beat the pants off me. They had me in bankruptcy in no time. Nevertheless, I had found a very effective way to get them to do their homework, playing monopoly with them AFTER they finished their homework.

It was a struggle, but I had the girls up, dressed, and eating cereal before I heard Jane stirring. They weren't too happy to eat cereal instead of their usual eggs, bacon and grits, but they understood the reason for their sacrifice and had visions of another game of Monopoly when I got home from work. Thank goodness Jane had selected their clothes and laid them out. I'm not good at that. Before we left for school, she checked them over and brushed their hair. I gave her a perfunctory hug and we made our way to the car.

The sun was peeking over the horizon through scudding clouds, and a light frost crunched under our feet as we walked. A picnic would not have been my first choice for this kind of day, but I couldn't contain my excitement at the thought of spending time with Maria. I was whistling "Hi ho, hi ho, it's off to work we go" as I put the girls into the car. Still whistling, I started the engine and backed out of the drive.

"Why are you whistling, Daddy?" Laurie asked.

"I guess I'm happy to take such cute little girls to school," I answered.

"Why don't you take us to school every day, then?" I should have expected that from Janet.

"Maybe I will, Jumper. Sounds like a good idea."

"No Daddy," Janet said. "We don't get up as early as you do."

"You're right, Jumper, but maybe on days I'm late, I can drive you to school."

Laurie spoke up. "Why don't you come home earlier instead? We could play monopoly like last night, and, when summer comes, we can play roll the bat. That's more fun than driving us to school."

"Yeah, why don't you just come home earlier?" asked Janet.

I had to think about that for a minute. "I'll try to do that. Last night was fun."

"Goody Daddy," Janet said. "How about tonight? Can you come home early?"

"I don't know about tonight, Jumper, but I promise I'll come home early some night this week." I hoped that would end this conversation. Fortunately, we were at the school and that would definitely end it. I pulled up to the entrance and stopped the car. "Be careful getting out. I don't want you hit by a car. Get out on the sidewalk side."

The doors opened and they popped out running. "Bye Daddy," Janet said. Laurie waved but said nothing. I watched them for a minute before driving off. I always felt a tug in my heart when I dropped them off. They were growing up so quickly, and I realized how precious every moment with them was. I had to find some balance in my life that provided me ample time to enjoy them.

As I drove off, my thoughts turned to Maria and the excitement returned. If I wanted to get any work done, I'd have to curb that. Working on her house would occupy my time, once I got started. I turned into the parking lot, parked and walked into the office. I was surprised that Martha was there, but I was a little later than normal.

"Hi Martha, anything going on?"

"Not yet, but I didn't see any fresh flowers this morning." She laughed. "Did I make you mad or something?"

Martha could get under my skin sometimes. "Maybe. I'll let you figure that out." I kept walking to the accompaniment of her laughter. At least, she could stop teasing me about it. I was sure as hell not going to tell her the truth.

I went upstairs and saw all of my sketches from last night. My God, I sure did a lot of work yesterday. My desk was covered with drawings and I had taped a bunch to the wall. My office looked like a senior class design project. I piled them up on my desk and went through them one at a time, selecting the most interesting ones. I studied the chosen ones and made careful notes in the margins, indicating what I liked and why.

Deciding my mind would work better with a cup of coffee and a cigarette, I hurried downstairs and found a pot of hot water on the hotplate. Good old Martha. Now I felt guilty for giving her a hard time this morning.

Nah.........she'd get over it. No need to waste an emotion. I'd save that for a better time. I fixed my coffee and lit a cigarette as I headed back upstairs. I was ready for work.

At twelve thirty or so, I heard Martha preparing to leave. She stood at the bottom of the stairs and shouted, "See you tomorrow. Hope you're in a better mood." She gave me that booming laugh. "Maybe the good fairy will bring me some more flowers." Her laughter followed her out the door. That was enough for me. I made a note in my calendar to get flowers for Martha, but not too soon.

A few minutes before one o'clock, I went into the restroom and brushed my teeth. Then, I went to the front door to watch for Maria. My heart was beating a hundred miles an hour. *If that isn't like high school, I don't know what is.* I grabbed my jacket and headed outside as Maria's car turned into the parking lot. I smiled, waved, and opened the door in one motion.

I slid into her car and patted her leg. "I guess a kiss is out of the question."

Maria laughed and said, "You'll have to be content with a pat on my leg. Remember, you're the one who said we must be careful."

I frowned. "You're right. Maybe later?"

"We'll see. Depends on how much you *ooh* and *aah* over my picnic lunch."

"If that's what it takes, I can handle it. Do you want me to start now?" I had a big smile on my face and the tension was easing away. "How long do we have for our picnic?"

"If you'll stop being silly, I'll tell you. I probably have more time than you. My neighbor is doing the car-pooling today and I told her I wanted to do some shopping. She's watching the kids till I get home. I could probably stay till four or five, but I don't want to wear out my welcome. I might need her again."

"Well, all I have to do is work on a house; I don't guess that 's important."

"If it's my house, it's OK. I'm the one who did the inviting. If it's somebody else's, I don't care. How do you like that?" She turned towards me and smiled.

"To tell the truth, I'd be here no matter whose house it was, and you know it." We were silent for a moment. "I've been waiting to see you all day. I may just be addicted to you. Being away from you gives me withdrawal symptoms."

"That's sweet, Terry. I feel the same way. But can we handle this? It's been a long time since I've been tuned so intensely into my emotions. I guess I'm playing it by ear…one day at a time. We have so many competing things – family, work, friends…and let's not forget our spouses. It's not going to be a picnic. Pardon the pun. I'm not sure I can manage all this. We need some rules that we can agree on, and I think one of them will be that our children come first."

"Maria, I'll never put you in a situation where a choice like that would ever come up. Our children will always be top priority. I don't want either of us feeling guilty. It didn't start out that way and I don't want it to ever be that way. I want you, but I know there's a limit to how much you can give. I'll learn how to be happy with that. I must. But, the rewards…" my voice trailed off. "They're greater than any price I'll have to pay. If what happened Monday was what I can expect from you and that was the alpha. I just hope that the omega is way down the road. It's a journey I'm willing, maybe compelled to take."

Maria eased on the brakes. "Isn't that the road to the lot?"

I leaned forward and peered over Maria's shoulder. "Yes, that's it; turn left at the power pole." I noticed the pines were swaying in the breeze. "It's going to be cold outside. You better get your coat on if you want to walk around the site." The sun was bright, but there wasn't much heat in it, probably no more than 45 degrees.

Maria turned the car off the road and drove well onto the site before stopping and shutting off the engine. "Why don't we have lunch first?'

"Suits me," I said. Then I put my hand on her neck and pulled her to me. I could smell shampoo in her hair and the faint aroma of her perfume. I kissed her gently and lingered over it. "Nothing like having dessert first," I said quietly.

"You can have seconds if you want," she said. Her eyes were half closed and her lips were open slightly, as if in a smile. She was the epitome of womankind, a feast for my eyes, provocative and beautiful. All of my senses ached to absorb her.

"I want." I kissed her again. This time it was a passionate kiss but not one of lust. I explored her sweet mouth with my tongue and was rewarded with hers. God was good to me and I savored every minute of it, hoping it would never end. I refused to break away from her until I was out of breath.

"Dessert wasn't half bad, was it?" she said. I was kissing her eyes as she spoke.

"You are a wonderful woman, Maria, and if I were Adam and you were Eve, I would be satisfied. I wouldn't need another woman. I wouldn't want another woman."

She moved away from me, but she had a big smile on her face. "Terry, you say such nice things. I think it's time I should reward you with this sumptuous repast." She laughed as she spoke. "After all, I labored long hours getting it ready, and all the time I was thinking that the way to a man's heart is through his stomach. That may not quite be right, but it's close."

Her eyes were sparkling. I hoped it mirrored her thoughts. "No need for that. My heart has already been captured, but I *could* be bribed a little more."

She opened the door and hopped out, straightening her slacks. I could feel the cold air entering the car. "Damn, it's cold. Need any help? I feel like I should be doing something."

She opened the back door. "Here," she said as she handed me a bottle of white wine. "There's a wine opener in the pocket on the side of my bag. You can do that. I never get the cork out without destroying it." She reached for the basket sitting on the floor and put it on the front seat. I moved over and shifted it to the center of the seat. She grabbed a bag, shut the back door and got back in the car. "Knife for the cheese and forks for cake," she said. "If we need them. Oh, goblets for the wine…that's important."

"Boy, I'm impressed," I said.

Maria removed an earring and put it in her pocketbook. "Darned thing is hurting." She rubbed her lobe, obviously relishing her relief, and turned toward me. "Don't be too impressed. You haven't eaten anything yet. Open the wine while I get the basket organized. We don't have enough room to spread things out, so we'll eat out of the basket. Sorry, but no candles."

I worked on the wine bottle without much success. "Damn, I hope I didn't leave cork in the bottle," I said as I finally removed it. "Never could get the corkscrew in the center of the cork. You've got to be a genius to get it just right."

Maria laughed. "Don't tell me I've finally found something you can't do."

I smiled. "Never said I was perfect. But I'm real good at eating, and something in there smells good."

She started unwrapping foil from the food and said, "It's getting a little cold. Mind if I start the engine and start the heater?"

"Good idea. As long as we're in the open, we won't die from carbon monoxide poisoning."

Maria looked startled. "Oh my God. There's no chance of that, is there? Wouldn't do for us to make the front page of the *State*. I can see the headline now: *Local Architect and Client Found Dead in Automobile.*" She hesitated and laughed. "Was it carbon monoxide or food poisoning?"

"That's very funny, Maria. I'm hungry; let's see if the food **is** poisonous."

"Now that's **not** funny," she said with a pout.

"I'm teasing," I said. I leaned across the basket and gave her a quick kiss. I wanted to grab her, but I thought better of it.

She handed me a sandwich and a goblet, and uncovered some potato chips and pickles. I filled her extended goblet and then mine, and took a big bite of my sandwich. It was chicken salad and it was very good. "Hey, this chicken salad is great. Did you make it?"

"Of course. Old family recipe. It's called 'Yankee chicken salad'." She grinned. "I'll bet you don't like that."

"Why? You're a Yankee and I like you. I wouldn't trade you for all the Southern belles in the world." I chuckled. "Besides, it's damn good Yankee chicken salad. I guess that's an oxymoron for a Southern boy to say, but lately I've come to like and appreciate many things with a Yankee flavor. I really didn't know what I was missing."

Maria leaned against the door with her arms crossed. "I believe I like that. I wonder what's going to happen if you like this cake I baked?" She had a relaxed smile on her face.

"Never know till I try it." I reached across the seat and touched the nape of her neck, playfully curling her hair with my fingers. "I think you'd better hurry with the cake. My self control has just about gone."

She unwrapped the cake and handed me a piece on a napkin. "Before you ask, it's Betty Crocker. I'm kidding. I made it from scratch."

I took a big bite. "Yummy! Boy that's good. I don't care if it's Yankee or Southern. If you fed me like this every day, I'd be big as a barn. I'd even have to give up Blizzard burgers."

"That's too much to ask. Could you pour me a little more wine?"

"Sure. Tell me when." I poured about half of the goblet before she said stop. "I could use a little more myself." I'm not a connoisseur, but it tasted good.

Maria started tidying up, putting things back in the basket. Then she turned, kneeling and leaning over the seat, and placed the basket on the back floor. The temptation was too great. I patted her rear playfully.

"Stop that," Maria said, slapping my hand. "Somebody might be watching."

"No way," I said. "There's no one within miles. Anyone who could see us would have to climb a tree and have powerful binoculars." I reached out for her and she slid across the seat. I kissed her and said, "Umm…you taste good, like warm Riesling wine."

"Maybe," she said with her eyes almost closed. "See if you know the year." We kissed again, only, this time nothing was held back. Her lips were warm, red, and inviting. I nuzzled my face into her hair and whispered, "Vintage 1952. That was a wonderful year. Over a hundred days of sunshine to bless the grapes. You could do that with one smile."

Maria rolled her head back and I kissed her neck. "You have such a way with words, Terry. Maybe you should have been a poet instead of an architect." She rubbed my neck and kissed me. I reached for the zipper on the side of her slacks. "Let me do that," she said. She slipped her shoes off and pulled her slacks down from her hips.

I had my trousers off in seconds, folded them and laid them on the back seat. "Take your slacks off. You'll wrinkle them if you let them hang there." It was getting warm in the car. I took time to cut off the heater and the engine. I slipped my boxers off and my excitement was obvious.

Without a word, Maria wiggled out of her panties and within the confines of the seat managed, somehow, to sit on my lap. I entered her immediately and it was pure magic. She held my head in both hands and kissed me.

"Are we really doing this?" she asked. Because of the small space and our position, I was immobile, but she wasn't. She moved slowly and with some apprehension, then she increased her pace and rhythm. It was wonderful. I was enjoying it, perhaps too much. I decided to put the brakes on.

"Wait Maria, I don't have a condom. We'll have to be careful."

"I told you at the cabin not to worry about that," she said.

"I don't understand. What do you mean?"

"I'm taking birth control pills. I started taking them just after the beach trip. That's all you need to know."

"Oh," I said a bit surprised. Why would she do that I wondered, but the first answer was obvious. She didn't want to get pregnant. No need to read anything into that. I'd get it wrong anyway. Besides, I had better things on my mind.

Maria kissed me, gently at first, then with increasing passion. Finally, she laid her head on my chest and began to make low, moaning sounds. I caught up with her before she stopped moving. We were both breathing hard. I held her tightly and rubbed her back until the rush subsided. She giggled and her first words were, "I can't believe we're doing this, but it sure is fun."

I kissed her smiling lips. "I sure hope we are. Otherwise, I've had one of the best dreams of my life."

She moved away but we remained connected. "**One** of the best?" Her voice was low and she had a devilish smile on her face.

"OK, I lied. It was the absolute best."

"That's much better. Now, what are we going to do about this mess we've made?" She pulled a handful of napkins from her bag and handed me several. "Here, this'll have to do." She moved away from me and, amidst a lot of laughter, we did what was necessary to clean up. "We're too old to do things like this," she said, slipping into her clothes.

"No, we're not too old. We just need to plan better. This isn't something I'm used to. And now that you're dressed, how about getting my clothes from the back so I don't have to show my ugly fanny to the world?"

She smiled. "I'd better. I sure don't want the world to have to see that!"

I got into my clothes and suddenly felt the need to move around. "Let's take a walk. I need some air and activity."

Maria had that devilish look in her eyes again. "Are you telling me you didn't get enough activity after all that?"

"No.....I just need to stretch my legs. It's close in here." I opened the door, stepped out of the car, and was greeted by frigid air. "Put on your coat if you're getting out. It's freezing."

Maria got out of the other side and put her coat on. "Hey, it **is** cold. I don't think I want to stay outside long." We met in front of the car and she grabbed my hand.

"Let's walk down to the lake. I want to see how the house will look from the water. I want to locate it around that big live oak, and I need to have a positive feeling about how to orient it for the best view of the water. The sun's orbit is almost as low as it will be. The shortest day of the year is only ten days away, so I can get a good idea of its position relative to the tree and the view." I dropped her hand and put my arm around her and we walked in lock step.

"You're pretty brave, holding me like this. We're not being careful."

"I know," I said, "but sometimes when we're together, I feel invisible. It's probably the wine. If anyone asks, I'll say you fell down and sprained your ankle. I'm just helping the needy."

"I don't think that'll fly, but don't stop."

We walked on, our warm breath forming a vapor trail in our path. I could feel my ears and nose becoming numb in the frigid air. "We'll make this a quick trip; I'm not into pain." We continued until we reached the edge of the lake, then I turned to look back at the oak tree. I lined it up with a large pine tree near the water to fix my location, and I was satisfied that I had selected the best place for the house. "OK, I've seen enough," I said, and we hurried back to the car.

We walked with our arms around each other and, except for a few words of caution about rough ground, had little to say. The cold air had something to do with that, but a quiet sense of belonging to one another made it unnecessary to speak. Her eyes glistened with tears from the cold, cutting air and sparkled like multi-faceted diamonds. It was hard for me, seeing her bundled up and walking energetically to the car, to imagine her a few minutes earlier, making love in the front seat of her car like a teenager. She still remained a mystery to me in so many strange and wonderful ways, even after our intimacy.

We stopped as we approached the car, and I pulled her to me. Her face was cold but her lips were warm as I kissed her. "I needed that," I said simply.

Her reply was one word. "Why?"

"Because I realize how much I love you. What could be more appropriate?"

"Maybe…doing it again," she said.

Her reply was perfect, and we did. A tender and loving kiss, so much so that it was tinged with a hint of pain. Not of the body, but of the spirit.

We moved apart and I opened the door for her. She jumped inside and started the engine before I could walk around the car and get inside. I knew she was cold. The temperature had dropped below freezing. Clouds had crept in from the west and obscured the afternoon sun, giving the air a gray tint that looked like snow as I remembered it from my tour in Germany. I knew that was not going to happen. I couldn't remember our last snowstorm. I got into the car blowing on my hands and rubbing them together briskly, my feet and ears numb from the cold.

"Maybe we stayed outside too long," I said.

She grimaced. "I didn't think it got this cold in the sunny South. I'm calling the Chamber of Commerce when I get home."

I smiled. "Won't do you any good. They'll tell you the average temperature is 67 degrees, year around."

"I can stand a few like this," she said. "I still remember spending winters in Pekin with skies like this and dirty snow littering the ground. I'm not going to gripe too much." She looked at the temperature gauge, saw the needle had moved up a notch, and switched on the heater

"Wait till we have one of those 100 plus degree days in late May. Then you'll wish for another day like today."

She was silent for a minute, and with her eyes locked onto mine, said, "I already do, and it has nothing to do with the weather." When she looked at me and said things like that, I became helpless.

Maria looked at her watch and said, "Gee, it's almost four. I guess we better get going. I've got to get home and clean up the picnic stuff before I can start dinner – excuse me, supper."

I had to chuckle. "You think I need an interpreter? I'm getting fluent in Yankee. I remember from my days in Germany that immersion is the best way to learn a new language."

"Judging your behavior in Germany, I'm not sure I like that."

"OK, we won't go there. I was suggesting that I learned German by listening and talking with my German personnel, same as with you. 'Nuff said."

"I was just kidding you. Didn't mean to hit a nerve. Will you forgive me?"

"Of course."

"Now that we've settled that, let's go. I have a lot to do before Pat gets home."

I was quiet until we were back on the highway. Then I said, "I know we can't use the cabin on Tuesday, and I usually play golf on Wednesday if the weather's decent, but I'd like to plan another visit next week. What do you think?"

"I'm not sure. It's too early to say. I think Pat's going to Savannah for a few days, but I don't know for sure or when. If I had to say now, I'd guess Thursday. He usually leaves on Tuesday and comes back on Thursday, sometimes early. If I can work it out, I'd like to. I'll try to find out if he's traveling, and let you know Monday."

"Fair enough. If push comes to shove, I could go on Wednesday, but I don't think it's a good idea to change my routine. It's one of those 'safe things'. But, rather than miss the opportunity, I'll find an excuse."

"No, I think you're right. Let's plan on Thursday and hope it works."

I reached for her hand and held it until she had to turn off the highway, then I moved to the door and watched the city come to meet us. Neither of us said much. It didn't seem necessary. I couldn't believe how quickly the afternoon had passed.

We drove up to my office at half past four and the parking lot, except for my car, was empty. She pulled up close to the door and after a hasty surveillance of the area, I leaned over and kissed her goodbye. As I exited her car, I said, "Call me when you can. I'm not sure I can wait until next Thursday to see you. Maybe we can have lunch at the Blizzard Friday. Give it some thought. I had a great day. See you."

She blew me a kiss and said, "I'll try. Bye."

I stood at the door, my breath fogging in my face, and watched her drive away. I knew whatever hold I had on her and this relationship was tenuous at best, and I felt helpless about it. I loved her and thought she loved me, but my assessment was based more on her actions than her words. Perhaps that was going to be the pattern, and maybe that was best for her. My problem was I was spending more time thinking about her than my work. That would have to change if I was going to make a living. The answer to that was simple. Find more lucrative work and hire some people. The hard part was finding better work. I could hire people if I could generate cash flow.

I went inside and made some notes on my *to do* list. The first one was to start cultivating new clients. I didn't think Jane had called, but I decided to ring her just in case.

"Hello," she answered. I didn't detect any anger in her voice.

"Hi. You didn't just call, did you? I was in the bathroom and the phone rang. I couldn't get to it in time." This was one of my standard ploys. I was becoming more devious and I didn't like it.

"No, I've been fixing supper. I hope you're not going to be late. I'm frying chicken and it won't be good cold."

"I'm getting ready to leave. Do you need anything?"

"How about getting some milk? We're about out."

"Sure. I've got a little to do here, but I'll be home in thirty minutes, tops."

"Don't be any later. Bye."

"Bye." I was relieved that she didn't know I hadn't been in the office all afternoon. I looked around the office, more from custom than reason, placed my list of things to do in the middle of my desk and left. It was time to go home.

41

Thursday morning I made it to the office early, in fact before Martha. I had a good night Wednesday, resting well after a tasty supper and an evening of Monopoly with the girls, and felt like I could accomplish anything. I checked my list and saw the note about cultivating new clients. I decided it was time to develop marketing skills, not my best suit but vitally important in my profession. I'd have to think about that. I needed a list of people who influenced the selection of architects by virtue of politics or financial standing in the community. The superintendent of city schools was a good place to start, and some of the members on county council. I had some family connections to the state adjutant general, but that was a long shot. At least I had a place to start.

I went through the mail Martha had put on my desk and found a change order request and three sets of shop drawing submittals. That would keep me busy for an hour or two. I was finishing up the second set of shop drawings when Martha made her appearance. I walked into the reception area with a smile. "Good morning, Martha. How are you this fine day?"

"Not fine at all," was her reply. "My daughter and her worthless husband are going to some convention today, and are leaving the children with me for the weekend. I'll have to take off tomorrow so you get to share in the fun. It wouldn't be so bad if I'd known about it earlier. At least I could have prepared for it. They never give me any warning. I guess they're afraid I'll say no."

"Gee, I'm sorry Martha, but I can do without you for a day." I wanted her to know I would miss her.

"I know," she said. "But I feel bad when I don't give you any more notice than this."

"It's OK, Martha. I know you didn't have a choice. Hey, you haven't had a day off that wasn't an emergency in a long time. Don't worry about it. We don't have much to do right now, so it's no big deal."

"I know, but I don't like it. They know they can take advantage of me whenever it suits them." She certainly had a point there!

I patted her shoulder. "Forget it. I always know I can count on you. You've done enough for me when I've really needed you. I remember how many hours you put in when we had to work a few nights and weekends. This just isn't a problem. Now, how about I fix you a cup of coffee? I was on my way to get me a cup when you came in. I'll be happy to get one for you."

"That would be very nice," she said, her voice trailing off.

"OK," I said and headed for the workroom. Martha never got upset over things like this. She got mad, but not upset. There was more to this than a weekend of baby-sitting, but being the private person that she was, I knew that I would never know the real problem. I made our coffees and took hers to her desk.

"Thanks," she said, and with no further words we returned to our work.

I made appointments with Dr. Merriweather, the Superintendent of City Schools, and the SC Adjutant General for Friday morning. I started putting a resume together. This would be a hard sell because most of my work was residential. Most of the work I did during my tenure with Bayer-Kline was commercial, institutional, or churches, but it would be unethical to take credit for any of them. But I would have to mention them to build up my experience or I wouldn't get to first base. *It's that same old story, no experience no job, but how in the hell can you get experience unless you get the job?* What a conundrum. I put some information together and gave it to Martha. She had done a few in her day, and I knew she would do it better than I could. She promised to finish before she left. Thank God for Martha.

Just before lunch Martha buzzed me and said I had a call. I thought it might be Maria. I picked up the phone with a big smile and said, "Terry Forte".

There was a pause; I was about to hang up when I heard a nervous female voice say, "Terry, is that you?"

"Yes, who **IS** this?"

"It's Ann."

"I'm sorry Ann. I didn't catch your voice."

"That's OK. I don't talk to you on the phone much so it's understandable."

"I hope nothing is wrong."

"No, nothing's wrong. The house hasn't burned down and nobody's sick. I just want to talk to you about something personal and I'd like to do it in private. Would it be possible to stop by your office this afternoon for about thirty minutes?"

"Sure. I'll be here until about six." I laughed. "Or until I get hungry.

"Thanks. I'll be in town in the afternoon to do some shopping. How about between two and three?"

"That's good. Just come on in when you get here. I'll be in the drafting room."

"OK. See you then. Bye."

What could she want? I *hope it's not a loan, but with her problem it could be anything. Whatever it is, Garth doesn't know about it. He would never let her come to me for help. He's got too much pride. Oh well, no need to try to figure it out. I'll know soon enough.*

The phone rang and I answered. "Design Concepts, Terry Forte speaking."

"What's my architect up to?" It was Maria.

"Nothing much. Just pining away waiting for my sweetheart to call. Hope she does before the day's over."

"Well now, I think you're trying to be rude. Maybe I ought to hang up so she can call."

"Uh oh, can't take a joke today. The truth is I've been waiting for you to call."

"That's better. Now that we've gotten your feeble attempt to be funny out of the way, we can move on to better things. Have you been working on my house?"

"No, I've been doing some grunt work and putting a resume together. I need to expand my client base."

"Are you telling me that I'm not enough for you?"

"Maybe we're not talking about the same thing."

"Would it make any difference?"

"Absolutely."

"Um...maybe we should discuss this more fully at lunch tomorrow."

"Wonderful! I was afraid you had forgotten about it."

"I didn't forget. I just had to get my ducks in a row. I have other tasks to take care of once in a while."

"I understand. You don't have to explain. I'm happy you can make it. What time can you meet me?"

"I've got a United Fund meeting at eleven so it may be late....probably one or one thirty. To be safe, let's meet at one thirty. If I get through before then, I'll find something to occupy my time or call you."

"I guess I can share you with United Fund, but don't let them keep you too long. Is this a special meeting?"

"Just a report meeting, but I have a committee meeting after that. If it gets too long I'll just leave. I'll get a headache or something. I'll be at the Blizzard Shop by one thirty."

"OK.....anything else going on?"

"Not really. I'm doing the PTA thing tonight. If I don't go I'll get elected to something."

"That's what happens to "do-gooders," especially carpetbaggers from up *Nawth!*"

"There you go, insulting me again. If you don't quit that I'm going to get angry."

"Come on. I'm just kidding; I wouldn't trade you for all the Scarlett O'Haras in the South."

She laughed before she replied. "I wouldn't trade you for all the 'Rhett Butlers either, only that's an insult for a Southern boy."

"That's not an insult. I'll accept it. Clark Gable's not chopped liver, you know."

"Enough of this. I feel like we're doing one of Abbot and Costello's routines. Are you working tonight?"

"Why?"

"Nothing special. If I'm alone tonight, I'll try to phone you. If not, I'll see you tomorrow."

"I don't think I'm coming back tonight. I promised the girls a Monopoly game. I think I'll save my night work until I know you can call. I don't want to waste a night if I don't know for sure you'll call."

"Makes sense. Let's leave it at that and look forward to lunch."

"OK, that's a winner. Oh, I'll be alone tomorrow, so if you have the urge and the opportunity, call me."

What's wrong with Martha?"

"She's babysitting her grandchildren; her daughter's going to a convention."

"OK, I'll call if I can. I'd better go. I've got a lot to do before I pick up the kids. See you tomorrow. Bye."

"Bye." I hung up and looked at my watch. It was twelve forty-five. Martha came into the drafting room and said, "I've finished with the resumes. Look them over and see if you have any changes so I can make them before I leave." She laid them on my desk.

I read them carefully, looking for any errors I may have made in my rough drafts. I knew Martha had corrected any spelling or grammar. When I was satisfied, I went out to Martha's desk and told her she could take off. "Looks great, as usual. Have a good time this weekend. I'll miss you, but I'll be OK. "

"I wish I could say the same. I love the kids, but I had other things I wanted to do this weekend. Now I've got to change my schedule so I can entertain them." She stood up and grabbed her pocketbook. "I'll see you Monday."

"Thanks for finishing the resumes. See you Monday."

She nodded a yes and smiled as she left.

I felt sorry for Martha. Her life hadn't been much since her husband's passing, but she should have the opportunity to spend it doing something besides babysitting.

I was working on Maria's house revising the floor plan when I heard Ann walk in. I turned and saw her as she entered the drafting room. She removed her scarf and unbuttoned her coat.

"Let me have your coat; I'll hang it in the closet."

She finished removing her coat and handed it to me. She was wearing a low cut green sweater, a form fitting gray skirt and black high heels, not the type attire I would expect from her. I put the coat and scarf in the closet and led her to the conference room. She sat down and crossed her legs, showing a little too much skin to suit me.

"How about a cup of coffee? It's instant so it won't take long to fix. Hot water's already on."

"That would be nice," she said. "A little sugar please."

My mind was racing as I fixed the coffee. Ann's appearance and manner disturbed me. This was definitely not the Ann I knew. I didn't want to read anything into this that wasn't intended, but I was worried.

"Here you go; service with a smile," I said and I was sporting a big one. I really didn't know what else to do, but I wanted this meeting to be relaxed and brief.

She was a beautiful woman but the ravages of alcohol were beginning to show. But she was attractive, and she was dressed to turn a male head. She leaned over her coffee and exposed a lot of cleavage. I was beginning to feel very uncomfortable and tried not to stare.

"Thanks, this hits the spot," she said. Except for her hand movements, she seemed relaxed and in control. I was not.

I decided it was time to kick the ball into her court. "Well. What do you want to talk to me about? I have a feeling that it's probably not architecture."

"You're very astute, Mr. Architect. It's not about architecture. It's about me. I need some advice and I don't want any of this conversation to leave this room. Is that agreed?" A serious look replaced her smile and her hands were clenched in her lap.

"Absolutely… this isn't about Garth, is it?"

"He's a major part of it."

"In view of our relationship, are you sure I'm the one you should talk to?"

"That's precisely why I want to talk to you. Also, I know I can trust you."

"True, but you may not like what I say."

"I understand and I'm prepared to deal with that."

"OK, what's the problem?"

She cleared her throat and licked her lips before she spoke. "It's no secret that I've had a drinking problem for some time. Socially I've become a pariah and if it weren't for Garth our friends wouldn't have wasted any time with me. I came to terms with that and stopped drinking three days after the country club dance. I swear to you, I haven't touched any alcohol since then. I'm sure you noticed that I didn't have a drink at your party."

"I did and I knew it wasn't easy for you or Garth. I was proud of you but I didn't want to make a big deal of it."

"Before I go any further, I want to apologize for my behavior at the dance. It's not much fun holding a drunk upright while pretending to dance." She laughed. "It's not too damn easy dragging a semi-dead body around. I'm surprised you didn't get a hernia."

"Come on, I was probably as drunk as you were. Besides, Jane said I was acting like a fool dancing with one of my clients. She was pretty embarrassed and damned mad."

"Well, I don't remember any of that, but it *was* the main topic of conversation for some time after the dance." She looked at me quizzically and said, "You're not having an affair with her, are you? She **is** very pretty."

I was shocked and visibly shaken. "Uh….what do you mean?" It was time to answer a question with a question, my usual line of defense. "Why would you think that?"

"To be honest, you and Jane seem to be drifting apart. That's a personal observation. Nobody else has said anything about it. I've always thought your marriage was the most solid one of our friends, but I'm not so sure anymore. I hope that's not the case, but I know things can happen when you're not happy."

"We've had a few problems, but nothing we can't fix. It's not anything that would push me into an affair. It's absurd to even think that."

"Forgive me. It's none of my business and I shouldn't have asked about it. What I need is some advice, and it has nothing to do with you and Jane. It's about me and Garth."

"OK. Let's talk about that. I have no interest in talking to you about Jane or me."

She smiled, leaned forward exposing more breast and said, "I agree." She stopped to take a sip of coffee. "I told you I've cleaned up my act, and I've done my best to make up for all the misery I've caused Garth. I'm sure he's been through hell taking care of a drunk, and I certainly haven't been a good wife during the last year, if you get my drift. The problem is that I'm trying desperately to respond to him, even to the point of being very aggressive sexually and he's rejecting me. I'm not strong enough to go through rejection, and I'm so afraid I'm going to fall off the wagon."

I was confused by her remarks. "I'm not sure what you expect from me, or even if I can help you. Do you want me to talk to Garth?"

"No, no! That would make him angry." She took another sip of coffee. "He may be trying to punish me, or he may have lost interest in me." Tears were welling up in her eyes.

"Look Ann. I can't solve your problem. I don't know if there's anything I can do. You're going to have to work this out yourself. Why don't you sit down with Garth and tell him what you're telling me? He may not realize how you feel. I'm sure he loves you very much and will do whatever he can to make you happy. My God, he's stayed with you through all this drinking. He's not going to leave you now."

She pulled a crumpled Kleenex tissue from her bag and dabbed at her eyes, they were beginning to streak from her mascara. She sighed and said, "Garth isn't treating me badly; he's just ignoring me. I've had so much rejection from men in my life – my father and now Garth. I just can't go through any more. I'm not a strong person and drinking is my way of coping with it."

She stood up and I assumed she was going to leave. I stood up and she moved toward me. She put her arms around me and rested her head on my chest. It was innocent enough, so I hugged her and patted her back to reassure her. That was a mistake. She pulled my head down and kissed me before I could move away. I pushed her away. "Hey, what's going on?"

She smiled as suddenly as she had begun crying. "What do you think is going on? I want you to make love to me."

I was stunned. I realized I was dealing with a very emotionally disturbed woman, and instinctively I knew I had better measure my words. "Ann, Jane is your friend and Garth is my oldest and probably my best friend. We've been buddies since grade school. I can't do that to him. I'd never be able to look him in the eyes again. It's not easy to say no to you. You're very beautiful and you sorely temp me. But you're not being fair to me."

She reached out to embrace me and I caught her hands. She said, "Why are you making such a big deal of this? How can it hurt them if they don't know? I'm not looking for a husband. I have as much to lose as you. We could meet discreetly every week or so and nobody would have to know." Her eyes were almost pleading.

I was in a no-win situation. I had to find a way to say no that she could accept. "Ann, I can't handle that kind of guilt. What you are offering me is a wonderful thing, but it isn't right for either of us. It would destroy a lifelong friendship. Is it worth that to you?"

She looked away and said in a monotone, "It's not a problem. When we're together socially, I would have no trouble ignoring you, especially if I knew I could have you when I wanted you."

"That's a pretty damned callous thing to say. Are you looking for a gigolo?"

"Of course not, but I have money and I could do a lot for you." For the first time, I thought she was not only crazy but also potentially dangerous. I could see that any further conversation was useless. "Look, let's just pretend this day never happened and maybe, after we've thought this through, we can discuss it again. I can't think about it anymore today."

Her eyes lit up. "Fair enough. I know I came on a little strong, but when you've had a chance to realize what I can give you, you'll come around. I'll call you in a week or so. By then I'll have something even better planned for you. Please get my coat. I've got to go."

Thank God, I thought as I hurried for her coat. She was a chameleon; her whole manner changed. She totally ignored me as I helped her with her coat. She made no further romantic overtures.

She turned as she reached the door and said flippantly, "I'll call you soon. Toodles." And she was gone.

I stood there for a minute, not fully comprehending what had happened. *I've known her for over ten years and never seen this side of her. She's always been quiet and reserved, never laughing at risqué jokes or taking part in any ribald conversation that emanates from too much liquor at late night parties. She's always come across as a little slow bordering on stupid, definitely wound too tight, or as a psychologist would say, anal-retentive. Maybe she's about to snap. She's definitely not normal.*

I didn't have a good feeling about her, and the thought was coming through that she could be very dangerous, especially if she saw Maria and me together. Garth should be told about her actions, but my heart wasn't in that resolution. The risk of losing his friendship was too great and I didn't want that to happen. No, I'd have to find another way. I needed some professional help. Suddenly I thought about Alma. She would be perfect.

Three years ago, two women had come to see me about renovation work for their house. They were middle aged and had been living together for many years in an old home near Five Points. Alma was a psychologist and her roommate, Charlene, was a librarian. Alma wore masculine clothes, kept her hair short, used no makeup, and was always in loafers or low heels. Charlene was very feminine, dressed stylishly and seemed to depend on Alma to make all their decisions. It was not difficult to determine that they were a dedicated, lesbian couple.

Their home was a typical vintage bungalow of the 1930s, a wood frame with stucco and painted wood exterior, a massive stone chimney, a large balustraded front porch and a steep shingled roof with dormers. Six large double-hung windows with twelve equal lights were spaced symmetrically across the front wall. It was a delightful, old home and had been maintained with loving care. Most of the work was remedial – plaster cracks, aging light fixtures, and defective hardware – and easy to fix. They also wanted to turn a bedroom into a den. I provided them with drawings and specifications, and recommended a building contractor I knew and trusted. The work took less than a month to complete and the ladies were thrilled with the results. That was the beginning of our friendship, and it became almost a ritual during the process to drop by on Thursday afternoons for a glass of scotch, conversation, and a few of Charlene's freshly baked cookies.

Most of the scotch drinking and conversation was between Alma and me while Charlene busied herself with domestic chores. Alma was an engaging conversationalist and a great listener, largely due to her training as a psychologist. She took a welcomed interest in the problems of a young and struggling architect with a growing family. She talked me through a number of problems and seemed to genuinely enjoy it. She became a surrogate mother to me. She would be perfect to talk to about Ann, and I just might mention Maria. I knew she never made moral judgments and would keep our conversations confidential.

I retrieved Alma's phone number from the rolodex and called her office. The receptionist answered and said she was with a patient, but she took my name and number and said she would have Alma call me. It was nearly five o'clock, so I knew it wouldn't be long.

I cleaned off my desk and drawing board and penciled in some items on my *to do* list. I wanted to review my resume once more, issue an addendum, call a few general contractors to request they bid on the Huguley residence, and catch up on any shop drawings I may have missed. The phone rang as I finished my last notation.

"Design Concepts, Terry Forte speaking."

"Terry.....Alma. I just finished my four o'clock and got your message. What's going on?"

"I'm not sure Alma. Maybe nothing, but I'm uncomfortable about a visit I had today from a good friend's wife. She's put me in a sticky situation and I don't know how to handle it. I need some advice."

"**Great** excuse to get together. We haven't seen you in some time and I just happen to have a fresh bottle of Glenlivet. Why don't you stop by in about thirty minutes? Charlene is going to be late, so we can have some time to ourselves."

Good old Alma, biggest heart in America. "I'll be there. Thanks Alma."

"See you in a little while. Bye."

Just talking to Alma made me feel better. She had a way of reducing situations to their essentials and letting **me** come up with the solutions. She asked questions and listened to my answers, guiding me along and getting me to focus on the problem. She did all this in a very relaxed manner, which made me feel comfortable in the process.

I grabbed the phone and called Jane. "Got to stop by Alma's on the way home. She's got a problem she wants me to look at. I'll be a little late," I said.

"Just be here by seven thirty. I'm cooking a roast and I just put it in the oven. If you're late we'll eat without you. And try to stay out of the scotch."

I laughed. "Think you know me like a book, eh? I won't promise not to have a scotch, but I'll keep it to a social minimum. Alma would be mad if I let her drink alone."

"Sure Terry. I'm certain she'll have to twist your arm. Anyway, just come as soon as you can."

"OK, I'll be there by seven thirty. Bye."

I took my usual tour around the office before grabbing my jacket, lowering the thermostat, and switching off the lights. I went outside and was greeted by a darkening sky with a wisp of light on the western horizon. The sun had made its exit and the temperature was falling. It was warmer than usual, the result of a warm front pushing through, but it would soon reach the forecast low of thirty-nine degrees.

I jumped in my car, pulled out of the parking lot and headed west toward Five Points. It was a short ride to Alma's, about ten minutes. The porch light was on and the front of the house was full of light all across the windows. I saw Alma walking around in the living room. She was watching for me, and met me at the door with two drinks of scotch and water in her hands. The front door entered into a living room full of antique furniture, oil paintings of European landscapes hung from picture molding, chair rails, and a deep crown molding at the soffit. This was obviously Charlene's touch. Alma was as much out of place here as a bale of hay.

"Can't beat that kind of service," I said with a big smile. She put both drinks down and gave me a familiar hug. "Well, a drink of scotch and a hug. What did I do to deserve that?" She had a wide smile on her round, ruddy face framed by her Dutch-boy hairstyle, and she had traded her trademark three-button jacket for a cardigan sweater.

"Nothing's too good for my favorite architect," she said as her eyes smiled into slits. "Let's sit in the den and do some serious drinking and talking. I haven't seen you in a while. We need to catch up." She motioned for me to sit in an overstuffed well-used chair with an ottoman; it had to be hers. "A tall drink of water like you needs some space." She sat opposite me and leaned forward in her chair. "Now, tell me what's going on with you that's so important?"

"Just like that, huh?"

"Why not?" She stopped just long enough to light a cigarette she had inserted into her holder. She exhaled a stream of smoke and said, "I'd like to hear what happened while it's fresh in your mind."

"You're right, Alma. I **would** like to forget it. I wish the whole thing had never happened. It seems like a bad dream." I lit a Kent and settled into the chair. "Before I start with this, it will help put things into perspective if I tell you what I know about her." I told her about Ann's family life, her search for her father's love, and her problems with alcohol. Alma smiled when I told her about my episode with her at the club dance. I even told her about getting in trouble with Maria. Then I went through the entire afternoon scenario, starting with the phone call and ending with Ann leaving. Alma said nothing while I progressed through the story, just nodding occasionally and smoking her cigarette, but I could see the wheels turning in her head.

"Terry, has she come on to you before? Or anybody else, for that matter?"

"No, she never has. She's shy and doesn't have much to say. Frankly, I didn't know she had it in her."

Alma blew a stream of smoke into the air. "Has she ever exhibited mood changes?"

"Not really. She's usually very quiet, very drunk, or both. If it weren't for Garth, she'd never be invited anywhere. He's a remarkable guy who everyone likes, so we put up with Ann. Fortunately, she's never caused any trouble. She just stays quiet and drinks herself into oblivion. For the most part, we ignore her."

Alma pushed her short hair back over her brow and stared at the ceiling. "Without knowing her medical history, I can't make a judgment, but I suspect she may have had similar symptoms in her youth. I believe she may be what we call bipolar, or at the worst, schizophrenic. She's definitely got some mental problems, but it could be associated with alcoholism. I'm surprised you haven't noticed it before."

"I haven't been around her alone when she's sober, until today. She's not the same person sober. Today, she was totally self-assured and aggressive. She didn't leave anything on the table. It's like she doesn't understand the meaning of NO."

"Well, you said her father gave her everything she wanted, except affection. That's not a prerequisite for NO. Do you think she might be jealous of your relationship with Garth? Seducing you might be a way to punish him. If you were older, it might be a father thing, but I don't see that as viable."

"Alma, she was pretty specific about not letting Garth know anything about her visit, and she let me know she just wanted to have an affair. Seems Garth is neglecting her since she's stopped drinking. I'm not sure why she's doing this."

Alma snorted. "Could be she's got a case of the seven-year itch. Don't rule out a case of the hornies. But she could be dangerous if she thinks she cares about you. Any gesture you make that could be construed by her as a return of affection will be interpreted that way, whether you mean it or not. Be very careful with her. She could cause you a lot of grief." She scratched her ear as she thought. "Some relationships are strange and sudden changes in behavior by one mate can provoke changes in the other. If her husband was always in control and lost that, he might retaliate by ignoring her, or even punishing her in some manner. Is he capable of that?"

"I don't think so Alma. He's the sweetest guy on earth, and has put up with her for a long time. It's not easy to stay with an alcoholic, and I don't think any change like hers would be anything but a plus as far as he is concerned. No, he would be pleased by her not drinking."

Alma smiled. "I'm just considering all the angles. I don't know him so I have to take your word about him. Of course, that may be a mistake and not very professional on my part. We'll leave it at that for now. Just be careful what you say to her."

"The last thing I want to do is encourage her; that would be a disaster. I told her having an affair was out of the question, but she wasn't listening. She doesn't care that Garth is one of my best friends, or that she has a relationship with Jane. She believes that we could pull it off and nobody would be the wiser. How can you reason with that?"

"You can't, but you can tell her that you're satisfied with your life and you're not interested. That probably won't do much good, but it will deter her to some extent. If she thinks your relationship with Jane is solid, she might give up. You can't get into trouble if you tell her that and mean it."

I gave her a wry smile. "I'm afraid I can't depend on that. She saw me dancing with a lady client of mine that went beyond normal behavior. In fact, since that time I've been having lunch with her, and it would really open up a can of worms if Ann knew it. She might use that to threaten me, or worse my client if I don't go along with her."

Alma tapped her cigarette out in the ashtray, and looked at me. "Would she suspect that something was going on between you and your client if she saw you together?"

"She might, but she IS my client. That's how I would explain it. I wouldn't want Jane to find out; after what happened at the dance, she would definitely suspect it wasn't totally kosher. But she's a very nice lady and I enjoy her company. She hasn't been here long, and she's already been recruited to help with the United Fund drive. You'd like her if you knew her."

Alma chuckled. "Give me one guess. Her first name isn't Maria, is it?"

I jerked forward in the chair. "You know her?" I said incredulously.

"You forget. My agency is part of United Fund. I sat with her at the first luncheon she attended. I can see why you like her. She's very attractive and intelligent." She stuck another cigarette into her holder, lit it and let the smoke trail upward from her mouth. "She and I got along famously and, in fact, have had lunch together once since then. I can't wait to tell her I know you." She said that with an impish smile.

"If you do, tell her I mentioned her as a new client. And don't mention this thing about Ann; I'm not sure if I should tell her about that."

Alma gave me a sideways look as if I had said a nasty word. "It's part of my job to be discreet. I won't get you in trouble and I won't mention this conversation, other than the drink and that we're old friends. She won't hear about Ann unless you tell her. The only information about you that she'll hear from me will be good."

I felt chastened and deserved it. "I'm sorry, Alma. I was reacting without thinking. I know whatever we talk about will never leave this room." I drank from my glass and smelled the malt aroma of the Glenlivet. The finger of warmth trickled down my throat to my stomach.

Alma stood and reached for my nearly empty glass. "How about one more?" she said.

"It's not often that I have the pleasure of Glenlivet, but unfortunately and with great sorrow, I have to refuse." I smiled and said, "The company ain't half bad either. But Jane's cooking a roast tonight and I promised her I'd be home when she opened the over door." I stood and finished my drink. "I really appreciate your listening to my problems. You always help me put things in perspective."

Alma patted my arm. "My door is always open anytime you want to talk.

Keep me posted on this Ann thing. I hope it dies a natural death, but I don't think it will."

I hugged her and started for the door. "You're right. I hope I don't do the wrong thing and make it worse."

"I know you well enough to know you won't. Keep in touch. It's been much too long since we've visited. I'll save the Glenlivet if you promise to come back soon."

I smiled at her. "That's an offer too good to turn down."

She closed the door behind me and the cold air embraced me. True to the forecast, the temperature had dropped significantly while I was at Alma's. At least the scotch had protected me from total shock. I drove away feeling a little better, but knowing my problem with Ann was far from over.

I pulled into the carport just as I was beginning to get comfortable. The heater was blasting and the windows were clouding up. I wasted no time striding swiftly to the back door, breathing in the heavy, cold air that was painful as it passed down my throat and into my lungs. Janet and Laurie had seen the car lights and were waiting for me as I burst through the door

"Hi Girls. It's getting cold outside. Not a good time for roll the bat."

Laurie made a face. "That's dumb, Daddy. Besides, it's too dark to play anyway."

I gave her a grin with lots of teeth. "I don't suppose for a minute that you didn't know I was kidding?"

"You tease so much, I never know."

I chuckled and pulled her ponytail. "How about a game of Monopoly after supper?"

Janet chimed in. "Can I get the game out and set it up on the dining room table?"

"If you want to, but no playing till after supper. Mom fixed a great supper for us and we don't want to mess it up. I can smell the roast," I said wrinkling up my nose in gratitude, "and I bet there's lots of potatoes, carrots, and onions in the pot, too."

"Yuk!" Laurie said. "You can have my onions."

"What's the matter? Think your boy friend might smell them?" I teased, jerking on her ponytail.

"Oh Daddy, you know I don't have a boyfriend."

"Oh yes she does Daddy," said Janet. "I saw her with him at recess yesterday. He gave her a candy bar. It was a Baby Ruth, one of those big ones."

"You didn't see anything Twerp," said Laurie.

I feigned interest with my eyes. "I don't believe I've heard about this. Who's the lucky boy?"

"I don't have a boyfriend," Laurie said. "He just sits next to me in class."

"So…who is he?" I asked.

Before she could answer, Janet replied with her hands on her hips and her face thrust forward for emphasis. "He **is too** your boyfriend, and his name is Jody Blankenship… so there!" Her defiant blue eyes were big as saucers.

"Wait a minute, Jumper. Let's hear what Laurie has to say."

"He's just a friend, Daddy. All of us play together at recess. He gave me the candy bar because he can't eat it. He's diabetic, or something like that, I don't know what it means. Anyway, I can't have a boyfriend because I'm just a third grader." She seemed satisfied with her rebuttal.

That's good enough for me," I said. "What about you, Jumper? Do you have a boyfriend?"

"Daddy, I don't ever want a boyfriend. I hate boys."

"OK," Jane said from the kitchen, "everything is ready. Go wash your hands Girls."

After the drink of scotch at Alma's and the fragrant odor of comfort food cooking, I was starving. "OK girls, chop chop. Dad's ready to eat." I was also looking forward to a game of Monopoly with the kids. Maybe we could entice Jane to play. I decided that helping to clean up after supper might help.

I woke up full throttle Friday morning and hit the floor with enthusiasm. I was full of paternal well-being after a wonderful supper and Monopoly with the family. I knew that part of that good feeling had to do with my impending luncheon with Maria, but I wanted to enjoy the paternal feeling while I had the opportunity.

I whistled through my morning routine and made my way to the kitchen, where Jane was hard at work preparing breakfast. The table was set for four so I assumed the children were awake. Jane, in her robe with her hair in rollers, was standing in front of the range frying eggs. A pot of grits was boiling, a plate heaping with bacon was on the counter, and toast was in the oven.

Jane smiled as I entered and said, "My, we're happy today. I haven't heard that kind of whistling since Mama's canary died. You went through every tune in your repertoire."

"I would have done more but the hot water gave out."

"I won't dignify that comment. Why don't you get the paper? Everything will be on the table when you get back."

"OK. I'll just be a minute." I jogged to the mailbox to minimize my exposure to the cold. The air was still frigid, heavy with what smelled like ozone after a summer storm. The sun was pulling itself reluctantly over the horizon, laying a hazy band of light across a darkened sky, but it didn't affect my happy countenance. I grabbed the paper and whistled every step back to the door. Big day coming!

When I returned the girls were sitting at the table, but they didn't reflect my exuberance. Janet was rubbing sleep from her eyes and Laurie was partially dressed but yawning with every breath. They were cute little munchkins, but I knew better than tease them. They didn't awaken well, just like their mother.

I smiled at each of them and said, "Laugh, and we'll play Monopoly tonight."

Janet stuck her tongue out and Laurie tried hard, but it came out "Ho, Ho."

"Now is that the best you can do?"

"Oh, Daddy," grumped Laurie. "That's not fair. Let us wake up. You know we want to play. It's just too hard to laugh when you get up."

"Yea," Janet said rubbing her eyes. "You don't always get up happy. Besides, you've had a shower and you're wide awake."

"You're right, Jumper. I guess I'll play whether you laugh or not." I graced them with another smile, expecting a rush of gratitude. It wasn't forthcoming.

"If I don't have much homework," Laurie said.

"I don't detect much enthusiasm," I said.

Janet grabbed my hand quickly and her clear blue eyes were suddenly wide open and awakened. "Please Daddy, we really want to play. We'll get our homework done as soon as we get home."

"First graders don't have homework," said Laurie.

"I'll clean up our room if you do your homework as soon as you get home from school," said a pleading Janet.

"Oh boy! That's a deal," said Laurie. She wasn't disposed to do any cleaning if she could help it. I had gained enough concessions. It was time to give them the final victory. Besides, it was Friday. Janet had all weekend to do homework.

"We'll have our game when I get home," I said magnanimously.

Janet jumped up from her chair and clapped her hands. "Goody, goody goody," she said. 'I'll have everything ready when you get home, Daddy."

I laughed and said, "Let's eat supper first. I can't play if I'm hungry." I finished the last of my eggs and said to Jane, "That was good. Should carry me through the day."

"Thanks, the cook appreciates that. Supper might not be as good."

I wrinkled my nose. "We'll see." I took my plate, juice glass and coffee cup to the sink. "Time to go; I'll see you tonight."

"Don't be late. I want the girls in bed before ten."

"I won't," I said as I got my jacket and made for the door. "See you later."

44

I drove quickly to the office, listening to the Beatles on the radio and feeling good all over. Even with a light haze, the sky was pretty with a scattering of low clouds and a broad band of light above the horizon. The temperature was rising and no frost was evident, a rarity for December. I parked and walked briskly to the office, whistling my way through the door. Inside, it was dark and cool and I suddenly realized why. Martha was at home with grandchildren.

I switched the lights on, set the thermostat to seventy-two degrees, and put the teapot on the hot plate. I felt the need for coffee and a cigarette. I was excited like a child on Christmas Eve. That was a little much, considering that lunch was five hours away, but Maria did that to me. I had to put a damper on the excitement if I wanted to get any work done. *Weird how a grown man can get so worked up over an hour of lunch in a public place with an attractive woman.* High school all over again. I heard the teapot whistling; perhaps coffee would help. I lit a cigarette, made a cup of coffee, and trudged upstairs to the loft. The morning sun was slashing through the blinds, forming ladder patterns on the wall. It was inviting. Maybe I would be able to work in such an appealing atmosphere. I switched on the desk lamp and my radio and, much to my surprise, heard the first Christmas music of the year. *White Christmas* played softly and it added to my feeling of well-being. Thanksgiving was hardly over. I wouldn't be surprised if it were skipped next year with Christmas being thrust upon us earlier each year. But the merchants won't let that happen. Got to get that Thanksgiving sale in before the Big One.

It was time to earn my keep. I snubbed out my cigarette, picked up a pencil and drew some lines. I tried to put Maria and lunch in the back of my mind. Fat chance!

45

Maria didn't call early so I left the office at one fifteen. The usual crowd – if you can call winos, vagrants, construction workers and two lovers usual – at the Blizzard Shop had thinned out when I arrived, but I didn't see Maria. I winked at Angie and took my place in the last booth, facing the door so I could see Maria when she came in. Angie didn't make any move to get my order. She knew I would be having company. I put some coins for the juke box on the table. When Maria came through the door, I would play *Stranger on the Shore.* I hoped she would be visible through the layer of cigarette smoke that was a permanent fixture of the restaurant.

She came through the door quickly, coat-tails flying, and gave me a big smile. I loved to watch her walk with her cat-like grace and athletic stride, and my heart skipped a beat or two before she sat down across from me. She motioned for me to sit by her, but I had begun that move, after dropping a dime into the juke box and punching C-3. I slid onto the bench and kissed her quickly, my reward for today. Acker Bilk played our song, *Stranger on the Shore.*

Maria grabbed my hand and said, "I've missed you." That was a perfect opening line. "I'm sorry I was late. I got trapped by the director and had to plead a headache." She hesitated. "But I love you."

"You really know how to start a conversation."

"I wasn't a speech major for nothing. Do you have a cigarette? I need to relax a minute before we eat. I feel like I've been running all day."

I grabbed two Kents and lit them both, doing my best Humphrey Bogart. I handed her one. "Here," I said. "I don't make you nervous, do I?" I put on a devilish face.

"Every time I see you," she said with a chuckle. "That's what makes you so interesting."

"I was hoping you'd say I made you passionate," I said.

"Oh, you do. But I'll have to control myself. They might not let us come back if I get too carried away."

"I believe I detect a bit of sarcasm."

"Well, don't ask silly questions." She blew smoke in my face.

I took a big drag off my cigarette and studied her face as I exhaled. Her amber-green eyes were sparkling and her full lips were turned up in a slight smile. She looked so young and exciting. I wanted to reach out for her. I wondered if she knew how attractive she was. I could look at her for hours, breathing her in like a beautiful, fragrant flower. Her hair smelled of scented shampoo and her perfume was almost understated as it reached out for me.

"Did I tell you I've missed you?" I asked.

"No, but I hope you have."

"I think we need to visit the cabin.......maybe next week? Maybe Monday?"

Maria hesitated. "I don't know about Monday. Too early in the week for me to know what Pat will be doing. I'd like to, but I won't know anything until Monday morning."

I frowned. "Well, Tuesday's out. That's Bill's day, and Wednesday's golf day. If Monday won't work, maybe Thursday will. Damn, I miss you. I'm not sure I can wait that long."

"This isn't easy," Maria said. "They're too many people in the equation. I could get away for a few hours, but I don't like to have to make up stories. It's dangerous."

"You're right. We can't take chances and we can't change our routines."

"While we think and plan," she said, "my routine says I'm hungry. Why don't we order something?"

I laughed. "I was trying my best to order YOU, but I'm striking out. I guess food is the next option." I motioned to Angie.

"I'd like to pursue that later. Now I'm hungry. One appetite at a time."

Angie shuffled over and took our order. It was becoming routine. Two cheese burgers without onions (my sacrifice), two Cokes, and a piece of apple pie to share. She had written it down before she came over. I put two dimes into the jukebox, punched B4 and C3. *Smokey Places* was up first.

Maria snubbed out her cigarette. Mine was gone. "If I can make it Monday, would the morning be a problem? It'll be easier if I can tie it in with taking the children to school. I've got some errands to run, so I wouldn't be noticed if I took some time then."

"I don't care about the time. I just want to see you. I'll need about twenty minutes with Martha. She'll want to know what's happened while she was off and what she can work on. I'll make a 'to do' list for her this afternoon. I can keep her busy until she leaves at noon. I kinda like that. She can take care of things until I return. That way, the office won't be unmanned."

I saw a sudden playful look on Maria's face. "Who says I'm going to let you go early?"

"I assumed you wouldn't have much time, but I can be flexible ...if you have the time and you aren't teasing me."

"You never know," Maria said. "If Pat's not around, I could stay until I have to pick up the kids. I might even bring some lunch for us. It won't be elaborate. I don't generally take lunch with me when I'm carpooling. The kids would ask a lot of questions."

"Don't bother with that. We can pick up something. Food is not an issue. I have other things on my mind."

"I should hope so." She blinked at me tilting her head down provocatively and licked her bottom lip.

"I wasn't kidding."

"I know. I was trying to add some levity. We can't get serious in here."

Angie appeared out of the layer of fog-like smoke, her shuffling gait reminiscent of my childhood recollections of Frankenstein movies. She put our order on the table. "Here you are," she said. "Enjoy." And she was gone. She left a bill for $1.42.

I didn't realize how hungry I was until the tantalizing aroma of the cheeseburger titillated my senses. Maria opened her burger, sprinkled it liberally with salt and pepper, added a dollop of catsup, and took a big bite.

"Umm...that's good. I'm glad you introduced me to the Blizzard Shop. As good as these burgers are, I guess it will remain one of our secrets."

I looked at her solemnly and said, "It's our place. I don't want anyone else to ever know about it. That probably sounds silly, but that's how I feel." I bit into my burger.

"No, I understand what you mean. Our place, our song, and our food. I want it to always be ours."

We finished the burgers and Maria split the apple pie with her fork and pushed the plate toward me. The crust was light and flaky, and the apples were sweet with a tiny bit of tartness.

"Couldn't be better," I said. "Almost as good as sex."

"I don't believe you said that," she said. She giggled and pushed her hair back from her forehead.

I glanced at my watch. It was nearly two thirty. My God, where had the time gone? It seemed as though it had been no more that 15 minutes. There was so much to talk about and so little time. My father was fond of saying that God gave mankind three score and ten years. By my reckoning, that's over 25,000 days. I had already used almost 11,000. If they continued at this speed, I really didn't have much time left.

"What are you planning for the weekend?" I asked.

"I'm not sure. We usually go out with Ricky and Harry and the rest of the bunch – the ones we went to the club dance with. We'll probably go to somebody's house and have drinks, then somewhere to have dinner. That's supper to you, Southern boy. That's not very definitive, but that's the best I can do on short notice. How about you?"

"Well, my social world isn't as definitive as yours. We'll probably eat **supper** at home and then watch television. Dinner's for Yankees."

She stuck out her tongue. "Don't get smart with me, Southern boy. I might not bring you a sandwich Monday."

"I hope you have the opportunity, but don't worry about the sandwich. My hunger is substantial, but a sandwich is not the answer."

"Umm........I think I like that answer," she said.

"It's honest," I said with a smile.

"Are you working over the weekend?" she asked.

"I may, probably Sunday afternoon. I need to do some things around the house. That will take care of Saturday. Call me if you have a chance, but make it after two."

"Sunday's difficult, but I will if I have an opportunity."

"Change the subject for a minute," I said. "I understand you know Alma, Alma Hooper."

She looked startled. "Alma who works with Mental Health?"

"Yep. She's a good friend of mine."

"Small world. I met her at a United Fund luncheon. I really like her. What do you know about her?"

"Let's see... she's gracious, interesting to talk to, good listener, likes people, keeps a secret...and is probably a lesbian. What else would you like to know?"

"The obvious. How do you know her?"

"She's an old client of mine. I stop by occasionally for a drink and some conversation with her and her roommate, Charlene. I stopped by last night. That's how I knew she had met you." I was hoping she wouldn't ask how her name came up or why I was there. I wasn't ready to tell her about Ann or my penchant for running my personal problems by Alma.

"We have the same opinion about her. I think she's a wonderful woman. I didn't know about the lesbian thing. I did notice her clothes were a bit severe and she eschews makeup, but that doesn't bother me. She's a delight to talk to and she **does** listen. I suppose that comes with being a psychologist."

"Probably. But I just enjoy her. Charlene's OK, but Alma's more open and comfortable without her. That's my personal opinion and it may be wrong. Alma likes her scotch and Charlene tries to cut her off."

"You're not upset about her being a lesbian, are you?"

"Of course not. I'm partial to women myself. Just don't like the competition."

Maria smiled. "I don't think that's competition."

"You might be a little bit prejudiced."

"I might be…Hey! I've got to go. It's almost three o'clock. My kids will think I've forgotten them." She gave me a nudge to get me out of her way.

"You're not getting away that easily," I said. I leaned over and kissed her. "Now you can go." I patted her leg and let my hand linger.

"Watch it Buddy. Don't get something started we can't finish. Monday's a long way off and it's going to be hard to keep you out of my mind until then." She moved my hand, but she did it in a way that indicated remorse.

"You're right, as usual. I just have trouble keeping my hands off you. I'm sorry."

"Don't be. I like it. This just isn't the place for it." She stood, smoothed her skirt, and put her coat on. "I'll try to call Sunday. It's a long shot, but you never know. I'll try my best to work things out for Monday. By then I'll need a day at the cabin. Terry Forte, you're beginning to be an addiction."

"Is that good or bad?"

"I'm not sure. When we're together, it's very good. When we're not, it can be very painful." She looked at me for a moment, kissed her fingertips and touched my mouth. "I'll see you Monday. To think otherwise is not a happy thought."

I whispered, "I love you," as she turned to go. She never looked back, a trait I had learned to live with.

I finished Martha's list of things to do, cleared my desk of routine tasks, and decided to leave the office early. I hadn't done that in a long time, but what the hell? Maybe I could spend some time outside with the girls. The weather had improved. My outside thermometer was sitting on 64 degrees, so it was warm enough to play roll the bat. That would make Janet happy and maybe it would help the depression I felt coming on. I hate it when I get depressed and don't know why. Maybe I did know. *Spending all my time waiting to see or talk to Maria might be the culprit, but I know I'll never get off that rollercoaster as long as she's part of my life. Kinda like a duck hunter who wears himself out waiting for that one shot at dawn before the ducks fly away. He keeps coming back and so will I. That's a poor comparison, but it's the only one I can come up with.*

I didn't waste any time getting home. I made it in record time. Jack Kochman and his hell drivers would have been envious – not for my skill, but for my recklessness. As though they had read my mind, both girls were in the front yard playing catch with the softball. That helped with my level of depression. I parked the car quickly and joined them.

"How about a quick game of roll the bat before the sun goes down?" I asked.

Janet came at me, wide-eyed, skipping and hopping. I didn't know how she did both at the same time, but her ability to do so was responsible for her nickname, Jumper. I caught her under her arms and twirled her around.

"Do it again, Daddy," she said. "That's fun."

"I don't think I can. I'll use up all my energy and not be able to play ball."

"Just once more, Daddy. Please!"

I couldn't say no to her enthusiastic pleading. "OK, but just once more." I gave her another twirl and pulled away. She wouldn't give up easily.

"Ok Daddy, but you have to play roll the bat with us. Laurie, do you want to play?"

"If we can still play Monopoly later. Can we do both, Daddy?"

"Sure, why not? It's Friday. We can sleep late tomorrow." The girls were helping my moodiness.

"I'll pitch. Laurie, you catch and let Jumper bat first. We're going to change the rules so both of you get to bat more. We're counting strikes, but four instead of three before you're out. No more just getting up there and swinging till you hit the ball. Get up to the plate, Jumper."

I lofted the first pitch underhanded and very slow. Janet swung at it before it arrived and missed it by a foot.

"Strike one. Three more to go." I threw another one and she popped it up right to me.

"You're out, Jumper," said Laurie. "Give me the bat." She did so grudgingly, but she knew she was out when I caught the ball.

Laurie took her place at the plate and I lofted the first pitch to her. She tipped it and it went over Jumper's head.

"Strike one," I said. Jumper retrieved the ball and threw it to me. I went into a windmill wind-up and threw her a slow pitch. Laurie didn't come close. That was Janet's signal to razz Laurie.

"You swing like a washer woman," Jumper said. She hooted and said, "Strike her out, Daddy."

"Oh shut up, Pipsqueak," Laurie said crowding the plate. I could tell she was determined to hit the next pitch. I tried my best to pitch it into her swing plane. She shut her eyes and swung as hard as she could, but she was way ahead of it.

Jumper cackled. "She can't hit it Daddy. Strike her out." She shoved the ball at Laurie's nose before throwing it back.

I knew with her determination Laurie would be swinging hard, so I threw it a little faster and chest high. The bat cracked against the ball and it sailed over my head. Slugger came through. Mudville would be a happy place today, at least for one. Janet was sulking, but I knew that was momentary sibling rivalry.

"Good hit," I said. Laurie was smiling from ear to ear, but didn't make any comment. She wasn't quite so lucky with her next attempt. After a strike, she hit it right back to me and I caught it easily. "OK, you're out. It's Janet's turn."

We played until the sun fell over the edge of the earth, pulling the warm air with it. It was a lot of fun for us, and I enjoyed the semi-combative banter between the girls. *Sometimes, I forget how much fun they are.* By the time we got inside and cleaned up, Jane had supper ready for us. She had fixed one of my favorites: hamburgers cooked in onions and gravy, rice, and English peas. She had my mother's recipe, and the familiar aroma lifted my spirits and filled me with sudden hunger. The world was becoming a happy place.

Friday night also was fun. After supper, I convinced the girls that if we helped clean up the kitchen, we could start Monopoly sooner. They took the bait, and without too much grumbling, did their part. We quit playing at ten o'clock, as Jane had suggested, and the girls were tired and ready for bed. School, roll the bat, and Monopoly had taken its toll.

Jane and I watched television until the news came on. Then we went to bed. Sleep came quickly for both of us.

Saturday morning was pleasant. I slept until ten thirty. After a breakfast of eggs, bacon, and grits, I put on work clothes and started on a list of work items Jane had prepared. She had them prioritized so I started with the top dog, washing the windows. I worked on the inside first so the temperature outside could get into a comfortable range. It was two o'clock before I was ready to tackle the outside. I started on the north side while the sun was at its warmest, and worked toward the south from the east. At four thirty, I had the job finished. With the little bit of daylight I had left, I decided to wash Jane's car. That wasn't the number two item, but it fit in the schedule better. It was dark before I could do anything on the inside, but the outside looked like new.

When I got inside, Jane was cooking supper. The house smelled wonderful – a mixture of smoked pork chops in a spicy tomato sauce, potatoes and corn. We had forgone lunch to maximize the work day, so I was inordinately hungry. I was pretty dirty, too, and Jane wrinkled up her nose in disgust when I walked into the kitchen.

"I know. I need a bath," I said.

"You sure do. We'll have to burn the bath water." She was laughing. "Your face is filthy. Don't look in the mirror. You look like a poor man's clown."

"But the windows are clean and your car looks good."

"True, but you don't look good. Get your bath. Supper's almost ready."

"Yassuh boss," I said and patted her on the butt with my clean hand. She retaliated with a glower, but it was done good-naturedly.

I went to the bathroom, stripped off my sweaty clothes and jumped into the shower. The warm jets of water felt invigorating, buffeting and vibrating the grime off my body. I stayed in the shower a long time, soaping and rinsing until

I felt totally clean. The depression I had felt Friday was slipping away. My grandmother always said, "Work is good for the soul." She was a smart woman.

I toweled off quickly, shaved, and brushed my teeth. I was a new man. I pulled an old pair of slacks and a lightweight sweater from the closet, slipped them over my under shorts and t-shirt, jumped into a comfortable pair of beat up moccasins, and headed for the kitchen.

Jane was standing at the kitchen cabinet, in the middle of a cornucopia of wonderful aromas, whipping potatoes in the mixer. Boy! That woman can cook. I couldn't wait to break bread.

"If that tastes half as good as it smells I'll be a happy man." I reached around her waist and gave her a hug.

"Careful" she said. "Don't hug the chef. Show some respect and your gratitude in other ways."

"I've already done that," I said, alluding to my completed work.

"What's done is done. Don't dwell in the past." She said that with a straight face. She smiled and said, "I was just kidding. I appreciate what you did."

I ran my fingers through my wet hair and stretched. "I didn't get many things on your list done. The sun gave out on me."

"You did enough. It would take me two days to wash all the windows. That's a job. And you washed the car, too." She smiled warmly and kissed me lightly on my mouth. "Now that you're all cleaned up, I can do that."

I laughed and said, "Now I know the secret. Cleanliness is next to Godliness."

"It is if you're as dirty as *you* were."

I walked to the stove and lifted the lid off the frying pan. It was full of smoked pork chops swimming in a rich sauce that smelled strongly of onions, catsup, vinegar and Tabasco sauce. "Um, um. That smells mighty good. I guess you'll make me wait until everything is ready before I can sample one?"

Jane slapped my hand and said, "Put the lid back on the pan. You can fill your plate first, but you'll have to wait on the rest of us before you do. Being first in line is your only privilege."

"How much longer?" I asked.

"Get the girls cleaned up. Everything's ready. Since you're so famished, we'll serve from the stove."

"Winner! I'm on my way."

I found the girls in the den watching television. "Supper's ready. Last one there's a rotten egg."

"Daddy, that's stupid," said Laurie, but she did disengage from the sofa and move toward the kitchen. Janet was really engrossed in whatever they were watching, so I tugged on her hair.

"Mashed potatoes," I whispered into her ear. That got her attention even though she missed the part about the rotten egg. I decided not to raise that issue again. Maybe Laurie was right. Problem was I was the last one to the kitchen. I guess I was the rotten egg.

47

Sunday morning came with its usual wild antics, everyone sleeping till the last minute before frantically trying to get ready for church. Everyone screamed at the top of their lungs for an advantage. *If my girls remember all this mayhem, they'll never want to go to church when they become adults.*

Somehow, we were out of the house with fifteen minutes to spare, and made it to church on time. If the preacher needed a miracle to preach about he could talk about how we did it. We settled into a pew looking like the perfect family, well dressed and groomed, with nary a sign of the conflict we suffered through getting there.

After church, we hurried to the Friendly in time to beat the folks from First Baptist, which is the largest church in town and the biggest contributor to the cafeteria dinner crowd. When we got inside, only a few people were in line. The fire and brimstone group must be suffering through a long sermon. We were in our seats and eating before the influx of diners filled up the serving line.

After lunch, I drove slowly down Main Street so Jane could see what was in the store windows. That was a habit we picked up from our parents. Taking advantage of the moderate weather, a few people in their Sunday finery were walking on the sidewalks to see and be seen. That also was part of the ritual.

When I reached the end of Main at the Capital building, I headed for home.

When I pulled into the driveway and stopped, I left the engine running. I patted Jane's hand and said, "I've got a few things I need to do at the office. I won't be long. Probably be back by four."

She pushed my hand away and answered, "For God's sake, Terry, it's Sunday! Can't you stay home just one weekend?" I could see the resignation in her eyes and I knew her question was more rhetorical than substantive. She wouldn't make a big issue of it.

Not so the girls. Janet said immediately, "Oh Daddy, why do you have to go to work? We could play roll the bat, or Monopoly."

"There will be time for that when I come back," I said, but I felt a bit of guilt. I knew that work had no part in my decision, but I had to go. I couldn't bear the thought of missing a call from Maria. The fact that she might not call was not important. I had to be there if she did.

Janet pouted. "No there won't," she said indignantly. "It'll be dark when you come home if you stay till four. Can't you come home earlier?"

"I'll try, Jumper," I said and I meant it. I rubbed her head but she moved away and jumped from the car. Her sudden dismissal caught me off guard and gave my heart a twinge, but my mind was made up. I watched them walk into the house and then I drove away. Twenty minutes later, I was in my office. Thirty minutes later when Maria called, my guilt was gone. She said Monday looked like a go. *Wonderful news.*

Was it worth going to the office? Would I do it again? You better believe it. Besides, I made it home before four.

I woke up Monday morning listening to raindrops tapping against the windowpanes. It would have been a good day to stay in bed a little longer, but the sudden realization that Maria might be able to go to the cabin today sent a wave of adrenaline through my body that literally jerked me out of bed. A whirlwind is the best way to describe my movements through showering and shaving, although I did spend more time showering and adding, perhaps a bit too much, cologne.

I was in the kitchen eating a bowl of cereal when Jane, in her bathrobe and rollers, walked in.

"You're either hungry or in a hurry. I had plenty of time to fix your breakfast." She appeared to be in a huff.

"A little bit of both," I said. "I have some early appointments and need some time to prepare for them."

Jane sniffed the air. "Well, whoever they are, I hope they like English Leather. Smells like you bathed in it. What's the occasion?"

"I poured too much of it in my hand and used it rather than waste it. I'll drive with the window open. That should take care of it."

"I should hope so," she said. "You smell like a bordello."

"Message received," I said. I moved to the sink, washed my hands vigorously, and wiped my face with paper towel after I dried my hands. Then I playfully slapped her on her derriere. "That's for knowing what a bordello smells like."

She smiled but I don't think she thought it was funny. "I guess since you're going to work to early, you can be home for an early supper?"

I wasn't sure whether it was a statement or a question, but I decided I'd better answer in the affirmative. "Sure, what are you planning for supper?" A question after an answer that I knew would be well received was a good way to change the direction of the conversation.

"I don't know... something quick and easy so you can spend some time with the girls. Maybe spaghetti and meat sauce. Pick up some French bread on the way home and I'll toast it with some garlic butter."

I pulled out my ever-present pocket calendar and noted the bread. "Sounds good." I put my bowl in the sink, kissed Jane on the cheek and said, "Good-bye."

"Get the paper for me before you go, please. I don't want to get out in the rain."

"No problem. If you wait at the door, I'll hand it to you." I jogged to the newspaper box at the street and ran back to the door. Jane was standing inside the door with it slightly ajar. I stuck it through the crack and ran to the car. The entire operation took less than thirty seconds.

I backed the car out of the carport into the turn around and started the windshield wipers. The rain was falling just hard enough to be a problem, but, on low speed, the wipers were more than adequate. The temperature was in the fifties, so the rain, a gray blanket snuggled around the car was pleasant. If Maria could get out, it would be a perfect day to be together. The excitement was building. I was so distracted that I turned into the parking lot not remembering how I got there. *That's what I call concentration!*

I jogged through the drizzle, bobbing and weaving to miss the pools that were forming in pavement depressions, went inside, and completed the litany of tasks – switching on the lights, setting the thermostat, and putting water on for coffee – that were part of my morning agenda. As soon as the water came to a boil, I made my first cup of coffee and lit a cigarette. It was the first of many that I would smoke during the day, but it was always the most enjoyable and the one I looked forward to. Of course, smoking after sex wasn't bad either, and I hoped I had that to look forward to also.

I was hoping Maria would call before Martha arrived so I could come up with a plausible reason to be out of the office if everything was a go. I don't know why I should worry about Martha. After all, I'm the boss. I guess it's because she's a woman and she's older. Some remnant of Southern culture that was planted in me at an early age.

Maria called fifteen minutes later. "Hi," she said. "Everything looks good. The kids just left, Pat's been gone about an hour, and I'm just sitting here all by myself, waiting for somebody to take advantage of me."

"I think you've reached the right person. I'm sorry you can't see the smile on my face."

She laughed. "I'm not too interested in your smile, Big Boy. When can you leave and where can we meet? I don't think across from the Governor's mansion is a good place this time of day."

"Not good," I said. "Do you know where the City Shopping Center is on North Main?"

"Ummm … I'm not sure. Give me some clues."

"Well, do you know where Main Street is?"

"Of course, I'm not stupid. I've been here long enough to know where Main Street is. How far is it from Elmwood?"

"Probably six or seven blocks. I'm not exactly sure, but that's close. There's a Winn-Dixie on the left end as you face it and it's on the right side of Main. I think there's a laundry on the other end. It's the only shopping center in that area."

"I'll find it. I may go early and get us something to snack on. I'll park in front of the Winn-Dixie."

"That's good. When can you leave?"

"Anytime. You tell me."

"It's eight thirty. I need about thirty minutes here, so lets say nine fifteen."

"Great! Just look for the lady in the raincoat and guess if there's anything under it." She was laughing.

"I know what's under it. I've seen the package without the wrapper….and I like it."

"Good, cause you're going to see a lot of it."

It was my turn to laugh. "I like the way you talk. A little obscene without a single bad word. That takes talent."

"Enough of this. I'll see you at nine-fifteen. Bye."

I heard dial tone before I could say goodbye. That was typical of her. I lit another cigarette and made my way to the workroom for more coffee. I needed a moment to think about something plausible to tell Martha, something that had some stretch in it in case I was gone longer than a few hours. It wouldn't take much. I needed something beyond the reach of the telephone to carry me past lunchtime. Martha would leave at noon. I could say that I had some errands to run and leave it at that unless she asked where I would be. I decided my backup would be that I was calling on a few legislators at the State House about state projects coming up that I might have a chance at. That was certainly vague enough and would allow me all the time I needed. I congratulated myself with a new cup of coffee and my third cigarette.

The door opened and shut and I heard Martha say, "Where's the fire?" There's enough smoke in here to choke a mule." Good old Martha.

"The place was full of mosquitoes when I came in. I think someone left the windows open. I'm smoking them out."

"Sure," she said. "I'm not going to honor that stupid statement. Just keep it up and you'll kill yourself with those coffin nails. And remember I told you so."

She was serious and I knew it. She probably was also right. "I'm going to quit, Martha. I just haven't made up my mind when."

"Yea, yea. I've heard that before. Just don't wait until you die to quit."

"Martha, you sound like you're on a mission."

"I wish I had been a long time ago and I don't' think I would have lost my husband. That's why I hate it. Think about all the people you know who died before they reached sixty and how many of them smoked. That's all the proof I need even if I don't have the facts or statistics to back it up."

In my mind I went through an inventory of people I knew who died young, other than accidents, and all of them smoked. "You're right, Martha. That makes sense."

She smiled. "You're too smart to let a bad habit kill you. Now, what's on tap for today?"

"I'm going down to the State House and see if I can buttonhole a few legislators about projects coming up this year. They're not in session yet so I can talk to them informally, if I can find any. I left some things for you and, if you have time, run me a set of the Huguley specs to use as an outline for the Watson house. I may not get back before you leave so leave them on my desk upstairs."

"Anything else you can think about?" she asked.

I looked quickly at my watch; it was almost nine o'clock. "No, if I think of anything I'll call."

Thankfully, she dismissed me with a nod and went to work without further words. I made my way to the closet and picked up my jacket. As I started for the door, Martha said, "It's raining pretty hard out there. Do you want to take my umbrella?"

"Thanks, but I'd better not. I don't know how long I'll be. I'd hate to be responsible for your getting wet when you leave. See you later." I didn't wait for Martha's answer. I bolted out the door into the rain. It was raining harder and the pools of water I walked around this morning had become more like a river. I jumped into the car and kicked off my shoes. They were full of water and my socks were soaking wet. Nevertheless, my enthusiasm was boundless. It was still warm for December, and being wet was not uncomfortable, merely a nuisance.

I cranked up the car (a quaint Southern expression from days gone by, started the wipers) and drove cautiously to the exit. Once onto the street, I headed for north Main. My watch indicated nine o'clock. The shopping center was ten minutes away, and I turned into the parking lot with five minutes to spare. Maria's car was easy to spot in front of Winn-Dixie. I parked on the driver's side. I was apprehensive about all the open space, but the rain provided a sense of protection that probably existed only in my mind. It spilled across the landscape coloring everything gray, obliterating the horizon. The engine remained running while I waited.

Maria emerged from the store wearing a hooded raincoat. She was carrying two grocery bags. She walked quickly to my car. I slid across the seat to open the door for her. She put the bags into the back seat before jumping in the front.

She smiled and patted my leg. "What an absolutely perfect day!"

I laughed. "It's more than appropriate, but it would be perfect without the rain. I'd like to help you get out of the coat, but I'm afraid to after what you said."

"Come on," she said. "I'm not that brave." She unbuttoned it and I slid it off her shoulders.

"What's in the bags?" I asked as I drove slowly from the parking lot.

"Not much. Ham, bread, mayonnaise, and mustard. I hope you like whole wheat bread."

"I do."

"I got a few Cokes. I didn't want to use any more of your friend's, and there's some fruit and cookies too. Oh I got some sliced Swiss. I like it with ham."

"Sounds like a gourmet meal to me, but I can wait for that."

She pouted. "I should hope so. It's just a little after nine."

I reached for her hand. "You know what I mean."

"I do, I do. Get this car moving," she said.

I drove as fast as I could under the circumstances. The rain was coming down harder and visibility was limited. "There's the turn-off," I said as I slowed and turned carefully. The front wheels bumped at the transition from asphalt to dirt.

"I'm just glad we were able to come," Maria said.

"Me too," I answered. I watched the road for washouts and managed to avoid most of them. I pulled up close to the door and killed the engine.

"Sit still while I unlock the door. I'll plug the heater in so the bedroom can warm up. I'll be back in few minutes. Maybe I can find an umbrella in there."

"Don't worry about that. Get the door open. I'll be right behind you."

It was really raining hard when I got out of the car, so I bolted for the door with the key in my hand. As soon as I got the door open and stepped inside, Maria was at my side with the grocery bags.

"I could have gotten that," I said as I took them from her and set them on the kitchenette counter.

"That's silly," she said. I'm the one with the raincoat. You're already wet enough." She brushed the water from my face and kissed me. Her lips were warm and soft.

I held her against me. "Umm........that's worth the trip." I kissed her again and lingered over it. I felt her breath quicken.

She pulled away and looked at me. Her eyes were pools of amber green. "Lets get the heater going." Her voice was just above a whisper.

I smiled and moved to the closet, removed the heater, and took it to the bedroom. I found a receptacle, plugged it in and set the control on high. I shut the door and returned to the big room. "It'll get warm faster with the door shut." I embraced her and kissed the tip of her nose.

Her words were simple and targeted. "Bet you can do better."

I kissed her, searching for her tongue. We clutched each other tightly. Her body was pressing against me with her hips thrusting to meet me. Her hair was a bouquet of fresh flowers.

"I can't wait for the heater," I said. We were breaking records for BTU release.

She reached for the doorknob, grabbed my hand, and pulled me into the room. I grabbed some clothes hangers from the closet and handed her one. We were out of our clothes and into each other's arms in seconds. The cold didn't exist anymore, or if it did we didn't feel it. The power of warm bodies can be intense. I pushed my knee between her legs gently, did a small knee bend and entered her standing up.

She gasped. "Oh my. ....that's.... a new experience........and I like it."

"As far as I'm concerned, everything we do is a new experience. And if it weren't, it's so different and perfect any other experience would be such a pale second it would be forgotten." I stopped moving and savored the feeling of being inside her. I put my arm around her hips to stop her movement. "I can't do too much of this. Let's stop for a minute. I'm not ready for the big eruption."

She smiled. "We've got plenty of time. No need to hurry." She moved slowly, keeping her tempo in rhythm, but that only aroused me more.

"I warned you; you'd better stop."

"Spoil sport," she said. "You started it."

"I know. I just don't want it to be over." I moved away and led her to the bed. As soon as she lay down, I knelt beside her and kissed her breasts. She rubbed my head and guided me as I dropped to her stomach. I could feel her thatch brushing softly against my chin. I teased her before I kissed her mons and felt her arching to me as I touched her with my tongue. Her response was deliberate, then intense as she moved into orgasm. She started with the soft moans I remembered and her body jerked softly. Her moans became groans, and then she lay still. I moved up on the bed and cradled her quiet body in my arms. She put her arms around me and kissed me.

"I love you," I whispered.

"That was wonderful," she said dreamily. "God, I love you!" She squeezed me. "Don't ever let me go. I want this moment to last forever."

"It will," I said. "This one and many more." There was magic here – when we talked, when we touched. I felt a oneness I'd never felt before. Sex had become the ultimate embrace, the dessert after a gourmet feast. We were seduced, not by sex, but by our ability to give without expecting a reward. We had discovered a new paradigm for love and we grasped it like children with a marvelous, new toy.

I felt her relax, then she stretched and slid away from me. "Lie on your back and close your eyes," she said. Her magnificent eyes were playful as she looked at me.

"Do you have a surprise for me?"

"Maybe. Just close your eyes and imagine you're in a beautiful place, your private garden of Eden."

"I thought I was," I said. "I don't need to imagine it."

She leaned over me and gently touched my eyelids. She drew a line on my chest with her finger, moving down my stomach. I felt her hair brush against me, then her lips surrounded me and time took a holiday. The excitement took my breath away. I knew I wouldn't last long with the pleasure she brought me.

"You have to stop," I said but I let the words out slowly. "Get on top of me."

My breath was labored. I entered her as she sat on me. I let her set the rhythm, slow and easy. With her hands on my chest, she increased her movement until a sea of pleasure rolled over me. I heard her moan and she fell on me. We held each other and let the moment slowly ebb away.

Without conversation, we held each other. I drifted into near sleep before she brought me back with a quiet kiss.

"You're not going to sleep on me, are you?"

"No......but I could. I'm totally relaxed, not a nerve in my body."

"I know, but this moment is so wonderful I don't want it to end. I feel so complete. I've never felt like this........ever "

"We should feel this way every time we're together, every time we make love," I said. "I believe that. I never thought when people were in love they heard beautiful music, or it was all that different. That's for the movies........ until now. I'm beginning to understand my life isn't much without you, Maria. You really are my soul mate, another term I always considered bogus. I love you more than I could ever imagine. I know what we're doing is not morally or socially acceptable, but I don't care. For whatever reason, our paths crossed, and as stupid and sappy as it sounds, I think it was our destiny. This is no accidental toss of the dice. There're many things I don't understand, like why I feel I've known you all my life, or why you're so easy to talk with. My only regret is that I didn't meet you earlier."

Maria looked a bit pensive. "Many people come together and think they're a perfect fit, and, after a long period of time seeing each other at their best and worst, fall victim to discord and disengagement. That's what fills up divorce courts, spawns unhappy, maladjusted children and makes two adults very unhappy. In the beginning in any courtship, everything is wonderful and life is easy. Do you think we're better than that?"

"I do. I think that seeing you every morning, before you put on your make-up, or kissing you awake before you brush your teeth, would be just as wonderful as seeing you at your best. We haven't had any real tests, but I think we have a bond even at this early stage that's pretty damn strong. There's a mystery about you that intrigues me, and that's a plus. You're very positive, you don't say bad things about people, and you can carry on an interesting and meaningful conversation. I appreciate that. You're smart, you listen, and you're not afraid to speak your mind. I enjoy everything we talk about and every minute we're together.

You've made sex a viable, beautiful part of my life, but you've made conversations and companionship even better. Life **is** good. It's just unfair."

"Terry, you have a way of finding simple solutions for complex situations; I can't do that. You also have a way of making me appreciate my role as a woman, in a warm and caring way. You're the answer to every characteristic I desire in a mate except two, and they're killers. You're somebody else's husband and you're the father of someone else's children. And I'm no better. So, can we survive circumstances like that? If we're so pure, can we survive the moral duplicity that's bound to come?"

"Maria, that's not a question I can answer. They're two people in the equation. If you want an honest opinion, it hasn't been a problem for me. Oh, I've had a few pangs of guilt and I may have more. But everything negative pales beside the rewards. When we're together, we're alone, in a parallel universe of our making, not in our real habitat. We never talk about our home life except in general terms. It's not part of our relationship so it's not necessary, and I think that's good. I don't have fear, but if we were discovered, our parallel universe would explode. Then we'd have tough decisions to make. My biggest problem would be explaining it to my girls, not Jane. It would be hard to tell her, but not impossible. My girls are insolated by an Aesopian envelope that society has created to protect them. They have no concept of their parents not loving each other. That should be forever and ever, like fairy tales. I'm not sure I could burst that bubble."

Maria sighed. "It's not a question of guilt. Maybe it's a mother thing....... nurturing and keeping children from hurt. It's not a dichotomy of good and evil. I can function normally at home. I still do all the things I would normally do. Except I go through the motions when it comes to sex. I do it but there's nothing there. I'm sure Pat notices it. He has to. I know that sounds horrible, but it's true. Sex at home is a duty. Sex with you is a reward. That sounds evil and it bothers me."

"Maria, you're not evil, for God's sake. You're a good woman or you wouldn't react as you do. We know what we're doing isn't right in a conventional sense. I won't even debate that. And I really don't want to know about your sex life. I know you feel the same about mine. But the one thing I'm certain of is I love you and will in twenty years, or forty years, or however many I live. That's sad because it's probably going to cause more hurt than happiness, but I DON'T

CARE. Coming from a person who deals in logic for a living, I know that sounds stupid, but I really don't care."

She looked away, expressionless and said slowly, "I wish I could be as positive as you are. My heart says you're right, but my brain takes exception. My perception of life, what I've grown up believing, is still in that fairy tale world you talk about. I have problems dealing with how I feel about you. This isn't something I can sit down and talk about with my mother."

"Look, Maria, let's not ruin a good day debating pluses and minuses. I know it's not always comfortable. Sometimes it gets downright diabolical with all the scheming. But for me, the alternative, not seeing you, is a life of darkness I can't face. You make the sun rise. You put a smile on my life. I'll live with whatever I must, but I can't make it without you in my life. Maybe there's a level of comfort that you can handle. I hope I can help you find it. I won't require more from you than you're willing to give. Didn't you tell me to love you when we're together? Let's try that. Let's love each other when we're together and stay out of our other life."

A sad smile crossed her face. "You are my life…that's the problem."

I laughed and broke the serious mode we had fallen prey to. "Now that's the first thing you've said that appeals to me." I kissed her on each eyelid.

"Forgive me," she said. "I didn't mean to get so morbid. How about a cigarette? Maybe that will get us back on track."

I walked over to the closet and pulled a pack of Kents from my trousers. "Here." I handed her a cigarette, stuck one in my mouth, lit them and dropped the pack on the floor. I lay down beside her, took a drag and let the smoke drift out of my mouth. "I told you a cigarette is better after sex."

"I know," she said lazily. "But the prerequisite is still the best part."

"Hum," I answered. "I can't argue with that." She was lying on her stomach with her chin braced on one hand, looking into my face. I put my hand across her waist. She had a definite delineation between her waist and her hips. An hourglass figure and I liked it. I dropped my hand to her buttocks and pinched her with just enough pressure to get her attention. She reacted with a giggle.

"Stop that, I'm ticklish."

"Sorry," I said. "I didn't know."

She smiled. "There's a lot you don't know about me."

"Probably, but I intend to find out."

She took a drag from her cigarette, blew the smoke away and stubbed it out.

"I like to make love with you. Did you know that?" She rolled over on her back and reached out for me.

50

The rain had passed and the sun was darting through the window blinds casting rows of light and shadow across the floor. Midday had come. The day was beginning to wind down. Maria was busy at the sink making sandwiches and had ham, cheese, and a row of condiments spread across the counter. Her hair was pinned up on her head and she had put on my shirt, carefully rolling up the sleeves. I've never seen my shirt look so attractive. I was more modestly attired in my trousers but nothing else.

"Are you hungry?" she asked.

"No more than a bear coming out of hibernation."

"I take it the answer is yes?"

"You'd make a great detective," I said.

"I think I'd make a better target for a detective, with all this sneaking around we do."

I laughed. "Detectives get paid by the hour. They'd go broke following us. We're too easy."

"What makes you think that?"

"Just kidding," I said. "Anything I can do to help?"

"I thought you'd never ask. Get some ice for the glasses and pour some soda."

I chuckled. "Soda? What kind of talk is that? It's a sacrilege to call Coke soda. That's Yankee talk."

She put her hands on her well-proportioned hips, which I took notice of, and glared at me. "Just pour the Coke," she said.

"OK, OK," I said putting my hands up in surrender. I held the glasses up in the light, checking their cleanliness. Then I dropped in the ice and filled them.

She finished making the sandwiches, cut them in halves and put them on a plate she found in the cabinet. The coup was an accompanying plate of sliced apples, grapes, and cheese. I retrieved two chairs from the big room and positioned them by the counter.

I took a bite of the sandwich and rubbed my stomach in appreciation. It was delicious. "Yummy," I said. "You know just what a hungry bear likes." I emphasized my remark by patting my stomach again.

She smiled. "Are we talking about food?"

"Absolutely. If we were talking about something else we already know the answer."

She stuck out her tongue playfully. "You're so smart. You always say such clever things."

"I can't help it. You're spoiling me, and that's an absolutely true statement."

"If I'm not, I intend to. Don't you forget it!"

I looked into her eyes, a doorway into a world I wanted to live in forever, and said, "Sometimes I think I could eat you alive."

She cocked her head. "Just sometimes?"

"I lied. All the time," I answered.

"Literally or figuratively?" Her eyes were twinkling.

"Not a fair question," I said. "What's your choice?"

"Not a fair question," she said and we both laughed. She glance at her wrist and said, "What time is it? I don't have my watch."

"About a quarter to one. Is that a problem?"

Maria started cleaning up our mess and said, "Not an immediate one, but borderline. I've got some cookies for dessert, but why don't we save them for the ride back?" She took off my shirt and draped it over her shoulder. She walked over to me, as innocently in her nakedness as Eve might have done before she bit the apple, and stood quietly. "Maybe we should clean up the bedroom first."

I pulled her to me and kissed her breast. I felt her nipple swell and harden under the pressure of my tongue. "Who needs cookies?" I said. "There're much better things than cookies."

We drove away from the cabin in silence, partly because we were satisfied and happy, and partly because we were sad that another magic moment was coming to its inevitable end. I wanted to say or do something that would bring perfect closure to this beautiful day, but I couldn't think of anything appropriate. I would save it for our next magic moment. We had said our goodbyes in the cabin with our actions. Words were not enough, would never be sufficient, and would only add to my heavy heart. I was already thinking ahead to our next time. That was the eternal optimist in me.

"Are you ready for a cookie?" Maria asked.

"No thanks." I had reached the end of the dirt road. I slowed and made a wide turn onto the highway.

"They're good," she said taking a bite.

"I know."

She was quiet for a moment. "Are you in a bad mood?"

"No, I just hate goodbyes."

"It's not goodbye. We'll never say goodbye, never."

"If my life were a book, it would be full of many blank pages, pages for every day we're apart. I hate that."

"That's not fair. I can't control that……and neither can you."

"I know, but I don't have to like it."

Maria put her hand on my leg. "We have a life when we're apart and we have a life when we're together. Let's leave it at that. What we do when we're apart is not relevant. It's in that parallel universe you talk about. I'm just a neophyte in this new world. Remember, it's something I've never done and never thought I would do."

"Sweetheart, I understand, but I still don't like being apart. It's not your fault or mine. It's the world we live in." I could feel depression coming.

"I don't like it either, but we have no choice. We've been very careful about our meetings. We're not invisible in your car, or in the Blizzard Shop, but no one's seen us...yet.......I think. We'll find time to be together. We have to be patient and careful."

"OK," I said, trying my best to head in another direction. "So what's for supper?" I slowed the car as we entered the city limits.

Maria laughed. "You sure can change the subject in a hurry. But it's **dinner**, not supper."

"I thought I might have converted you just a smidgen to the Southern point of view."

"Never, but you've converted me in many other ways."

"That's not a one-way street," I said.

"I know, but isn't it wonderful?"

"You bet........wonderful and exciting." I turned into the parking lot and stopped at her car. It was still in the middle of vacant spaces.

She gathered the left over lunch materials and kissed me quickly. "I'd better go. I feel like a duck in a shooting gallery."

"Call me tomorrow," I said. She was moving quickly out of the car and the warmth went with her.

"Maybe today after I get home, if the kids aren't there." She was gone before I could reply.

I drove straight to the office. The lights were still on when I arrived. Martha must have expected me back before five. I guess she bought my story about the State House. I parked, reached into my pocket for the door key and unlocked the door. Her desk was clean except for a pile of messages for me under a paperweight. Only one was a surprise, a call from Dr. Merriweather, Superintendent of City Schools, about a small project. The rest were routine. Jane wanted me to call her before I left to come home, not unusual. The call from Dr. Merriweather was promising. If I could get a small project, maybe it would lead to something bigger down the road. At least, it was the opportunity I was looking for. He wanted me to call his secretary for an appointment later this week. I called immediately and set up a meeting for Thursday morning at ten o'clock.

I put on the kettle, made a cup of coffee, and sat down at my desk. I lit a cigarette and took a sip of coffee before the telephone's ring interrupted my quiet moment.

"Design Concepts, Terry Forte speaking."

It was Maria. "What's going on?" she asked. She was angry and abrupt.

"I don't understand. What do you mean?"

"What I mean is I got three postcards from you from Las Vegas, three very colorful postcards with some vivid language – wish you were *here, I miss you, my room is bare without you.* I know you didn't write them. But what if I hadn't been the one to go to the mailbox? Somebody knows, Terry. That's frightening."

"That's not possible," I said.

"Well somebody sent them. If not you, then who?"

"I haven't the foggiest notion. No one's seen us at the Blizzard Shop or the cabin. It would take x-ray vision to see us in the car. Besides, you ARE my client. There's more than enough justification for us to be together."

"Maybe, but someone knows, and they're letting me know they know. Why would anyone send postcards anyone might read if they didn't have an agenda? I'm telling you someone knows and they mean to cause us trouble."

"Who ever did it had to have been in Las Vegas, or had a friend mail them. Could you tell anything from the handwriting?"

"Only that it doesn't look masculine. I believe it's from a female. That's just a guess."

"Have you thrown them away? I asked.

"Not yet, but I plan to. I wanted to talk to you first."

"I'd like to see them. I might recognize the handwriting. It's a long shot. Keep them if you have a safe place to hide them until you can give them to me. If you're afraid, get rid of them. Don't take any chances. Burning them might be the best idea."

"I can keep them for a day or two, but I'm afraid to go much longer."

"Why don't you come by tomorrow afternoon? I've got some new drawings I can give you. That's a good excuse. I want to see the cards."

"OK, but let's make it a point to stay in view while I'm there. I don't want to give anyone any ammunition."

I laughed. "Just act like a client."

"That's a joke and you know it, and it's not funny."

"It wasn't meant to be funny. I'm dead serious."

"Sure," she said. "I'll stop by tomorrow afternoon, dressed in my porcupine dress."

"Don't get too carried away."

"You can bet on that. OK, I'll see you about two. Goodbye."

I penciled in *Mrs. Champion* in my calendar for two o'clock and *Dr. Merriweather* for ten on Thursday. My hand was noticeably shaking as I wrote. I fixed another cup of coffee to replace the cold one and made my way to the loft. It was time to do some thinking, but I didn't know where to start. I was sure no one had seen us doing anything I couldn't justify and certainly not at the cabin. I doubted if Bill really knew absolutely that we were using it. Maria made sure it was spotless when we left. Maybe someone at the dance had put two and two together and was suspicious, but who would care? It could be someone who knows Maria. I had to keep that in mind. I was without a clue, so I decided not to waste any more time on it. I went to work on Maria's house.

I pulled the file and looked through my latest sketches. The floor plan worked well and was beginning to take on the type character I wanted; I had developed a few free hand perspectives to show Maria how the house would look from the lake. It was nestled against the highest part of the site creating a slight berm, expressing broad, horizontal lines with deep roof overhangs over generous windows exposed to the lake. It had a free spirit about it, reminding me of Maria. I was happy with my initial design. I stayed busy for two hours or more, studying materials and finishes until it was close to six o'clock. It was time to call Jane and go home. The postcards were not in my thoughts.

Maria showed up Tuesday afternoon, as she had promised, and brought the postcards. She kept her coat on but unbuttoned it, exposing black slacks, a pale violet sweater, and black loafers. She didn't have much to say and left after I gave her blueprints of my latest sketches. She was visibly nervous and made a point of keeping everything businesslike. I suppose that was best, but I didn't so much for my ego. She did smile and give me an obligatory pat on the arm before she left, but there was little warmth in her actions. She wasn't there long enough to look at the drawings, an indication of how upset she was.

I took the postcards into the conference room and spread them out on the table. They were standard fare souvenir cards, pictures of hotels and casinos that meant nothing to me, and offered little clues as to who the culprit might be. The handwriting was definitely feminine, but was not overtly familiar. The content was not blatantly prurient, but it definitely had sexual overtones. I could understand Maria's concern after seeing them. I locked them in my desk drawer, but my intentions were to destroy them after I determined there was nothing more to gain from them.

I put in a call to Bill. I wanted to play golf tomorrow. Garth and Jerry had indicated they wanted to play if the temperature was above fifty degrees. The temperature had reached fifty-five at noon so I felt good about tomorrow. The trusty weatherman had promised good weather, but that usually was the kiss of death. Bill's secretary answered on the fourth ring.

"Must be busy today. You usually answer before the fourth ring," I said.

"Hi, Terry. You wouldn't believe how busy it's been. Mr. Jackson says it's because the interest rate dropped half a point. I'm not sure what that means, but everyone and their brother has called about starting construction on their house. I guess that's good."

"Absolutely; might be for me too. Mortgage rates will drop so people will want to take advantage of it..........Where is he? Counting his money?"

She giggled. "No, he's on the other line. Nope, he's off. Hold on."

"Terry.......what's happening?" Bill was jovial. "I hope you're calling about golf. I need some easy money."

"Well," I answered. "You're not getting any from me. I've got a seventy-three saved up and tomorrow will be a great day to let it out."

Bill snorted. "Don't blow smoke up my butt. I know better. I think I could get away early......how about one or one thirty?"

"Sounds good. Jerry wants to play and he takes off Wednesday afternoons, so he's good to go. Why don't you call Garth and call for a tee time at the club? I'll tell Jerry and If I don't hear anything more from you, we'll see you at one. I'll probably eat lunch there, so I'll come early."

"Good idea. I'll meet you in the nineteenth hole about twelve-thirty. By the way, you left your cigarettes at the cabin. Want me to bring them?" Bill was snickering.

"What do you mean?" I asked.

"You know exactly what I mean. You're the only person I know who smokes Kents and has a key."

"So?" I said.

"I'm not prying. I don't want to know anything about it. I hope you're enjoying it. Hell, Susie's been acting a little strange lately, so you might have it all to yourself before long. I think she's getting a little tired of messing with a married man. She's been dating a guy off and on for about three months and I've been encouraging it. It's better for her in the long run. But I sure hate to give her up. It'll be like being hooked on dope and going cold turkey. I don't relish the thought, but, hell, nothing lasts forever. This morning might have been my last time for a while."

"I **guess** I'm sorry to hear that. You know my feelings are mixed because of Sandy, but I understand why you're seeing Susie. I would hate for Sandy to ever find out."

"You're the only one who knows...besides Susie. That's not a threat is it?"

"No, Asshole. You know I'd never tell her, or anyone else."

"Good, cause I'd never rat on you either."

"I appreciate the use of the cabin, but let's leave it at that. It's not something I want to talk about."

"I understand; I'm not asking any questions. Just leave Tuesday's alone, at least for a while."

I laughed. "Don't give it a thought. I'm not on a schedule. In fact, I'll be lucky if I use it more than twice a month. And if you still have my Kents, bring them to the club tomorrow."

"I left them at the cabin on the kitchen counter. You can get them next time. Oh well, I'd better get off the phone. Better call Garth. I've got to get him psyched up so we can kick your collective butts. I'm tired of contributing to your cash fund."

"He's not easy to psyche up," I suggested.

"Maybe I can this week. He's been on vacation, so he should be well rested and in a good mood."

"Oh? Where's he been?"

"Lucky guy won a sales contest and got a free trip to Las Vegas. How's that for a reward?"

"Did you say Las Vegas?"

I worked hard Wednesday morning, and, for the first time in a while, I didn't hear from Maria. I left the office at lunchtime and drove to the club. I was anxious to see Garth and find out whether Ann had gone with him to Las Vegas. If it were true, I had the answer to the post cards.

I changed clothes and met Bill in the nineteenth hole. He was eating a toasted BLT and having a beer with Jerry. They were laughing and betting cars and houses on our afternoon golf round. Garth hadn't arrived.

"Be careful, Jerry. I'm too poor for that," I said, indicating my disdain.

"Why the concern?" Jerry said. "These guys are all talk, kinda like my sex life."

Bill laughed. "I agree with the part about your sex life. The only women you drill are trapped in a dentist chair, sedated and can't fight back."

Jerry took a sip of his beer and wiped his mouth with his napkin. "Well, it sure beats none at all."

We were laughing pretty hard when Garth came in and sat down. "Have I got time for a sandwich?" he asked.

"Sure," Jerry said. "How can we deny you your last meal before the execution?"

Garth smiled and said, "Obviously, I've missed something."

"Our pal Jerry's threatening us. He wants to up the 'Nassau'. He doesn't know you cleaned house in Las Vegas last week."

"I didn't clean house, but I did OK at the blackjack table. Not enough to make any big bets today, though."

That gave me the entry I wanted. "Bill told me about your trip. Did you take the family?"

"Ann went, but the kids stayed with Mama. We had a great time, but once in Las Vegas is enough for me. Ann liked playing the slots and shopped when she got tired of the games."

I had my answer. I should have known all along. Now I really had some work to do and I didn't know how or where to start.

Jerry signed his bill and got up. He stretched and said, "Come on Terry. Let's hit some practice balls and get ready for the massacre."

"I'm ready," I said, and we made our way to the practice tees. I didn't have my mind on golf after finding out that Ann was the one sending postcards. She was a sick woman and could cause massive problems for Maria and me. I threw out a few balls and went through my usual warm up routine – bends, twists, knee bends, and swinging two clubs. I grabbed a five- iron from my bag and took a few practice swings. My first shot sliced wildly to the right, almost off the range.

"My God, Terry. I haven't seen you hit one that bad in a long time." Jerry walked over to me. "Try it again."

I hit another shot with the same results. Obviously I wasn't concentrating. "Damn, I can't get my hands to rotate and I'm swinging from the outside. Better strengthen my grip a little." My next shot was better. The ball sailed high and long.

"That's the way, kiddo. That looks like the Terry I want for my partner. Had a little draw on that one."

Ann was slowly creeping out of my thoughts and my focus was coming back. I hit a few more shots with my six, seven, and eight irons, and then tried my driver. I was hitting every shot solid and straight. "That's better," I said to no one in particular.

"Don't hit any more Terry," Jerry said. "Let's get over to the first tee. I don't want them to get any warm up shots. That's good for two holes." Jerry was in the cart turning it around. I slid my clubs into my bag and jumped into the moving cart.

"Whoa, Jerry. Don't kill us before we play." He eased off the pedal a little, making me feel more comfortable. "That's better. It's just a golf match."

"Relax Terry. How about getting a couple beers out of the cooler? It's time to start the celebration."

"I'll get you one. I'm not ready."

Jerry looked perplexed. "Why not?"

"It's too early in the day and it's too damn cold. The temperature is still in the low fifties and with this wind it feels like forty. Not my kind of weather for beer."

"OK, spoil sport. But I'm going to pop one when we get to the fourth tee, cold or not."

Bill and Garth were waiting at the first tee. They were laughing and talking. They didn't seem concerned that we had taken warm up shots and they hadn't.

Jerry pulled a coin from his pocket, flipped it into the air and said, "Call it."

"Heads," said Bill.

"You got it," Jerry said as he picked up his coin. "Hit away."

Jerry was right. We won the first three holes. We closed them out on the seventh hole, won the front, and two presses. They managed one press so we went into the back side up two bets.

Ann and the postcards kept coming back into my thoughts, so I had to really work to stay focused. Jerry kept us in the game, despite three beers, and we finished the day up five bets and eight dollars. We completed the festivities with two beers at the bar and we all left, tired and cold.

I drove home in the dark flipping radio stations, and was treated to Christmas music. I think I heard *Little Drummer Boy* at least twice, *White Christmas, Winter Wonderland,* and a plethora of others before I made it home. As I turned into the drive, I saw a Christmas tree. It was shining through the living room window as conspicuously as a lighthouse beacon on a dark night. *Dammit to hell.* Jane asked me last week to get a tree and I had forgotten it. I felt a twinge of guilt for my omission, because I looked forward to helping decorate the tree with the children. How could I have forgotten it? Was there a message here? You bet, and I was going to take my punishment like a man. I certainly had it coming.

The children mauled me when I walked into the house. It was reminiscent of a surprise party. They were proud of the tree and wanted me to see it.

"Come see the Christmas tree, Daddy," said Janet, grabbing my hand and pulling me into the living room. Jane was cleaning up boxes and litter left from lights, ornaments, and other decorations and didn't look up as I made my appearance. *Further evidence of* ***the message***.

"Wow! That's a great looking tree. Santa won't have any trouble finding our house." Laurie gave me one of those *ho hum* looks, but Janet's face was full of sparkling eyes and happiness. She still believed in Santa Claus and the excitement was evident. The true meaning of Christmas had long been replaced with this pagan version of a holiday, but somehow the excitement and wonder of receiving gifts from a fat old, bearded man in a red suit hauled around in a sleigh drawn by flying reindeer was a true miracle to those lucky enough to still believe it. It was a magic moment in the lives of children who would learn much too soon in their mad dash to maturity that it was all make believe. They would have a lifetime to learn the true meaning of Christmas, but only a short time to believe in Santa Claus.

I picked Janet up and said, "Only two more weeks and Santa'll be here. Wonder if he'll bring you anything."

"I've been good, Daddy. I helped Mama put up the tree and I even washed Inky. I want him to be clean for Christmas."

Laurie rolled her eyes. "She almost drowned him and he was about to freeze. She washed him in cold water."

"Liar, liar! Pants on fire!" said Janet. "The water was warm when I started." She was squirming around in my arms trying to kick Laurie.

"Stop that," I said. "Santa might be watching."

"Sure Daddy, and Superman can jump over tall buildings," said Laurie.

I put Janet down and she immediately stuck out her tongue and stood defiantly with her hands on her hips. "I hope you get switches and a bag of coal."

I decided it was time to diffuse the issue. "Enough!" I said. "Maybe we can get in a game of Monopoly tonight. Now, let's help Mama clean up the mess."

"Yes, let's," said Jane tersely. Her voice sounded low and disinterested, and she didn't look at me as she spoke. "Laurie, get the vacuum cleaner and clean up the tree needles. Janet, you can take the boxes to the garage store room. Be sure to put them on the shelves. I don't want them on the floor. Terry, you can help with the boxes. If it's not too much to ask."

"Sure," I said with a big old briar-eating grin. I was humble. I knew I had lost the war. "OK, Jumper, let's get them out of here."

I put the smaller boxes inside the bigger ones and we hauled them away in two trips. When we returned, Laurie had finished vacuuming and Jane was busy putting cotton around the bottom of the tree to hide the stand. The tree really looked good. I was beginning to feel the Christmas spirit.

"That's a beautiful tree, Jane. Where did you get it?" A compliment and a question was a good beginning to my redemption, if she would take the bait.

"The Optimist Club lot on Devine Street. They're seven dollars this year. They go up every year."

At least she had answered. "Maybe we ought to buy one of those artificial trees. They're about twenty-five dollars. Pay for itself in four years," I said.

Jane's eyes narrowed in disgust. "Not in my house. I hate those phony trees. They look like pipe cleaners. Besides, natural trees smell so good."

I had lost what little advantage I had gained with the question. "You're right. We'll stick with natural trees.....hey, I won eight dollars today. Let's go out to eat. I know you haven't had time to cook anything." *Maybe I could sneak back into the fold with a good deed!*

I had struck the right chord. Jane's face came to life and she smiled, a big, wide genuine smile. "That's a wonderful idea," she said. "Anything special in mind?"

"How about Captain's Kitchen? We haven't been there in a while, and the girls love the shrimp and hush puppies."

Another smile. "Well, that's something all of us like that we don't have at home often, and we can go as we are. That's a great idea." She came over and kissed me on the cheek. I hadn't expected that and I certainly didn't deserve it. Maybe food was the way to a woman's heart, too.

"Check out the girls while I comb my hair and fix my face. Make them wash their hands and faces. I'll fix their hair when I'm done. I'll just be a minute so hop to it."

I had my marching orders and I didn't need any motivation. Life was good again. Not perfect, but good. Maybe, just maybe, I had paid the proper penance. I would find out when the euphoria of the moment was over and we were alone. Oh well, at least the white flag was waving and I would take advantage of it.

I took the girls to the bathroom, supervised their hand washing, and scrubbed their faces. When I was satisfied, I took them to Jane for inspection. She gave them a good look, approved, brushed their hair and we grabbed our coats and headed for the car. I was in a good mood and it intensified when I suddenly remembered that I had an appointment with Dr. Merriweather tomorrow. Maybe good things were about to happen.

We had a good time at Captain's Kitchen. The food was mediocre and the children ate their weight in hush puppies. I didn't do too badly with the fried oysters either, ordering two refills. Jane didn't eat much. She spent her time moving food around in her plate and lecturing the girls on their behavior. I was beginning to worry that I hadn't paid sufficiently for my sins and needed to wallow around in propitiation some more. Perhaps she wanted another opportunity to berate me for forgetting the Christmas tree. The oysters that had been so comforting and filling were transforming themselves into a rock quarry in my stomach. I just couldn't face another conversation about the tree.

When we were first married, conversation was easy. Well, that's stretching it a bit. Most of the time we communicated by sex and didn't have to talk. After a year or two and a pregnancy, our conversations became more about our daily routine and less about feelings. Our sexual escapades became even more businesslike, more a matter of bartering an occasional night of half-hearted sex for some task Jane wanted done – the *carrot and stick* trick. It had gotten to the point where I wished my sexual appetite would fall into the same morass that Jane's had, because thinking about it all the time was wearing me out and playing havoc with my life.

Sometimes I suspected Jane secretly enjoyed my pain. At least she had been successful in subjugating **her** libido. Hers was probably justified because she was tired most of the time raising the girls and managing the house, and didn't have the energy it required to get her work done and please me too. I guess I was too immature to understand it and considered myself relegated to a very low point on the choice chain. Not good for self-esteem. Nevertheless, her lack of ardor and my increasing frustration over the years put me in a perpetual funk that I didn't understand and couldn't cope with, and now our relationship seemed hopeless. Neither of us could talk about it without getting angry, so we couldn't cure it. Now we hardly talked about anything, including sex. I hated it, but I was convinced it wouldn't get any better, with or without conversation. Now, I'd just as soon say nothing; it was easier that way. Whoever said "Silence is Golden" was either very smart, sexually repressed, or both. *And to be honest, Maria had changed my whole view on sex and made it easier.*

Jane still managed an occasional conversation, but it was usually to let me know I hadn't done something she asked me to do – the Christmas tree for instance – or, if I had, I hadn't don't it exactly right. I might have completed the task, but I left a tool out or some equally innocuous thing that somehow negated the large part that I had completed. Finally, I had come to understand that I would never be capable of doing anything right in her eyes, sexually or otherwise. Therefore, I decided that I may as well not attempt it. I thought that by some act of valor or finding a way to please her, I would be able to turn the situation around. Now, I had become astute enough to know that will never happen. *One thing for sure, it's either there or it isn't. You can't manufacture it.*

After Jane and I smoked a cigarette and the girls visited the bathroom, I signaled the waitress for the check. I left seventy-five cents on the table, paid six dollars at the cashier's stand, and drove us home. The girls sat quietly in the back seat. Janet fell asleep, and Laurie was yawning. Jane was sitting with her head back on the seat but her eyes were open.

"I can't wait to get home and go to bed. I've had a long day," she said.

I liked the sound of that, not a mention of the tree. "I'm pretty tired myself," I answered. "Playing golf in cold weather wears me out. I need to be rested for my meeting tomorrow with Dr. Merriweather. I have to be sharp for that." I hoped having said that might save me from any more harassment.

She turned toward me and asked, "Do you think he might give you a project?" Her voice was soft but inquiring.

"I think it's promising that he wants to talk to me. I know the school board is planning a new elementary school in our area, and, it will be budgeted about three hundred thousand dollars. That's a fee of eighteen thousand. If I could get it I could hire a draftsman full time and spend more time marketing. That's what I need to be doing. Architects can't make a good living doing nothing but houses."

"That would be wonderful, but you shouldn't get your hopes up."

"Why not? Architecture is a business of hopes and dreams. I have to keep trying to expand my clientele base. It won't kill me if I don't get it, but it will if I don't try."

Jane turned away and leaned back on the seat. "I have a good feeling about it. This may not be the job you get, but I think Dr. Merriweather will eventually give you one. He knows you did a lot of schools when you worked for Bayer-Kline. He'll take that into consideration."

"I'm hoping he will, or I'm dead in the water. I haven't done any schools since I've been on my own, so I can't claim any experience. That elementary school I did in Summerville in 1960 while I was at Bayer-Kline won several awards, and I designed it. Drew every line of working drawings and prepared the specifications. Doesn't matter, I can't take any credit for it. It would be unethical."

"Why do you have to be so honest all the time? Tell him you worked on it. That's the truth, and you wouldn't be taking credit for it."

"You don't understand, Jane. We operate under a rigid code of ethics, probably the most rigid of all the professions. We don't advertise, we don't cut fees to get work, and we don't take credit for work we did in other offices. The time will come when I'll have architects working for me, and I wouldn't want them taking credit for my designs."

"So...... I just think there's a way you can get the message across without killing the messenger. You don't have to take credit for the concept."

"I know, but I don't want people to ever think I'm dishonest. It's not like architectural ethics are arcane. Everyone knows about them. I want to know I've always fought the good fight and have the respect of my peers. A lot of firms have made tons of money by cutting corners on ethics. But believe me, they don't have the respect of their peers."

"You don't have to tell me how honest you are; I remember when the bank teller cashed a check for you and gave you a hundred dollars too much. When you realized it, you couldn't get back there quick enough. How many people would have done that?" Jane laughed. "I'm not sure I would."

"Sure you would. You wouldn't keep someone else's money."

"Maybe I just haven't reached my level of temptation. I know you're an honest person and I respect you for it. I'm just a housewife. You're the architect; you always do the right thing."

Jane's words awakened me like a pitcher of ice water in my face. I realized what a hypocrite I was, giving her a lecture on ethics and honesty. My life was totally out of control when it came to honesty and I knew, absolutely *knew*, that it wouldn't change. As sure as God created the universe, Maria had become my life, and I couldn't change that now or ever. I measured my response carefully.

"Don't throw the mantle of honesty over me so absolutely. It doesn't fit me well. Nobody's honest all the time. The Bible teaches us only one man is without sin and I'm a subscriber to that."

Jane looked at me intently. "Is this confession time? Do you have any specifics you want to tell me about?"

For a brief moment I considered it, but it wouldn't come out of my mouth. Instead I laughed and said, "Well, we took advantage of our golf opponents today and won eight dollars. I can't say that was honest. We didn't give them any time to warm up."

Jane sighed in disbelief. "For heaven's sake, that's not dishonest. That's gamesmanship. And....I'll bet it was Jerry's idea. I can't believe anything like that could ever enter your mind. Besides, they'd do it to you if they had the chance. You had me going for a minute. I was looking for a blockbuster. I should have known better."

This conversation needed closure and fortunately we were at our turn. There was a car behind me so I rolled the window down and gave a left turn signal with my arm. I wish the highway department would make blinkers legal. It's too cold to be rolling windows down. The Germans have the right idea with their "machs nichts."

Jane gasped when the cold hit her. "Wow, it's cold. I hope the children don't wake up. I'll get the door open and we can carry them inside. You get Laurie and I'll get Janet. Laurie's too heavy for me."

"It's OK Mama," Laurie said. "I'm awake; just get Jumper. She's really sleeping."

I opened the car door for Laurie and she came out yawning. I reached across the seat and picked up Jumper, shielding her face with my coat to protect her from the cold. I felt her warmth as she snuggled against my chest, and managed to kick the door shut and get her to her bed without totally awakening her. Jane had Jumper's pajamas out and got them on her with little protest. Both of the girls were in bed and asleep in minutes. Jane and I weren't much longer, marching off to dreamland aided by fatigue and a full stomachs.

Thursday was a day designed to punish Southerners and send tourists packing. It was very cold, a near record eighteen degrees. The sky was clear and cloudless, a cold blue shading from light to cobalt with a sun that wasn't prepared or capable of supplying heat perched grudgingly above the horizon. The air was heavy with cold and attacked exposed flesh, notably noses, ears and fingers, with a vengeance.

Jane bundled the children up in sweaters, coats, scarves, hats, and mittens and I drove them to school, giving her a reprieve from her normal day of carpooling. The car was just getting warm when I arrived at the office. I went inside and bumped the thermostat up to seventy-two. I had set it at sixty Wednesday when I left for golf but after leaving eighteen-degree weather, it felt warm.

I made a cup of coffee and set about preparing for my meeting with Dr. Merriweather. It would have to be perfect or my chances for a project would be nil. My portfolio consisted of expensive residential work, some small commercial work, but no schoolwork. My ability was all I had to sell him with, and that would be difficult without credible experience in school design. I couldn't ethically take any credit for the considerable number of schools I did at Bayer-Kline, but strangely enough I was considered reliable enough when I worked there to lead the office team that did most of the schools. Now, that couldn't be part of my resume.

Architecture is a difficult profession. If you don't have experience in a field, you can't get a job. If you can't get a job, you can't get experience. What a dilemma. It's the old *what comes first, the chicken or the egg?* thing. My hope was that Dr. Merriweather would remember that I was the one who met with him and his administrative staff when he worked with Bayer-Kline. That was probably my only hope at landing a commission.

I sorted through slides of my more expensive residences and all of my commercial work and loaded them into a carrousel. I had enough to do a twenty-minute presentation with appropriate commentary, and I allowed another ten minutes for my close and any questions Dr. Merriweather might have.

I went to my filing cabinet and rummaged through a marketing file I had compiled since starting practice. The first thing I pulled out was a list of significant questions clients tended to ask at interviews. Martha had typed them from hastily scribbled notes I had saved and modified. Most of them were related to fees and contract agreements, but some of them were probing questions about architectural philosophy. As an administrator, Dr. Merriweather had interviewed many architects and was knowledgeable about fees and contracts, so he probably would be more interested in my philosophy and how I processed a project. Knowledge is security and my years at Bayer-Kline had provided me with a plethora of information about school design. I was familiar with the jargon, types of construction, materials, finishes, applicable codes and procedures required by the state. If I wanted to distance myself from the rest of the pack, I would have to convince him I was the best man for the job. Not the easiest task with nothing significant to show.

I heard Martha typing away and looked at my watch. It was nine o'clock. I didn't have much time. I set up the projector on my desk and went through all the slides. I rearranged them until I was satisfied with their order, shut the projector off and put an extra bulb in the case. Having accomplished the logistical problems, I jotted down in outline form all the points I wanted to cover and moved everything to the door.

"Need any help?" Martha asked.

"I don't think so. It's not that much to carry."

"Put on your coat. It's too cold to go outside without it," she said. She sounded like my mother.

"OK," I said, a little annoyed, even though I knew she was right. I grabbed my topcoat from the closet, put it on, and hauled everything to the car. The cold was brutal; my eyes filled with tears and my breath vaporized in trailing tendrils from a reddening nose. After loading the car, I started the engine so it would have a chance to warm up before I left. I made for the warm confines of the office. I still had some time to kill.

"I told you it was cold. Now, aren't you glad you wore your coat?" Martha asked the question more for information than *I told you so.*

"I coulda used a scarf and gloves, too. Man, it's cold! Colder than I can remember for a long time. I left the engine running. I should have cut on the heater."

"Wouldn't do any good; the engine's still cold," she said.

I looked at my watch. It was twenty minutes to ten. "I'd better get going. I don't want to be late."

Martha smiled. "Especially for Dr. Merriweather. He's a very punctual man. Well..........good luck, and, as they say in show biz, 'Break a leg'. Don't be nervous. He puts his pants on just like you do."

I smiled real big for her. "Come on now...you know I'm not nervous. This is a big opportunity for me. I just don't want to screw it up."

"I know and you won't," she said. "Now get out of here."

"OK," I said, saluting smartly. I ran to the car and started the heater. Warm air circulated immediately around my feet and felt good.

It was a ten-minute drive to Dr. Merriweather's office. I found a parking place near the entrance. I grabbed everything but the roll-up screen, hoping they had one I could use and walked briskly to the door. A well-dressed woman about thirty – his receptionist or secretary – was sitting behind a large, ornate desk that was impressive and overpowering. Her black hair was twisted in a severe bun and her glasses encircled a pair of striking brown eyes. If her appearance was tailored to create a conservative air, it was a failure. She was young and attractive and nothing could change that.

"May I help you?" she asked.

"Yes thanks. I'm Terry Forte. I have a ten o'clock appointment with Dr. Merriweather." I laid my paraphernalia on the floor and handed her a card.

She smiled and said, "Dr. Merriweather's expecting you. Have a seat. I'll tell him you're here." She stood and walked to a paneled walnut door to my right, knocked twice and walked in. I heard her say, "Dr. Merriweather, your ten o'clock appointment is here. Dr. Merriweather followed her through the door, and walked toward me smiling, extending his hand. He was slender, tall, and bald except for a ring of thin curling gray hair. His red cheeks gave him an air of good health and his handshake was firm.

"How are you, Terry? It's good to see you. I'm sorry I picked such a dreadful day to have you here. Come in." He led me into his office and motioned for me to sit in a large, comfortable leather chair in front of his desk.

His desk was massive but well organized, and his office was spacious with a conference table to his right that seated four. Behind his desk was a matching credenza covered with what appeared to be family portraits and a wall decorated with diplomas and honors he had received over the years. An ornate chair rail at window stool level terminated a paneled wainscot stained to match his desk, and the wall above was painted in off white. Tasteful landscapes were placed sparingly on the other walls. One of them was a view of the battery in Charleston. The floors were covered with a thick rose-colored wool carpet. I was impressed.

I sat down and gazed around the office approvingly. "Very nice," I said. "Who did the carpentry work? It is really well done. I'd like to have workmanship like this on all my jobs."

"It's my pride and joy," he said. I had a man from Charleston who does restoration work do it. He insisted that all the moldings be run in a Charleston mill that uses authentic knives. He selected the lumber and wouldn't let me see the bill for any of it until everything was completed. I probably would have had a heart attack otherwise. I think the school board thought I lost my mind." He chuckled. "I told them I would never ask for any more raises if they overlooked my extravagance."

"Well, he did a magnificent job; the lumber is superb. It looks like all rift cut walnut. That's hard to find in those lengths. He had to have a good source."

Dr. Merriweather laughed. "He didn't tell me much. Probably didn't want to let me in on his trade secrets." He paused and relaxed into his chair. "Well, tell me a little bit about you and your firm. I remember you did some good work for us when you were with Bayer-Kline."

Wow! That was a break. "Thanks, Dr. Merriweather. I enjoyed working with you and Mr. Cathcart. Is he still here?"

He is, but he's getting close to retirement. I hope he stays on until I leave. He's a good man, knows construction and he's a registered mechanical engineer. He would be hard to replace. I remember he had a lot of nice things to say about you. He said you were the best young architect he'd worked with. He didn't have much patience with some of them."

I smiled. "Tell him I appreciate that. You probably know most of my work is residential. That's necessary when you're getting a practice started. It's hard for beginning firms to get commercial work, but that's the direction I have to go to be successful. I know I'm capable enough to do schools. I just need someone willing to give me a chance. I'm thorough in my work and my approach. I pride myself in not making mistakes. Nothing leaves my office until I'm satisfied that it's the best it can be. If you have anything you can let me do, even a small project, I promise you won't be disappointed."

Dr. Merriweather pulled a pipe from inside his coat. He poked at it with his pocketknife, filled it with tobacco, and lit it. It was quite a production and took some time. I didn't interrupt. It appeared to be as necessary to him as breathing. After puffing hard for a minute and filling the room with sweet, aromatic smoke, he said, "I see you have some slides. Let's see what you've got."

Relieved, I set up the projector and went through my slides, with suitable commentary, and went into my spiel about my practice and my thoughts about architecture. He seemed interested and didn't interrupt. He sat quietly, puffing away, staring at spot over my head. Finally, I asked, "Do you have any questions about anything I've said?" I was beginning to feel uneasy.

He smiled. "No, actually I was thinking about what we have coming up that I could give you. Hampton Elementary is in need of major alterations and four additional classrooms. It's not a big job, about eighty to a hundred thousand dollars, but we need it now so it will be ready for next year. It's a good entry level project and would give us a chance to see what you can do. A successful job here would give you legs up on the new elementary school we're planning for Westside."

I was stunned. "That's wonderful. I would really appreciate the opportunity." I took a deep breath to calm myself. "I can start tomorrow, Dr. Merriweather." The smile on my face was wide enough to encompass my whole head.

Dr. Merriweather threw both arms up, hands extended and laughed heartily. "That's what I call enthusiasm," he said. He stood and opened the door. "Debbie, get the file on Hampton Elementary and give Mr. Forte a copy of the program. Better give him two copies. Call Capital Blue and have them deliver two sets of prints of everything they have on Hampton to his office." He turned to face me and said, "That should be enough to get you started, Terry. If you have any questions, call Mr. Cathcart. He can fill you in on some of the problems we're having there."

I got up and shook his hand. "You don't know how much I appreciate this, Dr. Merriweather." I grabbed my projector and headed for the door.

"Leave a copy of your brochure and a business card for my file."

I dropped my brochure on his desk and fished in my wallet for a card. "Thanks again, Dr. Merriweather," I said as I handed it to him. He smiled and led me to his office door.

"Thanks for coming, Terry." He shut the door behind me. In my euphoria, I started for the door.

"Mr. Forte, don't leave without the program," Debbie said, stopping me in my tracks.

"Oh, excuse me. I'm sorry. I wasn't thinking."

"No problem," she said. She seemed amused. I guess my reaction was strange, but I was too happy to think straight. "Thanks," I said when she handed me the file, then I literally danced my way to the car. The cold that affected me earlier didn't faze me now. I drove back to the office whistling a happy tune like the seven dwarfs. I didn't have Snow White but I had Maria, and I wanted to tell her about my good luck. My trip to Dr. Merriweather's office had taken a little over an hour so nothing had changed at the office. Martha was still there, typing away, and didn't look up when I came in. She did ask without missing a beat, "How'd it go?"

I tried to be nonchalant. "About like I expected."

"Well, don't give up. Rome wasn't built in a day."

"Of course it wasn't. I wasn't the architect."

Martha winced. "That's the stupidest thing you've ever said."

"I won't take offense to that; I'm too happy. Dr. Merriweather gave me a project. How about that?"

Martha stopped typing. "You're kidding," she said.

I pulled out the material on the school and dropped on her desk. "Start a file for Hampton Elementary School." I was smiling like a monkey. "It's not a big job as far as dollars go, but it's big for me. My first school project. I've been waiting for this opportunity a long time."

Martha stood up and hugged me. Very sincerely she said, "I'm so proud of you, Terry! You're on your way."

I was taken aback for a moment. This wasn't vintage Martha. I seldom saw emotion from her, but I could tell she meant it.

"Thank you Martha. Coming from you, that's very special."

Then in typical fashion she said, "Don't get the big head; now you've got something to prove."

What God giveth, God can take away, I thought. Now I felt more comfortable. "Martha, you really know how to cut to the chase." We both laughed and she settled back in her chair and resumed typing.

"Well, get to work; you don't have all day. I've got a contract to type up," she said.

I was still laughing when I got to my desk. At least, she had me focused. I labeled a file drawer for Hampton School, and answered correspondence that had lain neglected. That would keep me busy for an hour or so. I wanted to call Maria and share my good fortune, but I wanted to be alone when I did it. It would wait until Martha left.

As soon as Martha closed the door behind her, I called Maria.

"Hello," she said. Her voice was soft and seductive.

"Hi." I have some good news that I want to share with you. I want you to be the first to know."

"Oh? And what might that be?"

"I had a meeting this morning with Dr. Merriweather. He's Superintendent of City Schools. I don't think I mentioned it to you. Anyway, I asked him to consider me for any future work he might have. It was more of a courtesy call than anything else. I didn't expect anything, but I was fishing for the future. Guess what? He ***gave*** me a project, right out of the blue. I couldn't believe it."

"That's **wonderful,** Terry**!** I'm so happy for you. How is this important for you? You know, I'm not an expert in your field, so I don't know what the impact is."

"It's a huge step for me, Maria. It's my first school project, my first job that isn't a residence. It will open doors for me unless I screw it up."

"Does this mean you won't be able to design my house?"

"Of course not. Nothing changes. It just broadens my opportunities. I'll be able to hire a full time draftsman, maybe two."

"Well, Terry, I'm happy for you. When are you going to open the champagne?"

"Now you're being sarcastic."

"I don't mean to be. I'm really happy for you. Obviously, this has been one of your goals. I wouldn't make fun of it. I guess this thing with the postcards has been on my mind, and I can't think straight. Forgive me Terry, I promise I didn't mean to be flippant."

"Oh. I'm the one who isn't thinking. I found out who sent the cards. I should have told you before I got caught up in my euphoria."

She interrupted me. "Who? What?"

"I found out on the golf course yesterday. One of my partners, Garth, told me he had been in Las Vegas during the time the cards were mailed. That was all I needed to know to figure it out."

Maria was quiet and I could tell she was confused. "I don't understand. Did your friend with the cabin tell him? How did he know about me? Did ***you*** tell him? Why would he send cards to me?"

"No, no.....nothing like that. It wasn't him. It was his wife."

"My God Terry, did you tell HER?"

"Of course not, Maria. I haven't told anyone. You know better than that."

Her voice softened. "I, uh.........I don't understand. How did she find out about me?"

"It's a long story. She didn't. She's guessing."

"I need a better explanation than that, Terry."

"I know...........I should have told you about what started this whole thing, but I didn't. I thought it would go away. I guess I was wrong."

"What in the world are you talking about? No more games. I want to know what's going on, **now**!"

"OK, OK." I cleared my throat and swallowed. "She hasn't seen us together. It's nothing like that."

"Terry, get to the point. Who is this woman? Have you been seeing her?"

"No, no.....just relax a minute and let me explain. It's going to take some time, so just listen. Remember the club dance? That's when it started, although I wasn't aware of it. Ann, Garth's wife, saw us dancing together and thought we were more than dance partners. She was so drunk I had to hold her up to dance with her. I'm surprised she even remembers being there. Anyway, from that, she suspects we're seeing each other. She called me about a week ago and said she wanted to talk to me and that it was important. I thought it might be about some problem she and Garth were having and said OK. We've been friends for a long time so I couldn't say no." I was measuring my words. I didn't want to say anything to upset Maria. "Do you remember the day I went by Alma's, and she told me she knew you?"

"Yes, but what does that have to do with it?"

"That was the reason I went to see her. I wanted her advice about it. I never told you. That was the day Ann came by the office. "

"I still don't understand," she said.

"When Ann came by, she came on to me. The bit about a problem was a ruse. She was looking for an affair. I couldn't believe it, but she was serious. The woman is mentally unbalanced, and I didn't know how to handle it. That's why I wanted to talk to Alma." I told Maria most of the details about Ann's visit as honestly as I could. I told her about Ann kissing me and offering me money for sex. She didn't interrupt me.

When I completed the story, she said, "I don't believe she could do all this without some provocation. Are you sure you didn't encourage her in some way?"

"I swear to you, it came out of the blue. She's always been a very private person. I've never seen her act so brazenly. She's usually quiet at parties, just gets drunk and says nothing. I promise you, I've never seen her act like that."

"Well, what did Alma think of it?"

"She thought Ann might be bipolar, schizophrenic, or it might be alcohol related."

"And what do you think?"

"I have no idea. I've known her for at least ten years, even before she and Garth married, and she's never acted this way......not to my knowledge."

"Um, have any of your friends said anything strange about her? Like coming on to them?"

"No. But I'm not sure they would. If she had, I would have noticed it. Our group is too close. Women pick up on stuff like that and they would talk about it. I tell you, this isn't the Ann any of us know."

"I know coming from me this is a stupid question, but why do you think she picked you out of the crowd?"

That was a good question. After a moment of introspection that produced nothing, I said, "If she really feels neglected, maybe she wants to punish Garth. He's my oldest friend. What better vehicle to inflict pain than an affair with your husband's best friend?"

Maria laughed. "You understand women more than I thought. It's a good hypothesis, but it would take a lot of nerve and courage to proposition you like she did. And I'm not sure she has that much moxie, not from your description of her."

"Well, that's the best I can come up with. What do you think it might be?"

"Wait a minute now, I didn't say I don't believe that. I just think there might be some other motivation."

"Like what?"

"Terry, you're not a flirt, OK? You've got that thing that women like, that little boy Southern charm, but it's not sexual… not in the beginning. Believe me, it grows on you, and it's powerful, but you're not the type to force your way on anyone. I don't even think you know what you're doing sometimes. Honestly, you'd be the first to run if things got out of hand. Our situation was different – a thing of destiny and no friends were involved. That's why it happened. Both of us wanted it to happen, or it wouldn't have. You were the one who said it was destiny. I believe you. It took a while to develop, and I think……I **know….** we stepped away quite a few times because we had so much to lose and we couldn't justify our moral behavior. You don't want to accept that, but deep down, you know it's true. We can't help it. That's how we were raised. "Now," she paused and swallowed, "In view of all that, maybe you did something. Don't get mad, something that set her off."

I was taken aback, hurt, and confused. "Are you saying I'm at fault? Do you have so little trust in me? I can't believe you could think that. I'm disappointed in you."

"Please, I want to believe you. More than anything. There just has to be more to this. Maybe she thinks you're more susceptible. It may not be anything you've done. Didn't she say she thought you and Jane were having problems, she thought we were seeing each other? Help me with this. I'm not looking for fault, just answers."

"Believe me, I spent plenty of time thinking about it. I'm telling you, I have no idea why she did it. I can't figure out why she sent you the cards, probably to smoke us out or make us stop seeing each other. I'm sure she'll let me know….. soon."

"What makes you so sure?"

"She's gone too far and she might think I'll tell Garth. The least she'll do is apologize and tell me it won't happen again. She's got to protect herself."

"I'm not so sure, but I don't know her. Look, we need to talk. Face to face. I'm confused with all of this, and talking on the phone isn't helping. If it's OK, I'll come by your office after I pick up the kids from school, probably about three thirty."

That sounded good to me. "That's good; I'll see you then."

"I've got to go. See you."

The pattern had become resolute. When she said goodbye, she meant it.

I thought about our conversation and felt it was more talk than substance. My biggest mistake was not telling her about Ann when it happened. I thought it would go away, and that was part of the justification. Yet, it went a lot further than that. I really felt some guilt and didn't know why. Part of me wanted to tell her and part of me didn't. She sensed that I had some guilt, probably because I didn't tell her. I could tell that from her questions. Truth was, I didn't have many answers for any of it.

I fixed a cup of coffee, lit a cigarette, and went to the loft. The phone was ringing.

"Design Concepts, Terry Forte speaking."

"High Terry; it's Ann. Long time no see." Her laughter was long and boisterous.

"Not long enough," I said in a monotone.

"Now, now. Don't pout." She was needling me.

"How do you think I should act after what you did?"

"All I did was offer you my feminine charms.......and YOU turned me down. Shame on you. You don't know what you're missing," she said coyly. I could visualize her batting her eyes.

"Knock it off, Ann. You know what I mean."

"I'm afraid I don't; perhaps you'd better tell me."

"The postcards, Ann. Don't you think that was a bit presumptuous?"

"What postcards?"

I was getting irritated. "Those damn cards you sent to Mrs. Champion. I know it was you. Garth told me about the trip to Las Vegas. It wasn't hard to figure out."

"Oh, the trip. I was there, but I was too busy to send any cards. If I'd sent any, it would have been to you and Jane."

My face was on fire. "OK, you can deny it if you want to, but I know it was you. I recognized your handwriting," I said, hoping she'd bite at my lie. She didn't.

"I'm sorry somebody sent Mrs. Champion postcards. Were they naughty?" She tried to muffle laughter.

"That doesn't deserve an answer," I said.

"Well then, let's stop talking about it. That's not why I called. I'm coming to your office. We need to talk."

I was flabbergasted. "Are you crazy? We have nothing to talk about."

"I think we do!" Her voice took on different tone, strident and menacing. "I wouldn't want anything else happen that would upset Mrs. Champion."

"That's it, Ann! It's time for me to have a talk with Garth, not you." For the first time, fear was creeping into my mind.

"I don't think that would be wise. I'll tell him how you got me to your office on a pretense and tried to put the make on me, and I'll cry and tell him how horrible it was. Who do you think he'll believe? What do you think Jane will believe? I assure you, it will be my finest hour, worthy of an Academy Award."

"You wouldn't do that."

"Like hell I wouldn't. Just try me."

She had raised the bar and I was unable to jump over it. "What do you want?"

"You know what I want, and you want it too. You just won't admit it. I can be reasonable."

"Reasonable?"

"I'm admitting nothing. I don't know anything about the cards, but maybe, just maybe, the gods might smile on Mrs. Champion… if we could get together. I think that's reasonable."

"Sounds more like a threat or bribe, I'm not sure which."

"Are you stupid?" Her voice was becoming strident again. "It's neither. It's a way of working things out for both of us. Your marriage is unhappy and so is mine. If you're not involved with Mrs. Champion, why do you care?"

"I care because the Champions are my client. I care because Garth is one of my friends. What you're doing could cause me, you, our families, irreparable damage. For no reason that I can determine, you're trying to destroy my reputation and Mrs. Champion's."

She laughed. "You're assuming way too much. All I'm saying is, if I **AM** involved, maybe it will stop **IF** I'm given the chance to succumb to your …shall I say significant charms."

I was not winning the argument. I needed time to figure out what to do. "I'll think about it and call you later. I need more time."

"NO! You've had plenty of time. I expect something positive from you now. Otherwise, I can't be responsible for what might happen. I'm coming to see you now, this afternoon."

"No, damn it, not today. I've got an appointment with a client this afternoon and don't know how long it will take. I need to sleep on it, maybe tomorrow afternoon." She had me in a box. I couldn't have her show up with Maria here. That would be a catastrophe. Sweat was forming on my brow and fear had me by my throat.

She was quiet for a moment, then she spoke. "OK……I'll wait. But you better be there tomorrow, at three o'clock. Oh….and be careful what you do and who you do it with. You never know who might be watching." She laughed as she hung up.

I was stunned. This woman I have known for years – this shy, quiet woman whose only vice was alcohol – had become sober and satanic. Her threat was totally out of character, but undeniably real and frightening. My brow was wet with perspiration and my stomach was churning. Fear was taking over and it was fear I couldn't define. I had no idea what this woman might do. I was powerless. I wanted to talk to her, to reason with her, but I knew it was probably futile. How do you reason with insanity?

Protecting Maria and myself – I had to remember that I was also at risk – was the first order of business, but would be difficult and dangerous. Ann had Maria in her sights and was capable of following her to prove her theory. But not seeing Maria was unacceptable, and I had to maintain a client relationship with her regardless. *That might be the answer. If we could keep our meetings under the guise of business, Ann might be lulled into believing nothing is happening between Maria and me.* Wishful thinking, perhaps, but better than nothing. The problem was dealing with an Ann I didn't know and couldn't predict. She had shown me how irrational her new persona could be.

I wasn't accomplishing much thinking about what might happen. I had to get to the defensive side of the coin. I needed something, anything that might give me some time. Short of agreeing to meeting her at some rendezvous of her choice, which I wouldn't do under any circumstances, there must be some ploy I could use to stall her without making her angry and distrustful. I had to make her concede to something that would indicate she could be trusted, something she would accept. Surely, in time she would come to her senses.

Suddenly, it came, the old *carrot and stick* trick. *It just might work, if, and that would be a big if, I could trust HER! She must prove to me that she could be trusted by not threatening Maria in any way. I couldn't be a party to an affair with someone I couldn't trust. She might buy it. She would certainly understand it. I would ask her to demonstrate her trustworthiness over a period of time, maybe a month. If she would agree I would have a breathing spell and Maria would be safe for the moment.*

Maria walked through the door, windblown and rosy-cheeked from the cold. It was three forty-five. I had forgotten she was coming … well, not forgotten, but the time had gotten chewed up with the Ann dilemma. She was dressed casually in gray slacks, powder blue sweater and loafers, and she smiled as she approached. Her gait was measured, athletic and fluid, a combination that never failed to intrigue and arouse me. She had a bundle of drawings under her arm.

"Hi, Architect. Long time no see."

"Hi yourself," I said. "More than a day is too long." My inclination was to reach out for her, but visions of Ann peaking through the window slowed my passion.

Her smile widened. "You can't help yourself, can you? That smarmy Southern charm just has to come out."

"I'm glad you consider it charm. I can't seem to help it when you're around."

"I'll give you two days to stop that." She batted her eyes coquettishly. "You know I like it, don't you? Do you talk like that to all your clients?"

"Of course not. There are clients, and there are clients, but there's only *one* of you." I snickered and said, "Besides, if I flirted with all my clients I would be locked up."

"Well, you're free so I'll have to believe you. Do you have any coffee in this joint?"

"The very best. *Maxwell House* instant in a jar. Have a seat in the conference room, the pot is on." I filled the kettle and put it on the warming hotplate. Maria walked into the break room as I finished, brushed her hair back with both hands and stretched. I caught her in the middle of it and kissed her. She put her arms around me but leaned away from me. Her perfume, faint but pleasing, played with my senses. I wanted more.

"Let's not start anything we can't finish," she said.

"Why?"

"This isn't the place for it, that's why."

"Why not?" I was smiling.

"This could go on forever," she said. "You know why not. I'm not going to honor the question. We have other things to talk about. Have you forgotten?"

I took a deep breath. "Unfortunately I haven't. Let me get the coffee made before we get into the Ann thing." Steam was funneling out of the rumbling kettle.

I spooned in coffee and poured. "How much sugar?"

"One medium spoonful."

I handed her the cup. "How can you drink it with so little sugar? I have to disguise it before I can drink it."

"That's because you don't like coffee. You just tolerate it because I like it."

"Not true. There other things besides taste. It keeps me awake, it's good with cigarettes and it keeps my hands warm." I offered her a cigarette, which she accepted, and fished one out for me. I lit both with a black Bic lighter lying on the table.

I pulled on the cigarette, inhaled deeply and let the smoke out in a slow stream. It rose through dust motes captured in light framed by the doorway. Subconsciously or purposely, I was putting off the inevitable.

"OK, OK. What's going on with Ann?"

I took a deep breath. "You're not going to like it."

"What does that mean?"

"She called me after I talked to you."

"And?" She was getting agitated.

"For starters, she grudgingly admitted to sending the cards. Then she threatened me if I didn't take advantage of her offer. That was prefaced with her word that she would leave you alone, it was up to me."

"That's certainly comforting."

"Hardly. She said she was watching me and I better be careful what I did and with whom."

Maria's eyes opened wide. "You let me come here after she said that?" Her voice was rising to match her incredulity.

"Wait a minute. I had no way to stop you. I couldn't get in touch with you. Besides, you **are** a client. You have a vested interest in being here. Before you get all upset, let me tell you what I said to her."

"I hope it's an improvement over what you've told me so far."

"I think it is. It's a plan, not the greatest one, but better than nothing. I think she'll buy into it. If so, it's promising."

She shook her head and ran her fingers through her hair. "Well?"

"I'll put the ball in her court. I'll tell her we'll talk about it in a month if she doesn't harass you during that time. My point is that I have to be able to trust her if anything further is going to develop. And, of course, it won't."

"What? You can't be serious."

I laughed. "Serious as a heart attack. That's a month's grace to plot new strategy, and during that time she won't be bothering you. That's not all bad."

Maria crossed her legs and pulled at some imaginary wrinkle in her slacks. "And of course, you trust her."

"No way, but it'll give me some to time to think of something else to do."

She rolled her eyes in disbelief. "What happens when she finds out you're playing games with her?"

"I didn't say it was a perfect plan. I said it's a plan. I'm gambling that she won't catch on. Maybe something good will happen."

"In the meanwhile, she may be decorating my yard with toilet paper or sending pictures to my husband."

"I don't think so. As long as she thinks we'll get together, why would she jeopardize the opportunity? She wants you out of the picture. I think she'll buy it. We'll have to be very careful how we handle ourselves, not give her anything to arouse suspicion."

"Terry, is it really worth all this? It makes everything seem so sordid."

Her words were like a blow to my stomach. "That's your decision to make. You know how I feel. .I've told you many times. Life without you or even contemplating it is out of the question for me. For good or bad, I love you.... unconditionally."

She rubbed my cheek with the back of her hand and a tear welled up in her eye. "It's not a question of love, Terry. Neither of us has anything to prove there. I hate all the scheming and hiding. And now we have to play games with a psychopath. That's pathetic."

I fished the cigarette pack from my pocket and offered her one.

"No thanks," she said.

I extracted one, tamped it against the table and examined it. I was framing my comment. It was crucial. "Why should we make any decisions now? Remember, you **are** my client. We have every reason to see each other. In fact, if we act like architect and client in public, we shouldn't raise any suspicions. To do otherwise would be the worst thing we can do." I lit the cigarette and watched the smoke rise toward the ceiling.

The corners of Maria's lips turned up slightly, suggesting a wistful smile. "You're right. If we'd made decisions in the beginning, none of this would have happened.......shouldn't have happened. Don't misunderstand. I'm not sorry. I'd do it over again even knowing what I know now. But we have so little time together and I want it to be just for us, not sullied by some idiot who has no business in our lives. I'm beginning to feel like the other woman. How crazy is that?" She clasped her hands together and looked away.

"I don't see that, but I do sometimes feel like we're part of a psychological exercise of reward and punishment. What ever it is, this relationship we stumbled into must be powerful to survive all the negative things we've been through."

She turned and focused unblinking amber eyes at me. "It is...because we nourish it. It's personal and private and must remain that way. The minute it becomes more than the two of us and threatens our families, it's over! I mean that. I love you and value our moments together. To think of losing them is devastating. But, my children come first. They're my ultimate responsibility. Ann threatens that and that's why I'm leery."

"I understand and agree. But give me some time. Please. I'll find a way to stop her. I promise I won't let anything happen that would hurt you or your family."

She sighed. "I wish I had your confidence." She raised her left arm and looked at her wrist. "Oh my gosh. I've got to go; it's almost five." She stood up and pushed the chair under the table. She gave me a rueful smile. "Time flies when you're having fun."

"I take it that's a cruelty joke?"

She gave me a pat on my shoulder. "No, of course not. Even a bad day with you has merit. It would have been better had it been a good one, but that's life."

As she started walking to the door, I said, "Wait a minute." When she stopped, I reached for her waist and turned her around. "That's better." She didn't resist my kiss and I lingered over it like it might be the last.

"Um.......see, even a bad day can be good," she said.

"Well," I said, "We didn't miss the best part." I kissed her again.

She pulled away. "That's enough; I've really got to go."

"Can we get together next week?" I asked. "We need some alone time."

"Maybe, if we CAN be alone! Let's work on Monday. I think I can get away in the afternoon. But what about Ann?"

"I'll take care of her. I know her car and, of course, I know her. I'll plan it so we won't have to worry about her. Monday sounds good. If we don't get to talk tomorrow or the weekend, call Monday morning as early as you can. I'm going to work on a new routine for meeting you."

"Sounds good. Oops…I've really got to run." She made her way to the door and turned before opening it. She chuckled and said, "Let's hope I look like a client. Never know who's watching." Then she was gone.

I sat quietly for a few minutes. I was not pleased with my world and what was happening to it. Ann was making a shambles of it. I suddenly remembered I had an appointment with the Adjutant General tomorrow and I wasn't prepared for it. I knew it wasn't good, but I decided to try to reschedule it, if possible.

I called his office and got his secretary, Mrs. Eubanks. "This is Terry Forte," I said. I'm having a problem getting things ready for my appointment with the General for tomorrow. Would it be possible to reschedule it for next week?"

"The General will be pretty busy until the end of the year. I think I can give you Thursday morning, January third. Hmmm……..how about ten thirty?"

"That would be great, Mrs. Eubanks. I'll be there."

"I think it's a good idea, Terry……changing the date. With the holidays upon us and all the other things he has on his mind, it'd be to your advantage meeting with him later. Also, and don't tell him I told you, there's a rumor that we're getting three more armories next year.

"Thanks Mrs. Eubanks; I won't say anything about it. Hope you have a wonderful Christmas and New Year."

"Same to you, Terry. Goodbye."

I earned brownie points with the girls and Jane Thursday night by taking them to Mack's for cheeseburgers and milkshakes. That ranks right up there with summer vacation. Nevertheless, I didn't sleep well thinking about Ann coming by the office Friday. I drove to the office with many things racing around in my mind doing their best to drive me crazy. My office seemed almost hostile instead of my usual place of refuge.

I busied myself with routine tasks until Martha arrived. Then I decided to start on Hampton Elementary School. I pulled the file Dr. Merriweather had provided, grabbed the drawings of the existing building and went into the conference room. I spent three hours meticulously going over them and making copious notes on a legal pad.

I had some big decisions to make. Would this project require that I hire fulltime help, or could I make it with temporary help from my usual consortium of friends? It was a question of cash flow and mine was marginal. I could carry myself, but I would have to borrow money to take on full time help. One possible solution would be to take on a partner, which was inevitable at some point if I wanted to keep the right people. With my workload, I could expect a partner to buy in and perhaps that would eliminate the need for going in debt. That gave me three options and all of them had pluses and minuses. Rather than rush into a decision that I wouldn't be happy with, I leaned toward using temporary help. That would provide me time to weigh out other options.

"I'm leaving now," Martha said loud enough for me to hear her in the conference room.

"OK, see you Monday," I said. She mumbled something that sounded like "thanks," but I wasn't sure. She was obviously ready to leave. She made no effort to come to the conference room to say goodbye.

I heard the door slam when she left and momentarily thought about locking the door. It was a wasted moment. I remembered Ann was coming and dread replaced my almost festive, *get ready for the weekend* mood. I managed to work through it until three o'clock. She walked in while I was making my last cup of coffee for the day.

"Surprise," she said, bowing and throwing her arms out as if she were on stage. "Aren't you going to help me with my coat?" She walked toward me smiling, turned and dropped her arms. I removed her coat, breathing too much perfume, sweet and heavy as honeysuckle on a warm summer morning. It was overpowering, almost noxious. I hung her coat in the closet, and, when I turned, she was in my face. She was wearing a tight red sweater and a short black skirt. The sweater offered mounds of cleavage punctuated with nipples hardened from the cold. She was not wearing a brassiere.

"Are you happy to see me?" she asked. "You could at least give me a friendly kiss."

I ignored her remark. "I'm always glad to see you, Ann."

"You didn't kiss me."

I leaned over and kissed her quickly on the cheek without touching her.

"Is this an act of piety for Jane?" she said slowly and precisely. "Or is it for *Mrs. Champion*?"

I smiled and said, "Don't you think it's appropriate for a married man to kiss his best friend's wife on the cheek, if he kisses her at all?"

"Don't try to trick me with your misguided logic, Terry. I know what you've been doing......with her." She spat the words out. "It's a lot more than kissing on the cheek, or anywhere else, for that matter."

"You don't know anything, Ann. There's nothing to know."

"Sure, Terry, And pigs don't have curly tails. I know you drive around together a lot, and it can't all be client relationship."

"That's where you're wrong. Your imagination is playing tricks. We've visited their lot and we've looked at building materials, but that's normal. When construction starts in a few weeks, there'll be more of that. None of it means anything." I was wasting my breath.

"Yeah? And how long will it take to build HER house?"

Where was this leading? She had veered off course. "About six months, why?"

"Because I want to know what kind of excuse you'll be using then."

My expression was full of anger. "I guess you'll just have to wait and see."

"Hell no I won't. By then I'll be part of the action..........ONE WAY OR THE OTHER!"

"Is that a threat?"

She flashed an arrogant smile. Not a threat, I never threaten. I…just… make…promises." Her expression was menacing and dark.

"Call it what you will. It's still a threat."

"No, a promise isn't a threat. I want you to know what you have to look forward to. You're going to like it, I *promise*." She let the last word, promise, roll off her tongue languidly for emphasis. "I'll make you forget you ever knew HER."

"She and her husband are my clients. There's nothing to forget. You and Garth are my friends, maybe our best friends. It's all together different."

She narrowed her eyes and thought for a minute. "OK, let's try it another way. I don't believe it, of course, but let's say you aren't having an affair with the charming Mrs. Champion. There's no reason we couldn't have a sexual involvement purely for pleasure. You will admit it's pleasurable, right?" She waved away my reply and continued. "If it were purely for sex and not for emotion, we wouldn't be hurting anybody. We could continue loving our spouses, enjoy our sexual moments, and no one would be wiser. That sounds like a good arrangement to me. It may even save our marriages. And, from the looks of yours, it needs saving."

For added emphasis, she moved closer and put her hand on the inside of my thigh.

"Hold on a minute, Ann. "I pushed her away. "You're conveniently forgetting that Garth IS my best friend. We've been best friends since we were six years old. I couldn't make him a cuckold and wouldn't. Sex **is** pleasurable. I don't know any men who think otherwise, but that doesn't make it right for us."

"Would you do it if I were married to someone you didn't know?

"It would be difficult for me not to." My answer was truthful but laden with caveats, the obvious and only necessary one for me being Maria.

"You're not answering the question. Yes or no?"

"If you're looking for one word, it's yes." I didn't want to antagonize her; no was not a safe answer.

"Do you find me attractive?" Her questions were incisive, surgical.

"Um…….yes."

"Do you find me physically appealing. Sexually appealing?" She thrust out her breasts provocatively.

"You know I can't answer that."

"Answer me! Yes or no!"

"Under other circumstances, yes."

"In other words, if Garth weren't my husband, you'd sleep with me. Is that right?"

"I didn't say that."

"Well that's what I hear from your comments."

"We've discussed Garth, but we haven't said anything about Jane. Don't you thing she's worth mentioning?"

"Crap, Terry. That's garbage and you know it. If you're doing what I think you are, Jane hasn't been a factor. Besides, I'm not stupid.....or blind. At the cookout, I could see and feel the tension between you two. You're not getting along and I'll bet it's related to your sex life."

Ann was right on target. She was a lot smarter than I realized. She had been sober that night. Had she been in her usual drunken stupor, she wouldn't have noticed. I had hoped our anger with one another hadn't been that obvious.

"Maybe," I said. "But she's still my wife."

"For God's sake, Terry." She lifted up her hair and fluffed it, giving me a sideways look of frustration as she did so. "Don't you understand? I don't give a damn about Jane or Garth. I'm not interested in you for keeps. Nothing personal. I'm just a frustrated housewife who needs some attention. Don't make anything more of it than that. In six months or so, we'll never think about it again. No one will ever know about it but you and me. I might even agree to share you with Mrs. Champion, if that's what it takes."

"Now you're being absurd. Nothing's going on with her. How many times do I have to tell you? If it were, why would I be having sexual problems with Jane?" I really wanted to grab her and shake her and tell her the truth – I loved Maria, but I didn't want to start the third world war.

"You can tell me that till you're blue in the face and I won't believe it. A woman can tell and I've seen enough to know. I'll find out for sure. It may take a while, but I have ways. When I do, I'll start with Jane, and then I'll tell anybody who'll listen. You can stop the bleeding by simply spending a little time with me, maybe just once a week for starters. That's all it would take to get Mrs. Champion an insurance policy. That's what you want, isn't it? Her protection?"

"She doesn't need any protection. She hasn't done anything wrong. If you slander her, she'll have her day in court, then you'll need protection."

She glared at me. "I'm not stupid, Terry. I won't fire until I have all the ammunition I need. Don't forget, I don't have to find proof. Dear old dad left me plenty enough cash to hire the best detective I can find. It won't be difficult to catch you."

"You're not endearing yourself to me."

"Oh, you're getting angry. You're kind of cute when you're angry." She pushed against me, pulling me closer by grabbing my side pockets. "You're wrong, I can be very endearing."

Before I could move, she kissed me, nibbling on my lips and stabbing me furiously in the mouth with her tongue. When I didn't return her ardor she moved away.

"You're not the best kisser I've known, but I can teach you," she said.

"What do you expect? You've been threatening me for an hour."

"No Sweets, I don't threaten. I make promises. There's a big difference."

"You promised to threaten me. What's the difference?"

"Are all architects obsessed with semantics?"

It was my turn to laugh. "As a profession, we're not that esoteric."

"Well, let's forget about semantics. I promise that if we can work out a mutually acceptable arrangement, I won't do anything to damage Mrs. Champion. But if we can't, I'm not responsible for my actions. That puts it all on your shoulders."

"I don't think so! I'll tell you what's going to happen before this goes any further." I glared at her with unblinking eyes. "As soon as I get home, I'm telling Jane everything you've said, all of it. I'll tell her I had to call Mr. And Mrs. Champion and apologize for the post cards you sent. That was your big mistake because I have them and I'm sure Garth would recognize your handwriting. And when I show them to Jane, any more threats you make will be academic. If it's necessary, I'll tell Garth and show him the cards. I don't want to because I value his friendship, but believe me, I will."

Her smile turned to fear. "You wouldn't. I… I don't believe …..you would…" Her voice trailed off and her eyes went blank.

"You bet I will. You can't threaten me into a relationship I know is wrong……for both of us. You're not going to use me to punish Garth."

The dam broke and the tears came. She put her head on my shoulder and wept like a child. "I'm sorry…..so sorry. I didn't mean to hurt anyone." Her words were choked and stumbling. "I'm so confused." She was a broken soul. I almost felt sorry for her.

"OK. It's OK. I think we can work this out so no one will get hurt." I patted her shoulder and held her protectively. "We can walk away from this like it never happened and no one will ever know."

I offered her my handkerchief and she took it. She dabbed at her eyes and wiped her nose while she tried to speak. "Please........don't tell anyone. I don't know what came over me. I'm so ashamed."

"Hey, it doesn't matter. We all do things we can't explain. It's no big deal. I'm sorry I came down on you so hard. I lost control."

"No, you did the right thing. That brought me to my senses, even if it took a threat from you to do it. I'm the one who lost control. I don't know why I did it. It wasn't driven by sex. I think, deep down, I really want to punish Garth. God knows why, he hasn't done anything to hurt me. He's always stood by me and we both know that hasn't been easy. I've been a drunk for the last two years. It's hard to be romantic with someone who's blitzed out of their mind or throwing up half the night. I've lost my self-esteem and I guess I thought an affair would help me. I really love Garth and you do too. You're a good friend."

"He's my best friend, and he means a lot to me. No way I could sleep with his wife. Ann, you've gotten your head on straight and you seem to have gotten control over alcohol. You're a very attractive woman. He'll come around. But it'll just take time. He loves you very much, but he needs time to adjust to the new you. I'm proud of you. What you've done isn't easy, but good things will happen if you stay sober."

She sniffed back a tear and gave me a weak smile. "I'm not sure I can do it......stay sober."

I gave her a big hug and laughed. "Sure you can. You might need some help. Have you thought about AA or some psychiatric help? I know a wonderful lady, a psychologist, who works with people with dependencies. She was a client of mine and we became very good friends. I think you'd like her. She's helped me out a few times."

She backed away and ruffled her hair with a flip of her hands. "A psychologist might be OK, but I associate AA with derelicts. I know I shouldn't, but that's how I perceive it."

"You'd be surprised at who goes. That's why it's anonymous, so anyone can go and not have to worry about others finding out. But, if you feel uncomfortable with it, it wouldn't do you any good."

She averted my face and looked down before she spoke. "I need to think about it. Seeing your psychologist friend sounds like the better idea. Do you have her phone number?"

"Sure do. Let me write it down for you." I grabbed a scratch pad and printed Alma's name and phone number in large block letters. I folded it and handed it to her.

She stuffed it in her pocketbook and said quietly, "I'd better go. I apologize for all the trouble I've caused you and your friend…."

"Client, not friend," I said quickly, stopping her in mid sentence.

"Well……whatever you say."

Her reply bothered me. Maybe her attitude change was a charade, a trick to lull me into false security. I wanted to accept it in good faith but I had concerns that bothered me. Alma said bi-polar people were like that, up one minute and down the next, but I could only judge it by what I considered normal behavior. This happened too fast to be normal. I would get some advice from Alma before Ann contacted her, if she ever did. If she became Alma's patient, she couldn't advise me………doctor-patient privilege. Maybe this was normal behavior for people like Ann.

With out a word, Ann got her coat and walked to the door. She seemed to be mesmerized by her thoughts, as though she were alone. Before opening the door, she turned and looked in my direction with unfocused eyes. "I'm sorry," she said. "You won't have to worry about me anymore." Her words came slowly with resignation and indifference, directed at me but not to me.

I watched her walk to her car and drive out of the parking lot. If I had opened my dictionary to "zombie" it would say "Ann". What a change! She came in like a lion and went out like a lamb like the Ides of March. Perhaps I had destroyed her with my tirade even though I felt it was justified. Nevertheless, my comfort level was not good. She was a fragile creature with unimaginable demons assaulting her in ways most of us will never know or understand. I found myself feeling sorry for her, which would have been impossible a few hours ago, and wishing I could help her. But, I knew she was beyond my help and I was trapped with that knowledge. My heart was filled with an abiding sense of sadness, but, for all my trepidation, I had the gut feeling that my problems with Ann were over.

It was time to go home.

When I got home, Jane was in the dining room up to her elbows wrapping presents. She had boxes, wrapping paper, scotch tape, and ribbons spread over the entire table.

"You've been busy," I said.

"Christmas is Tuesday," she said curtly. "Did you expect the good fairy would shop for our presents, wrap them, and put them under the tree?"

"No, I thought my pretty little wife would do it while her hubby was trying to make a living." The truth was that I hadn't thought much about Christmas.

"Well, you were right, and, as usual, you haven't been much help. But tomorrow you'll have to go to the Schwinn store and pick up the girls bicycles. I told Mr. Grady you'd pick them up at one o'clock. You can hide them in your office until Monday night."

"Did you ask him to put them together? I don't want that facing me Christmas Eve."

"Of course, but it will cost you two dollars more for each of them."

"Fair enough," I said. Christmas was four days away and I hadn't gotten Jane a present. I'd have to do it Saturday if I were going to the cabin with Maria Monday. That was all the motivation I needed. I also knew that, regardless of Maria, it had been that way most of our marriage. "Where're the girls?"

"They're out of school for the holidays and I needed to shop, so I called your mom and she picked them up. She wanted to take them to Belk's anyway to try on some clothes. That's what she's giving them for Christmas. She said not to worry about them. She would feed them supper and we could pick them up tonight. We're going to town and find something for your folks and eat at the Redwood. That will finish up our shopping and I won't have to cook."

"Sounds good to me. Maybe we could go to Sears and look for a new vacuum cleaner. You said you needed one. That's not much of a Christmas present but it's practical." I felt a little like Scrooge for suggesting it, but our financial condition didn't allow for much extravagance and I knew Jane would go for it because she's better with money than I am and she had complained enough about the vacuum cleaner.

"That would be wonderful, but can we afford it?"

I smiled. "Sure, I'll do it the American way. I'll put it on installments. Besides, now that I have a school to do, we'll have some cash."

Jane looked stunned. "A school? What school?

O my God! I hadn't told Jane. My biggest accomplishment, and I hadn't shared it with her. "Uh......I was saving it for the right time to tell you," I sputtered. "Dr. Merriweather gave me an addition to Hampton Elementary and promised if I did a good job to consider me for the new elementary school."

"That's wonderful, Terry, but why didn't you tell me? You should have called; I can't believe you kept that a secret from me."

"I wasn't trying to keep it a secret." That was the truth. The mess with Ann had temporarily removed it from my thought process

. "Sometimes I don't understand you," she said. "If I had gotten news like that I would have wanted you to know about it immediately. Martha knows and she's probably told everyone. I feel a little like a fool. What if someone had asked me about it?"

"Jane, I haven't told anyone." *A strategic lie*. "I wanted to make it special and we haven't had any special time."

"And whose fault is that?" she snapped. Her eyes grew cold and she said, "I guess you planned to wrap it up with the vacuum cleaner and put it under the tree."

I tried to smile. "Don't be silly. I just told you, didn't I? It's only been two days."

"Some special time **YOU** picked."

"Jane, don't give me a hard time. I told you now because I know how you are about spending money. You didn't think we could afford a vacuum cleaner. I wanted you to be comfortable with it, that's all." I had screwed up big time. The only way out was to get her a nice surprise for Christmas. Of course, I'd have to suffer until then but it would solve the problem.

"Forget it," she said. "Christmas is for the kids anyway. It's not a big deal for me. I'd like a new vacuum cleaner; my old one is about to quit on me. But I hate to spend that much on Christmas. We could wait until a better time, or until it stops working."

"Hey.....it's not that expensive and you really need one. It's not like we're spending just to be spending. Besides, it could be for both of us. There's nothing I really need." That was true, but Jane could use many things, and giving her a vacuum cleaner was a bit tacky. Maybe I could find her a piece of jewelry. She'd like that. "While we're looking for presents for Mom and Dad, we can look at vacuum cleaners. If we don't see anything we want we'll forget it."

"We'll see", she said.

The conversation was officially over and we left for better things, shopping.

I was up early Saturday morning and left for town as soon as the stores opened. I was a man on a mission. I knew Maria wouldn't be expecting a present from me but I had something in mind that I felt she would like. I wanted to get her an Acker Bilk album that had *Strangers on the Shore* on it and I had noticed she had a charm bracelet she wore often. If I could find one, a seahorse would be perfect to commemorate our first encounter at the infamous Seahorse Motel. Even though the last part of our night wasn't anything to brag about, it seemed appropriate. A second choice would be a conch shell, but it would be a little off the mark.

Finding something for Jane would be a problem. It would have to be small so I could hide it from her, and it would have to be a little ostentatious. Jewelry would probably fill the bill, but I would have to buy hers in a different store. It wouldn't do for anyone to recognize her and ask how she liked her ring, which I was thinking about getting her, and her charm. I decided to get her a ring from Sylvan's and find Maria's charm someplace I wasn't apt to be known. I wanted to get my shopping done before I picked up the bicycles. I could hide everything in my office.

I went by the office first to pick up two company checks. I had enough money in my account to pay for the gifts, but not in my personal account. I would have to make up an excuse for Martha, not that it was any of her business, because she posted my books and was very particular about it. I was only a minute, but I took time to see if any remnants of Ann's visit were evident. I picked up left over cigarette butts and flushed them down the toilet. Nothing else was visible.

I turned onto Hampton Street heading towards Main Street, the location of Sylvan's, and found myself behind a long line of automobiles inching along. It seemed that every car in Columbia was converging on Sylvan's. It took three changes of the traffic light for me to get to Main and a policeman standing in the intersection waved me across, not letting me turn onto Main. I gave him an ugly look but it didn't help. He kept on waving me across and blew his whistle when

I hesitated. Main Street was awash with people, Christmas lights, decorations, and unmoving cars for as far as I could see, so the policeman had no choice but to keep traffic moving across the intersection. I went around the block, extending it to three blocks each way and found a place to park two blocks away. The walk would do me good if I didn't freeze to death. It was thirty-eight degrees and I had on a light jacket. Not good planning.

With head down and hands in my pockets, I pushed through the crowd of last minute shoppers, mostly women dragging along sulking children. Their conversations, past pleading and entering into orders and prodding and the irate cacophony of auto horns, measured the mood of the participants who were desperately trying to finish up their shopping. Once again, the spirit of Christmas was losing its luster to procrastination.

I edged to the inside of the walk and entered Sylvan's. Iit wasn't crowded like the other stores – Belk's, Tapps, Penny's or Louries – largely because it catered to the more affluent who spent larger sums of money. Normally I would not be shopping there, but my current situation at home dictated more largesse in my gift selection. Bribery or penance, take your choice.

A man about my age wearing a dark gray suit, white shirt and bow tie met me at the counter. His wavy brown hair was parted in the middle and he wore glasses low on his nose. "May I help you, Sir?" He glanced at my hands and clothes as though taking inventory of my net worth. I was wearing my Clemson ring and a plain wedding band – my total compliment of jewelry, not too impressive.

"Yes, I'd like to look at rings. For my wife, not too gaudy but in good taste." Gaudy was my way of saying not too expensive, but I could see it wasn't a good choice by the look of distaste on his face.

"Perhaps……. a small diamond?" He reached for a tray of rings that were obviously beyond my means.

"No," I said curtly. "Maybe a pearl or ruby…..around two to three hundred dollars?"

"Oh. I think I have something that you'll like. An opal in a setting of small diamonds. I believe it's about two hundred and seventy dollars. Let me get it for you." He brought back a ring, making a big show of shining it with a jeweler's cloth and laying it on a piece of felt in front of me. "Do you know her ring size?"

"No," I said. I slipped it on my little finger. "I think this will do. Her finger is about the same as my little finger."

"Well, if it doesn't fit, we can size it.....for a small fee." He tilted his head back as though the air had suddenly filled with an unpleasant odor and said, "We have to charge for rings under five hundred."

His veiled insult didn't deter me. "I'll take it. Do you have a small box I can wrap it in?"

"Certainly, Sir. Will this be cash or charge?"

"Check, if that's OK?"

"Fine, Sir. That'll be two hundred and seventy-five dollars and forty cents, with tax. Do you have identification?"

"Sure." I wrote the check, fished out my wallet and handed over my driver's license and social security card with the check. He carried them to the manager, who gave them a cursory look and nodded affirmatively. He put the ring into a small box, bagged it, and brought it to me.

"Bring the ring back with the bill if you need to get it sized," he said. "Merry Christmas."

"Thank you, and merry Christmas to you." *One down and one more to go.*

I entered the crowd once again, and walked two blocks to a small jewelry store that catered to younger people, figuring they would have charms. My judgment was correct, but there were so many charms to choose from I didn't know where to start. In time a young woman, most certainly holiday help, came over to wait on me. "See what you want?" she asked. Blunt but pleasant.

"No, but maybe you can find it for me. I'm looking for a seahorse in silver. Do you have anything like that?"

"We don't have any on display, but last week I saw a few in the back. Let me check." She whisked away in her sweater, wool plaid skirt and bobby socks, obviously a young college student or high schooler. She was gone for about fifteen minutes, but she returned with one in her hand. "Last one; you're in luck."

It was a very detailed replica in sterling, just what I wanted. "That's wonderful. I'll take it."

She did some hasty figuring on a pad and said, "That comes to twenty-eight dollars and fifty-six cents with tax. Do you need a box for it?"

"That would be nice," I answered. I had the check written when she returned with it. "Do you want any identification?"

"No that's not necessary" She glanced at my check and said, "Thank you

Mr. Forte.....uh, is that right?"

I gave her a quick smile. "Absolutely. Thank you. Merry Christmas." I left the store felling good about my purchase. I knew Maria would like it. Now I had one more purchase to make. I crossed the street and walked three blocks to Mehlmans to find Acker Bilk's album. Mehlmans was easy to spot with the RCA mascot, a large black and white dog, standing placidly at the entrance. It was a madhouse. Every high school kid was inside. All the booths were full of youngsters playing the latest recordings – some dancing, others listening. The place hadn't changed much from my high school days. It was still a gathering place for youth. I knew what I wanted so a booth wasn't necessary.

I bounced through the crowd and found a rack labeled "instrumentals". They were in alphabetical order so Acker Bilk was easy to find. I selected one that included *Stranger on the Shore* and walked to the cashier. I gave her five dollars. She rang up the sale and gave me back a dollar and some change. Mission accomplished; I felt the rosy glow.

I threaded my way through the maddening crowd with a smile frozen across my face. I was as happy and secure as a suckling babe. I was invincible. One more stop at Schwinn's and I had reached the pinnacle. I wasn't sure what the pinnacle was that I had reached, but in my manic state it didn't matter. I found my car and drove the few miles to Schwinn's in ten minutes. Twenty minutes later, Mr. Grady miraculously managed to get one of the bikes in the back seat and the other tied down in the trunk. I watched carefully so I could remember how he did it. I didn't want to spend a lot of time Christmas Eve in the cold trying to figure it out. I paid him, this time in cash, and left for my office. I had everything stowed away in no time, but I had to think about a safe place for Maria's gifts. I put them in the Hampton Elementary School file. I knew no one would find them there. I decided to take Jane's ring home so I could wrap it and put it under the tree. It would be easy to hide from her.

I looked around the office, gave myself a mental pat on the back and went home. Santa, with a little help from the architect, had done his magic!! *Merry Christmas.*

Sunday arrived with the usual chaos created by our efforts to get ready for church. The girls didn't want to get up and neither did I. Jane was, as usual on Sunday, the matriarch who knew what to do and how to do it. She took on the persona of a drill sergeant and had us all dressed and ready to go with about ten minutes to spare. She could organize when it counted.

Actually, I enjoyed church when it was over and felt like I was better for having gone. Our minister preached an appropriate sermon, "The true meaning of Christmas," and his delivery was outstanding for a change. The church was beginning to attract more members and would be overflowing on Christmas Eve. All those who came twice a year, Christmas Eve and Easter, would be in attendance. I guess, in Christian terms, it's a good thing, but it sure made it hard to get a seat for those who come regularly.

After the service, we spent a few minutes in the church parlor having a cup of coffee and chatting with friends before we picked up the girls. Then we made our usual pilgrimage to the Friendly for dinner. It was not a unique thing for us. On the contrary, it was a generational thing passed on from our parents and theirs before them. I can remember my parents leaving church early on the Sundays we went to the Friendly just to beat the people from First Baptist.

After dinner, we drove down Main Street to see the Christmas decorations. It was a far cry from yesterday. The throngs of traffic were non-existent. We could have been on another planet. If it were not for the blue laws, the streets would have been crowded like yesterday.

It was impressive to see lights and garlands strung across Main Street and the State House with its thirty-foot tall Christmas tree, all ablaze with lights and decorations, anchoring the end of the street.

"Daddy, don't drive so fast," said Jumper. "We might get to see Santa." She was searching both sides of the street with her luminous eyes.

"I don't think so, Jumper. Even Santa needs to rest on Sunday. He'll be real busy Monday night."

"Are you staying home today so you can rest, Daddy?" Her pretty blue eyes were pleading.

"Sure am," I said turning and giving her a quick smile.

"Oh goody! Can we play Monopoly? Mama can play, too, cause she doesn't have to cook."

"Sounds like a winner," I said still smiling.

I woke up early Monday and fixed my breakfast: orange juice, a quick bowl of corn flakes, and coffee, and took my time reading the paper. I let Jane and the girls sleep; no reason for them to get up. All the shopping was done and the girls didn't have school.

When I left, the sun was in the low part of its winter arc peeking through scattered clouds, turning them into gray and pink slashes simultaneously. The ground and rooftops were covered with frost that would soon burn off, but the temperature would remain just above freezing all day. Didn't matter; what I had in mind had nothing to do with freezing. I was upbeat and sang to myself most of the way to the office. It came out, *The wind is blowing, the snow is snowing, but I can weather the storm. What matters dear how much it may storm; I've got my love to keep me warm.* I really let it go on the last line. Not much talent or technique, but lots of gusto.

The office wasn't cold. I had set the thermostat at sixty-five when I left Saturday afternoon. I pushed it to seventy-two and heard it click on. I wasn't sure how long I would be there. Not long, I hoped. I cut the hot plate on for coffee water and dug Maria's gifts out of the Hampton Elementary file. I found wrapping paper, ribbon, clear tape and stick-on ribbon flowers in Martha's desk, and hastily wrapped them. It wasn't professional, but it would pass. Satisfied, I lit a cigarette and had a cup of instant.

Shortly after nine, Maria called. Her voice was effusive and quick to the point. "I can be ready to leave here in ten minutes. Is that too early for you?"

"No. The sooner the better."

"Well, what's the plan?" she asked. "Do you think Ann might still be a problem?"

"I don't think so, but no need to take a chance. Drive to town and circle a few blocks. If you don't see a bright red Plymouth or a dark blue ford Fairlane behind you, head for that shopping center on lower main. I'll meet you there. I doubt that Ann knows your car. She would more than likely follow me. I won't pick you up until I feel safe."

"OK. Oh! I hope you're not hungry. I didn't have time to fix anything and I can't stay past twelve anyway. Can you live with that?"

I laughed. "Are you kidding? I'm surprised you can get away that long. It **IS** Christmas Eve, you know."

"Just didn't want you mad at me."

"That's not worthy of a comment; just get moving."

"I'm gone," she said and hung up.

I cleaned up the wrapping mess and put the paper, ribbon, and tape back in Martha's desk. I burned the remnants of wrapping paper into the sink and washed it out. I didn't want to leave anything that would provoke questions. I would be coming back so I left the lights on and the thermostat set at seventy-two.

I didn't see any cars as I exited the parking lot, but just to be sure, I drove to town and turned a few blocks as I had told Maria to do. Satisfied that I didn't have a tail, I drove to lower Main and the shopping center and waited for Maria. I felt like a character out of a Dashell Hammett book. I saw her car turning in and watched her park in front of the Winn-Dixie Store. I was moving before she stopped and pulled up beside her, pushing the door open. I laid her presents on the back floor before she entered.

She jumped in with a huge grin on her face. "Nobody followed me," she said patting me on the knee. "Maybe I wasn't worth it." Her smile remained.

"You are to the only one who's playing this game."

"Playing?" she said with her eyes arched.

"You know what I mean."

She slid away from me. "No I don't. Explain."

"I just mean I'm your lover, soul mate, partner – whatever, and I think you **ARE** worth it."

Her smile returned and she slid back toward me. "I'll accept that. Besides, I was kidding. I believe I ruffled your feathers."

"No, but you had me going for a minute. I wasn't sure what you were thinking."

"A little mystery's good for you," she said coyly.

"If you want my opinion, there's too much mystery right now to suit me."

"And what might that be?"

I laughed. "Too many clothes."

"You don't want me to freeze, do you?" She slipped her coat off. "Is that better?"

"Good start." I rubbed her leg just above her knee. She was wearing a light gray sweater, charcoal skirt and black pumps. Dressed for shopping.

"That's not a bad start, either," she said. She grabbed my hand and held it with both of hers, kneading my fingers softly. "If you're not at the cabin in fifteen minutes, I'm a pumpkin."

"Umm…I like pumpkin."

"Watch that wicked smile, Buster, or you'll get a pumpkin in your face."

"Then I hope you turn into a pumpkin." Now I was laughing.

"OK, I give up. I can see where this conversation is going…..and I like it." She had her happy face on and she continued to rub my fingers.

"There's the turn," I said. I checked the rearview mirror for familiar cars. Seeing none, I slowed and turned onto the rutted roadway. The trees, most of which were bare of leaves, didn't offer much visual protection until we were near the cabin. That would change when summer came. I pulled up near the front door and parked. "It's going to be cold in there. Stay in the car until I get the heater going. It'll only take a minute."

"Uh-uh, I want the full course. We haven't been here in a while." She beat me out of the car.

"OK, but stand at the door until I get the power on." I opened the door and made my way to the panel in the closet. I felt for the main switch and pushed the toggle button. "Turn on the lights." Maria hit the wall switch and two of the lamps came on.

"That's not much light," she said.

"The other lamps aren't on that circuit. I moved around the room and switched on two more lamps. "How's that?"

"Better. Now I can see you."

"Let me get the heaters going, then you'll see more of me. Maybe more than you want to."

"Promises, promises," she said laughing. Her laughter was like a young girl's, uninhibited and honest.

I got the two heaters from the closet, put one in the bedroom and one in the big room and turned them on high. Warmth from the electric coils was immediate. "Bill needs built-in heaters and a thermostat. He could set it a little above freezing so the water pipes couldn't freeze. He's taking a big chance. Well……

maybe not. He may have cut the water off." I opened the cold-water valve and water flowed into the sink. "We're in luck."

"I didn't think it ever got that cold in South Carolina," she said.

"Sure it does. I can remember some days below zero when I was in college. 'Course Clemson's in the Blue Ridge foothills and it's not uncommon to have snow a few times in the winter. Columbia's a bit iffy, but usually never below the middle teens."

"Well, I don't need anymore snow. I saw enough in Pekin. I hated those gray winters with dirty snow on the ground. Fresh snow's beautiful but it doesn't stay white."

Damn. I had forgotten about my gifts. Talking about snow reminded me of Christmas and that jogged my memory. "I left something in the car I want to show you. Excuse me for a minute."

I was back in a second and handed her the gifts.

"What's this?" she asked.

"Just a little something for Christmas. Well, it's not really for Christmas. It's just a gift. You can open them. You can take them home without a problem."

She sat down and opened the bigger one first. She smiled and said, "Acker Bilk.......and *Stranger on the Shore.* That's perfect.......our song. I like that. Thanks Sweetheart." She stood and kissed me. It was a light touch but powerful in its quiet dignity.

"Open the other one."

She sat back down and slipped the ribbon and tape off. She did it very carefully. I would have ripped it off. Women are definitely gentler than men. When she pulled the charm out of the box, her eyes opened wide and she stared at me before she spoke. "I don't know what to say. This is the most wonderful gift I've ever gotten. It's absolutely perfect." She stood, tears welling in her eyes sparkling with happiness, but this time she kissed me with total abandonment, as though she was surrendering her spirit to me. When her kiss ended, she put her head on my chest and held me a long time. "How in the world did you find it?" she said in a hushed voice.

"It wasn't hard. I knew exactly what I wanted. I asked and the saleslady found it. I was lucky. If they hadn't had a seahorse, I would have gotten a conch shell."

"No. The seahorse is the only right one. How did you decide on a charm?"

"That was the easy part. I noticed your charm bracelet the night we were in Pete's Bar. I also knew you wouldn't have any trouble hiding it on your bracelet. It was an easy decision."

"You're so smart. That's why I love you. I wish I had something to give you that meaningful."

I smiled. "Oh, but you do!" And after she kissed me, she did.

We lay in a cocoon of afterglow, quiet and introspective after our mating. Dust motes played in the light flowing through the blind slats, the light bending over the slats like a Dali painting. I watched smoke trailing from my cigarette; she had stubbed hers out.

Every part of my body, mind, and spirit was relaxed and satisfied. A state of nirvana. Our lovemaking had been quiet, almost lazy, but, as always, consuming. It was never the same, each time surpassing the last "How do you feel?" I asked. She was lying quietly on my arm.

"Um……..how do you think?" Her question came with closed eyes and lips turned up in a smile.

"Maybe like children too excited to go to sleep tonight?" I propped up on one arm and stroked her tummy with extended fingers.

"Not excited," she said. I'm past that stage. I got just what I wanted and now I'm content." She smiled at me with languid eyes, those amber green portals to her soul. Even now, there was an aura of mystery about them, but it was good. Something that I would always cherish.

I tickled her playfully. "Was it the record album or the charm that made you content?"

She stuck her tongue out. "If I didn't know you better, I'd think you were a tease."

"Huh?" I blurted.

"The charm, of course." She laughed as only she could, warm, responsive and playful. "The lovemaking came in third, just behind the album." She watched my eyes for reaction and must have sensed my confusion. "Oh silly, I'm just kidding." She put her arms around me and pulled me to her. She was really laughing now. "The presents are wonderful, but nothing, absolutely nothing is close to our lovemaking. And the presents would lose their meaning without it."

"For a minute, I thought I was losing my touch."

"Touch has a lot to do with it and you definitely haven't lost it."

I moved closer and kissed her. Her response was instant, encouraging. "Let's pretend I lost it so I can find it again." I closed her eyelids with a kiss, and then kissed the tips of her breasts. Her eyes remained closed.

"Sounds good to me," she whispered. "Let's just do that."

While I was dressing and using the bathroom, Maria found some instant coffee and brewed us a cup. We spent our last minutes at the cabin sipping it, smoking a cigarette, and engaging in non-specific conversation. We sat on the sofa holding hands, and that's hard to do when you're smoking and drinking coffee.

"What's on your agenda for the rest of the day?" I asked.

"Lots, but I haven't gotten organized yet. That's not like me, but I just couldn't think about it until after we had our morning. Now that you've cleaned out all the cobwebs, it'll be easier." She picked up her cup and crossed her legs. Even in my satiated state they got my attention.

"Sweetheart, have I ever told you what gorgeous legs you have? It should be against the law to have legs that long and shapely."

"I'm so glad you finally noticed. I've been trying to entice you with them for so long." She leaned over and kissed me. "You know..........flattery will get you anything."

"Really?" I broke into song. "All I want for Christmas is your two great legs, your two great legs. Now what a present that would be!"

"Uggh! That's so silly." She giggled and said, "Cute, but silly."

I flashed one of my best smiles. "Sometimes the truth is silly. But silly or not, I mean it. And it's not just your legs I want. I want it all."

"Don't get so serious; I've got to go. It's Christmas Eve and we have much to do."

"I know." That was all I could say. She was right but I hated to leave her. "I'll be back in the office Wednesday. Maybe you can call."

"I'm not sure. The kids will be there and Pat's not working till after New Years. The only way I can do it is from a pay phone."

"What if I call you about your house?"

"Not good. I'm uncomfortable when Pat's around. I know it's silly, but that's the way it is. I couldn't say much anyway, so what's the point?"

I shook my head in the affirmative. "You're right. I'll wait till after New Year's……... Do you have any plans for New Year's?"

"Pat invited our friends over; looks like I'll be cooking. It would have been nice if he had asked me first. That's not my idea of a good time. How about you? Anything exciting?"

"No, not really. Same thing as last year. Jerry Lieb gets us tickets to the Jewish Center, thirty dollars a couple. That includes drinks, a band, champagne and noisemakers at midnight and a buffet breakfast. Not a bad deal."

Maria gave me a wry grin. "Better than me cooking, that's for sure. Want some excitement?"

"Like what?"

"Do they have a telephone?"

"There's a pay phone in the lobby."

"Great. Call me between eleven thirty and midnight. I'll make sure I answer. We can at least say happy New Year."

"I can't promise, because I'll be with a lot of people, but I'll try to slip away. It'll be closer to eleven thirty than twelve."

She extended her arms out, palms up and said, "So…….either it works or it doesn't. It won't be the end of the world if it doesn't………but it'll be a wonderful surprise if it does. If it doesn't work out, at midnight let's close our eyes, shut out everything around us, and think about this day and each other."

I smiled though my heart wasn't in it. "Good, but the hard part for me will be waiting that long."

She put her hand on my arm and squeezed. "I have a feeling it'll work out. Now let's go! I've got a lot to do."

I left the office early and got home before three o'clock. The house was a beehive of activity. Jane was baking pies for Christmas dinner and the children were trying to help. Good way to burn off some of the excitement of Christmas Eve.

Jane glanced up as I came into the kitchen and wiped her brow with the back of her hand. I could tell she was tired. "God, I'm glad to see you. I need some help. I'm trying to get a head start on tomorrow's dinner. Could you do some peeling and slicing for me? It would really be a big help."

"Sure," I said. "Let me change clothes and I'll be right there." Christmas dinner is a big thing at our house. Both of our parents come over for what has become a ritual. Sometimes they come early to watch the kids get their gifts. I think they enjoy it as much as the children do. That means breakfast too, but it's usually doughnuts and coffee so that's not a problem. They don't stay long if they come early, preferring to go home and come back for dinner.

"Don't tarry. I need help now."

"Be just a minute," I said. I changed into cotton slacks and a tee-shirt, washed my hands, and hurried back to the kitchen.

Jane didn't look up. She was busy coring and slicing apples for her pie. "Grab those bags on the table and start with the carrots. Peel them and slice them into quarter inch rings. The peeler is in the drawer with the knives."

"Gotcha. Do I need to wash them?"

"No. Why would they need to be washed? Peeling them will take care of that. Sometimes I wonder about you."

"You don't need to wonder. You know I'm a klutz in the kitchen."

"Well, today you're going to be Julia Child. Now hop to it."

I went to work with the peeler and after three carrots I got the hang of it. I made it through the peeling, but slicing them into small circles was another matter. The engineering side of my brain was measuring them into exact sizes and that took too much time.

"Hey, get another knife; that one's too small. And don't be so meticulous. You're not building a house. Just slice them; don't measure them."

The bigger knife was a help, but I hard a hard time not measuring each cut. I finished about twenty minutes later and dropped the knife on the cutting board with a flourish. "Ta da! I'm finished."

"No you're not." She handed me a plastic bowl. "Put them in here, then seal them with aluminum foil and put them into the fridge. Let me pour some water in there before you seal them so they won't dry out."

I stretched the foil tightly over the top of the bowl and meticulously folded it around the edge. After I put it into the fridge I asked, "What's next?"

"Peel the potatoes in the other bag, quarter them and put them into the large pot on the stove. You'll need a small paring knife to get the eyes out after you peel them."

"No sweat," I said. I was getting good with the peeler, but potatoes were more difficult to peel and there were a lot of them. It took more time to remove the eyes, but with due diligence, I got it done. I quartered them, put them into the pot, and washed the starch off my hands.

Jane put the pot into the sink and covered the potatoes with water. "Would you mind putting them on the stove? They're kinda heavy."

"Just call me Hercules, the great chef. Ugh, they are heavy. I think I've gotten a hernia."

Jane smiled one of those *told you so's*. "You're not getting off that easy. Put the cover on and set the heat on medium."

"I'm stupid. What's medium?"

"Just move out of the way; I'll do it." She pushed me out of the way with her hip. "Men are worthless in the kitchen."

"What do you mean? Look at all I did."

"Should I pay you by the hour, or give you a medal?"

"I'll have to think about that. What do you think I'm worth?"

"Not much." She laughed like it was all a big joke.

"I think I'm good at some things."

"Like what? Oh for heaven sakes. I'm just kidding. Get that hangdog look off your face."

I flashed the old briar-eating smile, almost swallowed my face. "I was beginning to wonder."

"Silly goose," she said dropping her hand towel on the counter top and hugging me tightly around the waist. "But don't get any ideas; we've got lots to do. I've still got to make eggnog for the girls……..and you, Santa. I shorted you on the cookies this year. I bought some from the bakery instead of making them. However, I'm prepared to spike Santa's eggnog with some *Southern Comfort.* It gets cold riding around in a sleigh all night."

"Now you're talking. Maybe Mrs. Claus could help me with the eggnog, the *Southern Comfort* part."

"I might just do that after the girls go to sleep, **IF** they go to sleep. They get so excited. Remember, last year we had to stay up till two o'clock before they finally got to sleep."

"Yep, I do, but we let them go to bed too early. They were in bed at eight o'clock trying to get to sleep. That didn't work. We need to keep them up till at least ten."

Jane thought for a minute. "Why don't you see if you can get them interested in a game of Monopoly? That might take their minds off Santa."

"Guess again, Kemosabi. That ain't going to happen. Tell you what; how about Kirk's? I could call and get him to fix something to go. They love Kirk's cheeseburgers. That'd get their attention and fill up their stomachs to boot. Monopoly on top of that might do it."

Jane smiled. "It sure gets mine. I don't have anything to fix anyway. Besides, I've been in the kitchen all day and I need a break."

"Consider it done. Where's the phone book?"

"Look in the drawer left of the sink, all the way to the end. But you better ask the girls what they want before you call. They can get strange sometimes."

"You're right." I wrote the number down on a piece of scratch pad and went to find the girls. Shock, shock. They were sitting quietly in the den watching television. "OK ladies, I know you probably aren't interested, but I'm ordering something for supper from Kirk's. If you want anything, now's the time to ask or forever hold your peace."

They came out of their semi-stupor like ravenous wild animals. Janet was first to reply. "Kirk's?" A pause. Then "Wow, yummy. I want a cheeseburger, smothered in onions. And a chocolate milkshake. And can I have a slice of strawberry crème pie? It's sooooo good. Please Daddy, pretty please."

She reminded me of the puppy, panting and jumping around. "If you want it, you can have it, but don't let your eyes get bigger than your stomach. You know we're going to have your mother's special eggnog later. She'll be upset if you don't drink any."

Laurie snickered under her breath. "She'll never eat all that. She won't eat **HALF** of it."

Jumper was furious. "Liar, liar. Just watch me. You don't know everything."

"I know you can't eat that much." Janet looked down her nose at Jumper.

I decided to intervene. "OK, that's enough. I don't think Santa would like to hear this conversation. Just cool it. Both of you can have what you want. What's for you, Laurie?"

"Oh Daddy, Santa doesn't care about what we eat. Get me a cheeseburger without onions and a strawberry milkshake."

"What? No pie? You like the chocolate crème. If you don't eat it you can save it till tomorrow. Or you can leave it for Santa."

"Sure, Daddy. OK, I'll take chocolate.'"

Jumper stuck out her tongue at Laurie. "If I don't eat my pie, I'll put it out for Santa."

"OK, I've got it. Anything else or any changes of mind? Last chance." I waited and looked into their faces. "I'm making the call. Anybody want to ride with me?"

Jumper was up and running towards me. "I do, I do!" she said. "Can I go inside with you?"

"Of course, if I leave you in the car, Santa might grab you up to help him."

She giggled. "You're teasing me, Daddy."

I made the call and Kirk said it would be ready in twenty minutes. He was having a slow night because of Christmas Eve, and would probably close after I came by. I got Jumper and we took off. It was about a twenty-minute ride.

We managed the complete trip in a little over an hour. Kirk took about a half hour to get everything ready, so we were a little later getting home. Jane had finished in the kitchen and had set up the dining room table for us, including the monopoly board. We decided to eat our burgers and pie before we started playing because of the mess the food and participants would make. Believe it or not, Jumper polished off her cheeseburger, pie, and milkshake without difficulty, much to Laurie's chagrin. She did have trouble with Jane's eggnog, but finished it off like a brave soldier. I was proud of her. After a quick cleanup, we got into

Monopoly and played until the girls started yawning. We had kept them up, filled their stomachs, and tired them out. They would sleep through the excitement tonight.

At eleven o'clock and after we finished a glass or two of eggnog with libation added, I left to pick up the bicycles. I felt more like going to bed than going out into the weather, but it had to be done. I slipped into the bedroom and got Jane's ring from the inside of my bedroom slipper where I had hidden it, and put the box into my pocket. I hadn't been able to wrap it at home so I would do it at the office. Thank God for Martha and her wrapping paper.

Actually, the cold air was refreshing after the warm house, and it woke me up. It was a small price to pay for all the fun Christmas day would bring. I never tired of seeing the surprise and happiness on the girls' faces. *Too bad it will come to an end when the fantasy is over for them. Unfortunately, it's already over for Laurie, but I hope Jumper can hang on for a few more years. The wonderful part is that parents can re-live the wonder of their Christmases past through their children and grandchildren.*

When I got to the office, I wrapped Jane's ring. I wanted to be ready to leave when I put the bicycles into the car. Thank goodness Mr. Grady showed me how to get the bicycles in the car, or it would have taken me all night. It still took me a lot more time than it took him, but, with the help of a few, choice four-letter words and a lot of luck, I made it and was on my way home in thirty minutes. I decided it would be wise to leave the bicycles in the garage until I had the opportunity to check on the girls. I wanted to be sure they were asleep.

The house was quiet and Jane, bless her, was asleep in the chair, and the girls were down and asleep also. It was time for old Santa to relax and enjoy a little Southern Comfort.....with water instead of eggnog. I fixed a small drink and sat on the sofa sipping and watching Jane sleep. I could hear the faint sound of her snoring, but that was the only sound in the house and actually welcome. She must have really been tired to conk out like that. It wasn't her style to sleep with a job not done.

I sat quietly, looking around the room, in an ambiance of comforting odors – Kirk's burgers, Jane's cooking, and good old bourbon and branch. What could be better? It was Christmas Eve and all was well with the world. I thought about Maria and what she was doing, and wondered whether she was enjoying Christmas as much as I was. She was probably busy doing the same things we were. I thought back on our morning at the cabin and felt a wistful feeling. It would be a long time before we would have that luxury again, and I already missed it.

Begrudgingly, I separated myself from my daydreams and leisure, walked into the kitchen and rinsed out the remnants of my drink from my glass. It was time to get to work. I returned to the den and gently massaged Jane's shoulder. She came out of her sleep without movement and with her eyes shut.

"How long have I been asleep?" She yawned and stretched as she spoke.

"Well, let's see," I said pointedly looking at my watch. "I'd say about three hours from the looks of you. I thought about leaving you there; you looked so comfortable."

"I know better. If I had slept three hours you would be asleep too. Where are the bikes?" She was still yawning.

"I left them in the garage. I wanted to be sure the girls were sleeping. I'll get them." I went to the garage and brought them inside. Jane was good enough to hold the door open for me, and we each rolled a bike into the living room. I put the kickstands down and arranged them on each side of the tree. Jane tidied up the presents, filled stockings for the mantelpiece and set out cookies and eggnog for Santa, which I immediately downed. I surveyed our work and felt good about it. When Jane went into the kitchen for water and to turn off the lights, I hid her ring between two large presents. We took one last look at our work, turned off the lights and went to bed, weary but satisfied.

I woke up at six o'clock Christmas morning. My biological clock didn't know the difference between a holiday and a working day. I was in the bathroom before I realized what day it was, and, groggy or not, I had to get up if I wanted to see the children's reaction to their presents. I rinsed my face with cold water and returned to the bedroom and gently rubbed Jane's head to awaken her. I was careful to stand away from her just in case she took a swing at me. Sometimes she could be vicious coming out of a sound sleep.

"What are you doing?" she said in disbelief. "It's still dark."

"Black as a coal mine, but it's Christmas. Don't you want to see the children when they get up?"

"Not now I don't." She turned on her side and pulled the pillow over her head. She was still for a second, and then she bounded out of the bed. "What time is it?"

"It's a little after six, but, by the time we get dressed and you get coffee on, it'll be six thirty and time to call your folks. If I know them, they're already up, dressed, and ready to leave. I can't keep the girls away from their gifts very long……besides, it's not fair to them." Jane's parents had never missed witnessing the children's Christmas. I think they enjoyed it more than the children did. My parents would come later; they weren't obsessive about it and took their time.

"I'm not dressing now." She was trying to repress a pout, but not doing it very well. "A housecoat and bedroom slippers is good enough for now. I'm not dressing twice. I still have a lot to do in the kitchen."

"That's fine. I'm going to put on cotton work pants and an old shirt. I'll probably be chasing bicycles down the road in a little while. Whatever we do, we'd better be quiet. God help us if we wake the girls. Keeping them out of the living room will be like trying to stuff the genie back in the bottle."

Jane brushed her hair, put on some lipstick, and made quick work of getting into her housecoat and slippers. "I'll start coffee and get the doughnuts out.

Why don't you call Mom and Dad from our bedroom phone so the children can't hear you? That might keep them in bed a little longer."

"Good idea." I was dialing as Jane left the room. What a surprise – her father answered on the first ring. "I hope I didn't wake you," I said tongue-in-cheek.

"No, no. We've been up for a while. Have the girls gotten up?"

"No, I think I can keep them down for a little while, but you'd better hurry. You know how they are."

"We're on our way; don't let them get up till we get there."

"I'll do my best. See you." I wasted a perfectly good "see you." He had already hung up.

When I got to the kitchen, Jane was busy getting the coffee on. I got orange juice out of the fridge and poured a small glass. It tasted unusually good. *Must be the after-effects of the Southern Comfort.* I could feel acid in my stomach mixing with the acid in the orange juice and grabbed a doughnut to stop the unwelcome chemical reaction.

Jane slapped my hand. "Stop eating the doughnuts. We can have some cereal before the folks come."

"Fat chance," I said. "They'll be here too soon for that. Besides, I ate the doughnut for medicinal purposes."

She laughed. "No way. You ate it because you wanted it."

I winked at her. "Have it your way," I said. I walked over to the corridor and stood silent for a moment. "I don't hear any noise; I think they're still asleep. I'll stand here so I can catch them before they can make it to the living room. Maybe I can hold them off until your folks get here."

"Good luck! I hope they come in through the back door. Surely they wouldn't try the front."

"You better watch for them. It's a crap shoot which way they'll come." Jane sighed. "You watch for the girls and I'll watch for Mom and Dad."

Mother used to tell me a watched pot never boils; she was right: No folks and no kids. In this case, we were ahead of the game if Jane's folks made it before the girls woke up. Normally, I would have bet my life the girls would be up before daybreak. Maybe late supper and Monopoly had done the trick.

Jane signaled me from the kitchen and gave me the *shush* sign. She was silently mouthing, "They're here." She disappeared out the back door to head them off. Now, the trick was for me to keep the girls out of the living room until they got into the house. Her folks came in quietly, waved and took off their coats. That was my cue to wake up the girls.

I slipped into their bedroom and found them sleeping like angels. I stood to the side of the door, I didn't want to be trampled, and in a stentorian voice announced, "Santa's been here. Time to rise and shine!"

Jumper hit the deck, making the change from sleep to wide awake as if by magic and headed for the door. I caught her in my arms and said, "Don't you want to wait on Laurie?"

"Huh?" That was the first indication that she might still be a little groggy. "Oh, OK." She turned in Laurie's direction. "Get up Laurie; let's see what Santa brought."

Laurie was rolling out, but it required some effort on her part. She rolled her head around, stretched and stifled a yawn. Then she rubbed her big, blue eyes open. "OK, I'm ready. Are Ma-Ma (she didn't like to be called Grandmother) and Grandpa here?" She knew the routine.

"Ready and waiting," I said. "Get moving." That was all it took. They bolted out of the room like the bulls at Pamplona. I had to move quickly to get there with them. I wasn't about to miss the yearly show.

Jumper turned into the living room, stopped, and started her jumping routine. "Wow, bicycles! How did Santa get them down the chimney?" She was all smiles and probably didn't care how Santa managed the miracle of getting two large articles through a small hole. Santa was also smart enough to tag each bicycle with their names. They were identical but of different color, green for Laurie and blue for Janet. Arguing over ownership on Christmas was not a good way to start the day.

I almost let it slide but decided to make a quick comment. "He has his ways." As lame as it was, it was enough. Or else she really didn't care. Laurie didn't say anything, but her pleasure showed in her eyes.

"Can we take them outside?" Laurie asked.

"Sure, but you need to put on some warm clothes. It's very cold."

Good old Grandpa came to the rescue. "Why don't you open your other presents before you dress? We can have some coffee and doughnuts while you open them. Then we can go outside and watch you ride."

They grabbed presents and started ripping the wrapping paper off them unceremoniously, scattering shoes, skirts, pants, sweaters, blouses and other articles of clothing around the tree. We managed to get our first cup of coffee and doughnuts, my second, during the whirling dervish created by the destroyers.

"Whose present is this?" asked Laurie. She was holding up the small box. Jane's present.

"That's your mother's," I said. "Let her open it."

"Obviously that's not a vacuum cleaner," Jane said. She looked perplexed but it came with a smile.

"No, it's not; it's a surprise."

Jumper went into her ubiquitous jumping routine again. "Open it, Mama, open it!!" She grabbed it from Laurie and ran to her mother, extending the present to her.

"It's not a vacuum cleaner and it's too small for an elephant. What could it possibly be?" She was teasing the girls and it was too much for them. The stood in front of her as though she were the pied piper.

"Open it, please Mama," Jumper begged. She was really jumping now.

Jane untied the bow and carefully stripped away the wrapping paper, savoring each moment and heightening the surprise. She snapped open the box and with widening eyes said, "Oh my gosh, an opal ring. It's beautiful.......I can't believe it. It's just gorgeous. Did you pick it out?"

My "of course" and the girls' "Let us see it, Mama" came out in unison. I looked on as though it was nothing.

"You shouldn't have done this; the vacuum cleaner was enough. I don't know what to say. Now I feel bad; I didn't get you anything." Her lips were quivering as she spoke. I felt good, but a bit disingenuous.

"The smile on your face when you saw it is gift enough for me. You deserved a surprise. You worked so hard on Christmas for the rest of us."

Jane's mother reached for the ring. "Terry, that's just beautiful! Jane, does it fit?"

"It's just perfect," Jane said sliding the ring on her finger. She held her hand out and viewed the ring from all angles. Her smile indicated her happiness. The girls were pulling at her arm so they could see it.

Jumper looked at the ring with widening eyes. "Wow, Mama. Is that an engagement ring?"

Jane laughed. "No, Jumper. I'm already married; it's too late for that."

When the laughter died down, Grandpa cleared his throat and said, "OK Betty Jo, we need to get out of here so the kids can enjoy their gifts. I've been up a long time and could use a nap before we come back for dinner. What time do you want us back?"

Betty Jo looked at Grandpa angrily. "Sam, you're so rude; we just got here." She looked at Jane and shrugged. "He's your father. You know how he is. I guess we better go."

"It's all right, Mother. Come back around two. Everything will be ready by then. Don't worry about Daddy."

He had forgotten about wanting to watch the girls ride their bicycles and that suited me. We would have enough family togetherness before the day was over. I decided to walk them to the door and made a move for their coats. Sam was two steps ahead of me and had his on and was waving Betty Jo's coat like a cape in front of a bull. It was a novel move and it worked. They were gone in minutes.

"Well, can I have another doughnut now?" I asked.

Jane was still examining her new ring. "Sure. You can eat them all if you want."

"That might be a bit much, but two won't hurt me. I'll be hungry by dinnertime if we're waiting until two. After I chase the girls up and down the street, I'll really be hungry." I expected they would be on me like fly paper as soon as they got dressed. They had disappeared as soon as the grandparents left.

I polished off two doughnuts and was contemplating a third when Laurie and Jumper came out of their room. They had listened to me and had on pants, sweaters and jackets. Jumper had on her ski cap, but Laurie was bareheaded. "Girls, are you ready hit the streets?"

Laurie walked to her bicycle. "We're ready, Daddy. Help us get the bikes outside. I can roll mine to the porch, but I can't get it down the steps by myself." Laurie grabbed the handlebars, kicked up the stand and started toward the front door.

I held the door open for her, grabbed the other side of the bike and helped Laurie guide it down the steps. "Wait here until I get Jumper's bike. We need some ground rules before the riding starts."

I went back for Janet and her bike and moved it to the walk. This was her first bike, and her ability to ride it depended on Daddy's ability to teach her how. Past experience with Laurie, if it were any indication of my teaching method, meant a lot of holding the bicycle up and running along side it. It was just plain hard work. Nevertheless, I was able, willing and looking forward to it.

"OK, Jumper, let me get a jacket and we'll be ready to start. I'll be right back." I ran into the house, grabbed a windbreaker from the coat closet and went back outside. It was cold but windless, and with the sun just above the horizon, my lightweight jacket was not appropriate. But I would be running most of the time, and that would keep me warm.

I held the bike upright and patted the seat for Jumper to get on it. "Come on Jumper, it's now or never. Let's get started."

She hopped on the seat with eyes big as saucers, somewhere between absolute fear and total exhilaration. Her cheeks were two red circles, rouged by the cold. She was afraid but determined. "Don't let me fall, daddy."

"I won't Baby; just relax and start peddling. Not so fast. Do it slowly." I walked along at a rapid rate, extending my gait into a jog as she picked up speed. "That's it. Don't try to stand up. Sit on the seat and try to balance the bike. You're doing real good."

When I felt her balancing, I let go for a minute until she lost control. As soon as she regained control, I would repeat the process. It took fifteen or twenty minutes for her to get the hang of it. She took a few spills, but got up, brushed off, and got back on. Finally, she understood about balance and managed about a hundred yards without my hand on the seat.

"Let go, Daddy. I can do it by myself. Just run by me so I won't fall."

"OK," I said. I was beginning to breathe heavier. "Don't ride faster than I can run; I'm getting tired." I had about reached my limit and was getting exhausted. My tongue was lolling about like a tired dog's.

She was concentrating hard with her tongue protruding from one side of her mouth. "Look at me, Laurie," she shouted. She stood up on the pedals and gave them a few revolutions. The bike started wobbling and she lost control. I grabbed for the seat, but the best I could do was soften the fall. She hit the ground hard but bounced up quickly.

"Are you OK, Jumper?" I brushed her off and picked up the bike.

"It didn't hurt, but I need to rest for a minute." The fall had frightened her, but she wasn't going to admit it. She needed a little time to get her courage and determination back.

"You're really doing good, Jumper, a lot better than I did when I first started. I fell down a million times." Well, maybe not a million, but it would sound good to her and give her some encouragement. "Let's take a break and get some water. I'm thirsty."

"If we stop for water, will you come back outside?"

"Sure I will. I just need a short break. I won't be more than ten minutes, I promise."

Jumper looked at me. "Cross your heart and hope to die?"

"Absolutely. Would I fib to you?" With that sacred vow, we went inside and had out drink of water. I sat down for a few minutes and then we trudged out to renew our work. Jumper rode for another hour and improved enough to make it on her own. After that, she not only didn't need me, she ignored me. I had become old news and she had become an expert rider. I was pleased but now that she no longer needed me I was filled with a pervasive sense of sadness. I would have to find something else to teach her.

Our parents arrived about one thirty and were thrilled to find Janet riding so expertly. I told them it was my superb instruction, but they opined that it was Jumper's innate athletic ability. I suggested it might have something to do with my genes. That didn't make much headway either, so I dropped it. We adjourned from bicycle to dinner, opened other presents, which we were obliged to *ooh* and *ahhh* over, proclaiming they were perfect, and thought about where we might hide them until next year. Jane brought out her pies, which were wonderful and truly deserved *oohs* and *ahhs*, and ended out delightful repast. We had completed another Christmas in grand style.

I thought about our Christmas and realized it might be the last one Jumper might have still relishing the mystery of Santa. What a shame that children are deprived of all that fun because someone feels it necessary to free them from their ignorance. We live and die through our children and we are also the victims when something so magical is taken away from them at such a tender age.

I managed to work hard for the balance of the week, fighting a battle with depression and melancholy that was to become a pattern in later years for me after Christmas. I mesmerized myself into thinking it was connected somehow with not being able to see Maria until the New Year, but that wasn't the reason. It certainly was aided and abetted by it, but I knew it went deeper than that. I could taste it, smell it and feel it, but I couldn't define it. What brought it on remained out of reach and resisted my efforts to unearth it. It lasted till the weekend and disappeared just as it had originated, without any discernable reason.

I worked through my mental mischief and completed a unique and functional preliminary plan for Hampton School additions. I was pleased with it and instinctively knew Dr. Merriweather would like it. Since the exterior character of the original building was established and would never be an architectural icon, I kept the elevations simple and used matching materials. No purpose would be served making it into the Taj Mahal. I would have my chance later if I did a good job with this one.

I also found time to move Maria's house plans further along in the pipeline, but it was becoming obvious to me that I needed help if I planned to stay abreast of my workload. I was beginning to accept the idea that I needed full-time people, even though I fretted about the cost. I didn't want to give up ownership or lose my design identity, but I knew I needed an experienced hand and that meant partnership. I guess I couldn't have my cake and eat it too. But that decision would have to wait until next year.

I worked through the weekend, and with few interruptions, accomplished quantities of work that seemed unfathomable. Maria didn't call. She said it would be hard to do, and I suffered abominably because of it. She had spoiled me. She had always found a way to keep in touch with me, and it was hard to accept her silence. Nevertheless, I swallowed my resentment and sorrow and worked on. Sunday was a good day, quiet and conducive to working, with Martha off and the phone not ringing. I was beginning to feel the excitement of New Years Eve building. My depression was leveling off and I was feeling the party mode coming on. I went home at five o'clock and told Jane I wasn't going to work Monday. I knew she had errands to run, and would be going to her hairdresser's, getting fashionable for our night out at the Jewish Center with our pals. She had to look her best at the big celebration. This would be the third consecutive year we would bring in the New Year together at the center.

She was pleased that I would be home and could look after the children. I was happy because I wanted to hang out with the girls, get away from the grind, and try to keep Maria out of my thoughts. The girls were overjoyed because they knew good old Dad would let them do pretty much what they wanted to, and would, in fact, join them. With the cooperation of the weather, warm for December and clear skied, we managed to play roll-the-bat until the early afternoon, and when it got cooler, we played a spirited game of Monopoly. In the middle of it all, I used my considerable culinary ability to make us peanut butter and jelly sandwiches which we downed with copious quantities of milk. It's amazing how hunger can change a mediocre meal into a five-star event.

Jane rolled in at five o'clock, hung her coat in the closet and made a dash for the bedroom with words cascading at us over her shoulder. "Get on the stick," she said. "We have to be at Bill and Sandy's at seven for cocktails. Girls, get your baths."

"Oh Mom, why do we have to do it now?" said a disgruntled Laurie.

"Don't ask why. Just do it," screamed Jane from the bedroom.

"When did this come about?" I asked. "I thought we were going straight to the Jewish Center. You should have told me."

"It was a sudden thing. Sandy called this morning and I forgot to tell you. I'm sorry. I had too many things on my mind. I thought I would be back in plenty of time. It didn't work out that way."

"If I'd known, I would have stopped playing with the kids and taken a shower. Now I've got to rush. It's a thirty-minute ride to pick up Jessie. How can I shower, get dressed, and pick her up in time to get to a cocktail party at seven?" The tone of my voice was strident with anger.

"You're in luck," Jane answered. "Jessie is driving herself. You don't have to pick her up."

"OH Kayyyyyyy," I said with relief. "Now I might make it. Maybe even have time to polish my shoes. And by the way, I like your hair. You look like Marilyn Monroe in that do. In fact you look better than her."

"Yeh sure," she said from the bedroom. "You either did something bad or you want something. It's not going to work so forget it."

"Not true," I said. "I'm just giving a compliment where a compliment is due. I think you look great."

"If you really want to make points, get the girls in the tub. After playing with you all day, I'm sure they're filthy."

"Who's going to feed them?"

"I asked Jessie to bring something from the drive-in. They'll like that. I hope you have enough cash to pay her. I told her you would."

"You're in luck," I said fanning through the few bills in my wallet. I've got one extra five-dollar bill, and it's burning a hole in my pocket. That was a great idea. We don't have time to get food if we're going to make the cocktail party."

"True. Now get them bathed so you can get your shower."

"Are you going to shower?"

"I already have," she said. You don't think I'm going to ruin a seven-dollar haircut and curl with all that humidity, do you? I took a shower before I went to the beauty parlor."

"OK, let me see what I can do with the girls." I found them in the den watching television, and with a little bribery I got them moving to the bathroom. I left them in the tub arguing about who would get to stay up until midnight. Laurie argued that Jumper was too young to stay up that late. Actually, both of them would probably be sleeping long before twelve after the workout I had given them.

I decided to polish my black wingtips before I showered. I kept them almost "spit shined" a delicate term from my cadet corps years at Clemson. I only wore them a few times a year, so it was an easy job. In ten minutes I was ready to shave, brush my teeth, and jump into the shower. After all the exercise with the children, my hair was sweaty and in need of a quick shampoo. Waiting for it to dry would take some time, but it didn't matter. I had to do it.

We were ready shortly before seven, and with the arrival of Jessie with cheeseburgers and milkshakes, we made our adieus. My five dollars covered the cost and left Jessie with a little change. She appreciated that. Quick kisses later, we were on our way.

70

The temperature had dropped noticeably since we had played roll-the-bat, but it was still above freezing. The sky was clear and full of stars. With the absence of cloud cover, the temperature would be below freezing before we returned home.

"I'm glad I wore my coat," said Jane. "It's freezing. You should have brought your topcoat." She shivered as she spoke adding emphasis to her comment.

"We'll be inside or in the car. I'll be all right."

"But if you're wet and sweaty when we leave you'll catch a cold."

I laughed. "I'll have enough antifreeze in me by that time to protect me to minus 5 degrees."

She gave me a stern look. "I'm not sure I like that. Promise me you won't get out on the dance floor with some strange female like you did at the club dance. That was embarrassing."

Her comment sent a wave of guilt through me that manifested itself in fraudulent self-righteous anger. "For God's sake Jane, can't you forget about that? I told you I was sorry. What more do you want? Don't start the evening off beating me over the head with that crap. I told you I wouldn't do it again." My voice was reaching a crescendo. "Now damn it, that's enough. I don't want to hear any more about it."

"OK. I won't say anymore about it...if you don't embarrass me again, and that's a promise."

I'm sure she could see the anger in my eyes. "Suppose we just forget about this conversation and start over. Otherwise, we're going to ruin a perfectly good evening."

She fixed her gaze straight ahead and started humming in a soft voice. When she stopped, she said slowly, "I'm glad I brought my coat; it's going to be cold tonight."

That broke me up and I started giggling. "That's certainly an ice breaker. You win the prize."

She shrugged her shoulders and a smile spread over her face. "That was easy enough." Then we both laughed.

I snuggled the car against the curb in front of Bill and Sandy's; there was plenty of room. We were the second couple to arrive. Only Jerry and Toni had been more punctual. Being the gentleman that I am, I exited quickly and opened the door for Jane. It was time for me to make points; I might need them later. I picked up her coat and draped it cloak like over her shoulders, being careful not to wrinkle her new gown. It was knee length to emphasize her legs, blue to bring out her eye color, and strapless to show her ample cleavage in a conservative manner. She looked stunning and she knew it. I had to admit, I was proud.

It wasn't necessary to ring the doorbell. Bill was standing in the doorway with a New Year's smile on his face and a drink in his hand. He kissed Jane on the cheek, shook my hand, and took Jane's coat. "Well guys, are we ready to party?"

"Better believe it," I answered as we made our way through the living room and went through the same routine with Toni and Jerry. "Show me the bar and I'll get this show on the road," I said.

Bill led the way to the kitchen and Jerry guided me with his hand on my back. The women remained in the living room *oohing* and *ahhing* over their outfits. Jane had managed to tell me quietly before I made my exit that she wanted vodka and lots of orange juice.

"What's your pleasure?" Bill asked. "I only mix the first drink; then you're on your own."

"Scotch and water for me and vodka and orange juice for Jane. Easy on the vodka."

Bill smiled and gave me a wink. "Sounds more like a pacer than a partier." He poured a small amount of vodka in a glass and filled it with ice and orange juice. "This ought to do the trick." He gave it a good stir and handed it to me.

While Bill was fixing my drink, I took Jane's to her in the living room. Win and Patti Gage and Ken and Judy Clyburn arrived together as I was about to return to the kitchen. "Hey guys, drinks on me in the kitchen," I said. The men followed me and immediately queued up to the bar.

I fetched my drink and said," Everybody's here except Garth and Ann."

Bill shrugged his shoulders and pondered an answer. "I think they had babysitter problems. Garth said they would meet us at the Center." He shifted his gaze toward me and rolled his eyes. I took that to mean he had made up the excuse. The he leaned over and whispered to me, "Ann is off the wagon again. I think Garth is trying to prolong the agony. Maybe he can keep her on her feet till ten o'clock."

I didn't like the sound of that. I just hoped she would keep her mouth shut about our recent conversations. "Damn, I'm sorry to hear that. She was doing so well."

"Such is life," Bill said. He hoisted his glass and proposed his usual toast to an agreeable group. "To all of us: Good health and prosperity in the new year."

I grabbed Jerry by the sleeve. "Who's playing tonight?"

"Would you believe.......the Beatles?" I assumed he was trying to be funny.

Bill's head snapped around. "The WHO? Are they a local group? I've never heard of them."

"He's putting you on," I replied quickly.

Jerry grinned. "I was just trying to see who knew what was going on in the music world."

"I've heard of them," Ken said. "They're from Europe."

"So?" Bill said. "If I've never heard of them, they can't be too important."

Jerry was roaring. "They're about the hottest thing to come down the pike since Sinatra or Elvis. If they were a stock company and you bought a nickel's worth of their stock, you could probably retire in five years."

"Now that you've proven we're all stupid, who IS playing?" Bill was getting a bit testy. Sometimes his disdain for Jerry's humor showed.

"Those guys from Sumter, Southern Comfort. But what do you expect for thirty bucks a couple, Guy Lombardo?"

"Didn't they play last year?" Bill asked. Southern Comfort, not Guy Lombardo."

It was time for me to break up the debate. "Yeah and they're very good. They play a good mix of music. Let's have a toter and get moving. The party starts in ten minutes and I want to get my thirty bucks worth."

"I'll drink to that," Bill answered. "If you're carrying one out, use the paper cups on the counter. Mama gets mad when her cocktail glasses disappear."

Jane and I took our time driving to the Jewish Center so Jerry and Toni could get our table set up. They were our link to the Jewish community and were responsible for our attending our first New Year's party there. Now it had grown to encompass our entire group. Although predominantly supported by the Jewish community, it required more numbers than they could bring to the table to make it feasible. Now, through marketing and word of mouth, it attracted a larger, more diverse group because it was affordable, well planned, and offered a good band.

From childhood through adolescence, I had had few Jewish friends. Those who I did get to know were either very gregarious or athletes. The rest seemed guarded or clannish, either subconsciously or by design. My guess now is that adults on both sides who didn't trust each other directed it. My peers only noticed Jews went to church (we weren't astute enough to know they were called synagogues) on Friday evenings and had some strange holidays. I do recall my father's saying that Jews were not allowed to live in some neighborhoods and wondering how that could be.

Jane and Toni had been friends since junior high. Their special bond included family summer vacations together in high school, rooming together in college, and being in each other's weddings. Toni brought Jerry into our life and he has become on of my best friends. He is bright, funny and totally unselfish. He would literally give you the shirt off his back, and not many can pass that test. My father loves Jerry and when he first met him uttered these now famous words, 'Son, that boy's OK for a Jew'. Jerry and I had many laughs over those words. Perhaps it never entered my father's mind that a Jew could be like anyone else. Jerry had introduced me to many Jewish businessmen and professionals who became clients and has always included us in social events attended or sponsored by the Jewish community. He always introduces me with the flip comment that all my friends were Jewish. He got a big kick out of that.

We pulled into a nearly full parking lot and walked quickly into the building. A foyer with coatroom, toilets, and kitchen stretched across the front. We hung Jane's coat in the coatroom and made our way into the party area, a gymnasium used primarily for basketball with a high-trussed ceiling, exposed brick walls, and a gleaming wood floor perfect for dancing. Bars were located under the basketball goals at each end of the floor and both were accumulating growing groups of revelers. Laughter and conversation, increasing in volume directly proportional to the alcohol being consumed, was at party level and cigarette smoke was stratifying in the upper levels of the trusses. A bandstand was centered on the floor against the wall and was without musicians. They would appear magically at nine o'clock.

Jane spotted our group, with drinks in hand near the center of the floor milling around our table. "There they are," she said pointing with her finger. She walked toward them with me in hot pursuit.

"Looks like Jerry has them enthralled; they're all laughing. Probably telling some of his filthy jokes."

"Good," she said. "Maybe he'll run through them before we get there." Jane was not a fan of Jerry's jokes. She tolerated them, but she didn't like them. *Personally, I think they're funny, but they might be a bit risqué for some women.*

Bill spotted us first. "Better get to the bar if you want a drink; the line's not getting any shorter."

"I think I will. What would you like, Honey? Same ole, same ole?'

Jane shrugged. "Vodka and orange juice for now. Maybe I'll change later."

Bill fell in behind me. "I'll walk with you. I'm almost ready for another one. By the time you get to the head of the line, my drink'll be gone. How about you Sandy?" he shouted over his shoulder.

"I'm OK," Sandy answered and returned to the women's chatter. No doubt they were discussing who looked the best... and worst.

Bill nudged me with his elbow and whispered. "How's the romance going?"

"What romance?" I countered.

"Don't play dumb with me. You know what romance I'm talking about. I know you're still using the cabin, probably more than I am."

It's something I'd rather not discuss. No offense, but I'd rather keep it to myself."

He smiled. "Getting serious, eh?"

I stopped and looked him straight in the eyes. "I didn't say that. I said I'd rather keep it private. Look.....we've been friends a long time and we know a lot about each other. This just isn't any of your business.......or anyone else's. If it was something I wanted to talk about, you'd be the first guy I'd turn to."

"OK," he said. "I get the message. I was going to tell you that I might have to give the cabin up, that's all."

I blinked my eyes in disbelief and almost choked. "What?"

"Susie and I split. She's dating some guy she met at church and it's getting serious. It's the right thing for her, but that doesn't make it any easier. I haven't seen her in a while and it's killing me. I'll swear I feel like a drug addict taking the cure cold turkey."

"Gee Bill, I'm sorry, but what's that got to do with giving up the cabin?"

"I've had some good offers for the property over the last two years. The only reason I haven't sold it is Susie. There's no reason to keep it without her in the picture. I bought it with resale in mind anyway, and now might be the time to get rid of it. I would make a good profit if I sold it."

"When are you going to do it?"

"I doubt before the summer. I'm getting prices on the timber next week and if I can make anything on it I'll do that before I sell the land. I figure if I cut it selectively, it won't reduce the value of the land that much. I might pick up twenty or thirty thousand dollars for the timber."

As we neared the bar, I thought it better if we changed the subject. Too many ears made me uncomfortable. "Let's discuss this later when we can talk."

Bill nodded. "Good. We'll catch a smoke outside later. Right now, I need a new drink. I told you I'd finish mine before you got to the bar."

I laughed. "Good timing. With the line like it is, maybe we ought to get two."

Bill grinned. "Not a bad idea," he said.

We got our drinks and made our way back to the table. We spotted Garth near the end of the diminishing queue. We stopped just long enough to shake his hand.

"Hey Buddy; glad to see you. I was afraid you were going to be late. See you at the table." He smiled and said he would see us shortly.

When we got to the table, all the women were on one side and the men on the other, fairly typical for our group. The noise level was building to a crescendo, with men yelling to be heard and drowning out almost all of the women's quieter gossip, but the topics of conversation couldn't have been more divergent. I reached across a table full of noisemakers and crazy hats and handed Jane her drink. She acknowledged it with a smile and rejoined the women.

I took a sip of my drink and moved into the men's group. They were talking about the bowl games.....naturally. Jerry, who liked to bet the games, was holding court.

"If you don't bet on the Rose Bowl, you're crazy. Southern Cal is favored by six, but they'll win big time. The big ten always tanks when they get out in California and this year is no different. I'm betting all I can on USC, might even mortgage the house. Wisconsin will find a way to lose," he said with authority. "It won't even be close."

That brought a large chuckle from the group. "Remember, we're not dentists. We don't have all those mouths to mine in like you. We have mouths to feed," I said. "Besides, nobody here has enough equity in their house to get a second mortgage except you."

"Don't give me that poor mouth, architect. We know you're not hurting. You're just tight." A big smile ignited his face as he finished his dig.

"Yeah? Well a wiser man than any of us, my father, told me once: 'If you can't afford to lose, you can't afford to win.' I think he's absolutely right."

"Then, why do you bet on the golf course?" He was baiting me.

I laughed. "That's easy," I said. A sure thing isn't a bet, and you're my partner so it's a sure thing we're going to win."

"By God, I like that answer," Jerry said and gave me a bear hug.

At eleven o'clock I began to get nervous. It was getting time to figure out how I could call Maria. There was a pay phone in the foyer, but it was close to the men's toilet. I visited the men's toilet a few times during the evening and hadn't seen anyone using the phone. I didn't expect much action as it got closer to midnight, but you never know. Some overprotective mother might want to check on her child…or the babysitter. I didn't want company when I made my call.

The odds were in my favor if I made the call between eleven thirty and midnight. It would be more difficult as midnight approached. Shortly after eleven thirty, I slipped away from the group and went to the telephone. Fortunately, no one was in the foyer as I dialed Maria's number. I was prepared to hang up if Maria didn't answer, but she did on the fourth ring.

I cupped my hand over the mouthpiece and whispered, "Can you talk?"

"Hi Genny," she said. "Happy New Year. I wish you could have made the party." Then she whispered, "I miss you."

"I miss you too. It's been a long time…too long."

"I know. If I have to hang up you'll understand?"

"Sure. I'm just glad to talk to you. I love you, Maria. I wish we could be together."

"Maybe next week," she said.

"Count on it," I whispered. "Think about me when twelve o'clock comes."

"Of course I will. That's all I've been doing all night."

"Maria, call me Wednesday as early as you can. Maybe we can go to the cabin."

"I think that will work. Pat's going to Atlanta for a few days. If we could make it early, I'm sure I can."

"I'll make it work." The thought of it filled me with delight.

"Uh oh, I've got to go. Bye, Genny and Happy New Year."

"I love you," I said to a dead line. She was gone. I looked around guilty as a thief, but no one was in sight. I quickly inserted a dime in the phone and dialed my house. Jesse answered on the third ring.

"Forte residence." She sounded a bit disturbed.

"Hi Jessie, it's Mr. Forte. Are the children up?"

"No sir. They've been asleep about an hour."

"OK. I was going to wish them a happy new year if they were still up."

"Should I wake them?"

"No, don't do that. I thought I would let you know we might be late."

"Don't worry Mr. Forte. If I get tired I'll sleep on the sofa."

It was quarter till twelve and time to get back to the party. When I returned to the table, a few were dancing and the rest were talking. I hadn't been missed. I eased up to Jane and asked her if she wanted a fresh drink.

"I'm fine. "Where were you? I was about to come looking for you."

I took a deep breath and cleared my throat before replying and tried to smile away my guilt. "I had to go to the men's room." I kept my reply casual.

"You were gone over fifteen minutes. Is your stomach upset?"

"No, and when did you start clocking my toilet visits?"

"Does that bother you?" she asked. Her eyes narrowed, searching for anything unusual in my manner. I felt like I was being backed into a corner. It was time to play my trump card before I stepped on a land mine. "No it doesn't. Why should it? I called home to tell the kids happy New Year but they were already asleep. I didn't wake them."

"That was fatherly of you," she said. The tone of her voice and her eyes said she didn't believe me.

Undaunted, I persisted. "I told Jesse we'd be late, and she said she would sleep on the sofa if we were." I walked away looking at her over my shoulder. "I'm getting a drink."

"Hurry up," she said. "It's almost midnight. I'd like you here at the countdown."

I looked at my watch. She was right. It was three minutes before midnight. "I'll make it; don't worry. Why don't you put the stopwatch on me?" Dumb, dumb, I thought. Why do I have to say stupid things like that? I think I have the moth and candle syndrome. I just can't leave things alone.

I got back in time to see Jerry pouring champagne to toast the New Year and heard someone on the bandstand counting off the seconds. When he reached one, the band played *Auld Lang Syne* amidst a cacophony of sounds – shouts, whistles and noisemakers. I finished my champagne, grabbed Jane by the waist, and moved onto the heavily populated dance floor.

"Happy New Year," she said. Her smile was radiant - a 'no malice intended, let's enjoy the evening' smile.

"Happy New Year," I answered and we stopped dancing for the obligatory kiss. It wasn't long and it wasn't passionate, but it was appropriate. I wondered if Maria was going through the same routine and how she might be responding. I was piqued with jealousy, hoping shamelessly that another man's wife, a woman I dearly loved, was thinking about me instead of him. It was a grim thought, a wake-up call, that Maria and I would probably never share together a new year, a Christmas, or any other important day that families shared. Our feelings were real and we could share many things, but all would remain forever outside that realm.

Did I love her enough to leave my family? Did she? I believe so, but I also believe that our love would never survive the pain or shame we would cause our children. That was forever cast in stone and was not acceptable to either of us.

As I danced with Jane to the haunting and melancholy sound of *Auld Lang Syne,* I knew she was not my soul mate, but she would always be my life mate, as unfair as that may have been for both of us.

The music stopped and we walked away from the dance floor, leaving my sobering thoughts behind. I smiled at Jane and said, "Let's get this party started."

She looked puzzled. "I thought we already had."

"That was last year; this is 1963."

She waved me away with her hand. "OK, but that's silly."

"I know, but it makes good sense to me." I watched her take her place at the table and become absorbed into the world of women talk. It was time for me to do some serious drinking. *Maria, I love you, wherever you are.*

Jane and I danced with everyone at our table before breakfast was served at two. I even managed one dance with Ann. She had returned to her old ways, but seemed to be moderating her drinks and didn't appear intoxicated. That was an improvement over her usual imbibing. Our conversation was lifeless and mundane, but devoid of any mention of our recent conversations. She didn't bring it up and neither did I, but I could feel the tension under the surface. Her brooding eyes glazed with alcohol said it all. One dance with her was enough. She and Garth made short shrift of breakfast and left just as soon as they had eaten.

Breakfast was good and I sampled everything: grits, eggs, country fried steak, hash browns, biscuits, bagels and tons of Jewish breads. Gluttony was my ally because the food in my stomach was like a giant sponge absorbing all the excess quantities of alcohol I had imbibed. After a large, hot cup of black coffee with lots of sugar and a very satisfying cigarette, I was almost back to normal. At any rate, the party was over for me, and with some encouragement from Jane we excused ourselves, making the last obligatory round of kisses, hugs, and "Happy New Years," and left for home. It was three-thirty and we woke up the babysitter twenty minutes later. I told Jessie she was welcome to stay the night, but she was ready to leave. I gave her ten dollars, walked her to her car, and Jane and I were asleep before her car made the main road. That's an exaggeration, but pretty close to the truth.

The children were quiet and kind to us, letting us make Tuesday a short day. We got out of bed just before midday. I was surprised to be without any trace of a hangover, just a hint of nasal congestion and fatigue. Jane fared even better because she had limited her intake of alcohol, but she complained about needing more sleep. A quick shower and brushing my teeth was enough to get me going, but I chose to eschew shaving, regarding it as cruel and unusual punishment for a holiday and justified it by convincing myself that it wouldn't improve my ability to watch football games on the TV.

Jane slipped into the kitchen and fixed sandwiches for lunch. Laurie and Janet had treated themselves earlier to raisin bran, but were hungry again when we got up. I opted to open a can of Campbell's tomato soup to go with my sandwich. It was a perfect combination for a cold day.

I went into the den, turned the TV on and ran through the channels. LSU was leading Texas seven to nothing in the Cotton, Old Miss and Arkansas were tied seven to seven in the Sugar and Missouri was leading Georgia Tech seven to three in the Bluebonnet. The games looked interesting. I grabbed a TV tray and set it up by my chair, a large, comfortable, overstuffed, nondescript chair with an ottoman. I flipped the channel back to the LSU-Texas game and went to the kitchen for my soup and sandwich.

"I guess you've found a place for the rest of the day," Jane said. "And by the looks of that scruffy face, I don't suppose you're going out."

"You're right and you're very observant," I answered. "You know I always watch the bowl games. What did you think I'd be doing?"

"I don't know," she answered, "But it doesn't matter. I've got to cook supper anyway."

"What are you fixing?"

"The usual – pork roast, black-eyed peas, rice, and collards."

"Sounds good. Anyone invited for supper?"

"If they were, I'd un-invite them. You look too wild for company."

I laughed. "So? A man's home is his castle. Lighten up; it's a holiday for God's sake. At least I showered and brushed my teeth. You're still in your nightie."

She prefaced her remark with a malevolent smile, a little teeth, and hard eyes. "I had to have lunch ready for the king so he could entertain himself. When I eat and clean up the mess, I'll shower and get dressed."

"I thought you were the queen," I said sarcastically. "I didn't know you were the maid."

"Whatever," she said and her voice trailed off.

I took that to mean I was dismissed, so I ambled back to the den with my spoils like a wounded lion. The conversation was better ended. It was going nowhere. I let the games absorb my frustration. Hell of a way to start the New Year.

All of the games but the Rose Bowl were over when we sat for supper. I could stand that, because I didn't care who won. I didn't have any interest in Southern California and Wisconsin. Of course, my pal Jerry was betting his house on Southern California so I'm sure his adrenalin was flowing in high gear at the moment, and I'm sure he was certainly glued to the TV. The fact that all the Southern teams – LSU, Alabama and Mississippi – except Georgia Tech won, and that I didn't have much love for them, because they beat Clemson most of the time, nourished my Southern heritage.

We sat together at the table like any typical family and I didn't sense any more bitterness except in the collards, and there was no way I would have said anything about it to the chef. I sprinkled mine liberally with hot vinegar and shoveled them down like Sherman marching through Georgia. Everything else was delicious, enticing me into several helpings, so I wrote the disappointing collards off as a mental error that I probably was responsible for.

I expressed my admiration for the delightful repast and left the table to return to the Rose Bowl. I could hardly breathe from all the food I had consumed. It hadn't stopped me from literally cramming in a piece of my favorite lemon pie made from condensed evaporated milk. It was so rich it should pay taxes. I left a table full of dirty dishes and messy pots and pans for my wife to clean up, as any properly raised Southern boy would do. After all, she had made the mess and she had two daughters to help clean. It was her Southern duty to prepare them for their legacy in life to do the same when they married. It was almost criminal, but I wasn't going to complain.

My eyes tried to close, but I managed to finish watching the game. It was exciting to the end, but Southern California won the game and with it the national championship, beating Wisconsin 42 to 37. I knew Jerry was happy because he said that's how it would come out and he had bet on Southern California. I didn't remember the point spread, but it didn't matter. He said he had to give only a few points. I figured it was less than four and that would be a winner.

It was almost ten o'clock but I knew Jerry would be up, so I gave him a quick call. Toni answered.

"Hello," she said.

"Hi Toni; Terry. Is the big winner in?"

"Oh Hi Terry. I think he's in the den making out a deposit slip," she said laughing.

"Do you think the tycoon will talk to a poor architect?"

"Absolutely. He needs someone besides me to brag to. Let me get him." I heard the phone *plunk* as she laid it down. I didn't have to wait long.

"Terry, my man", he said playfully. "I told you USC would win. Won me a cool dime." (A dime, for those of us who don't bet, is slang for a thousand dollars.) "I spotted three and it was touch and go for a little while. I was glad when it was over."

"That's great Jerry. I don't have the nerve. A twenty-dollar bet would make me so nervous I wouldn't be able to sleep. I don't know how you do it."

"Nothing to it, my boy," he said. "It was money in the bank all the way. The big ten never wins a Rose Bowl."

"But didn't Wisconsin beat them pretty big during the regular season?"

"No, that was the last time they played in the Rose Bowl and Southern Cal whipped the dog shit out of them. It was a lot closer this time than I though it would be and I was scared for a while. But a one point over the spot victory is as good as a thousand."

"Well," I said. "It's still a gutsy thing to do. Damn man, you could have lost a thousand bucks. That's a month's pay for me..........in a good month. What would you have done if you had lost?"

"Maybe cry a little. Hell, I've done it before, but this time I just knew I was going to win. Gamblers get that gut feeling sometimes and they have to bet it. You wouldn't understand. My dad used to tell me you have to play your hunches, and I did. It was never in doubt."

"Well congratulations pal. That's all I can say."

"Thanks Terry. How about tomorrow? It's Wednesday. Are we playing golf?"

His question caught me off guard. "I can't tomorrow. I've got too much to do." My mind suddenly turned to thoughts of Maria and her promise to meet me tomorrow. "Maybe next week if the weather's good."

"OK. I thought with my new wealth I could talk the guys into doubling the bet. When you're on a roll you have to strike."

"We'll see next week, but I doubt if we can get them to bite. We've been whipping them like yard dogs lately."

"You're right, but I think I'll try anyway. Might make for a fun day."

"Suits me. Well, I've got to go. I've got a long day tomorrow." I hoped that wasn't wishful thinking, especially if I could spend it at the cabin.

"OK Buddy. Thanks for the call. Bye"

I drank a glass of water and started for the bedroom. Maria was filling up my thought world and I could feel the nervous tension building. I was ready to let sleep ease my way through the night until I could be with her. It had been a long time.

Wednesday arrived and I embraced it enthusiastically. I sprang out of bed quickly and jumped into the shower. I didn't feel as though I had slept well. My night had been filled with fleeting dreams of frightful experiences that left me fatigued, but there was no desire to remain in bed. I was too excited to think about anything but seeing Maria, and a shower would be sufficient to get my blood flowing and wake me up.

I went through my morning routine by rote, my mind too full of Maria to think about anything else. I had difficulty picking out my clothes, matching colors and selecting a tie, but somehow I muddled through it. I can't remember being so obsessed about anything in my life. When I got to the kitchen, Jane had two sleepy girls in tow, encouraging them to eat breakfast, but not having much luck.

"Janet, quit playing with your food. You're not getting up from the table until you eat some of your eggs," Jane said. She reminded me of a mess sergeant.

"I'm not hungry, Mama," she said, "and I don't like eggs."

"Well, you better get hungry and eat your eggs whether you like them or not. Now get with it. I don't have all day."

"Rats," she said but she started shoveling them down, swallowing them quickly with facial expressions suggesting she was taking some foul tasting medicine.

"That's better. Now get dressed and don't forget to brush your teeth. I'll be there in a minute to brush your hair."

"My, my," I said. "You're not in a good mood this morning."

"No, I'm not. It's hard enough to get them up, feed and dress them on a regular school day, but after a holiday, they're impossible. How about dropping them off at school on your way to work? I'll never get them ready if I have to dress."

"Fair enough," I answered. "While you're standing in front of the stove, how about scrambling me a couple of eggs?"

"Are you trying to bargain with me, or are you just hungry?"

I smiled. "A little of both, but I'll take the girls to school whether you cook me eggs or not."

"If you're patronizing me, stop."

The goblins had returned. "You really are in a bad mood. What's the problem?"

"If you really must know, I started my period this morning."

"Cramps?" I asked.

She took my eggs off the range, dumped them in a plate and thrust them in front of me. A single word burst from her lips. "Yes."

"I'm sorry." *What I should have said was I'm sorry I bothered to ask, but I didn't need any more aggravation.* I thought that but I knew she didn't deserve that kind of retort. She didn't answer so I let it drop. I busied myself eating eggs and reading the newspaper.

"Well, I'd better get going." I rinsed my plate and dropped it in the sink. "See you this afternoon."

I walked to the living room and yelled, "Let's get moving."

"We're ready," Janet answered.

"Don't forget your coats; it's cold outside."

Jumper bounded from the back supercharged as always with Laurie reluctantly following her. "Let's go, Daddy." She grabbed my hand and we marched off to face the day.

I arrived at the office a little after eight and walked into a cold, unfriendly building. I set the thermostat at 72 degrees and walked through the office turning on lights as I made my way through each room. I stopped long enough to fill the kettle with water and set it on the hot plate. Architects are inveterate coffee drinkers, learning early in college to appreciate its innate ability to keep you awake for long stretches of time when projects are due. Architectural students were also procrastinators who put off completion of their projects until the last minute. Getting paid for your efforts puts an end to that.

I was going through mail, enjoying my coffee and third cigarette of the day, when Martha arrived.

"Happy New Year, Martha." She didn't reply. "I *said* Happy New Year."

She looked at me blankly and said, "What?"

"I said Happy New Year. Damn.....Jane hardly spoke to me this morning and now you come in all grumpy. What's with you women?"

She looked puzzled. "I don't know. I guess I need to be retrained. I didn't mean to be rude; I'm just not here yet."

"Well, I wish you would hurry up and get here. On second thought, if you're this grumpy when you're not here, you may be worse when you get here." I laughed and she gave me a smile. That was reassuring. "I left the pot on if you want coffee. I'll be in the conference room if you need me."

Her reply was abrupt. "I don't need any coffee and I don't need you. My nerves need a rest. Cut off the pot, if you don't mind."

"Sure," I said walking away shaking my head. It seemed I had struck out with the first two women in my day.

At nine thirty the phone rang. Martha answered it, put the call on hold and buzzed me in the conference room.

"Terry Forte speaking," I answered.

Maria's voice washed over me like warm honey. "What are your plans for today? I hope not drawing lines," she said.

"Anything you desire," I said almost too quickly but with conviction.

"Umm.........that sounds interesting. How about meeting a grocery shopper in front of the Winn-Dixie in about thirty minutes."

"I'm not sure I can."

"Is that serious or are you kidding?" she asked. I sensed surprise.

"Not really.....What I mean is I don't know if I can wait that long."

She was quiet. Then she said simply, "I'll try to hurry."

She said nothing more and the line went dead. I put the phone in the cradle and immediately felt the excitement building. I fought it, but it was just too powerful, like capping a volcano with a cork. I let the emotion run free for a moment; I had no choice.

I went to the toilet and rinsed my face with cold water. I needed time to come up with an excuse for Martha and cold water helped. She knew the call was from Maria and I didn't want her to connect my leaving the office with our conversation.

I went to the blueprint machine and ran off two copies of the latest floor plan of Maria's house. I rolled them carefully, secured them with rubber bands and took them to Martha.

"Mrs. Champion will be coming by for these. If she comes by before I get back, give them to her and tell her I'll call her later. I'm going to look at a used car I'm interested in and, if it's a good deal, I may take it over to Smitty's garage to get it checked out. I shouldn't be long, but if I don't get back before you leave, lock up the office."

Martha looked at me as though I was losing my mind. "There's nothing wrong with the one you've got. Why in the world do you need another one?" Martha had an inkling I was up to something, or my conscience was taking umbrage at my tall tale.

"Well curiosity, if you must know, I was thinking about it for Jane. I didn't want to tell you because I want to keep it a secret. I know how you talk and I didn't want you having to keep a secret. Now, you can forget I told you...OK?"

"Sorry I asked," she said with a touch of anger in her voice. That was all right, as far as I was concerned. A little anger helped with the deception.

"Don't get all bent out of shape. It's no big deal. I'll be back in a little while." I grabbed my coat and left. I whistled all the way to my car, thinking how crafty I had been......or hoped I had been.

In fifteen minutes I pulled into the Winn-Dixie parking lot and looked for

Maria's car. She was parked between two cars, but conveniently left an empty space on the Driver's side. I nosed in beside her car, leaned across the seat, and opened the door for her. She gave me a big smile as she entered, and reached over to touch my hand.

"My hands are cold," she said. "My heater isn't working."

"Good, that gives me an excuse to warm you up."

After we turned out of the parking lot and headed away from town, she snuggled against me. She smelled of fresh soap and perfume. "My you smell good. I hope you didn't do that just for me." I smiled at her as I spoke.

"No…actually I did it for the milk man. He hasn't been very attentive lately. Come to think of it, you haven't either."

I laughed. "Well then, I guess I'd better make up for lost time."

She batted her eyes and said, "Talk's cheap, Rhett Butler." For emphasis, she wiggled against me.

"For a Yankee that's pretty cute, but I think I prefer you in your natural state. I'm getting kinda fond of Northern women."

She stuck her tongue out playfully. "That's for not knowing any better. Illinois is Midwestern, not Northern."

"Anybody from a state that fought against the south in the War Between the States is a Yankee to me, but I sure won't hold it against you. I'd surrender to you anytime."

"Promises, promises." She shook her head, letting her loose hair fall freely and pushed it back away from her face.

"Uh oh, I'm about to miss the turn." I slowed for the turn and drove slowly down the rutted roadway. "It seems like forever since we were here. The road's a little rougher than I remembered." I navigated the bumps and ruts as best as I could and pulled up to the cabin.

"I'll go get the heaters started. Wait in the car and stay warm."

Maria said, "No way. I'm going with you." To make her point, she hopped out of the car before I could open my door.

"OK, but it's going to be cold."

She smiled. "So? I'll find something to do."

It was cold when we entered, but much better than outside. I felt my way along the wall to the closet, pulled the main breaker and punched all the circuits on the panel board. "Cut on the lights," I called to Maria.

"Done," she said and the lamps lit up the room. "That's a lot better."

I went to the bedroom and plugged in the heater. Maria was watching me from the door.

"It's not as cold as I thought it would be," she said. She took off her coat and draped it over a chair. "I think I can do without this." Her lips were parted in a soft, provocative smile. She was gorgeous. Her black slacks were form fitting, revealing her small waist and rounded hips and her pink sweater was a perfect choice, emphasizing her breasts.

"You don't know what a pleasure it is to look at you. You're always beautiful, but always different. There is magic about you that no women I've ever known possesses. I never tire of seeing you, and if that were all it could be, it would be enough. I love you, Maria. I've missed you so much."

She walked to me and we embraced. "But what if I don't want it to be enough," she whispered.

"Then it won't be," I said, holding her close. I kissed her and, as our lips met, felt the rapture emanating from the ethereal bond of our oneness. It was not a new feeling. I experienced it in some form every time we were together, but now, each time, it was gaining momentum.

I backed away and removed her clothes slowly, one garment at a time. It was a labor of love and she made no effort to help or impede me. As I exposed her body, I reveled in her beauty, feasting like a gourmet on each part with my lips and hands and inhaling her delicate bouquet of soap, shampoo, and perfume. Her eyes were closed and occasionally she caught her breath, but her soft smile remained.

When I finished, I stood back and admired her uninhibited nakedness. She was stunning. "You really don't know how beautiful you are," I said.

Maria lay down on the bed and said, "You're prejudiced." Her eyes were alive with humor and impishness. "Now, let's see how fast you can get over here…undressed."

I did so hurriedly, but the haste ended there. Our lovemaking was long, languid, and inventive. We put Kama Sutra to the test and then some. The end came almost casually, like an afterthought, but when the moment arrived, it was golden.

Afterwards, we shared a Coke we found in the fridge. In our haste and excitement, neither of us had thought about lunch. It was warm in the bedroom, so we remained in the bed, Maria wearing my shirt and her panties, and me in my shorts.

"Bill told me he might sell the cabin," I said. "That will put a crimp in our meetings."

"When?" she asked.

"He thinks summer will be the best time to sell the property, but he may sell timber early in the spring."

"That's plenty of time," she said without looking at me.

"What? Why do you say that?" Her comment caught me by surprise. It had cryptic overtones.

Biting her lip and staring into space, she replied in a monotone, "I'm not sure I want to talk about this, or even if it's the right time."

"What is it? Don't leave me hanging." I sat up on the edge of the bed.

"Pat got a call from headquarters last Friday. They want to know if he would accept a move to Florida to start up a new plant. He has a week to make a decision. I don't want to move, but Pat says if he refuses he'll never get another promotion." Tears were welling up in her eyes. "I can't stand thinking about it. It's tearing me apart. And even worse, I think Pat is beginning to think something is going on. He's been questioning me a lot lately about how much time I spend at your office, and why it's taking so long to finish the drawings. I'm between the proverbial rock and a hard place. I can't protest too much about moving with him thinking we might be having an affair. He's not stupid."

Her words hit me like a sledgehammer. "Why didn't you tell me?"

Maria walked to the window. My shirt was hanging like a sail on her shoulders. She turned, eyes pleading for understanding and said, "How could I? Today's the first day we've talked, other than New Year's Eve, and it's not something to talk about on the phone. Besides, it's not a done deal yet, and I just want it to go away." She sniffled and wiped away tears with the back of her hand. "If I had told you earlier, it would have ruined our day. I guess I was being selfish, but I wanted today to be happy."

I was stunned and speechless. The silence that followed was like fingernails on a chalkboard. Cold sweat broke out on my forehead and I swallowed hard before words would come. "This isn't possible. You can't leave. I won't accept it. I can't."

"We have no choice. It's called fate, and that's what brought us together. It can just as well take us apart. We've been on borrowed time anyway. I'm really surprised Jane or Pat hasn't caught us. Neither of us is prepared to leave out families, and that's our only remedy. That's not going to happen. No matter how much we love each other, that's not a sacrifice we could make in good conscience. And neither of us could stand what we'd have to go through if we were caught. I'd like to think that we aren't capable of building our happiness on the sorrow and pain of others, especially our children. You may think there's no guilt here, but it would soon materialize. That's what's at stake. That's quicksand for any future we might have together. Our children are just babies. They wouldn't accept or understand how we feel about each other. If it was only Pat, I leave in a second."

I couldn't bear to look in her direction as I spoke. "That's all true and logical, but this isn't about logic. The heart isn't logical. If it were, we would never have done this. My feeling for you jumped over the logic fence when we met. **YOU** filled a void in my life, and, if you leave, the vacuum will be like a black hole in space. It will crush me. I'm not suicidal, but life won't be the same." I felt a wash in my eyes and a catch in my throat, but I wouldn't cry.

Maria brushed her hair away from her face and rubbed her nose. A tear wandered slowly down her cheek. "You do what you have to do, and we'll face whatever happens and find a way to cope. Don't court trouble; it may not happen."

"Maybe, but that doesn't keep me from feeling like Damocles waiting for the sword to fall." The glow of the day was fading.

She walked over to me and held my face in both of her hands. "Why do you think everything is over for us if we are separated? It's only space. Surely, if our feelings are what we say they are, we'll still love each other." She turned my face and caught my eyes with hers in a viselike grip. "Is that all there is to our relationship? A union of flesh? I'm disappointed in you."

"That's not fair. You know that's not the case at all. I came to love you kicking and screaming. It's not something I would have embraced if I didn't believe in it. There's a lot of minuses in our relationship, but dammit........one plus cancels out a million minuses."

"I've told you a MILLION times not to exaggerate." She said it with a timid smile. It was one of her favorite expressions.

"This time it's true," I said.

She lay back on the bed and reached out for me. "Come here and hold me. Our time is too valuable to squander."

I agreed, but I was having a hard time getting out of my funk. I reached out for her and held her tightly in my arms. I kissed her and when I felt her exploring tongue in my mouth, the dark feeling began to slip away. We held our embrace for a long time, kissing and stroking each other, fighting to return to our earlier mood. We clung to each other like two drowning people, but it was a tender moment. Once again, we made love, both feeling like it might be the last time.

There had been no time for foreplay; we joined together lovingly and passionately, and, when it was over, both of us shed tears of happiness, sadness and relief. I couldn't remember the last time I had cried about anything, but this wasn't just anything.

Something about the possible finality of this act, the most wonderful unity of body and spirit imaginable, tore at my soul. How could I survive without her? We held on to each other as the warmth of passion slowly ebbed away, and the calm of spiritual unity took passion's place. I knew, regardless of separation, this union would never die. I suddenly remembered her saying, *Love me when we're together* and I understood.

For the next few months, Maria and I were together as often as possible. Most of the time we went to the cabin and even did a little clean up and decorating. Bill still planned to sell, but his plans to sell timber pushed the sale of the land off in his time frame. We also continued to meet at least once a week at the Blizzard Shop for lunch. It was astounding that no one ever saw us there together.

My practice flourished, even though I stopped working on Maria's house at her request until Pat's decision was finalized. At the end of January I hired an architect, Hardy Thompson, dangling the seed of partnership in a year if we were both satisfied with each other and could work out an agreement. That allowed me to get Hampton Elementary School additions out for bid in record breaking time, bringing it in under estimate. Dr. Merriweather was so impressed, he convinced the school board to commission me for the new elementary school to be located near my neighborhood.

My reputation was given instant credibility and recognition with Dr. Merriweather's action, and a number of new, unsolicited projects drifted into the office. Suddenly, we had at least a year of work, and that was plenty of time for me to judge Hardy's architectural ability. He wasn't a totally unknown person to me; we were classmates and friends in college. He had a good personality, excellent work habits, and would be an asset in marketing. He wasn't a good designer, but was an excellent detailer. That would be a good fit for me if it worked out.

Spring came, bringing with it an array of fresh green foliage, dogwood blossoms, and gorgeously adorned azaleas. It also brought the answer to the dread that remained constantly with me. Pat accepted the move to Florida and a "For Sale" sign was placed on their lot. Maria spent two weekends in Florida looking at houses and picked one in a new development near Fort Lauderdale. She stayed with Pat in an apartment his company had provided him until they moved; he was commuting, working two weeks and coming back to Columbia on the weekend.

It's hard to be sad at springtime, but even with a flourishing business, I was. Reality was here, and now I would have to learn to cope without Maria in my life. I had always heard that when tragedy comes, work is great solace. It had better be, because that's all I had to look forward to. I dreaded the day when we would say our last goodbye. But early in June, the time came.

The move was set for two days after school closed for the summer. With all the activity of packing, Maria had little time to see me the week before she left. She and the children were leaving Friday morning, June 7, 1963 – a date I will always remember – as soon as the moving vans finished loading and left. Pat had taken Maria's Ford and left her his Buick so she would have more room and a newer car to travel back to Fort Lauderdale. Maria was planning to stop overnight in Jacksonville and stay with an old friend of hers from Pekin. That was a good place and time to take a break in her trip.

Thursday night, Maria planned to drop her children off at a movie and come by my office. Hardy had taken the week off for a vacation at the beach with his family, so we knew we would be alone. I ordered cheeseburgers, without onions of course, from the Blizzard Shop and picked them up before she arrived. I wasn't very hungry, but it seemed the appropriate thing to do since we spent so much time there.

She came in a little after seven dressed in a white blouse and a pair of old denim shorts, looking a bit disheveled, but exuding her usual aroma of soap, shampoo, and perfume. She embraced me and we kissed, but it was more of a greeting than anything akin to passion. She responded as though she were fatigued.

"Ummmm," she said. "I smell something good, like Blizzard burgers and I'm famished. I haven't eaten a bite all day."

"I thought you might like one; it might be your last."

"Please don't say things like that. It's hard enough as it is," she said. She bit her lip and stared into space.

"I'm sorry. I didn't mean anything by it; I don't know what to say. It's not like I do this every day."

"I know, but we're not dying. Let's don't make it sound like it's our last meal." She nibbled at the edges of her burger, and then put it down on her napkin. She dabbed at her mouth with her napkin and took a swallow of Coke. "I'm not as hungry as I thought." Her eyes seemed to focus above my head.

"I got this off on the wrong foot," I said. "That's not what I want. It's important we talk about what's going to happen to us. It's not time for flippant statements or clichés. I want to talk about what this means to us. I have to think there's a purpose for you leaving, otherwise I'll go nuts. I always assumed we'd be together. And now I'm not emotionally capable of coping with your not being here. Intellectually, I knew our relationship couldn't go on much longer without being discovered, but I didn't have the intestinal fortitude to face that either. It's fair to say we've been in a wine and roses existence because neither of us wanted to face reality. Well, reality is here and it hurts like hell." I rubbed my hair in despair and tried to look at her.

Maria answered my despair with a lingering sigh. "Terry, I might say some things you won't understand. I'm tired and tomorrow is going to be hard for me. Not as much as right now. I've got a lot on my mind, but I can tell you I've thought about us a lot in the last few days. I don't want to leave. I was prepared, even before we met, to make Columbia my home for many years. Pat led me to believe that, because that's what management told him. That's why I wanted to build a house. Given the choice, I wouldn't move, but it was not mine to make. The times we've been together have been wonderful, but in terms of time, we spend more time apart than together. Under the circumstances, that's not always pleasant."

I interrupted her as she took a breath. "Wait a minute. You're right. We don't spend much time together, but I could always look forward to being with you another time. We also talked a lot on the telephone. You were at least accessible. Now, I don't have anything to look forward to."

"We can still talk on the phone. It won't be easy, but it's possible."

"And how will we do that? That's not an option for me. I have no way of knowing when I can call you." I snapped a pencil in half in disgust.

She put her hand on my arm. "I'll call you collect, during the day. I know where you are."

I laughed. "Yeah? I can just hear Martha now: 'Mrs. Champion is calling collect, do we want to accept?'"

"I won't call in the morning. And I won't use my real name. Surely you can give me the name of some company you deal with."

My lips tightened as I thought. "That might work…how about Blakely, Ward and Stuckey? We did business with them when I was with Bayer-Kline. That sounds legitimate."

She took a small pad out of her pocketbook and wrote their name down.

"See, that wasn't so difficult. And if you want to call me, you could dial me and let the phone ring one time. If I can talk, I'll ring you back one time. Then you can call me back. The worst thing that could happen is that you would have to say 'wrong number' or hang-up."

"Damn, you're good. Sounds like you've had some practice at this."

She flashed me an ugly glare. "I resent that. I told you this has been on my mind all week." She reached in her pocketbook and brought out a folded sheet of paper. "I made notes."

"I'm impressed. What else do you have on there?"

"I can write you and I'll rent a PO box so you can write me back."

"Anything else?"

"One more thing. Maybe once or twice a year we could meet in a place somewhere in between, like Jacksonville or Atlanta. That will be hard and it will take some careful planning, but it could happen. I could work that out and it would be worth it."

I showed her my first smile of the evening. "I like that. I can always drum up a business trip."

She rubbed my hand. "See, where there's a will we'll find a way." She slipped out of her chair, sat on my lap and kissed me, rubbing the back of my neck softly. This time it was not a kiss of greeting.

She stood and walked to the light switch, plunging the room into half light. "We don't have a lot of time; let's make the most of it." She took off her blouse and bra before I could get out of my chair. I could see her breasts silhouetted in the dim light and barely make out her erect nipples. My mind flashed back to Garden City and our first encounter. I took off my shirt and t-shirt and we embraced. Her soft bosom felt warm against my flesh. I couldn't help thinking about our beginning and now, our end – alpha and omega. It was sad, but time was too precious to waste with those thoughts. We broke apart long enough to get our remaining clothes off and sat on the carpet. She gently pushed me onto my back, and straddling me at knee level took me in her mouth. The pleasure and tenderness of her act wiped away all my sadness. Then she sat on my erect member, moving slowly with her eyes closed and a slight smile on her face. I forced her to stop, and, after rolling her over on her back, covered her body with kisses until she lifted my head in her hands.

"We don't need to rush this," she said. "I want it to last a long time."

"When's the witching hour?"

"The movie's out at nine o'clock, but I can be a little late."

"Good. Then let's practice until we get it right."

The corners of her lips formed a smile and she closed her eyes. "Sounds good to me."

I walked her to her car, hand in hand, trying hard not to think it was the last time. We didn't say much. There wasn't much left to talk about. She unlocked the door and I held it open for her. As she settled back into the seat she looked at me with a face so full of sadness and pain I had trouble recognizing her. Her eyes swelled with tears and she said, "Terry Forte, I love you. You may think this is over, but it's not. It never will be. When we're old we'll think about what we've had in this very short time and know it was the defining moment of our lives. I'll never be able to love a man like I've loved you. There's no substitute for perfection and that's what this has been. You're my lover and my best friend. I didn't know that was possible. We may never be together again, never touch one another again, but *you* touched my soul and I will always, always, be grateful for that."

I wiped away a tear with the back of my hand and swallowed before I could speak. "I love you Maria. I must have known and loved you in another life, and I hope it happens to me again. God help me, I will miss you so."

She tried to force a smile, but it wouldn't come. She turned away from me, gave a little wave, and drove away. I stood in the parking lot watching her car disappear and then its taillights. There was nothing I could do but stand there immobile and empty, watching my life leave me. She had come into my life like gentle zephyr and left it the same way. But the aftermath would be more like a tornado's wake.

I would never stop loving or thinking about her, but, somehow, I had to return to the world I knew before her. It would be difficult, but it had to be. I turned and with a heavy heart walked slowly back to the office. The air was turning cooler and smelled of rain. Sheet lightning streaked across the sky in the distance followed by muted thunder. How ironic, I thought. *Even Mother Nature is sad and trying to cry.*

I was a total wreck the first few months after Maria left. I thought surely Jane and the children would notice my mood swings and reticence to communicate with them, but they tended to ignore me. I tried not to think about Maria, but everything reminded me of her. I continued to work at night as I had done when Maria was in my life, preferring work to moping around the house. I would have periods of highs when Maria would call me collect when she had the opportunity or would write me short notes. But those moments were seldom, and served only to boost my morale for short periods of time.

As the months and years went by, things became easier. Time does heal old wounds. I thought about Maria often, but the destructive thoughts morphed into pleasant memories of our times together. Jane and I began to put our life back together, and we learned to live with and accept our differences. Our threads would never blend into whole fabric, and we recognized that. But with determination and understanding we worked hard to grow as a family. The children were the catalyst for our efforts and the glue that held us together.

Laurie and Janet grew up entirely too quickly, and one by one they left the nest to go to college. Laurie, who was always more studious than Janet, majored in law and worked in a local firm after her graduation from law school. It was there she met her future husband, Richard Belton. Janet's love for animals led her to be a veterinarian and her athletic ability helped her find her mate. She met Marshall Cosgrove while playing in a mixed softball league. I guess all that roll-the-bat we played in the yard was responsible for that.

When the babies started coming, Jane and I got the grand parenting crazies and spent our time going to recitals and little league games. I do believe I could have played every character's part in *The Nutcracker* and I had a reputation of driving umpires crazy. (I'm not sure I'm proud of that.)

My business prospered and kept me busy. And Maria and I managed to keep in touch just enough to know how things were going in each of our lives. Our infrequent conversations changed gradually over the years from undying love to everyday problems and our families. We loved each other, but we talked about it less and less, and soon became more like best friends. Our contacts eventually diminished, limited to birthday cards and an occasional phone call. Time, distance, and family affairs finally had exacted a toll we couldn't overcome.

Jane and I found and bought a lovely beachfront condominium near Charleston in March of 1995 and spent most of our weekends there, especially in the spring and fall. It was time for me to ratchet down my workload and I started thinking about retirement. I entered into a contract with my partners to sell them my shares of the business over a three year period, effective December 31, 1998, with the caveat of trimming my work schedule to three days a week and expanding my vacation to three months each year. That gave Jane and me ample time to spend at the beach and to travel to all the places we had dreamed about during our marriage. Those were our best years.

In July of 2001, Jane suffered a massive stroke totally unexpectedly, and died three weeks later. I was devastated. It was then that I realized what a treasure she had been, and I missed her terribly. All the things she had done for me suddenly became my responsibility and I was not prepared. I felt some lingering guilt for my transgressions of infidelity, something I had not felt when Maria was part of my life. I went through a period of time mentally blaming myself for my sinfulness and I sought solitude for my propitiation. I couldn't force myself to take part in any social activities. My children, grandchildren, golf at the club with old friends and my church were my umbilical cord to the world, and eventually brought me back to the land of the living.

I sold our home and moved into a smaller house with enough yard to allow a small garden and a minimal lawn. By the summer of 2002, I had become quite a farmer and had a wonderful summer garden. I enjoyed that immensely, but I still missed Jane and wished she could have seen the fruits of my labor. She would have been surprised to see what I had become.

In the fall of that year, in the evening after I had cleaned out the remnants of my garden, I took a long shower, slipped on a bathrobe, and prepared supper. Just after eight as I was finishing my meal, the telephone rang. My first intention was to ignore it, figuring it was one of those annoying telemarketing calls, but, in a magnanimous moment, I answered it.

"Hello," I said. No one spoke and I was about to hang up when I heard sounds of sobbing. Then I heard a familiar voice.

"Oh Terry, Terry. Please don't hang up. It's me …Maria." Her voice sounded far away and full of pain. "Pat passed away two days ago."

In the early hours of a spring day in March of 2004, an elderly couple, holding hands and in animated conversation, walked from the door of their condominium in south Florida, to a large heated swimming pool. He was dressed in a soft blue jogging suit and she in a white robe. He set his newspaper and cup of coffee on a table near the pool and helped her remove her robe, exposing a surprisingly trim body in a one-piece bathing suit of solid black. She walked to the top of the empty pool, adjusted her bathing cap over her gray hair, and dove into the water. He sat at the table, turning his chair so he could watch her as she swam, drinking his coffee and intermittently reading his paper.

When she completed her routine of fifty laps, he picked up her robe and met her as she came out of the water, wrapping her lovingly with it, and hugged her. She removed her bathing cap, rubbed her hands through her hair and gave him a big smile.

"Well, what would you like to do today?" she asked.

"I feel like cooking dinner tonight; maybe something special. Let's go to the market for some fresh vegetables and then to that seafood store on Cappriotti Street. You know, the one we tried last week. Damn, I can't remember the name of it. I'm having another senior moment. Anyway, I need fresh flounder, scallops and a bottle of expensive Riesling. Maybe leeks for soup, if we can find some fresh ones."

"I like the sound of that," she said, "but that won't take much time. How about doing some shopping at the mall?"

"Shopping? You never buy anything. You just like to touch things."

"That's not true. I like to see what's new and the prices. Besides, shopping is a woman thing and how she does it is her prerogative."

He laughed and shrugged his shoulders. His piercing blue eyes were filled with love for her. "Whatever pleases you," he said. He adjusted her robe and rubbed her back.

It was her turn to laugh. "Come on now, you like seeing all the people, even if you don't like to shop."

"Architects are structured people. We shop with a plan."

"Humor me a little," she said. "Don't you think I'm worth it?" She had a tease in her smile and a few wrinkles in her laugh line.

He grabbed her hand and gave it a squeeze as they walked back to the condominium. His eyes twinkled as he said, "Why else would I be here with an old woman?" His jocular comment ended with laughter.

Then both of them laughed as though it were a private joke. Then she said, "You'll pay for that, Big Boy."

"And how might I do that, Maria Forte?"

"Terry, a Southern gentlemen should have more imagination than that. But since you don't, how about a quiet walk on the beach at sunset? We might even take along a cold bottle of chardonnay."

He was quiet for a moment, and then he smiled broadly as though he were the luckiest man in the world. "That sounds just about perfect."

He had his arm around her waist as they disappeared through the front door.

www.ingramcontent.com/pod-product-compliance
Lightning Source LLC
LaVergne TN
LVHW050930080826
845145LV00001B/290

* 9 7 8 1 5 9 9 3 2 0 2 8 1 *